JENNILEE'S LIGHT

H S SKINNER

Copyright © 2018 by H S Skinner

All rights reserved.

No part of this book may be reproduced in any form or by any electronic or mechanical means, including information storage and retrieval systems, without written permission from the author, except for the use of brief quotations in a book review.

This is a work of fiction. Any resemblance to people and/ or places are figments of the author's imagination, or used in a fictitious manner.

❦ Created with Vellum

To all my family and friends who believed in me more than I believed in myself.

And to Josie. You had no idea what a torrent you were unleashing with your simple question: "Will you write a column for me?"

Thank you, one and all, for your support and your efforts to see my dream realized.

PROLOGUE

*L*ate Summer, 1968

Putting her baby blue 1964 Nash Rambler in park and switching the ignition off, Cynthia McRae Lee rested her head on the steering wheel. Stepped out, took a deep, calming breath. A beautiful spot, one of her favorites—at the end of a long, winding dirt road, no one around, peaceful, right at the river's edge.

Peace she desperately needed right now.

The tang of saltwater and Loblolly pines and wind filled her senses. Keeping a cautious eye out for copperheads and rattlers, picking her way carefully through the broom straw and catbriars to the water's edge, she found a dry spot and sat down.

Hugging her knees, letting her thoughts drift, Cynthia watched as the outgoing tide steadily siphoned away the brackish river water, leaving a rapidly widening beach.

She wished—a futile waste—that her best friend was here.

Iris had disappeared a couple months ago. Consensus was she'd tired of being a wife and mother in the backwater town of Chinquapin Ridge and hightailed it for parts unknown.

That was nothing but a bald-faced lie.

No woman born ever loved being a wife and mother more than Iris Meyers. Cynthia had no doubts Iris was dead.

Iris' disappearance had dredged up old memories, re-opened festering wounds.

Campbell College. Albert Marvin Lee.

Two things Cynthia loved.

One she'd left behind when she graduated, the other she'd...lost. A loss that hurt as much, seemed as fresh five years later as if it'd just happened.

She had her degree, gained from her years spent at college.

From her short-lived marriage, her beloved daughter, Jennilee.

While she was wasting wishes, she wished for the millionth time she knew what had happened to Albert.

He'd just...disappeared in the time it took Cynthia to come home and check on her father when the Judge suffered another stroke.

How could someone just disappear like that? With no trace?

She didn't know, but Albert had, and now Iris.

Too restless to sit, Cynthia meandered down the shore. She loved Jennilee, more than she'd loved Albert, more than she knew you could love another person.

Shivering as she felt a goose walk over her grave, Cynthia sent a heartfelt thanks winging heavenward for Grandy.

Didn't know what she'd do without Grandy. Surrogate mother, grandma, friend, confidant, as well as being Iris' mother-in-law, Cynthia sent another heartfelt thanks up for Del—Adele Taylor Meyers.

If anything happened to Cynthia, she knew Grandy'd take care of her baby. Uneasy, and growing uneasier by the day after the loss of both her husband and best friend, Cynthia'd made her will. Grandy was to have custody of Jennilee should anything happen to Cynthia.

The Judge barely tolerated Jennilee, was in no shape to take care of her. Celie, Cynthia's younger sister—taking care of Jennilee—that thought didn't bear thinking. Celie could see nothing but herself and her own daughter, Sylvia.

Continuing down the shoreline, throwing shells and sticks in the water, Cynthia picked up a large chunk of driftwood. Giving it a fling, she laughed out loud at the big splash it made, finding joy in the childish pleasure. Stepping around some large myrkle bushes, she almost fell over a blanket spread on the sand. Judging by the clothes scattered around and the beached skiff, she'd surprised some couple in the middle of things. Red-faced, Cynthia spun on her heel and headed back the way she'd come.

Almost to her car when the first blow struck the back of her head, she dropped to her knees and fought the blackness. Another blow and she fell flat in the sandy road, tried to squirm under her car. Dragging her back out, her attacker continued to land blows.

Cynthia's last thought was of Jennilee. Grandy would take care of her.

CHAPTER 1

ctober 1968

Sitting between her Uncle Mort and cousin Sylvia, Jennilee listened to the preacher drone on and on about Heaven and Hell. Swinging her leg, every time Sylvia swung her foot back, the sharp heel of her Mary Janes connected with the front of Jennilee's shin.

Every time Jennilee flinched and squirmed, Aunt Celie, who had her arm around Sylvia, pinched the back of Jennilee's arm—hard. Jennilee might only be four and a half years old, but she already had very definite ideas about Heaven and Hell. Jennilee's empty stomach growled, earning her another hard pinch and firming her convictions.

Heaven was all light and laughter and love. Hell was dark and cold and silent, and the two were separated by a high privet hedge.

CHAPTER 2

ctober, 1971

SAGGING AGAINST THE WALL, arms and legs leaden, Jennilee heaved a silent, exhausted sigh. Her practiced eye ruthlessly scanned the spotless kitchen and she mentally checked off her long, long to-do list. One she'd only accomplished by staying up far past midnight and rising not too long after.

On top of all the usual—washing and ironing, sweeping, mopping, dusting, dishes and bathrooms—Celie'd piled more chores on Jennilee's slender shoulders before she'd agree to let Jennilee take off with Charlie and Grandy. The good silver had suddenly needed an immediate polishing, the floors a thorough waxing, the windows a streak-free washing.

Jennilee mused wryly, at least no vacuuming or making beds today. Celie and Sylvie were still asleep, and Mort was out of town.

Jennilee'd even swept the porches and walks, not that anyone but herself would notice.

She could have skimped on the chores and the doing of them, but Celie would've made Jennilee pay in spades.

Taking one last look around, making certain sure, just as sure that Celie'd find fault no matter what, Jennilee eased out the kitchen door like a ghost. Careful not to let the wooden screen door squeak or slam, eyes locked on Grandy's kitchen door, she completely missed the pinks and golds of a spectacular sunrise.

Bolting across the dew wet expanse separating the two houses, through the gap in the hedge between the yards, she pelted up the back steps. Hitting the door like she was being chased by a pack of demons, she burst into Grandy's warm and welcoming kitchen.

Sneakers squeaking, she skidded right into Charlie's bear hug, standing sentinel a step inside the door. Breathing in his beloved scent, she melted against him, eyes on Grandy's familiar form.

Brown hair with reddish-gold overtones, shoulder length and softly waved, blue-gray eyes the color of a dawn sky that could be sharp as slate but always looked at Jennilee with nothing but love. Wearing shiny penny loafers and neatly pressed slacks and a flowered blouse with a lacy collar, Jennilee figured Grandy's picture should be in the encyclopedia beside the word perfect.

Moving away long before she wanted to, Jennilee hugged Grandy, pressed her face against the older woman and wrapped her arms around Grandy's comforting softness. Gratefully inhaled Grandy's everyday perfume of fresh baked bread and cookies and love mixed with a hint of honeysuckle and a tickle of pressed powder.

Around Grandy's embrace, Jennilee saw Charlie stretching on tiptoe to reach the yellow bottle of Jergens lotion Grandy kept beside the sink. Returning to Charlie like they were a couple of magnets forcibly separated, Jennilee closed her eyes in bliss as Charlie caught her hands in his and rubbed the soothing lotion in.

"You guys want some cinnamon toast? I'll make you some as soon as I finish this. We were starting to wonder if you were coming, Jennilee." Flashing Jennilee a teasing grin, Grandy focused her attention once more on the makings for sandwiches.

Jennilee's gaze held Charlie's, silent messages passing back and forth.

Mouth watering, Jennilee watched with all the fixed attention of a starving hound as Grandy buttered several pieces of bread heavily. Coating it with sugar and sprinkling it liberally with cinnamon Grandy popped the bread beneath the broiler for just a minute. Pouring two big glasses of milk, she set the feast on the table.

A few short minutes later, bellies full, after eagerly helping load the Ford Falcon wood-sided stationwagon affectionately known as Woody, Jennilee clambered into the front, taking her usual spot between Charlie and Grandy.

"Look at me, guys." Both kids looked up at Grandy's call and she snapped a picture with her Swinger. The thick, waxy paper popped out with a mechanical whir and Grandy laid it on the dash.

"Ready?"

Charlie and Jennilee nodded as one.

"State Fair, here we come!"

Pulling out of the drive, they wound through Chinquapin Ridge, passed the sign that read, Population 1,572 and pulled out on Highway 70.

"See if the picture's ready."

Peeling the paper off, Charlie waved the picture back and

forth until colors solidified. Heads together, Charlie shared the image with Jennilee.

Grandy held out her hand. "Let me see." There they were, caught in time. Charlie, her very own tow headed cherub with eyes as dark as marsh mud and Jennilee, their angel with hair of spun gold and ocean eyes.

Jennilee nestled contentedly against Charlie, the ruthless bands around her heart loosening with each mile they put behind them. Listened with half an ear as Charlie kept them entertained with local historical facts and did-you-knows into Havelock, past Cherry Point Marine Corps Air Station and all the way through New Bern. Nudging Charlie once he wound down, she cut her eyes toward Grandy.

Nodding, Charlie asked, "Grandy, what's an obishry?"

"A what?" Taking her eyes off the road long enough to return her grandson's earnest stare, Grandy tried to make sense of his question. Puzzled, she looked back at the road, glanced back at him.

Jennilee stared at Grandy just as intently.

"Say it again. I didn't understand what you asked me."

"An obishry."

Drawing a blank again, Grandy turned her eyes to the road, mulled possibilities. With these two, you never knew what they were up to, or what question their too intelligent minds would come up with next. Most babies were born young and aged slowly and naturally, but these two…

She'd swear they'd been born old and wise in young bodies. Talk about old souls. The two of them were seventy going on seven if they were a day, and she loved them fiercely. Charlie, son of her only son, and Jennilee, child of her heart and light of their lives. For all intents and purposes both orphans, Grandy tried to be everything to both of them.

"Where'd you hear it? Maybe if you told me that I could figure out what you're asking."

"We were playing behind the camellias when you were on the porch. When Miz Lily was visiting."

It clicked then. Sounding like Olde English spoken with a heavy dose of Scottish brogue, Mrs. Lily Gillikin's distinct Cedar Island accent combined with Charlie's soft Southern drawl to mangle the most obvious of words. Let alone one a seven and a half year old had no business wanting to know about.

"An obituary?"

"That's it!"

"An obituary is a death notice. When someone dies, there's always a notice in the paper, kind of an honor listing their accomplishments and their family, and to let everyone else in the community know about funeral arrangements and such."

"Spell it please, Grandy."

Charlie and Jennilee shared a look as she did, more silent messages flowing.

"Enough gloomy thoughts! We're supposed to be having fun!" Grandy started singing *We're Off To See The Wizard*.

Jennilee giggled, a brief sound, too quickly cut off.

Listening to Charlie and Grandy playing *Twenty Questions*, then *I Spy*, safe between them, Jennilee gradually drifted into thankfully dreamless sleep.

GLANCING at the two beside her, Grandy smiled to herself as memories surfaced. One of the few fits her even tempered Charlie'd ever pitched had been over Jennilee's name. Both toddlers splashing in the galvanized washtub Iris and Cynthia were using for a wading pool, Cynthia'd calmly remarked it was time for Jenny to get out.

Charlie'd gone mulish. All three women talked until they

were laughing too hard to catch their breath. The harder they talked, the redder Charlie's face became, the louder his protests. Not even Jennilee's crying could sway him.

His shouts had bounced off the house, echoed off the huge live oaks scattered through the yard. "Jeni*lee*, just like Char*lie*."

Jenny-no-middle-name-Lee on her birth certificate, he must've heard Cynthia sing-songing it and adapted it to his own agenda.

She'd been Jennilee ever since—to everyone except Celie.

Lordy, but she loved these two, even more than she'd loved their mothers.

More happy images flickered across her mind.

Iris and Cynthia, pregnant together, going into labor together, having their babies the same day in the same room of the hospital. Charlie being born scant minutes ahead of Jennilee.

The babies, napping on the same blanket, playing in the same playpen, sharing clothes and toys and mothers and Grandy. When Iris wasn't spoiling them, Cynthia was.

The train in Kinston caught them and Grandy tucked those memories away, like a fragrant sachet in a cedar chest.

Stretching a little, she took a longer look at her quiet passengers. Charlie, arm around Jennilee, counting train cars. Jennilee, slumped against him, fast asleep.

Grandy shook her head. Having known Celie since she'd been a devious toddler bent on getting her own way and getting her older sister in trouble, Grandy didn't have to be told life was no bed of roses for Jennilee. A bright, talkative toddler, Jennilee'd pretty much quit speaking after her mother died.

More memories intruded, ones that set Grandy's blood to boiling all over again. She could see the unfortunate string of events unfolding as clearly as she could see the clacking, swaying train cars rumbling by in front of her. Noisy, lumbering, locked into their path and their destination as surely as Jennilee's fate, every single memory chiseled, clear-cut as the individual train cars.

Cynthia's death and the Judge's debilitating stroke.

Celie, along with her husband and daughter, moving back in to take care of Jennilee and the Judge.

A scant month later, the Judge passing away.

Jennilee coming over not too long after. Standing dumb as a stump in Grandy's kitchen, ghost-white pale, remaining rigidly upright and refusing to sit even when Grandy urged her to eat.

Charlie, instantly tuning into whatever was bothering Jennilee.

Jennilee excusing herself to the bathroom, Charlie bursting into heart wrenching sobs.

Making sense of his sobbing tale, Grandy'd followed Jennilee straight away. Coaxing Jennilee to pull her pants down, she'd taken one look at the bloody horseshoe shaped welts and bruises up and down the backs of Jennilee's legs, covering her buttocks, and seen red.

Doctoring Jennilee.

Herself, marching over to the Judge's house and nearly wrenching the screen door off its hinges, slamming the inside kitchen door open hard enough to crack two of the three bottom panes of glass.

The state of the normally spotless kitchen taking her breath.

Plowing through the once pristine house until she found Celie.

Putting the fear of Grandy, never mind God, into her.

Jennilee hadn't come over with welts on her again, but she wouldn't get near a flyswatter for love nor money.

Heaving a sigh, Grandy locked those memories away. No

sense dredging up the past, she couldn't change it. All she could do was remain vigilant and help in the here and now.

STILL ASLEEP when they reached the fairgrounds, Jennilee blinked and sat up when Charlie called her name softly.

Putting the back window and the tailgate down, Grandy pulled thick bologna and cheese sandwiches out of the cooler, with an Orange Crush and an apple for each.

Bracing the rim of the glass bottles against the tailgate, one at a time, Charlie smacked them on top to open them. Unwrapping the wax paper around their sandwiches, they sat on the tailgate, Jennilee once more firmly entrenched between Charlie and Grandy.

Helping Charlie and Grandy do simple things, just being with them, the soul-deep frozenness inside Jennilee began thawing. Drip by drip, each small act of normalcy contributing to the thaw.

Munching contentedly, Charlie and Jennilee swung their legs in time to their chewing, watched the other fairgoers avidly.

Joining the throng entering the gate, Grandy cautioned, "You two make sure you know where the car is in case we get separated."

Nodding, happily swinging Jennilee's hand, Charlie enthused, "Ooh, Grandy. Can we go to the Village of Yesteryear, and the Old Farm Machinery Barn? And the trial gardens and the handicraft barn, and we wanna see the biggest pumpkin again."

Taking their time, strolling and enjoying, making one final lap around the light bedecked midway as day faded into night, they headed back to the car.

At a quiet rest stop just outside Raleigh, using one of the

picnic area grills, they roasted hotdogs on straightened out clothes hangers before climbing into the back of the stationwagon.

Changing into their PJs, stretching out on the pallet of sleeping bags, Grandy reminded them, "Say your prayers, kids, and let's go to sleep. We've had a busy day."

Charlie and Jennilee said their Now-I-Lay-Me's, Charlie saying an extra, silent prayer for Jennilee like he did every night. Curling up side by side, Charlie and Grandy sandwiched Jennilee. Bookended her, as they'd been doing all day, as they always did, every chance they got.

Breakfasting on cold pop tarts, washing them down with instant Tang in paper cups, they headed to the Museum of Natural Sciences and the Capitol building. Spent the day exploring and just being together.

When Grandy finally pointed the stationwagon back towards the coast, Charlie asked, "Grandy, can we stop at King's? I'm really hungry for some BBQ, and they have some of the best in the state."

"Sure, Charlie."

Rejoicing at her overflowing plate, filled with generous portions of pork BBQ, hush puppies, cole slaw, and baked beans, served with lots and lots of iced tea with a wedge of pecan pie for dessert, the tight bands around Jennilee's heart eased a little more.

Heading for the car, squeezing Charlie's hand for courage, the bands loosened enough to make speech possible. Looking hopefully at Grandy, Jennilee ventured hesitantly, "Grandy, that was good, but not nearly as good as anything you cook. Will you teach me to cook like you do?"

Surprised by Jennilee's first words in...days, tears prickling her eyes, Grandy pulled Jennilee close. "Thank you for a very nice compliment. I'll be glad to."

Somewhere between Dover and New Bern, the cold

began to reclaim Jennilee. Feeling the first shiver run through Jennilee's slender body and the steady trembling since, Charlie'd kept his arms around her since the first quiver.

Grandy knew only because she could see both kids in the faint backwash of light from the instrument panel. Neither child said a word.

Pulling into their driveway, he whispered, a promise and an oath, "Someday…"

Jennilee nodded jerkily and let Charlie help her out.

Staring through the gap in the hedge at the house she knew was there but couldn't see because it was totally dark, not a light on anywhere and certainly not on anywhere in the kitchen area, she wondered how two mirror image houses, so identical outside, could be so different on the inside. Both old, built in the early 1800s, both L-shaped and two story, both adorned with spacious porches.

Forcing her feet to cover the distance, Jennilee pondered dismally at a further anomaly. Going toward Charlie and Grandy and into their light seemed to only take a few steps on solid ground while the return trip into the nightmare dark seemed to be miles long, all of it through sucking, grasping marsh mud.

Knowing Charlie was watching her, Jennilee didn't have the fortitude to turn around and wave. If she did, she'd be right back through that gap in the hedge and they'd have to pry her off Charlie, screaming.

From his bedroom window, Charlie watched as lights came on in certain rooms of the Judge's house, stayed on awhile and went off only for another light in a different room to come on. Jennilee'd need more lotion tomorrow for sure.

CHAPTER 3

*H*olding the shiny black phone at arm's length, Del could still hear the strident voice on the other end.

"*Do you know what those two heathens of yours are up to?!*"

"Calm down, Bertha, and tell me what's wrong." Rolling her eyes, Del wondered how anyone could make so much noise through a face and lips that were constantly pruned in disapproval, as if Bertha thrived on a steady diet of lemons and censure.

"Don't you tell me to calm down, Del Meyers! You come down here and get them right now!" The phone made a loud sound of protest as its twin was slammed into its cradle on Bertha's end.

Head librarian and also mother to Celie's best friend Tracy, Bertha Rogers was eminently predisposed to hate Jennilee. Driving there, Grandy was loath to believe the kids could get into much trouble at the library.

Stepping through the front door of the Chinquapin Ridge Library, Del followed the sound of Bertha's agitated voice,

JENNILEE'S LIGHT

sounding like an aggravated wasp caught on the inside of a window and just looking for a hapless victim in order to deliver a vicious sting. In her office, sitting on straight-backed wooden chairs, Charlie and Jennilee were calmly listening to her irate buzzing, politely mulish looks on both their faces.

Both stood when Grandy entered the cramped office.

Giving Bertha's protruding teeth, bouffant hair and cat-eye glasses on a chain a disparaging glance, Grandy inquired, "Charlie? What's going on? You two upend the card file or tear the pages out of all the books?"

Charlie snickered, covered it with a cough. Jennilee's eyes lit and her lips twitched the slightest bit.

Bertha opened her mouth, Grandy held up a hand. "Charlie?"

"No ma'am. We wanted to look up something. Miz Bertha told us no."

Grandy turned ice cold eyes on Bertha, taking in at a glance the evidence of Bertha's lunch clinging to the front of her sweater, a spot of mustard and an unidentifiable blot. Tried not to stare at the piece of lettuce caught between Bertha's crooked front teeth. "Imagine that, people wanting to look something up at a library."

"Do you have any idea what they want?" Face mottled red, spittle flew with each word Bertha screeched, followed by a blast of halitosis that screamed rotten teeth. Or maybe it was just Bertha's winning personality coming out.

Crossing her arms, trying to breathe through her mouth, Grandy cocked her head. "Bertha, this *is* a library and they both have their library cards. Lower your voice, and no, I don't."

"Obituaries! The two of them asked me…"

"I doubt if the *two* of them asked you anything. The

purpose of a library is to dispense information, in case you've forgotten."

"They don't need to…"

"Don't need to what? Learn? If people can't come to the library to find out something, then there isn't much reason to have a library now, is there?" Uncrossing her arms, Grandy held out a hand to each child. Thought about letting Bertha know she needed to check her appearance, uncharitably and somewhat gleefully decided the witch was on her own.

Bertha stuttered and stammered.

"Come on kids. There's more than one way for a fox to get in a henhouse."

Loading their bikes in the back of the stationwagon, Grandy asked, "What did you want to know about obituaries?"

Two words she should've been expecting. Two words that dropped the ground right out from under her, never the less.

"Our mothers."

"Oh, my babies. Come here." Wrapping an arm around both of them, Grandy pulled them close. She'd known this day would come, dreaded it, hoped it would be a long while in the making. Not with these two. They'd been working their way around to this on the way to the State Fair.

"Get in the car."

Grandy tried to compose herself. It was hard—so hard. Closing her eyes, willing back the tears, she tried to swallow through a throat that'd suddenly become way too small.

How did you tell a child his mother didn't have an obituary because she'd never been declared dead and they'd never found a body? And Jennilee—sweet Jennilee—the details weren't spelled out, but smart little Jennilee would read between the lines.

Heart clenched in pain, Grandy firmed her lips and tried

to breathe. Putting the car in drive, she headed for the town's newspaper office.

She had the clippings at home, but Charlie and Jennilee needed to do this, finish what they'd started. Wouldn't be satisfied otherwise, and she'd just get another irate call from Bertha.

The newspaper office smelled of ink and paper and grease and other unidentifiable but not unpleasant odors.

Matt Holmes, butterball round and bald as a cue ball, owner, editor, and chief reporter of the Ridgerunner, merely raised his bushy eyebrows at Del's request. Showing them to the small room that housed the microfiche reader, he got them the films and left them to it.

Grandy settled both kids in her lap, one on each leg, an arm around both. Getting too big for her to hold like this, right now they all needed the closeness and comfort.

"Charlie, before we get started, there's something you need to know." Grandy swallowed, took a couple deep breaths. "Charlie Bear, there is no obituary for your mom."

"She's dead. You said so. Daddy said so."

"She is. Charlie, your mom loved you. The only way she'd go away and never come back is if she was dead." Reaching around them, Grandy put the film in the reader and scrolled until she found the tiny article on the back page.

Local Woman Missing.

Jennilee wove her fingers through Charlie's, held Charlie's hand in a tight grip. Leaning forward, they read the whole paragraph, read it again.

"That's why Daddy drinks so much."

Grandy kissed him on the crown of his head in confirmation.

"He's imagining what happened to her and it's tearing him apart inside." Jennilee spoke, almost too soft to hear.

"The paper makes it sound like she just…left."

"I know, Charlie. Your mom would never leave you. I know in my heart she's dead, no matter what anyone else thinks. She left you with me to go shopping and she never came back. That was the last time anyone saw her."

Jennilee stated, "Somebody saw her."

Two speeches, in the same day!

Charlie demanded politely, "Tell me what happened."

"Iris said she was going to New Bern, had a very special present in mind for…" …*Cynthia…* "…someone she was very close to. We didn't get too anxious at first, thought maybe she'd had a flat or car trouble, run out of gas. It just got later and later. Your dad borrowed my car, drove to New Bern and back several times."

Grandy swallowed the pain. "Days passed and we were frantic. We organized search parties and combed every patch of woods, every ditch, every side road between here and New Bern. Even enlisted the help of search dogs and half the Marines on the base. Never found the least trace."

"What about her car?"

Whoa. Three!

"Honey, they even dragged all the ditches, checked the junkyards, everything we could think of. You know those ditches are more like canals, and we had a horrible storm the week before so they were full to overflowing. It would've been easy for a car to disappear in one, even a big old Buick like Iris'."

Charlie took a deep breath. "So we don't know what happened to my mom, except that she's dead. What about Jennilee's?"

Unable to force any words past the lump in her throat, Grandy squeezed both kids so hard they squeaked. She'd thought she'd have more time than this, that they'd be older, the pain farther away and easier to talk about, if there was such a thing.

Her voice low and gravelly, she resumed. "Iris wasn't from here. Donnie married her while he was in the service and brought her home when he got out. I loved her the moment I saw her. We'd written back and forth, talked on the phone. As soon as I laid eyes on her, I knew why Donnie couldn't wait. They were so perfect for each other, and so much in love."

Grandy paused, lost in memories. "As much as your dad loved her, and as much as I loved her, when she met Jennilee's mom Cynthia, it was like they were twins separated at birth. Cynthia brought a pie over to welcome Donnie and his new bride home. She crossed the yards just like you do, Jennilee, came into my kitchen."

"Iris and Cynthia took one look at each other and started talking. Neither one came up for air for days. When I say twins, I don't mean they looked alike or anything. Their souls…mirrored. Jennilee, you're the spitting image of your mother, except for the color of your eyes, and Charlie, you look so much like your mom it isn't funny. Iris had dark hair, and you've got your daddy's white blonde, but other than that…"

"They were best friends." Charlie squeezed Jennilee's hand.

"They sure were. The two of them were just like the two of you. They did everything together, talked over each other, finished each other's sentences. Took long walks, played cards, went to the movies, picnicked together. When they found out they were both expecting, well, that was icing on the cake. What mischief one didn't think of, the other did. Not meanness, but jokes, always jokes. Those two kept all of us laughing, even the Judge. When they weren't at my house, they were at the Judge's. After the two of you were born, Iris and Cynthia grew even closer. They loved the two of you so much."

Taking out one film and exchanging it for another, Grandy could only pray Jennilee wouldn't ask. Wasn't ready to deal with it today, maybe not ever.

The obituary for Cynthia McRae read short and sweet. Daughter of Judge Daniel McRae, graduate of Campbell University. Preceded in death by her mother, survived by her father, sister, niece, and daughter.

The kids read it twice, their silence deafening. Grandy braced herself. Maybe Jennilee'd stop with this question.

Fat chance.

"How come my last name's not the same as my mom's?"

"You've got your daddy's last name."

"Grandy, what about my daddy?"

"Nobody knows, sweetie. Your mom graduated from college, moved back in with the Judge shortly after. Everybody in town had a fit when she announced she was pregnant. Some of them even refused to speak to her for coming home with a bun in the oven and no husband. Cynthia claimed until the day she died she was married."

"Would my mom lie?"

My, my. Jennilee was turning into a real chatterbox. "I don't think so, Jennilee. She never lied about anything else, I can't see her lying about this."

Grandy tensed a little more, tried to think of something else, anything else. Willed Jennilee's thoughts in another direction.

"How'd she die?"

Heart constricting, Grandy didn't know a body could feel this much pain and not be mortally wounded. "Jennilee, I do my best to answer all your questions truthfully, but I'm not sure you're ready for this."

Ancient eyes in young faces turned to Grandy, Jennilee's ocean eyes locking on Grandy's soft blue-gray, pain-filled in her oval face. "Tell us, Grandy. No matter how bad it is, knowing is better than imagining."

Putting the next film in, she scrolled to the article, didn't have to go far. It took up most of the front page, the headline in huge, bold type.

LOCAL WOMAN BRUTALLY SLAIN. NO MOTIVE, NO SUSPECT.

Grandy couldn't hold the tears back any longer. They streamed down her face, dripped off her chin.

Charlie and Jennilee read the long, detailed article. Finishing first, Jennilee's eyes fastened on the picture of her mom accompanying the article.

Reaching out, she brushed the tip of one finger across her mother's smiling face. Aunt Celie'd gotten rid of all the old stuff. Pictures, furniture, everything.

Leaning back against Grandy, Jennilee tucked her face into Grandy's neck. Charlie mirrored her. The three of them sat that way for what seemed ages. Jennilee spoke again, in what had to be a record for her. "I'm sorry, Grandy."

"For what, Jennilee?"

"I know this was hard for you, but we appreciate it. It helps."

Grandy figured Jennilee must've used her quota of words for the entire month, maybe the year.

A solemn crew thanked Mr. Matt and climbed back into the stationwagon. Grandy drove home, called Celie and told her in no uncertain terms Jennilee was staying for supper and staying the night.

In the short time she spent on the phone, the kids disappeared. No need to bother looking for them. Any time either of them was upset, they both headed for the rocking chair in the family room, and she could hear the rhythmic sound all the way down the hall.

Big and comfortable, with a perfectly soothing two-note squeak, the rocker had belonged to Grandy's great-grandmother, a wedding present from her soon to be husband. It'd rocked away worlds of hurt for generations of adults and babies alike.

Grandy could see the two kids as clearly as if she'd peeked in on them. Jennilee in Charlie's lap, scrunched in a ball, arms and legs tucked close, face buried against Charlie. Charlie's arms wrapped tight around Jennilee, rocking both of them, his cheek resting on her head.

Leaving them to it, Grandy started chicken and dumplings. Definitely a comfort food, and they definitely needed comfort tonight.

Charlie rocked Jennilee, both of them absorbing the information they'd gleaned. Untangling herself, Jennilee sat up. Sharing a look, they got up, went upstairs hand in hand to Grandy's bedroom.

The silence alerted Grandy—no more squeaking. Having a pretty good idea what they were up to, she left the chicken simmering and headed upstairs.

Just as she thought. The two of them stood side by side holding hands and gazing at a picture of Iris and Cynthia laughing into the camera, arms around each other.

"I've got albums full of pictures, if you want to look at them."

Nodding in unison, Charlie and Jennilee waited expectantly.

Pulling the albums out of her cedar chest, Grandy paged through them with Charlie and Jennilee. Framed pictures were all over her bedroom, on the dresser, on the wall, on the nightstand, but she'd put away the ones downstairs.

There were loads of pictures, all showing laughing, smiling adults and happy babies, the love palpable. Looking poured salt on raw wounds, but a great weight lifted off Grandy with the sharing.

"You know where the albums are now. Any time you want, you're welcome to go through them. Just put them back when you're done and try not to have them out if Donnie comes over."

"Daddy doesn't come around much because I look so much like my mom."

Another spasm of pain clenched Grandy's heart. "Charlie, your dad loves you, but sometimes grief makes people do strange things. I don't have any excuses for his behavior."

"He hurts like I'd hurt if something happened to you." Putting a hand to Charlie's cheek, Jennilee shared an intense look with him.

Feeling like she'd intruded on an intimate moment between a long married couple, Grandy couldn't tear her gaze away.

Charlie blinked and the moment disappeared like smoke. "Enough gloom and doom. I'm hungry."

"You're always hungry."

Tension broken by shared laughter, they put the albums away.

"Jennilee, when I called Celie and told her you were eating supper here, I also told her you were spending the night."

Throwing her arms around Grandy's waist, Jennilee hugged her tight. She'd pay for this reprieve, but it'd be worth it.

BACK IN THE KITCHEN, splurging on a few more words, Jennilee asked, "Grandy, how do you make chicken and dumplings?"

Setting Jennilee to mixing the dumplings while she deboned the chicken, Grandy instructed, "Cover your chicken with water, and remember to use a fairly big pot so you'll have room for the dumplings. I used a whole chicken because that's what I had, but pieces work just as well. There's no set recipe. Usually I mince an onion, celery if I have it, add that and salt and pepper to the water and cook the chicken until it's done. I like to take the chicken out and debone it, but you don't have to. I personally don't like chomping down on a piece of bone or gristle while I'm trying to eat."

Dumping the chicken back into the pot, Grandy turned up the heat.

"This is like making biscuits." One of the first things Grandy'd taught Jennilee to make, right after they got back from the State Fair, Jennilee'd mastered the art.

"Pretty much, only you don't want the dough as solid. You want the dumplings to be light and fluffy."

Chicken and broth coming to a boil, Grandy helped Jennilee spoon the dumplings onto the liquid.

"This has to cook uncovered for ten minutes, then covered for ten more. Charlie, would you get a jar of peas and one of applesauce out of the pantry, please?"

Jumping off the stool she used so she could help, Jennilee dragged it around the kitchen and used it to get Charlie things he needed to set the table.

Almost flat, shallow bowls for the chicken and dumplings, small serving bowls for the applesauce and peas, silverware. Grandy poured three glasses of milk and set one at each place.

Putting the stool back in the spot reserved for it, Jennilee stroked it like a beloved pet. She loved that stool, loved standing on it to help. Looking like a miniature chair on tall chrome legs, underneath the shiny red vinyl seat were two pull-out steps.

Unscrewing the rings on the jars, popping the airtight metal lids off, Charlie handed one jar to Grandy and one to Jennilee. Putting the applesauce in a pretty blue bowl, Jennilee sprinkled it with cinnamon, watched closely as Grandy put the peas and a dab of butter in a pan and put them on the stove.

Grandy sneaked a look while Charlie said the blessing. The kids took turns, with the honor falling to whichever one set the table. Side by side, both precious heads bowed and hands folded, Grandy sent up a fervent prayer of her own.

Jennilee cleared, Grandy put away the leftovers, Charlie dragged two chairs over to the sink. Tonight Charlie washed and Jennilee rinsed while Grandy dried and put away.

Singing as they worked, starting with *Amazing Grace,* they segued into *Will The Circle Be Unbroken,* finished with *I Will Meet You In The Morning.* Jennilee's throat would loosen up enough to sing where she'd hardly speak a word, especially with Charlie.

Reading them stories before bedtime, Grandy chose one of their very favorites from when they were small, *Little Black Sambo.* Following that with some *Uncle Remus,* she did all the voices, made the stories come alive.

Charlie and Jennilee could both read, and well, Grandy'd seen to that. Both able to read long before they started school, all of them enjoyed the ritual of snuggling close and sharing great literature.

Deep into *Tom Sawyer,* postponed for tonight, they'd read *The Hobbit,* and *Lord of the Rings,* and *To Kill A Mockingbird,* and *My Friend Flicka,* all of the *Black Stallion* series, the *Bobbsey Twins,* all the *Old Mother West Wind* stories, tons of others.

Grandy snorted to herself. Bertha could complain about

these two, call them heathens all she wanted, but Charlie and Jennilee were probably better read than most of the adults in town. Including Bertha.

Celie and Bertha might have it in for Jennilee, but Grandy fully intended to do everything in her power to thwart their evil.

CHAPTER 4

Both kids came down with chickenpox for Christmas vacation, spent the week on the pull out bed on the couch in the family room.

Their enforced confinement a joy rather than a hardship, Charlie and Jennilee played endless games. Grandy's wall to wall, floor to ceiling bookshelves in the family room had enclosed cabinets on the bottom, rivaling the games section at the toy store. Games the kids had long ago organized into some order that made sense only to the two of them.

Mother Goose, Monopoly, Chutes and Ladders, Risk, and Trouble resided in one cabinet. Mousetrap, Scrabble, Operation, Yahtzee, and Battleship filled the next. Clue, Candyland, Cootie, Barrel of Monkeys, checkers—both regular and Chinese—lived next door. The next cabinet held all manner of card games and dominoes.

Puzzles. Big ones. The harder the better, nothing less than a thousand pieces. A card table stayed in one corner all the time, usually with a puzzle in progress.

The current jigsaw consisted of all greens and purples

and blues with splashes of white, flowering shrubs reflected in a pond.

Working on it together, not recognizing the colorful blooms, Charlie asked before Jennilee had a chance to nudge him. "What kind of flowers are those, Grandy?"

"Lilacs. They're a northern shrub, smell like Heaven."

CHRISTMAS DAY FOUND Jennilee still at Grandy's. Absolutely the best Christmas she could remember, usually her aunt insisted Jennilee wait until late in the afternoon to come to Grandy's.

Not today! Up at the crack of dawn, Charlie and Jennilee tiptoed into the front parlor. The huge, beautifully decorated cedar tree stood regally in the corner. Looking like something out of a fairy tale, all covered in paper chains and strings of popcorn, lights and tinsel and a mixture of old and new ornaments, handmade and store-bought.

Presents piled high beneath the tree, their stockings hung full and bulging from the mantle. The empty plate holding a few cookie crumbs, the empty glass of milk, a few carrot leaves and a single bite of carrot beside them had the kids sharing a look of amazed astonishment.

Turning, they bolted up the stairs. Hearing them moving around, Grandy pretended to be sleeping when they quietly opened her bedroom door and crept in.

Christmas hadn't been this much fun since Donnie was their age.

"Grandy, you have to come see. Santa came! The milk and cookies are gone, and so are the carrots!" Charlie did the talking, as usual, but Jennilee's eyes were shining like the star on top of the tree.

Charlie and Jennilee took turns passing out presents from Santa and opening them, one at a time. Decided who'd go first just like they decided everything else—paper, scissors, rock.

Santa brought the kids Twister and a new puzzle, a paint-by-number kit for each—puppies for Charlie and Holly Hobbie for Jennilee. A transistor radio for Charlie and a music box for Jennilee. Both stockings held unshelled nuts, an apple, an orange, individually wrapped candies. Marbles for Charlie and Jacks for Jennilee.

Taking pictures until they made her stop, Grandy's eyes filled with tears at the lumpy, clumsily wrapped packages Charlie and Jennilee presented her with. A bar of her favorite perfumed soap from Jennilee, and a couple handkerchiefs with flowers embroidered in the corners.

"Jennilee—where…how?" Not really expecting an answer, Grandy figured Santa had given her an extra-special gift when Jennilee started chattering.

"We raked pine straw and did chores for Miz Ethel and she paid us. I bought the soap, 'cause I know it's your favorite, and the handkerchiefs were plain. Miz Sadie taught me how to do the fancy stitching, 'cept she called it 'broidery."

Jennilee shook her head. "*Em*broidery. I made some for her, too, on account of she taught me." When Grandy didn't say anything, Jennilee tensed like a dog that's been whipped too many times and is expecting more of the same.

Before Grandy could respond to the speech, to the insecurity and upset on Jennilee's face, Charlie danced eagerly from foot to foot. Throwing his arms around Jennilee, he locked her in place. "Open mine!"

Unwrapping Charlie's presents, Grandy burst into tears. A bottle of perfume and a crude but recognizable pelican carved out of driftwood.

"Grandy? We can get you something else." Charlie sounded as insecure as Jennilee looked.

"Don't you dare! These are the best presents I've gotten in a long time. You know what the only presents better than this that I've ever gotten are?"

Charlie and Jennilee shook their heads.

"Why, the two of you, of course!"

Reaching under the tree, Grandy handed Charlie and Jennilee their presents from her.

Charlie opened his—a dress shirt and tie, a pair of flannel pajamas, all sewn by Grandy.

Jennilee opened hers—a soft wool jumper in blue and brown and cream plaid and a flannel nightgown, again, sewn by Grandy. A pair of cream knee socks.

Grandy had also knitted both a sweater, dark brown with a light tan stripe around the neck and cuffs for Charlie, dove gray with aquamarine trim for Jennilee.

Charlie and Jennilee put their sweaters on over their pajamas. Grandy dabbed a little of Charlie's perfume behind her ears, tucked one of Jennilee's handkerchiefs in the pocket of her robe, the flowers hanging over the edge.

"What did you two get each other?"

Charlie handed Jennilee two presents, she handed him two. PSR, Charlie won. Jennilee smiled as she watched him open the first one.

"A harmonica!" Blowing a long train-whistle sound, Charlie gave Jennilee a jubilant hug. "You go now."

Jennilee took her time opening her first present from Charlie. "Bubble bath!" Jennilee's face matched Charlie's, joy for joy.

Each looked at their remaining present. "Together."

Starting at the same time, finishing at the same time, they turned the items over at the same time. Grandy knew what each held, because she'd helped them both.

Charlie had a tight grip on a picture of Iris holding his baby self, Jennilee stared at a picture of Cynthia holding her baby self. Both women were smiling, both babies wore adorable, nearly toothless grins and a diaper.

Grandy blinked back tears. "Let's get this mess cleaned up. You two put your new things in your rooms and get dressed, then we'll get some breakfast going."

∽

MEASURING the ingredients for hot cocoa—sugar, cocoa, vanilla and milk with just a dash of salt, Jennilee stirred it on the stove 'til it was ready.

Charlie was on standby with the marshmallows and mugs.

Cooking the oatmeal just the way they all liked it, Grandy added honey and a dab of butter and a bit of milk.

Breakfast over, Jennilee helped Grandy make the stuffing, stuff the turkey, get the turkey in the oven and the ham boiling on the stove. Charlie started peeling potatoes, Jennilee cut them up as soon as she finished helping Grandy.

Next came pies—apple, sweet potato, pecan, chocolate. They mixed and rolled the pie dough out, made the fillings. Cut apple shapes out of dough to put on top of the apple pie, made whipped cream to put on the sweet potato and chocolate.

"You guys want some cinnamon twists?"

"Cinnamon twists?"

"Sure. Watch this." Rolling out the leftover pie dough, Grandy buttered it, sprinkled it with cinnamon and sugar. Rolled the pieces into cylinders, slashed the tops, put them in a pie pan and popped them in the oven for a few minutes.

Putting a pot of water and and a slab of salt pork on to boil, Grandy instructed the kids, "We have to wash the collards good, get all the sand out. After the water boils for an hour or so and gets seasoned good, we'll add the collards."

Pulling a bowl of dough out of the frig, they shaped light rolls. Jennilee sniffed appreciatively. Even cold the rolls smelled delicious. Once they started baking, the scent would fill the kitchen. Draping a dishtowel over them, Grandy set them in the warming oven over a bowl of hot water.

"How many people are coming this year, Grandy?"

Rattling off names, even though Jennilee appeared absorbed in what she was doing, Grandy knew the tables would be set with the proper amount of plates, glasses, and silverware.

A mixture of family and friends started arriving and organized chaos ensued.

Opening the pocket doors in the dining room doubled its size and the men carried in sawhorses and wide boards for makeshift tables. Adding the sawhorse tables to the end of the dining room table stretched its length until it would hold twenty or more adults, and the kids had their own table.

Jennilee got out the good tablecloths, then the good china and glasses and silver. All the beautiful things residing in the built-in hutch, waiting for such occasions.

Everyone contributing to the feast, Grandy's frig and countertops were soon groaning with the abundance. The kids were shooed outside, the men headed to the porch to smoke and talk or into the living room to watch TV while the women bustled around the kitchen.

Amidst all the chatter and laughter, a voice spoke up. "Del, you must've stayed up all night to get all this done before we got here."

"I can't take credit for all of this. Charlie and Jennilee are great helpers."

A wave of silence and disbelief met her statement, followed by a ripple of laughter.

"You're kidding, right? I can't stand to have mine in the kitchen at the same time. All they do is bicker."

"Charlie and Jennilee are all the help I've got, and they never bicker."

Another wave of disbelieving laughter and shaking heads and the conversation was forgotten as the women put the finishing touches on the meal. Calling the men and children to wash up, steaming platters and bowls were relayed to the waiting table and the sideboard, glasses were filled with ice and sweet tea poured.

Amid complaints of *do I have to sit with the babies* and jockeying for seats, everyone found their place. Waited while the blessing was said.

Grandy gazed around. The only person missing was Donnie. She'd invited him, as she did every year, and he'd given her the same reply he always did.

"I'll try, Mom."

Leftovers put away, kitchen cleaned up, the women drifted out to the porch to sit with the men and join in the music making. Shouts and laughter rang throughout the the yard. Grandy figured it wouldn't be long before Charlie and Jennilee were drawn by the sounds of music, and it wasn't.

Jennilee added her voice to the medley, Charlie played a soft accompaniment on his harmonica, learning as he went. The music and laughter lasted a long while, people coming and going, some to sing or play, some to just enjoy.

Looking around, Grandy frowned to herself.

Jennilee wasn't with the rest of the kids, wasn't in the house, either. Grandy'd checked. Knew Jennilee wouldn't have gone back to the Judge's house voluntarily, and normally she wouldn't get more than a few steps from Charlie.

JENNILEE PEDALED HER BIKE HARD, careful not to spill the contents of her basket. Braking to a cautious stop, she looked at the dark windows of the apartment over the closed Garage. Climbed the outside stairs, knocked.

Blinking his eyes open, Donnie rolled off the couch. Who would be knocking on his door on Christmas day? Persistent, he'd give them that. Opening his door, not seeing anyone, he focused his bleary gaze down and blinked.

"Jennilee? Something wrong?"

Jennilee shook her head, held out a large paper grocery sack.

Donnie looked from her to the sack.

"Mom need something?"

Jennilee shook her head again, her eyes locked on Donnie's, her young face fresh and full of hope, his face lined and eyes clouded with pain. When Donnie made no move to take what she offered, she gave him a lopsided smile. Carefully setting the bag on the floor of the landing, she slipped silently back down the stairs.

Donnie shook his head, figured he must be either still asleep or suffering drunken hallucinations. Crouching slowly so his head wouldn't explode, he picked up the sack, got a whiff of…food. Stomach growling, he stepped back into his apartment and closed the door, delving deeper as he went.

On top of the myriad Tupperware containers of every size rested a homemade card on red construction paper. The message had been traced out with glue and sprinkled with glitter.

Merry Christmas. Love, Grandy, Charlie, and Jennilee.

Pedaling as hard as she could back to Charlie and Grandy, almost there, a familiar sounding car came up behind Jennilee and blared the horn.

Her blood turned to ice, her limbs to jelly as Celie's strident voice informed her, "If you're well enough to be out riding your bike, it's past time for you to come back from Del's. You've got ten minutes, and plenty of chores waiting."

Flooring it, cutting close enough to Jennilee's bike that Jennilee had to yank her leg back, Celie disappeared in a cloud of exhaust that left Jennilee choking.

Breathless by the time she reached Grandy's, heartsick, Jennilee headed inside. Company having gone home, Charlie and Grandy were in the kitchen. Spotting her, Charlie stood, resignation written all over his face.

Grandy, watching Charlie, turned to see Jennilee, looking like a parolee who'd just learned his parole had been revoked. "Gotta go?"

Jennilee swallowed and nodded.

Grandy caught her up in a fierce hug. "We've enjoyed having you this past week. Come back when you can."

Pressing her face into Grandy's neck, Jennilee inhaled like a swimmer going under for the last time.

Charlie took his turn holding Jennilee and Grandy again had the uncomfortable sensation of intruding on a private moment between lovers. Shuddering once, Jennilee molded herself to Charlie. Tightening his hold, he stroked a hand down her long hair. Jennilee reluctantly pulled away.

"Aren't you going to take any of your presents?"

At Grandy's question, Charlie and Jennilee shared a look. Both darted a glance at the goldfish swimming lazily around his bowl. Not the goldfish Charlie'd won for Jennilee at the State Fair, but his replacement.

Grandy, impressed when the goldfish made it home alive, sprung for a bowl and some fish food. The kids'd had a ball watching him, taking care of him. Charlie won PSR, got first dibs.

Taking Goldie to the Judge's when it was her turn, Jennilee'd come back the next day, white-faced, and told them Goldie'd died. Grandy didn't think to ask how and

Jennilee refused to tell Charlie when he did ask. He had a pretty good idea, and he was on the right track, but even Charlie's conjectures fell short.

Placing Goldie in her room, Jennilee'd gone to work on her never ending chores. Returning to find Goldie gone—fish, bowl, and food, Jennilee found Goldie in Sylvie's room. Jennilee tried to take Goldie back, Sylvie pitched a fit. A long, loud fit that resulted in Celie's appearance, and Jennilee being dragged downstairs to face the music.

Celie finally let Jennilee out, only because Uncle Mort was due home any minute and there were Things That Needed To Be Done.

Mort walked in the front door before Jennilee had a chance to get started.

Making sure she was on the stairs, party to the whole debacle, Sylvie smirked over the banister, just loud enough for Jennilee to hear. "You can have your stupid fish back. I put him in your room."

Not trusting her cousin's generosity, Jennilee tore up the stairs.

Sylvia'd given Goldie back, alright. In pieces. His beautiful tail and fins had been hacked off, the fish equivalent of pulling the wings off a fly. Pinned to Jennilee's dresser with a nail through his eye socket, gills searching desperately for oxygen, mutilated body twitching horribly.

Removing the nail with shaking hands, Jennilee gathered the pieces and gently held Goldie 'til he breathed his last, standing deep in grief over the torture and loss.

Uncle Mort stormed into her room.

"I thought Celie and Sylvie were lying when they told me what you did."

Jennilee thought, *they were*, but she didn't move, didn't say anything. Heard the sound of a belt being unbuckled and zipping through belt loops. Didn't make a peep as the belt struck her repeatedly.

Coming back to the here-and-now, Jennilee headed across the yards. Take her beautiful, wonderful presents to that house? No way. Charlie's mournful harmonica serenade followed her.

CHAPTER 5

Spring came, and Easter vacation. Heading south, the threesome hit Wilmington for the Azalea Festival, toured Airlee Gardens and Orton Plantation and the USS North Carolina Battleship Memorial.

School let out, summertime arrived, and Grandy's house became a child magnet. Grandy stayed busy making kool-aid and lemonade and PBJs, passing out popsicles and band-aids. Any parent in town who couldn't locate their kids had only to call Del.

Staying equally busy, Charlie led the others in endless games of tag, hide-and-seek, cowboys-and-Indians, Robinhood and Maid Marian, cops-and-robbers.

Swimming in the river at high tide, cannon-balling off Grandy's dock, in between tides the kids clammed and crabbed and fished. Played in the sprinkler and the hose, filled their squirt guns and threw water balloons to their heart's content. Marking off a playing field in the huge side yard, they set up bases, played kickball and baseball for hours.

Grandy's yard rang with shouts and squeals until it sounded like an amusement park.

Passing out Mason jars at dusk, Grandy dutifully admired how many lightning bugs were caught before insisting they be released. The kids turned her back porch into a science lab and she didn't make a peep. Tadpoles and baby rabbits and minnows and fiddler crabs and all manner of critters took up residence at one time or another.

Using old clothes and junk from Grandy's attic and the back porch as their stage, the kids wrote and acted out plays.

Built fires on the sandy shore down near the river's edge, roasted hotdogs and marshmallows, made s'mores, rinsed off the sticky in the river. Played flashlight tag until the parents insisted their kids come home, only to rise at the crack of dawn and head back to Grandy's.

Jennilee was always the last to arrive and the first to leave.

Miserably hot and humid this day, even for coastal North Carolina, the tide was out, way out, so swimming wasn't an option. Most of the other kids had drifted off, maybe home, to see if they could find a cooler spot. Just as well. A thunderstorm was brewing for sure.

Charlie and Jennilee reclined side by side in the hammock strung beneath a couple of ancient live oaks, sideways, feet touching the ground just enough to keep them swinging.

Charlie whispered, Grandy saw the sudden fierce shaking of Jennilee's head. Arguing his case fervently, no matter what he said, Jennilee kept shaking her head.

"What's up, guys?"

Jennilee turned away. Shooting her an aggravated look, Charlie clamped his lips, turned his head the other way.

Maybe they were just having a tiff. Lord knew, this heat was enough to make anyone argumentative. It was just so unusual. Charlie and Jennilee never quarreled.

Grandy shrugged. "How 'bout making some ice cream? You two can help turn the crank."

Nodding, getting out of the hammock as one, they headed for the porch.

Separating to collect the ice cube trays, the ice cream maker and the salt, they regrouped at the kitchen table.

"Peach?" Grandy answered herself when both kids refused to say anything. "Peach it is."

Both grabbing a metal ice cube tray and flipping the lever back to dislodge the ice cubes, Charlie and Jennilee dumped those in a bowl, grabbed another tray.

"Grandy, if someone's keeping a secret that's hurting them, is it okay to tell it?"

Shooting Charlie a keep-your-mouth-shut look, Jennilee reached for another tray, tucked her head.

Antenna vibrating, Grandy asked, "Jennilee? Is something wrong?"

Staring fixedly at the tray she held, at her hands working the lever, Jennilee shook her head.

Face a picture of misery, Charlie coaxed, "Jennilee."

Grandy put a hand on Jennilee's shoulder.

Jerking away so hard she tripped and fell, ice cubes going everywhere, Jennilee crabbed away from them until she hit the wall, eyes huge, tears streaming down her pale face.

Grandy froze. Oh, Lordy. Something was definitely wrong.

Reaching Jennilee before Grandy could move, Charlie dropped to his knees. "I'm sorry, Jennilee. Don't cry." Cautiously reached out and touched her.

Remaining stiff for a blink, she threw herself at him, wound her arms around his neck and held on for dear life.

Scooping Jennilee up, Charlie headed for the family room and the rocking chair.

Cleaning up the mess, Grandy finished mixing the ingredients, poured it into the cylinder, surrounded the cylinder with ice and salt, carried the whole mess out on the porch.

Watched the storm close in while she cranked. The rhythmic creaking of the old rocking chair carried to her through the open windows, a pleasant counterpart to the grinding noise of the ice cream maker.

No point in asking Jennilee again. She wouldn't answer and it'd only upset her. Ten to one, Celie was behind whatever was upsetting Jennilee. Maybe it was time for Grandy to have another heart to heart.

She was going to get her ducks in a row and then she was going hunting—for bear.

∼

THE STORM the other afternoon more bluster than substance, the one building up this afternoon promised to be a great deal worse.

The air hung heavy, completely still, a stage curtain waiting for the play to begin. Impossibly tall thunderheads kept building, building, pushing higher and higher, moving in from the west. Gleaming white on the tops where the sun still touched them, pewter in the middle, the underbellies of the towering clouds were black as the inside of a coal mine.

Keeping a wary eye on the darkening sky, Grandy urged Charlie and Jennilee to hurry. She'd be real surprised if they didn't get some hail out of this one. All the extra kids had been sent home with a strict warning not to dawdle.

Helping put away anything in the yard that might blow around or away, Jennilee entered the shed with an armful of aluminum lawn chairs. The wind gusted up out of nowhere and just as suddenly it went nearly pitch dark. The door to the shed blew shut, slammed hard and stuck.

Dropping the croquet set, Charlie ran to the shed and

wrenched open the door, but the damage was done. Wild-eyed, mouth stretched open in a silent scream, Jennilee launched herself, knocked Charlie down and took off running. Jumping up, Charlie sprinted after her.

Grandy had most of her answer. Celie wasn't beating the child anymore. She was locking her in somewhere. Somewhere dark.

No one around here had a basement, the water table lay too close to the surface. Not the attic—it was too light.

A closet. It had to be.

Catching up to Jennilee, Charlie grabbed her arm, shouting to make Jennilee hear him over the now rushing wind. She fought him mindlessly. Heaving her over his shoulder, he staggered to the house and collapsed on the floor just as the first hail struck and the icy rain started falling in sideways sheets. Hail pounded the roof, covered the ground, the wind shrieked like an angry banshee.

Jennilee curled into herself, unresponsive to voice or touch. Struggling to catch his breath, Charlie scooped her up, just like he'd done the other day, headed for the rocking chair.

Scrambling to close windows, upstairs and downstairs, by the time Grandy made it back, Charlie had Jennilee wrapped in the afghan off the back of the couch, rocking her, crooning wordlessly.

The storm settled in as quickly as it'd flared up, lightning flashing and thunder booming before the flash of light disappeared. Between the thunder and the hail still pounding down, the world became a discordant cacophony punctuated by brilliant strobes of blue-white light.

Grandy's first call was to Doctor Stanley Mason. The second was to Chief of Police Mac Williams and the third to the Judge's lawyer—Jennilee's now—Tom Stimpson. Grandy fumed and cleaned up wet floors.

Arriving first, Doc rushed gingerly to the house, careful not to slip on the hailstones still littering the walkway. Holding the flap of his raincoat over his head with one arm to keep off the sheeting rain, Grandy met him at the door, opened it before he knocked.

Draping his sopping raincoat over a porch chair, looking like a disgruntled blue heron, all gangly legs and gray streaked hair, Doc scolded, "Del, it better be life-threatening to drag me out in this."

Leading him to the family room and Jennilee, Doc took one look at Jennilee's shape beneath the afghan. Ordered Charlie, "Bring her over here son, and lay her on the couch."

Charlie shook his head.

"You want me to carry her?"

Charlie shook his head again.

Doc reached for Jennilee. Charlie snarled and tightened his grip. Doc pulled his hand back and looked to Del.

"Charlie, Doc can't help Jennilee if you won't let him near her."

Charlie looked at Grandy beseechingly. "If we try to move her, she's gonna go crazy again."

Doc coaxed softly, "Tell me exactly what happened, Charlie."

"Jennilee wouldn't want me to."

"Is she bleeding anywhere?"

Charlie shook his head. It seemed Jennilee's lack of words had rubbed off on the normally loquacious Charlie, at the worst possible time.

A loud pounding distracted the tableau. Jennilee didn't flinch, didn't stir, didn't give any sign she heard.

Grandy and Doc stepped into the hallway just as Mac opened the front door, stuck his head in, and hollered. "Del?"

Rushing toward Mac's solid, reassuring bulk, made even more reassuring by his khaki uniform and gleaming badge,

Doc in tow, Del started explaining. Through the wavy glass sidelight she caught a watery glimpse of Tom, all business in his dark three piece suit. "Hold on just a minute until Tom gets in here. You all need to hear this, and I'd rather only tell it once."

Starting with the bruises and the bloody horseshoe marks on Jennilee right after the Judge died, including her subsequent dressing down of Celie, Del told them of Jennilee's strange behavior earlier in the week. Brought them up to date.

"Jennilee's always quiet. Lately she's been downright mute. I knew something was bothering her, Charlie's tried to wheedle it out of her, but Jennilee clammed up, wouldn't say anything. This afternoon, just as the storm hit, the wind caught the shed door and slammed it so hard it stuck. Jennilee'd just stepped inside. She went berserk. I could hear her throwing herself against the door. Charlie opened it, Jennilee bolted out, knocked Charlie down and took off running. Charlie caught her and she...she fought him. He practically had to drag her into the house."

Mac and Tom exchanged grim looks. Looking puzzled for a minute, Doc caught on. "You think Celie..."

Del shook her head. "I don't think, I know."

Trooping grimly back to the family room, Mac and Tom hovered in the doorway. Stepping close to Charlie, Doc went down on one knee. "Charlie, do you think Jennilee'd let me look at her with you holding her?"

"If it upsets her, you have to stop."

"Fair enough. Uncover her."

Charlie eased the afghan off to reveal Jennilee pressed against his chest. Hair obscuring all traces of skin, curled in a ball, knees bumping her chin, arms tucked tight.

Doc ran a hand through his hair. "Can you turn her head so I can see her face?"

Gently smoothing Jennilee's hair back, Charlie tucked it behind her ear. The visible curve of cheek pasty gray, Charlie gently tried to turn her head. Jennilee held her position like a barnacle.

Doc scrubbed a hand over his raw-boned face. "Well, we'll give her a little time. Let me doctor those scratches, Charlie."

Jennilee stirred, the slightest whisper of movement. They all held their breath, but nothing further happened. Opening his case, Doc started taking out salve and other things. Disappearing, Grandy returned with a washcloth and a basin of hot water.

At the first touch of the washcloth, Charlie sucked in a breath. Jennilee shifted, her eyelashes fluttered. Opening her eyes, the first thing she saw was Charlie's arm, covered in bloody weals. The second thing was Doc, leaning close.

Charlie's name came out a moan of distress.

"Shh, Jennilee. It's just scratches."

"Charlie—what?" Putting both hands on Charlie's chest, Jennilee tried to push away.

Clamping his arms tight, Charlie refused to let her. "Jennilee-honey, they're not that bad."

"Then why is Doc here?"

"Doc's here for you."

Jennilee froze, then fought harder, arms and legs churning.

"Jennilee-sweet, if you don't sit still, you're really going to hurt me." Charlie's sincere tone got through to her.

Jennilee knew exactly what Charlie meant. One of the boys had taken a screaming line drive to the groin during one of their baseball games—with predictable results. All the girls cried because they thought Billy was killed, the boys instinctively clamped their thighs together and cupped their hands protectively over their privates.

Making a fireman's chair out of their arms like they'd

learned in Boy Scouts, Charlie and Jeff carried Billy while Jennilee'd bolted for the house and Grandy.

Jennilee tried to push away again. "I'm okay."

"No you're not." Whispering something in Jennilee's ear, whatever Charlie said, his magic worked. Helping Jennilee turn around in his lap, he hauled her back against himself, wrapped his arms around her.

Jennilee stared fixedly at Doc's shirt pocket.

Penlight in hand, Doc shifted closer. Jennilee's face lost even more color. Talking soothingly, he explained exactly what he was doing.

"Jennilee, you want to tell me what's going on?"

Giving Doc no answer, she tried to meld her body into Charlie's.

Whispering in her ear again, Charlie tightened his hold and looked at Doc. "She can't."

"Jennilee, you don't have to talk, just shake or nod your head."

A high pitched, distressed whine, like the first sounds from a steaming teakettle, escaped before Jennilee could contain it. Trembling, she buried her face in Charlie's neck.

"It's not that she won't talk, she can't tell you."

"Sure she can."

Charlie shook his head, his voice bitter, eyes full of anger. "She'll get in lots of trouble. Jennilee won't even tell me."

Nothing any of them said could convince Jennilee otherwise.

The adults pulled back out into the hall for a conference. A peek into the family room showed Jennilee curled in Charlie's lap again in her original position, the bright Granny square afghan once again securely wrapped around her. Jennilee's behavior solidified their resolve.

Grandy stuck her head in. "Charlie, we'll be back."

As soon as the front door closed, Charlie urged Jennilee to her feet. "Come on, Jennilee. They're going to your aunt's."

Jennilee shook her head, eyes huge in her pale face.

"Yes, Jennilee. This concerns you. We need to know what's going on."

Shaking her head again, Jennilee clung to Charlie's hand. Charlie wrapped her in a quick hug. "If you can't come with me, I understand, but I've gotta go. They won't tell us anything when they get back. We need to know, Jennilee."

CHAPTER 6

*H*ail mostly melted, rain softened to a fine mist, the four adults crossed the distance separating the houses. Tom looked at Del, all enraged mama bear, at the furiously determined set to her face and walk, tried to reason with her.

"Del, calm down. Just because Jennilee's scared of dark, enclosed places… No judge will take our word for what's going on. You know we can't prove a damn thing."

Del turned her hot gaze on him, flicked a glance over his habitual bow tie—baby yellow with tiny elephants on it today, totally ludicrous on anyone else but Tom pulled it off admirably and with great aplomb—and settled on his green eyes. "Don't you think I know that? We might not be able to prove anything, but we might be able to scare Celie enough that she'll let up."

Flanked by the three powerful authority figures, a force to be reckoned with herself, Del stalked up Celie's front walk. Mac pounded the side of his fist against the door, an age-old, unmistakable summons.

Through the sidelights, they could see Celie, a rather

blowzy Marilyn Monroe wannabe, taking her own sweet time coming down the stairs. Seeing who was at the door, she stopped on the landing, cigarette dangling, one foot lifted. Mac Williams, Stanley Mason, Tom Stimpson and Adele Meyers showing up on her doorstep any time, much less in the aftermath of a ferocious storm, was not good news.

Opening the door, Celie eyed the foursome. "Whaddaya want?"

Del answered. "We need to talk."

"Has something happened to Sylvie? Something happened to my Sylvie?" A flicker of genuine emotion crossed Celie's features.

"As far as we know, Sylvia, and Mort, are fine. It's Jennilee."

Face going as thunderous as the clouds earlier, taking a heavy drag, Celie blew smoke in their faces. Demanded, "What's she done now?"

"We need to come in, Celie." Militarily stiff, Mac Williams held his hat in both hands, used his official Chief of Police voice.

"I knew it. She's done something really bad this time." Turning away and stomping off, Celie stubbed out her cigarette in the ashtray beside the phone on the hall table. Spun to face them, hands on hips.

Doc defended Jennilee. "Jennilee hasn't done anything. It's your behavior we need to talk about."

"Me? I haven't done anything. You can't believe a word she says. Everything that comes out of her mouth is a lie."

Grandy got in a dig for Jennilee. "Well, since Jennilee never says anything, she can't be telling too many lies. And while we're here, that's something else that needs to be addressed. Jennilee has an extensive vocabulary, used it frequently—until you took custody. Now she barely speaks.

You've got some explaining to do, for that, and other things."

Tossing her head, Celie tried for innocence, fell flat. "I have no idea what you're talking about, Del. I want you out of my house this instant."

Tom Stimpson cleared his throat, adjusted his perfectly placed bow tie and straightened his already rigid spine. "Don't you mean Jennilee's house? Technically, you're only here to take care of Jennilee until she reaches her majority. You can talk to us here, or Mac can arrest you and we'll talk in front of a judge."

Celie stared daggers at Tom's trim form, looking court-ready in his spiffy suit, not a dark brown hair out of place. "Arrest me? Arrest me for what?"

"Child abuse, misuse of funds entrusted to you for a minor, slander, take your pick. Give me a minute, I can come up with a truckload of other reasons. If I get so much as a whiff of anything like what I witnessed today, I'll file on Jennilee's behalf to have her removed from your custody."

Celie tried to bluff her way out. "You can't do that! Daddy's will said if something happened to Cynthia, I was to have custody *and* this house *and* everything that goes with it."

Tom smiled, but it was the smile of a hungry predator. "Ah, but the will states you have to take care of Jennilee in exchange for those things. I'm not seeing that you are."

"The Judge is spinning in his grave right now." Grandy's heart was breaking all over again. "Cynthia'd have a conniption if she knew how you're treating her daughter."

Celie tried tears. "You have no idea what she's really like. She behaves for you, puts on this goody-two-shoes act for everyone else. I get to see the real child. She's hateful and disobedient, stubborn and willful and destructive and mouthy."

Might've gotten some smidgen of understanding if she hadn't included mouthy.

Fighting to keep her tone even, Del retorted, "I suspect Jennilee reacts badly to how you treat her. Children know when they're not loved or wanted. Jennilee never gives me or anyone else a bit of lip or trouble. She's one of the politest, most loving, most helpful children I've ever had the pleasure of knowing, not to mention—the quietest. I've told you before and I'll say it again in front of witnesses—you don't want Jennilee. Let me take her."

At Celie's drop-dead glare, Del pushed on. "I don't care about the money or the house—just Jennilee. I'll sign whatever you want, be responsible for everything she needs."

Celie sneered. "She put you up to this? Forget it. You'll never get a damn thing from me—and that includes her."

Del faced Celie's hate calmly. Losing her temper and pounding Celie's bleached blond head against the floor would be gratifying but it sure wouldn't help Jennilee's cause.

"Jennilee didn't put me up to anything. Doesn't know about us coming over here, never says a word about anything that goes on, but nothing would surprise me. Jennilee doesn't have to. I know you Celie, your black heart and your lying ways."

Celie sneered, "Go home, Adele. Take your accusations and your lapdogs with you."

"Mac, Tom, Doc—you're my witnesses. I offered to take Jennilee and it's not the first time. I give you fair warning, Celie. Keep your hands to yourself and quit using Jennilee as your personal whipping boy."

"Or what? You can't prove a thing. All you have are groundless accusations."

Doc gave Celie a hard look. "Enough, Celie. We know exactly what we saw, and we're willing to testify to that effect. You have to decide what you want more—the prestige that goes with this house and your father's name and all the benefits you reap from those, or to torment Jennilee. You can't have both."

Regaining her composure, Celie bitched, "What exactly is it that you think you saw? She left early this morning and hasn't been back since. When is it I'm supposed to have done whatever you think I've done?"

The whole group standing in the wide hallway bisecting the house, looking around while Doc talked to Celie, Del could see into the front parlor on her left and to her right the room that had been the Judge's den.

All the fine antiques were gone, replaced by cheap modern furniture, and not even good stuff. It might be tasteless, but the house was once again spotless, cleaner than the last time she'd reamed Celie.

Del's eyes followed the line of the hallway toward the back of the house, shifted up to the top of the stairs, followed the angle as the balcony cut to the right over the hallway. Zeroing in on the closet under the stairs, she didn't have to be told—this was the one. Headed for it.

Celie's shriek cut the air, reverberated in the hallway. "What do you think you're doing? You can't just…"

"That's the one." Del spoke to everyone and no one.

Celie didn't look to see what *one* Del was talking about but her eyes darted about like a trapped animal's.

Taking a deep breath, Del opened the solid wood closet door, swung it wide. Wasn't sure what she expected to see, but there was nothing except the usual coats and boots and her unwavering conviction that Jennilee spent an inordinate amount of time in this cramped space. No *Let Me Out* carved into the wooden door, no bloody scratches marring the varnish.

Del's voice, low and fervent, carried to every corner. "Cecelia McRae Johnson, I swear to you, if you ever—*ever*—

lock Jennilee in this or any other closet again, I will stop at nothing until you've lost everything you value and you are rotting in prison."

Del switched to her best Drill Sergeant voice. "Front room—now." Spinning on her heel, she headed for the room that had been the Judge's den.

Didn't look back to see if Celie followed, couldn't see anything but red right now anyway. Del's vision finally cleared, and she wished it hadn't. Where there'd once been a huge, floor to ceiling collection of fine, leatherbound volumes, volumes the Judge had treasured, now even the shelves were gone.

The Judge's fine leather furniture and mahogany desk had been replaced by chrome and vinyl ugliness. The highly polished heart pine floor and fine old Oriental rug were long gone, replaced by shag carpet in a shade of puce that should've been physically impossible. The exquisitely carved marble mantle with a full mirror of beveled glass over it had been torn out, the fireplace bricked over. Some hideous piece of sculpture on a pedestal resided there.

The entire room looked like some Better Homes and Gardens section on *Decorating Faux Pas, or How Not To Decorate.*

Del mentally shook herself. They weren't here to discuss Celie's taste in decorating, or lack of. Jennilee. Focus.

Celie started whining, making Del want to cover her ears. That particular tone coming from a child sounded bad enough. Coming from an adult, it was atrocious. "I haven't done anything. I don't care what you think. I'm not some ogre. I do the best I can with her."

"Celie, before you dig yourself any deeper, consider who's here. You're not fooling any of us. We've all known you since you were a baby, watched you grow up. You were a whiny, vindictive child and you're a whinier, even more vindictive adult. Did you ever stop to wonder why you don't have many friends?" Mac faced Celie, arms crossed, face stern.

"I never had many friends because everyone loved Princess Cynthia, She-Who-Could-Do-No-Wrong."

Mac ran a hand across his crew cut, blew out a breath. "That's exactly the kind of attitude I'm talking about. You got Cynthia in a lot of trouble when the two of you were growing up. Just because the Judge didn't pay attention to what went on doesn't mean the rest of us didn't."

Celie started whining again.

Del cut her off. "Speaking of Cynthia, had your situations been reversed, she'd never, ever, have treated Sylvia the way you treat Jennilee. Cynthia would've loved Sylvia just like her own. Whatever childish rivalries existed between the two of you would've been forgiven for the sake of the child."

"Sylvie isn't a bastard." Celie's voice was so venom-filled the others could only stare.

"That's what this is about—why you hate Jennilee so much?" Del sounded incredulous.

Celie flung her head. Sniffed, "Isn't that reason enough?"

"Cynthia said she was married, and I for one, believe her."

"Prove it. She never could. Where's the marriage certificate? Where's the husband? Miss-Goody-Two-Shoes comes home knocked up and Daddy welcomes her with open arms, lets her move back in. Supports her and her bastard."

Del shook her head. "Celie, your father had a stroke and Cynthia came home to take care of him."

"You'd believe anything she told you, just like you believe her lying bitch of a daughter. Daddy had a stroke when he found out about Cynthia and her little unwanted surprise."

Without touching her, Del crowded close and backed Celie against the wall. "Is this the kind of rubbish you spout to Jennilee? Jennilee's not a bastard and she's not unwanted, not then and not now. She's loved and wanted by everyone except you, her own mother's sister. Doesn't that shame you at all?"

"I have nothing to be ashamed of."

"More than we know, I suspect." Del sighed wearily, turned away. It took all kinds, but she'd never understand why there had to be people like Celie. "You just keep your hands and your hatefulness to yourself where Jennilee's concerned."

"And if I don't?"

Del whirled and with nothing more than the fierce look on her face, backed Celie to the wall again. "See that you do, or I'll drag your name so deep in the mud you're slinging you'll never get clean. The Judge might not be alive to be shamed by this, but your husband and daughter will never get over it. Mort might even leave you. In fact, he'd probably get custody of Sylvia. If word gets out what a terrible guardian you are, people'd probably think you aren't much of a mother, either."

Appealing to Mac, all six-plus very handsome and fit feet of him, tears trembling on her thickly mascara'd lashes, Celie entreated, "Mac, you're the Chief of Police. Do something! Arrest her. You all heard her threaten me." Celie looked from one to the other.

Mac shook his head, dark eyes solemn. "You heard Del. You lay off Jennilee."

"Your choice, Celie. I suggest you tell Mort about today, or one of us will. Keep in mind that when I file, you lose everything—*everything*—right down to the roof over your head." Tom turned to leave.

"Tom, I'll walk out with you. Same here, Celie. I'd think long and hard if I were you. If Jennilee comes up with so much as a hangnail, I want to know about it. The fact you refused to have anything to do with her while she had chickenpox won't help your case in the least."

Doc and Tom walked out, Doc playing Mutt to Tom's Jeff.

Left staring at their departing backs, and Del and Mac, Celie burst into tears. "Everybody hates me. Y'all are so mean to me."

"Dry it up, Celie. What goes around comes around, and I expect you've got a lot that's going to boomerang back on you. Sit down and listen up. There are going to be changes around here. Starting with the fact your niece has a name." Face grim, Del started outlining her demands.

∽

BACK ON DEL'S front porch, leaning against the rail, long legs crossed at the ankle and arms crossed over his broad chest, Mac sighed and watched Del pace furiously. "You know we can't make any of those accusations stick if Celie decides to fight back. If Cynthia'd just left a will..."

Pausing long enough to give him a heated glare, Del snapped, "I know that." Heaved a sigh and softened, body and tone. "I'm just hoping we scared her enough to give Jennilee some respite. Tom threatening to take away the house and the stipend Celie'll lose if she loses custody, besides the fact that everyone will know, might be enough to make her behave for awhile. The Judge could never see it but Celie hated Cynthia. She's transferred that hate to Jennilee. Did you see her face when we threatened to tell Mort?"

Mac scrubbed a hand over his crew cut in a familiar gesture of frustration and nodded. "I'll say something to him. He might be able to shorten her leash some."

Del sighed again. "When he's home. He doesn't have a clue what goes on when he's not here, only what Celie tells him, and I can just imagine." Resumed pacing and started winding back up. "Did you hear how she distorted that bit about the Judge's stroke? His first stroke happened long before Cynthia got pregnant. He's the one who insisted she finish, graduate with her class."

Catching her shoulders, stopping her, Mac soothed, "I heard, Del. Don't get all worked up again. Go take care of those two miscreants of yours." Grinned as he said it. Charlie and Jennilee were two of his favorite munchkins around.

Del grinned in return. "Thanks for everything, Mac."

Slipping inside, Del closed the door and leaned back against it, drained but jubilant. Celie'd caved to most of Del's demands. Del didn't know how long it would last, would bet anything Celie was even now plotting new ways to torment Jennilee, but for now Del had won Jennilee some measure of freedom.

Peeking quietly around the door to the family room, Del found the kids right where she'd left them. In the rocking chair, sound asleep. Walking through her house, humming softly and re-opening windows, her thoughts wandered back to the Judge's house and the wonderful antiques and treasures it'd once held.

The Judge's grandfather had captained a clipper ship, had brought untold treasures back from his voyages. Del sighed, wondering where they'd ended up. In the trash, more than likely.

There was nothing wrong with getting tired of old stuff and getting new. She'd done it herself, on more than one occasion. The trick was to use some common sense and replace what you'd gotten rid of with things of equal or greater value, not to replace real diamonds with paste. Oh, well. Celie'd never been accused of having any common sense.

Charlie wasn't asleep and neither was Jennilee. They didn't move, didn't make a peep as they listened to Grandy moving around the house. Jennilee drew a shuddering breath, Charlie tightened his hold. Having barely beaten the adults back here, almost getting caught had been worth it. They had a lot more pieces of the puzzle now.

Charlie could feel Jennilee's heart knocking against her ribs, a kind of Morse code pounded out in heartbeats from her soul to his. The message struck fear deep in his heart, repeated over and over.

She's gonna kill me now.

CHAPTER 7

*J*ennilee was reborn that summer. Grandy must've scared Celie more than they dreamed possible. Jennilee still had loads of chores to do, but... Joy! No more closet, and as long as Jennilee's chores were done, Celie didn't want Jennilee anywhere around.

Staying on top of her chores and out of Celie's way, the longer Jennilee was free, the more she talked, at least around Charlie and Grandy. Reveling in her newfound freedom, she blossomed like a sorely neglected plant that's suddenly noticed and taken care of.

Charlie and Jennilee rode their bikes a million miles that summer, until they knew every street, every road in or close to town. Until they knew every shortcut and pothole.

A body could learn a lot riding a bike. Charlie and Jennilee became a familiar sight, and a great many of the townspeople became more familiar to them.

Looking like a monk dropped in the wrong century, portly Brother Anderson, minus a cassock and already possessing the tonsure, didn't think anything about it when the two of them parked their bikes beside the foot high cement wall surrounding Oak Grove cemetery. Smiled to himself at the way they held hands and walked in synch across the grass, their faces radiating happiness and contentment. The thought briefly crossed his mind they looked more like a long time happily married couple than a couple little kids.

With a quick *hi,* they both fell to, helping him pull weeds and tend headstones. Nothing more was said. Jennilee looked at Charlie, and they shared a grin. Both loved this old cemetery, had made it one of their favorite stops on their regular rounds. Even if Jennilee's mom hadn't been buried here, they still would've come regularly. Huge live oaks shaded the better part of it, with a camellia or gardenia, a hydrangea or azalea or cedar planted at a great many of the graves.

Headstones ranged from crude cedar markers nearly defeated by time to elaborate marble angels. Small, plain stones marked some graves, ballast stones from the sailing ships used to carry goods from England and other parts of the world. Instead of grass, some of the older graves had cement arches covering the whole thing to keep the coffins from popping out of the ground during a hurricane.

The sense of peace tangible, as thick in this cemetery as the humid heat, Jennilee and Charlie worked companionably with Brother Anderson for a good hour or two. Hot, but here under the live oaks, there was a good breeze and plenty of shade. Kept pace until Brother Anderson finally sat on one of the concrete benches scattered around.

Charlie and Jennilee dropped at his feet, first checking carefully for fireants.

Mopping his cherry pie round face with a linen square, Brother Anderson looked at the two. There weren't many children who'd voluntarily spend a morning helping clean up a cemetery. Sister Del was doing a marvelous job raising them. Though there were five churches in town—Baptist, Pentecostal, Primitive Baptist, and the negro church—Del, along with most of her large extended family attended his, First Methodist.

Charlie smiled at Jennilee, a slow *I love you smile* fully returned by Jennilee. Taking Jennilee's hand in his, he asked, "Will you marry us, Brother Anderson?"

Still trying to get over the depth of love in their eyes and on their faces, trying to reconcile two children with a look of such intense love that he felt like a peeping Tom, he choked at Charlie's question.

Jennilee's laughter chimed out, pure and sweet as church bells on Sunday morning. "Not right now. After Charlie graduates from college."

Charlie grinned. "We know preachers get shuffled around, we just wanted to know if you'd come back when we need you."

After a flustered moment, Brother Anderson smiled hugely. "I give you my word. As long as I'm able, I'd be honored." Cleared his throat. "Aren't the two of you jumping the gun?"

"There is no other for me." Charlie's solemn declaration rang with sincerity.

"Nor for me." Jennilee agreed, just as sure. Their gazes never wavered off each other as Charlie lifted Jennilee's hand to his lips.

Brother Anderson felt like he'd just witnessed a...*betrothal* was the only word that fit. A mental picture of a fair maiden and a great warrior plighting their troth popped into his head.

Charlie stood, tugged Jennilee to her feet. Brother Anderson completely forgotten, they turned to leave.

Brother Anderson stopped them with a word. "Jennilee."

"Yessir?"

"You said when Charlie graduates. Aren't you going to college?"

Her certainty was absolute. "I have no need to."

"Surely you do—to learn…things."

Jennilee smiled radiantly. "But I already know how to love Charlie. That's all I need to know."

Jennilee's serene answer shook Brother Anderson to his core.

With the faith of a child… That these two should be so sure of their life's course at such a young age… Brother Anderson could do nothing but shake his head as the two walked toward their bikes, hand in hand. Pedaled off, leaving him wondering if they'd really been there or if he'd been working too hard in the heat.

Their next stop was the office of the Ridgerunner. Mr. Matt had become one of their favorite people, a veritable treasure trove of information. With Grandy's permission, he answered their questions, and they were insatiably curious.

Mr. Matt had shown them how to run the presses, taught them the rudiments of a good story, given them all the details he could remember about their mothers, everyday things that never made the paper. Things Charlie and Jennilee wouldn't ask Grandy or Charlie's daddy.

They didn't stay long with Mr. Matt today, had another destination in mind, had been working their way there all day. Charlie's dad, when he wasn't working at the Base or blind drunk, was a top notch mechanic. Owned his own garage, lived in the apartment over it.

The wide double doors of the garage bay open, after the over-bright sunshine outside, it took their eyes a minute to adjust to the comparative gloom inside.

"Dad."

The banging noises and sounds of tools continued for a moment, stopped abruptly. Charlie's dad slid out from under the car on his Jeepers Creepers.

"Hey, you two. What are you up to?"

"We were out riding our bikes and thought we'd stop and say hi."

"Glad you did. Thirsty?"

The kids nodded, said *yessir* as one.

Finishing, he put his tools up, washed the grease and dirt off his face and hands, stepped out into the sunshine. The kids were nowhere in sight and his heart skipped a beat. Maybe they'd gotten tired of waiting. Hearing laughter, he followed the sound around the corner.

Looking at their smiling faces, Donnie wished bitterly for the millionth time that Iris was here to watch their boy growing up. A pang of guilt struck him as he thought about what Iris would have to say about the way he neglected Charlie, about the way he was drinking himself into an early grave.

Uncannily observant, Jennilee nudged Charlie in his dad's direction. Grinning at her, he gave his dad a shy hug. Donnie kept an arm around Charlie's shoulders and kept Jennilee's hand in his.

Climbing the steps, slanting a long look at the two males beside her so engrossed in each other, Jennilee smiled to herself, well satisfied.

Sitting at his tiny kitchen table, drinking lemonade, Jennilee looked around while Charlie and his dad kept throwing surreptitious glances at each other, both pretending to look at anything but.

Definitely a bachelor's apartment, it wasn't filthy, but neither was it up to Jennilee's impeccable standards. No plants anywhere, or knickknacks. A lopsided pile of magazines and newspapers leaned against the room's only comfortable chair. Mr. Donnie probably slept in that ratty recliner a great deal more than he slept in his bed—the unmade one she could see through the open bedroom door.

Donnie studied the two in front of him, felt his heart wrench painfully. Charlie looked more like his mother every day, if that was possible. Jennilee was the spitting image of Cynthia. The two of them were thicker even than Iris and Cynthia had been.

"What have you two been up to?"

Charlie and Jennilee gave him a rundown of their day, talking over each other, finishing each other's sentences. Listening with half an ear, Donnie watched Charlie with hungry eyes.

Exchanging a look, the kids drained their glasses and stood.

Still lost in thought and regret, Donnie wasn't ready to let Charlie go, didn't have any good reason to keep him here. What could he say? *Sit still son, I just want to look at you?*

Jennilee hugged Donnie's thin frame. "We're cooking hamburgers and hotdogs on the grill tonight. We'd love to have you."

"Please, Dad. Grandy'd really like to see you."

"I'll try. Thanks for asking. Hey, you two come back any time. I mean it."

Standing at the window, Donnie watched them ride off.

"Think he'll come?"

Heart hurting at the wistful tone in Charlie's voice, Jennilee couldn't look at him right now or she'd cry. Spouted one of Grandy's favorite sayings, "Nothing ventured, nothing gained." She'd seen the hungry look on Mr. Donnie's face, the same hungry look Charlie had on his.

"Race you!" Standing on her pedals, Jennilee put everything she had into making her bike go faster.

Grandy watched them fly up the long driveway, neck and neck. Sliding to a stop, they dropped their bikes as one and ran for the porch. Hit the steps at the same time, both shouting *I won, I won!* before collapsing on the porch in a laughing, panting heap.

Grandy opened the screen door, grinning, their happiness contagious. "Hey, you two! Why don't you get your suits on and go for a swim before supper? Tide's high and you've got plenty of time."

The tangle of arms and legs wiggled and squirmed, looked up at Grandy. "Will you come with us?"

"Please?" Jennilee added her voice to Charlie's.

"All right, you twisted my arm. Bet I can get my suit on before you!" Screen door slamming like a starting pistol as Grandy turned and ran, Charlie and Jennilee scrambled to their feet. The three of them dashed madly through the house, laughing like hyenas.

Charlie practiced cannonballs off the dock, Jennilee practiced holding her breath. Grandy swam, climbed out to lay on the dock. She loved listening to Charlie and Jennilee. *Watch me's* interspersed with *start counting* and splashing and laughter. Lots of laughter.

Drying off reluctantly, they headed back to the house. Reluctant until they saw who was waiting on the porch. Grandy thought her eyes were playing tricks on her. Exchanging a gleeful look, Charlie and Jennilee took off running, came to a breathless stop in front of Donnie.

"You came."

Donnie nodded, watched his mother walking across the yard. The wide, welcoming smiles wreathing their faces instantly banished any doubts he had about intruding.

Donnie fidgeted. "Charlie and Jennilee...came by the garage today and invited me to supper."

"Well, we're certainly glad you came! Perfect timing, too.

We're starving!" Grandy gave Donnie a quick, fierce hug, blinked away tears. "Donnie, if you and Charlie will light the charcoal, we'll get the burgers ready."

Giving Charlie a wink, Jennilee headed inside with Grandy.

CHAPTER 8

*C*harlie and Jennilee wove invisible designs on the pavement with their bikes, swooping back and forth from one side of the road to the other and in and out between the lines in the middle. As always, their seemingly aimless meanderings had a definite destination. They weren't headed to the cemetery today, or the Ridgerunner, or even to the garage.

The First National Bank their destination on this fine summer day, both had been in here plenty of times with Grandy. Knew lots about the bank just from that. The hours of business, 9:00-1:00 and 3:00-5:00 every week day except Wednesday. Wednesday the bank closed at noon.

The polished marble floor was always spotless and gleaming, the interior cool and hushed as a church, the deposit and withdrawal slips neatly lined up in their berths with a pen on a chain close by. One of the few places in town that was air conditioned, had in fact been one of the first. Many people lingered for that very reason, gossiping with the clerks behind the counter, drawing their business out much longer than necessary.

Always neatly dressed, the men in suits and shiny shoes, the women in demure dresses or skirts and heels, the people who worked in the bank were a stark contrast to most of the customers. Knee boots and bib overalls were more likely to be seen on this side of the counter. When the farmers and fishermen put on their good clothes to come to the bank, everyone knew it was serious.

Dressed this morning in clothes usually reserved for church, Charlie wore a pair of dress slacks with a plaid button up shirt and shiny penny loafers. Jennilee wore a navy blue dress with lace edging the Peter Pan collar and the sleeves, shiny black patent leather shoes with lacy white ankle socks.

Standing patiently in line, when they got up to the window, they stood side by side and looked up at the clerk.

Mrs. Mamie Brown, looking extremely professional with her perfectly coiffed hair and elegant dress, a single strand of pearls gleaming, leaned over the counter. "Are you two waiting for Del? I haven't seen her this morning."

Charlie said politely, "No, ma'am. We'd like to open an account, please."

"You both want to open..."

Charlie shook his head. "We want to open one account —together."

"Only married couples can open joint accounts, and since you two are way too young to be married, I don't see how I can help you. Run along and go play."

Polite but firm, Charlie countered, "Business partners can open joint accounts, and they don't have to be married. Jennilee and I can be business partners."

"You don't *have* a business, so you can't open a business account."

"We will." Charlie and Jennilee smiled up at her.

Everyone in the bank avidly eavesdropping, Miz Mamie

tried another tack. "Del can come in and open an account for you, Charlie, since you're a minor. Jennilee, your aunt could come in and open one for you."

"We want our own account. Together."

An old farmer, wearing the requisite bibs and boots, shifted his tobacco, spit into his spit cup and remarked dryly, "Ain't never seen no bank what refused to take someone's money afore." That brought outright laughter from the other patrons, hastily smothered giggles and titters from the other clerks.

It also brought Mr. Whipple out of his office, starched and suited like a department store mannequin. As bank manager, much like any true librarian, he frowned on excessive noise in his sanctum. "Mrs. Brown, what's the meaning of this?"

The same old farmer spoke up again, gesturing with his spit cup. "These two younguns here are trying to put money in your bank and this here clerk is givin' them reasons why they can't. Seems like the bank manager could find a way around that little problem so's the rest of us could finish our business and get outta here." Scratched his leathery face and mused, "Can't remember when a trip to the bank was this entertainin', though."

"Mrs. Brown, I'll handle this. Charlie, Jennilee, does Del know what you're up to?"

"Yessir, Mr. Whipple." Charlie faced Mr. Whipple, matched him solemn look for solemn look. "We told her we wanted to open an account. Grandy said that was a good idea and to see Miz Mamie, since she's the Head Teller. She also said Miz Mamie's a stickler for the rules and if we couldn't get her to bend, we should speak with you."

Charlie's innocent statement brought another round of laughter from the assembled crowd, growing larger by the moment.

"Come into my office, children."

Turning back to Mrs. Mamie Brown, they thanked her politely and followed Mr. Whipple into his corner office, all mahogany and leather and sailing prints done in heavy oils.

Walking around behind his gleaming desk, Mr. Whipple indicated for Charlie and Jennilee to take the two seats facing him. He sat, they sat, and they stared at each other.

"Do the two of you know what a joint account is?"

"Yessir, Mr. Whipple."

Mr. Whipple raised a brow.

"A joint account means both people have access to the account, either to deposit money or to withdraw it. Married people or business partners can have a joint account, and relatives if so needed."

"You and Jennilee are neither married, business partners, nor relatives."

"We're partners, and we're getting married when we're old enough."

"I see." Mr. Whipple steepled his fingers. "Charlie, you trust Jennilee with your money?"

"I trust Jennilee with my life."

"Jennilee, you trust Charlie enough to open a joint account with him?"

Other than her thank you to Miz Mamie, Jennilee had yet to say a word. "The money means nothing without Charlie."

"This a most unusual request." Both children regarded Mr. Whipple solemnly as he eyed them.

Sounding more like a seasoned lawyer than a child, Charlie stated, "Mr. Whipple, whether you let us open an account or not, we will save our money, and it will be a joint effort. The only difference will be whether or not you reap the benefit of using our hard earned money while it's sitting in your bank."

Stifling a laugh, Mr. Whipple opened a drawer and took

out an application form. "Have you ever considered becoming a banker or a lawyer, Charlie?"

"Nossir, I have other plans. Bankers and lawyers work too many hours. I'm not willing to be away from Jennilee that long every day."

Grinning, Mr. Whipple initialed several areas on the application. "Fill this out and sign here, here, and here, both of you, then we'll take this and your money to Mrs. Brown. You won't have any more trouble. I'm obligated by law to get Del to sign for you, since this is a minor's account, so her name will be on it as well."

"We understand that, sir. Until we're eighteen and then it's ours alone."

Taking the application and the pen, Jennilee carefully filled out the required areas. Signed her name, passed pen and paper to Charlie. Signing in the appropriate spaces, he passed the application back to Mr. Whipple.

Checking to make sure all the i's were dotted and the t's crossed, Mr. Whipple rose. Shook hands with Jennilee, then Charlie. "If you ever change your mind…"

"Thank you, sir, but I won't."

Mr. Whipple accompanied them to Mrs. Brown's window. Quite a few people lingered in the lobby, but there wasn't anyone in line.

"Mrs. Brown, these fine customers would like to make a deposit. I'm leaving them in your capable hands. Their paperwork is in order. Charlie, Jennilee, thank you. Please don't hesitate to call on me if I can be of any further assistance."

"Thank you, sir."

Miz Mamie asked, "How much would you like to deposit today, Charlie? I need to know so I can write the amount in your savings account book."

"We already filled out our deposit slips, except the

account number. Grandy showed us how." Charlie dug in one pocket, produced a neat wad of bills. Mostly ones, several rolls of coins, a nickel, and a deposit slip. Dug in his other pocket, handed Jennilee the same.

Putting his on the counter, Charlie watched while Miz Mamie counted it. "I suppose you have exactly the same amount, Jennilee."

"Yes ma'am."

Charlie and Jennilee walked out of the bank, oblivious to the grins and chuckles coming from the other customers. They were now the proud owners of a savings account that held not just the tidy sum of fifty six dollars and ten cents, but the seeds of their dreams.

The old farmer walked out with them. "Aren't you Del Meyer's grandson?"

"Yessir, I'm Charlie."

"Who's your quiet lady friend?"

"I'm Jennilee, sir. Judge McRae's granddaughter."

"Sorry about the Judge. He was a fine man. Son, you tell your grandma Cyrus Adams said hello. Now, it's none of my business and you can tell me so if you've a mind, but where'd two younguns your age get that much money?"

"We've been saving awhile. Some's birthday money, some's from turning in drink bottles for the refund, mostly it's from working. Raking pine straw, running errands, stuff like that."

"Workin' that hard and being so good about savin' your money, you gotta have somethin' special in mind. You two savin' for new bikes?"

Grinning up at their new-found friend, Charlie twined his fingers with Jennilee's. "We've got bikes. We're savin' our money so when we get married, I don't have to work all the time and be away from Jennilee."

A slow grin creased Cyrus' face. "That's the best reason I ever heard for savin' money. Y'all have a good day."

"You too, Mr. Cyrus."

Retrieving their bikes, they headed for their next planned stop. Chief Mac would be in his office, and if he wasn't, he'd be at the Family Diner drinking coffee, or the barber shop or the hardware store, jawing with anyone who came in, benignly keeping a finger on the town's pulse.

Sharing matching grins, they flew past the library. Prune-faced as a starving piranha, Bertha still hadn't forgiven them for their fiasco with their mothers' obituaries. The fact that Grandy'd sided with them still rankled her. They were careful to only use the library on Bertha's day off.

In his office this morning, Chief Mac rose and grinned in welcome, his dark eyes lighting as Charlie knocked and stuck his head around the door.

"Mornin', you two. What in the world are you up to this early in the morning' and all dressed up to boot?"

Jennilee gave Chief Mac a hug, Charlie shook his hand. "We had business at the bank and we wanted to stop and see you."

Resting a hip on his scarred and battered desk, getting a mental image of Sheriff Andy talking to Opie and one of his pals, Chief grinned wider. "Well, I'm mighty glad you did."

"We wanted to say hi, but we have a question."

Mac eyed them warily. With these two, you never could tell what they'd come up with next and Charlie's innocent sounding words came out far too adult.

"Chief Mac, we were wondering if we could get some of the merchants to install bike racks. That is, if they'd agree, and if it's ok with you. We always have to park around the side so our bikes aren't in the way."

Mac's eyebrows shot up. Not just at the idea, which was a

good one, but because Jennilee was the one to voice it. "It is a good idea."

Jennilee spoke again. "We'd be willing to do the work, put the bike stands up in front of any business that wanted them, but we wanted to check with you first. The business owners might be more amenable if you suggested it."

To his credit, Mac didn't bat an eyelash.

"Dad said he'd donate the materials and weld the racks, help us distribute them."

"You two have put a lot of thought into this project, haven't you?"

"Yessir."

"I'll let you know."

"Thank you, sir. You have a good day."

"You, too, kids."

Mac watched them leave, shook his head.

Next stop, Tom Stimpson's office. Miss Judy Jones, blond, cute as a button and barely two years out of secretarial school looked up when the door chimed. "Hey, kids. Miz Del isn't here. Is she supposed to be?"

"Hey, Miss Judy. No, ma'am. How're the wedding plans going?"

"Just fine, counting down the days. Thanks for asking. What can I do for you?"

"We'd like to speak with Mr. Tom if he's not busy."

"He's got a few minutes before his next client. I'll buzz him."

Hitting a button, Miss Judy spoke for a moment, listened and smiled. "He'll see you. Go right in." Waved them to the door behind her. "Give Miz Del my best."

"Yes ma'am."

Dressed to the nines, looking ready to head to court in his pinstripe suit and wingtips, his bow tie colorful fishing lures on a blue background today, Tom smiled at the two.

"Charlie, Jennilee. To what do I owe the honor of this visit?"

As they'd done with Chief Mac, Jennilee hugged him, Charlie shook Mr. Tom's hand. Charlie stepped back and indicated Jennilee.

"We need to ask you a question, please."

Tom's antennae vibrated. "Everything all right, Jennilee?"

"Yessir. I appreciate you asking." Unspoken messages flowed back and forth between the three of them. Charlie nodded, confirming Jennilee's answer.

Mentally comparing the smiling, talkative Jennilee in front of him with the terrified little girl he'd seen at Del's, Tom asked, "What can I help you with?"

"Charlie and I just opened a savings account. I want to make sure that…no one else can get their hands on it just because my name's on it." *Celie* hung in the air like echoes from an unseen gong.

"You opened an account with both your names on it?"

"Yessir. We know Grandy has to be on it because we're minors. I just don't want anyone else to have access to it. Is there anything we can do legally?"

"You're worried that because your name's on the account, your aunt might try to withdraw the money."

"Yessir. She can have every cent my grandfather left and welcome to it, but she'll not get a penny more. I need you to figure out how to keep this from her and still be legal—pay the taxes and stuff." Jennilee faced him, proud and determined.

"Let me see what I can come up with and I'll let you know."

"Thank you, sir. Since I already have a guardian, can I make it so you have Power of Attorney? Grandy already signs all my permission slips and such, and thank you for fixing it so she can, but Grandy has enough on her."

"I'll check into it. Jennilee, you know if there's ever anything I can do… Your aunt may have custody, but I'm your lawyer."

"I understand that, sir, and there will come a time when I need you on that matter. Oh, are you paid a retainer out of the estate or do we need to pay you?"

"Out of the estate, Jennilee." *Even if I wasn't, I'd do this anyway.*

Charlie stepped forward to shake hands again. "Thank you for your time and your help, sir."

"We promised Grandy we'd help her as soon as we were done conducting our business."

Eyes glowing, impish grins appearing on both their faces, Charlie and Jennilee… transformed, as if someone switched channels on the TV and just like that the miniature adults were gone and two little kids stood in their place.

"Bye, Mr. Tom."

"Bye, kids."

Door closing behind them, Tom unknowingly mirrored Mac's earlier position, shaking his head as he bent over the never-ending paperwork on his glossy desk. Those two were something else.

CHAPTER 9

Charlie and Jennilee pedaled home, satisfied with their accomplishments so far.

Grinning at the sight of them, Grandy gave them both a hug.

"How'd it go?"

"You were right. Miz Mamie wouldn't budge an inch. Mr. Whipple came out of his office and helped us."

"He was awful nice about everything, said the next time you come into the bank there's a form you have to sign, please."

Grandy grinned wider as she thought of the by-the-book, Head Teller Mamie confronted with two immoveable forces like her Charlie and Jennilee.

"We gotta go change. We'll be right back."

Grandy shook her head, kept mixing. Listening to them race up the stairs, she checked the clock. They'd be back in three minutes or less.

Sure enough, nearly three minutes to the second, they reappeared. Washing their hands they started firing questions.

"What are we baking today?"

"What have you already finished?"

"What can we do?"

Grandy answered their questions in the order she'd heard them. "Triple layer chocolate cake with cream cheese frosting, lemon meringue pie, chocolate chip cookies, and nothing except the cake batter. Charlie, you get the pans out and grease and flour them. Jennilee, get the smaller mixing bowl out and start on the frosting."

Clatter and chatter filled the air.

"Hey, you two—how 'bout when we finish this and get it delivered to the diner, we head for Fort Macon?"

Both faces lit, and they moved faster. One of their very favorite places to explore, Charlie, ever the local history buff, rattled off what he knew.

Jennilee drifted, listening with half an ear. Charlie was all about historic significance. She just liked the fort because it was old. Loved the cobblestone drive that led to the fort, the drawbridge, the thick, thick entrance doors and the wood tiles that comprised the entryway. Made from blocks sawed off the ends of huge logs, squared off, the tiles showed the tree rings, had seen more foot traffic than Jennilee could imagine.

Laughing, Grandy told him, "Overload, overload. Enough history!"

While the cake baked, they rolled out the crust for the pies. Jennilee loved to stir the lemon filling as it cooked, watching it get thicker and thicker. Mixing the chocolate chip cookies, they greased cookie trays and began spooning dough onto the trays while Grandy made meringue.

By the time the pies and cookies were done, the cake had cooled enough to ice. Grandy did that while Charlie and Jennilee carefully transferred the cookies into a waiting box.

Making PBJs and fixing a milk jug of tea for their picnic,

Grandy grabbed a bag of chips, some paper cups and napkins. Winking at the kids, she put some of the chocolate chip cookies in a Tupperware bowl for them.

Dropping the baked goods off, they set out for Atlantic Beach.

Windows down, singing and joking, they got to Morehead only to find the Atlantic Beach drawbridge open and traffic at a standstill. Not that they could see the bridge from here—they were a good two miles from actually getting on it. Resigned to the wait, they made bets on how long it'd take for the bridge to close.

"Grandy, you're such a good cook, why don't you open a restaurant instead of just baking for the one out on the by-pass?"

Grandy grinned. "Thanks for the compliment, Jennilee. I've thought about it. It takes a lot of time to run a restaurant properly."

"You're not doing it because of us, huh, Grandy?" Charlie boasted, "We're not babies anymore. We can take care of ourselves."

"I will someday. It's because you're not babies anymore that I've been putting it off."

"Huh?" Charlie sounded confused.

Jennilee answered softly. "We're growing up fast and Grandy doesn't want to miss anything. In a few years, it won't matter. We'll be bigger and Grandy has plenty of time for opening her own restaurant."

Reaching out, Grandy hugged Jennilee, tousled Charlie's hair. "That's exactly right. I don't want to miss a single minute with you two."

Traffic started moving and it seemed to take forever, but they finally made it across the bridge, all three cheering when they finally turned left at the stoplight and headed down the island.

Spending an enjoyable hour or two exploring the fort, headed back to the parking lot Charlie asked, "Grandy, can we go out on the jetty?"

"Sure, guys. You know the deal. Stay out of the water. Every summer at least one swimmer, usually more, drowns here. We'll swim at the Oceanana."

Topping the dunes, they looked out at Beaufort Inlet and the water boiling through the channel, at the various boats, and the surf fishermen.

Driving to the Oceanana Pier, Charlie gibed wickedly, "Know how you can tell the locals from the tourists? Besides their flaming sunburns, all the tourists say Ocean Anna, not O-she-anna."

Jennilee grinned. "I don't care how you say it, I love this place."

"Pier first?"

"Yeah."

Kicking their shoes off, they hot-footed across the asphalt. Winding through the grill and bait shop, darting out the other side, they immediately felt the sway of the ocean pushing and pulling relentlessly on the huge pilings holding the pier. Strolling all the way to the end they meandered back, seeing what the fishermen lining the sides of the pier were catching. Sand sharks, a few spots and croakers. Nothing big on the chalkboard that listed the day's biggest catch and what had been caught in general.

Blinking like owls, they re-entered the dark grill, passed through and headed for the beach.

Shucking the clothes they had on over their suits, dropping them in a pile on the hot sand, Charlie and Jennilee headed for the slack surf at a dead run. Splashed out and dove in as one, frolicked like dolphins with legs for a long time.

Tiring, Jennilee dug in the edge of the surf for the tiny

coquina clams, no bigger than the tip end of your little finger. Admiring their beauty, all the pastel colors of the rainbow with light purple bands, she gently returned them to the surf.

Partial to the sand fleas, Charlie searched just as intently. Not really fleas, although there were fleas that lived in the beach sand, he dug up the small, many legged crustaceans that lived in the edge of the surf. Harmless and fun to catch, many of the surf fishermen used them for bait.

Face alight, arms in the air, head thrown back, Jennilee spun in giddy circles while Charlie watched with a dopey grin on his own face.

Strolling along in the edge of the surf, talking about everything and nothing, the threesome walked past two other piers before turning around and heading back.

Making use of the Oceanana's outside showers, they got most of the sand off before heading back past the cinderblock changing rooms—marked Gulls and Buoys—just outside the bait shop. Drip-dried by the time they reached the car, they wrapped their towels around their waists and climbed in.

"Hey guys. Wanna eat at El's?"

Grinning hugely at Jennilee, Charlie started intoning like Captain Kirk reciting the Star Trek intro. "El's—the perfect drive-in—has THE best shrimp burgers in the world. Established in 1959, El's carries on a fine tradition of good food and good service."

Pulling into El's, Grandy parked under one of the majestic live oaks. Seagulls hovered, raucously daring bandits who'd snatch a french fry right out of your hand if you held it out the window.

None of them needed to look at the menu board over the top of the window. When the carhop came to their car, Grandy and Jennilee both ordered shrimp burgers and fries,

Charlie opted for a Superburger and onion rings. Three of El's thick shakes.

Passing out the food, all three took the paper off their straws, put their straws in their shakes, set them on the dash. It'd be awhile before they melted enough to actually drink.

Unwrapping their shrimp burgers, Grandy and Jennilee sighed in anticipation. Fried shrimp, coleslaw and ketchup on a huge hamburger bun.

Charlie unwrapped his giant hamburger, loaded with mustard, slaw, chili, and onion—it was a local institution.

Polishing off every bite, right down to the very last fry and onion ring, they drove home sucking on the straws imbedded in their shakes. Laughter rang when they sucked so hard the straws collapsed on themselves.

Taking quick turns in the one upstairs bathtub, they bathed and rinsed their suits out, hung them on the clothesline. Coaxing Jennilee to sit on the steps in the waning sunshine, Charlie sat behind her and brushed her glorious hair.

Somnolent with the day's activities and the attention, Jennilee rested in the open vee of Charlie's legs, Grandy beside them. Perfectly content, Jennilee's elbows on Charlie's knees and his chin on her head, his wrists crossed in front of her, brush dangling from one hand.

The hot, humid air wasn't so bad after you'd spent the afternoon at the beach, and it was cooling off some with the approaching evening. Feeling Jennilee shiver, Charlie knew it wasn't the weather. Didn't have to look very hard to see what set Jennilee off.

Celie—standing at her kitchen door, her hatred as visible as the path between the hedges from one house to the other, leading just as surely straight to Jennilee.

Celie jerked her head. With that one small movement, all the warmth and color of the day fled.

Jennilee scrambled up. "I gotta go."

Grandy, leaning back on her elbows, eyes closed, missed the whole by-play. "Ah, Jennilee. Sorry. We've enjoyed having you, as always. Come back when you can."

"Thanks, Grandy. I will. Bye, guys." Jennilee spoke absently, her mind already across the way.

Charlie watched Jennilee leaving, head up and back straight. A tanned, barefoot princess in shorts and a t shirt, her cloud of golden hair reaching all the way to the pockets of her shorts.

A princess going knowingly to her doom, a willing sacrifice to the wicked witch.

CHAPTER 10

Jennilee seldom asked Grandy for help, never admitted everything wasn't hunky-dory next door, but she asked this time.

Waiting until Jennilee wasn't expecting anything, Celie broadsided her.

A week or so after their beach trip, Jennilee slipped in the kitchen door, started directly on her chores. Froze at her aunt's voice, Celie's smugness warning Jennilee whatever she wanted concerned her and was not good.

"Mort wants to see you."

Following her aunt, Jennilee passed her despicable cousin lurking in the hall and openly gloating, a wide grin on her piggish little face.

Mort, the insufferable prick, still riding the receding wave of his unremarkable high school football career like a tsunami that had long since come and gone, already going to fat and cultivating a distinct comb-over, lectured while Celie looked on piously. "Celie tells me you're not taking care of your hair, not brushing it or anything, and she's right. Look at yourself—your hair's all greasy and smelly. If you can't take care of it, you'll have to cut it. Celie's already made an appointment for you. Go get in the car."

She went—with Celie's fingers locked around Jennilee's upper arm in a punishing grip. Jennilee didn't pull away, didn't make a sound.

Sylvia climbed in the front seat of the car, gloating and smirking. Dragging Jennilee around to the driver's side, Celie opened the back door, tried to shove Jennilee inside.

Jennilee came to life then, like a cat trying to be forced into a sink full of water. Hissing and spitting, she wrenched her arm out of Celie's grip and streaked for Grandy's.

In the kitchen, right where she'd been when Jennilee left, one look at Jennilee's distraught face told Grandy all she needed to know. Throwing her arms around Grandy's waist, Jennilee clung like a leech. Grandy wrapped her arms around the shaking child.

Not far behind Jennilee, Celie wrenched open the screen door and started screeching.

Grandy held Jennilee tighter as Jennilee's shaking turned into shuddering and she tried to burrow into Grandy's skin.

"Celie!" Shouting to make herself heard over Celie's caterwauling, Grandy demanded, "What on earth is going on?"

Appearing behind Celie, Mort added his voice to the fray. "Jennilee, I told you to go get in the car! What the hell do you think you're doing?"

Grandy put Jennilee behind her. "Go upstairs to my bedroom, lock the door, and call Chief Mac. Do it now."

"Mac? What the hell does he need to come out here for?" Puffed up with his own importance, Mort took a step, Jennilee bolted. Picking up the large butcher knife she'd been using and dropped in order to enfold Jennilee, Grandy pointed it at Mort.

"Stop right there, Mort."

"Have you lost your mind, Del?"

"Have you? Bursting in here, chasing after Jennilee like she's number one on the FBI's most wanted list? What is wrong with the two of you? Celie's always been dumber than a stump, but you… I thought you had a little bit of sense, at least."

"Wrong with us? I told Jennilee she had to get a haircut and she pitched a hissy fit."

"Jennilee doesn't need to cut her hair. She obviously doesn't want to."

Mort gestured, Grandy tightened her grip on the haft of the knife. "It's stringy with grease and it smells."

Grandy ignored Mort. "Celie, this is pathetic, even for you."

"Del, what are you talking about?" Mort looked back and forth between the two women, glaring daggers at each other.

"Mort, open your eyes and see for yourself. Jennilee takes fine care of her hair. Washes it just about every day, and Charlie or I, one, brush it for her and put it up."

"It doesn't look like it."

"Damn you, Celie. I told you to open your eyes, Mort! Of course it's stringy right now! The kids just did get out of the river. Jennilee's hair isn't greasy, it's wet. And the only thing it smells like is river water!"

"Celie said…"

"Use a little bit of the brain God gave you for something besides a hat rack! Celie hates Jennilee, always has. You don't know the half of what goes on right under your nose. Celie dangles a carrot, and you follow her as blindly as a witless jackass."

"Now see here…"

"No, you see. I don't know what lies Celie feeds you, but I can pretty well guess. Omission's a lie, too, Celie. Why don't you tell Mort what happens if you lose custody of Jennilee, or shall I?"

Celie burst into tears, right on cue. Mort turned to comfort her. "See what you've done, Del? This is all so unnecessary. All Celie's trying to do is take care of Jennilee. Stop interfering."

"Dry up, Celie, or I'll give you something to cry about. Somebody has to interfere for that child. Mort, I want your word, right now, that Jennilee's hair stays uncut and she won't be punished for this, or I'm calling not only Mac, but Tom and Stanley as well. You won't like the fallout, I can promise you that."

"S…sh…sheee h…h…hates m…m…meee!" Pressing herself against Mort, Celie wailed louder.

Mort comforted Celie, patting her on the back and murmuring.

Grandy shook her head. "Ask yourself, Mort. Is this the normal reaction of a happy child who's just been told she's getting a haircut? Do you think Sylvia'd act this way? Do you think Celie'd treat Sylvia like this if Sylvia didn't want her hair cut?"

"Jennilee? Normal? She's the most difficult, cantankerous child I've ever had the misfortune to deal with. With Jennilee, it's one thing right after another."

Grandy rolled her eyes and gave up. She needed to be upstairs with Jennilee, didn't dare leave these two idiots down here by themselves. Grandy and Mort stared at each other until they heard the crunch of tires on gravel, heard the front door open. The only sound until then had been Celie's braying.

"Del?"

Without moving or taking her eyes off Mort and Celie, she called out, "Back here, in the kitchen."

"Del, what in tarnation…" Mac, looking all spiffy and

official in his uniform, hand instinctively going to the butt of his weapon at Del's tone, froze at the sight that greeted him—Del holding a very large knife, pointed at Mort and Celie. Mort holding Celie, bawling for all she was worth.

"Mac, stay with these two, will you? I have to go check on Jennilee." Taking the knife with her, Del headed upstairs.

Furious, Mac nodded. "What've you two done to Jennilee this time? Celie, turn it off. Now!"

"Don't talk to my wife that way!"

"Then either someone tell me what's going on, or Celie's getting a courtesy ride in the back of my car!"

"You're supposed to be the police chief. Uphold the law!"

Mac's lips stretched in a grim parody of a smile. "Gladly. You better get a good lawyer, Mort." Reaching for the handcuffs on his belt, Mac stepped toward Celie.

Mort sputtered. "Wait. What are you talking about? Jennilee is…"

"You don't have to tell me about Jennilee. We've got a pretty good idea of the hell Celie puts her through."

"Jennilee? What about Celie? Why are all of you taking Jennilee's side? You don't even know what happened and you're trying to arrest Celie. What do you mean—get a good lawyer?"

Celie cranked it up a notch.

Mac shook his head in disgust. "Take her back to your house and meet me in my car. Five minutes, Mort, or I'm taking her in."

Waiting until they were to the hedge before tearing upstairs, Mac heard Del's soft voice, silence from Jennilee. "Del?"

"In here, Mac."

Grandy knelt on one knee in front of Jennilee, hands on her shoulders, talking earnestly.

Jennilee looked up at Mac. "I'm sorry. I panicked. She said... I didn't know what else to do."

Mac eased closer. "It's okay, baby. You did exactly right."

Most kids would've been bawling their eyes out. Not Jennilee. She just looked at him, her too-old eyes wide in her pasty face.

"Easy, Jennilee. You want to tell me what happened?" Afraid she'd retreat into herself like she'd done earlier in the summer, Mac went down on one knee beside Del.

Jennilee tipped her head back, closed her eyes. Sighed, and opened them. "She told him I don't take care of my hair and he said I had to have it cut. She already m...made the appointment."

Except for that one stutter, Jennilee might've been reciting her times tables. Mac knew exactly how deep her panic went. He'd seen Charlie, many times, playing with her hair. Wrapping a long braid around his hand, giving it a gentle tug, stroking a hand down the unbound length of it, pleasure plain on both their faces.

"I'll go talk to Mort."

"It doesn't matter. He's leaving in two days. He'll be on the road for the next week."

"Jennilee, you listen to me. I will do everything in my power..."

Never rude to anyone, especially adults, Jennilee's interruption took Grandy and Mac by surprise. "You can't do *anything*, Mr. Mac. If you do, and she loses custody, I become a ward of the state. *A foster kid.* That means I'll be sent away and I'll never see Charlie again. I can take anything as long as..."

Backing away from the two concerned adults, her voice escalated, emotion breaking through at last. "Promise me! You won't do anything. You can't! I should never have come over here. I should've just let them cut my hair."

Gritting her teeth, Del held her arms out. "Mac, when you talk to Mort, tell him Jennilee's staying here 'til he gets back."

"Done. Don't worry, Jennilee. I'll handle this."

Neither moving, Grandy and Jennilee listened as Mac's footsteps faded.

"Jennilee, come here, baby." Coaxing Jennilee closer, Grandy saw the tremors wracking the slender body, knew the slightest move would send Jennilee running for cover.

Panicked words came pouring out. "You can't tell Charlie! You have to promise me. I don't want him to know about this —not any of it."

"Okay, Jennilee." Grandy would've promised her anything. "Come here, sweetie. I won't say a word."

Eyes darting from object to object, shaking like a leaf in a hurricane, Jennilee was breaking their hearts. Grandy, like Mac, feared Jennilee'd retreat within herself again.

Desperate to keep her from going that route, Grandy offered, "Honeybunch, how about a nice warm bubble bath? Come on, I'll help you." Slowly held out a hand.

Focusing on Grandy, taking a couple deep breaths, Jennilee came a step closer. Grandy waited. Another step, she touched Grandy's outstretched fingers, launched.

Grandy caught Jennilee, held her tight, rocked her as a muffled sob escaped. "Let it out, baby. Let it out."

Jennilee pulled back, face studiously blank. "I'd like that bath now, if you please."

"Jennilee, it's okay to cry."

Giving no sign she heard, Jennilee asked, "Will you wash my hair? I don't want to give them any excuse."

"Sure honey."

"Grandy? Thank you. I'm sorry I bothered you. I didn't know what else to do."

"Jennilee, you hush that talk right now. You are never any

bother to me. I love you, baby. I wish your momma could see you now. She'd be so proud."

"Tell me about her, please." *Good things—not the hateful diatribes Celie's always spouting.*

Herding Jennilee down the hall toward the bathroom, Grandy got her undressed and into the tub. Talking about Cynthia all the while, she'd just finished rinsing Jennilee's hair when Mac called out.

"Coming. Jennilee, will you be okay long enough for me to talk to Mac?"

Jennilee nodded, face still showing all the emotion of a marble statue, ingrained manners kicking in. "Tell him thanks."

"Sure. I'll be right outside if you need me."

Jennilee sank down in the bubbles, closed her eyes.

"Well?" Grandy looked at Mac expectantly but without much hope.

Mac shook his head. "I tried, Del. Mort's so brainwashed, I don't think he heard anything I said. I told him if Celie loses custody, she loses not only the house, but the money. He wanted to know who told me that garbage. Said he'd seen the will and it said no such thing."

"Mac, I thought they were going to kill her right there in the kitchen in front of me, the poor kid—no wonder she's like she is. The real wonder is that she isn't an axe murderer or something."

"Any bruises this time?"

"Yeah. You should see her arm—clearly delineated fingerprints. I'm so scared for her, Mac. What are we going to do?"

"Unfortunately, Jennilee's right. If Celie loses custody, Jennilee'll end up in foster care, then right back with Celie. You know as well as I do, the system likes to keep kids with their families. Celie'd probably have to take a couple parenting classes and promise not to do it again. If I thought you had a chance of getting her, I'd urge you to go for it. Celie's a good enough actress she could persuade a judge to torture his own momma and then have her jailed for harassment. She'd come up with some cockamamie story about you and you'd probably end up with a restraining order against you."

"It's not fair, Mac. It's just not fair!"

"I know it, Del, as well as you do. If life was fair, Celie'd be the one at Oak Grove, and Cynthia'd be raising Sylvia."

"Jennilee doesn't want Charlie to know."

Mac promised, "Charlie won't hear it from me."

∾

JENNILEE SAT on a small stool in front of Grandy.

"Braid it tighter, Grandy."

"I can't get it any tighter, Jennilee—not without pulling it out." Grandy kept her touch light, her voice even, while visions of plucking Celie bald flickered in her mind's eye.

The kitchen door squeaked and slammed. Jennilee half rose, sank back when she heard Charlie's voice. He came pounding up the stairs, his face aglow.

"Guess what? I got to help Dad... What's wrong, Jennilee? Grandy? Tell me!"

"I'm braiding Jennilee's hair. *Guess what* yourself. Jennilee gets to stay here for a week."

Happiness illuminated Charlie's face just before fear darkened it. "Why?"

Jennilee whispered, her tone as even as her facial expression. "I had a go round with *her* today."

Charlie dropped to his knees in front of Jennilee and covered her hands with his, squeezed. "Are you alright?"

Eyes full of pain, she managed a flicker of a smile. "I am now, and I get to stay."

"I should never've gone with Dad. I should've stayed here."

"*No*, Charlie. You couldn't have done anything. You're here now. Tell me what you were going to tell me and when Grandy's done, we'll go rock. Please?"

Reaching out, Charlie brushed his fingertips across her cheek.

∼

JENNILEE COULDN'T SLEEP. Charlie'd rocked her for a long while, they'd eaten tomato soup and grilled cheese sandwiches for supper, watched *Name That Tune*. Grandy'd read to them while Charlie rocked Jennilee some more.

Jennilee looked at the piece of paper in front of her. She'd been scribbling for a long time.

Seven days.

One hundred and sixty eight hours.

Ten thousand, eighty minutes.

How many seconds?

How many? Her exhausted brain couldn't do the math. Seconds made it seem like a long time. However many it was, that's how long her parole was going to last this time.

Didn't have to be a genius to figure out her punishment would last a lot longer than her reprieve.

CHAPTER 11

Grandy checked on the kids, went to bed, left all their doors cracked just in case. Woke to the rhythmic squeaking of the rocking chair, listened to it for a long, long time before falling back asleep to the comforting sound.

Charlie stayed close, closer than usual the entire week Jennilee was with them. The night before Mort was due home, Grandy heard the rocker most of the night. At breakfast the next morning, Charlie and Grandy watched Jennilee rearrange her food on her plate, divide it up, regroup it, ask to be excused without taking a bite.

Charlie, eating no more than Jennilee, was a hairsbreadth behind her when she rose.

Giving him no explanation, Jennilee'd gotten Charlie to braid her hair tight every day. Between the two of them, they'd worked out a method of concealing just how much hair she had. Charlie French braided it in two braids, one on each side of her part, then pinned them around her head in a tight coronet.

Braiding it today, they headed for the rocker. Crooning to

Jennilee, some of their current favorites by the Oak Ridge Boys, Charlie started with *Dream On*, chased it with *Lovin' You*, finished with *Sail Away*.

The last notes faded. Remaining still for just a moment, Jennilee sat up in Charlie's lap, leaned forward until they touched foreheads.

"Go, Charlie. Go to your Dad's, or Jeff's. Just...go."

"Un uh. No way. I'm staying right here until…"

"Charlie, you can't. If you don't go, if I know you're here, I'll never be able to walk across that yard. Not today, not any day. You know I'll come back as soon as I can."

"Jennilee…"

"I have to catch up on my chores. Promise me something."

"Anything, Jennilee-sweet."

"Play for me. Sit on the back steps and play for me. Light my way, just like the song says."

"You're breaking my heart, Jennilee-love."

"Every time I have to leave you it breaks mine."

"Someday…"

Jennilee affirmed his promise. "Someday."

Setting Jennilee on her feet, Charlie got up, left as she'd asked. Jennilee sank back down in the rocker, took deep breath after deep breath, braced her hands on her knees and stood up. Head high, back straight, she walked into the hall.

The sight of Grandy, tears streaming down her face, stopped Jennilee in her tracks.

Grandy opened her arms.

Jennilee shook her head in a desolate, I'm hanging on by the tips of my fingers gesture, skirted around Grandy. Walked out through the kitchen, trailing hands and eyes over all the things she loved best about the room. The scarred and polished table, the chrome stool, the spotless counters, the wonderful stove. The kitchen was truly the heart of any home, and hers was here—her heart and her home.

∼

ON THE NIGHT of the third day after Jennilee walked back across the yards, Grandy woke to the rhythmic creaking of the rocking chair. Getting up, she didn't go downstairs, went instead to the window that looked out at the house across the way. The sky was lightening around the edges when she at last glimpsed a slight figure flit across the yard and back through the gap. Perhaps she dreamed it, but the rocking chair had gone quiet.

Three days after that—three more endless days full of worrying—passed before Charlie, alerted by some nebulous sign Grandy could neither see nor hear, rose from his station at the table to stand staring out the door toward the other house. Three interminable days before Jennilee appeared at the kitchen door, after dark, silent as a moonbeam.

Stepping inside, she stood motionless, spooky as a twelve point buck during hunting season. Nostrils flared, white to the lips, trembling like a leaf, eyes dominating her pixie face.

Charlie eased toward her, holding a hand out, palm up.

Grandy froze, fearing her slightest movement would send Jennilee bolting out the door. Jennilee looked like she had when she'd gotten trapped in the shed.

"I played for you. Every evening."

Jennilee nodded jerkily, her eyes locked on Charlie's, soaking him up, storing visual and auditory memories.

Snagging the lotion, he squirted some into his hands and waited.

Jennilee took one hesitant step, then another. Catching her hands in his Charlie spread the lotion around. The barest whisper of sound came from her, like the echo of a ghost. "I can't stay."

"I understand." Charlie rubbed gently and started singing, low, the Oak Ridge Boy's *Come On In.*

Grandy just could hear the words, but Jennilee breathed easier.

Tugging her closer, Charlie pressed his lips to her forehead. "Go, sweeting. I'll be right here."

Jennilee backed out the screen door as quietly as she'd come.

Grandy blinked. Jennilee—here and gone, just that quick. If not for the lingering scent of Jergens, she'd think she'd hallucinated the entire episode.

Giving Jennilee time to get back, Charlie followed her out the door and played for her, the mournful wail of his harmonica a bittersweet harmony to the crickets.

CHAPTER 12

School started shortly afterward. Third grade.
Third grade, and being eight years old, meant Charlie was old enough to play Pee Wee Football.

Jennilee was all for anything that got Charlie and his dad together, and Mr. Donnie'd volunteered to be assistant coach for Charlie's team.

Practice lasted a couple hours, which meant Jennilee had time to get her afternoon chores done before Charlie got home. After that, she was free to go to Grandy's, eat supper over there and do her homework, study with Charlie.

It also meant she rode her bike home alone, since practice started right after school. This particular day, stopping at the hardware store to pick up something for Grandy, Jennilee parked her bike around the corner of the building.

They still hadn't gotten the go-ahead for the bike racks, but at least some of the merchants were interested. She watched as Mr. Roy wrote a ticket, put the item on Grandy's account.

Head down, thoughts miles away on the chores she had to complete and how fast she could get them done and hightail it to Grandy's, Jennilee put the package in her basket, swiped a foot across her kickstand. From out of nowhere a hard hand grabbed her arm. Dropping her bike, she swung, her other hand already fisted. She connected, but the open handed slap she got in return did far more damage, knocking her to the ground in an ungainly sprawl.

Trying to crab backward, Jennilee was hemmed in, trapped between her bike and her assailant and the wall of the store. A series of swift, hard kicks to her ribs insured she couldn't draw breath enough to scream.

Butch Jones! Her thoughts hammered and beat, as hard as her pulse was throbbing in her bruised cheek. *The most feared bully in school—what could he possibly want with me?* Older by several years, Jennilee and the other younger kids made it a point to avoid him like the plague. Mean and ornery as a nest of antagonized ground hornets, Butch lived to torment the younger kids.

Sensing more than Butch's normal hatred, Jennilee kicked and scratched and fought in vain. Almost as if he was...on a mission, Butch toyed with her, let her think she was going to get away, dragged her back.

Flat on her stomach with Butch's weight squarely in the middle of her back, his knees pinning her arms to her sides, Jennilee was completely at his mercy. Knew this went above and beyond his normal meanness when he started yanking pins out of her hair, hurting her, taking pleasure in ripping the pins out.

Struggling furiously, futilely, as she realized his intent, helpless to prevent what he did next, Jennilee could only stare in shock as one of her braids hit the sandy dirt beside her.

Not quite finished, Butch pushed off her, making sure one of his knees dug into her back with enough force to expel what little bit of breath she had left.

Crouching over her, he grabbed a handful of her chopped off hair, waved his switchblade in front of her eyes. "You tell a soul what happened, I'll come after you again."

Hitting the back of her head, hard, slamming her face into the dirt, he left. Jennilee heard him laughing as he sauntered around to the front of the building. Trying to catch her breath, she reached out a hand and clutched her hacked off braid. Charlie was going to kill Butch for this.

Not if he didn't know who did it!

Considering her options, Jennilee realized she didn't have any. She wouldn't tell a soul, but not because Butch had threatened her. Dropping her head back down on her arm for a minute, she pushed resolutely to her knees and got to her feet.

Oh, well—there were lots of things she didn't tell Charlie.

On automatic pilot now, she picked up her bike, put her package back in the basket.

Walked her bike for a good ways on the back street, was still walking, in a daze, when a car pulled up beside her. Jennilee didn't pay it any mind. It wasn't Celie—that fact registered—about the same time she began to get a sneaking suspicion that Butch had been put up to his mean trick. Mean enough by himself, he'd never gone this far before. Her stomach roiled and her vision grayed.

Jennilee turned dull eyes to the car—no, truck—as the horn tooted lightly. Stared blankly as the driver walked around the truck toward her.

"Jennilee? Is that you, child?"

An adult, male. Old. Bib overalls. A familiar voice. Knowing she should be able to put a name to the face, Jennilee was drawing a blank.

"Jennilee, what in the world's going on here? You need a ride home?"

Jennilee shook her head, found her voice. "I'm not allowed to accept rides from strangers."

Bracing both hands on his knees, the old man looked her in the eye. "I'm no stranger, Jennilee. Don't you remember? We met at the bank the day you and Charlie opened your joint bank account."

"Mr. Cyrus?"

Cyrus stared at the dirty, bruised child in front of him. Recognizing her walking and pushing her bike, he'd thought only to tap the horn and wave. Seeing Jennilee's distraught face when she turned at the sound of the horn had him slamming on the brakes and getting out.

"Yes, Jennilee. Let me take you home. I'll put your bike in the back of the truck."

White-knuckled grip on the handlebars, braid hanging from one hand, Jennilee shook her head. "Grandy wouldn't like it."

"Honey, Del and I are first cousins. She won't get mad at you, I promise. She will get mad at me if I let you go by yourself."

Jennilee stared blankly.

"If you won't let me take you, I'm going to follow you home."

Cyrus waited patiently, knowing Jennilee was only peripherally aware of what was going on. Judging from the braid dangling from her fist and the dirt smudges on her face and knees and clothes, she'd had a serious run-in with a bully.

"Honey, where's Charlie?"

At last, a spark of life. "He's at football practice. You can't tell him!"

Looking from the hacked off braid to the chopped off mess of Jennilee's hair, Cyrus' bushy brows shot up. "I think he'll probably notice all by himself."

Going from frozen and unable to move to panicked and ready to bolt in the blink of an eye, Jennilee agreed. "Yeah, he'll notice. Can I have that ride home, please? I have to get cleaned up."

Swinging Jennilee's bike into the bed of his truck, Cyrus helped her into the front seat. Jennilee didn't say anything else and Cyrus didn't either. He did wonder why Jennilee made no mention of going to her aunt's house. He'd mentioned home, and Jennilee'd assumed Grandy's. Del didn't say much against Celie, but Cyrus figured Jennilee's omission said plenty, loud and clear.

Pulling up, Cyrus tapped the horn. Opened Jennilee's door just as Del stepped out on the back porch. "Del, c'mere a minute, would you?"

Lifting Jennilee's bike out, he scooped up the package.

Jennilee hadn't moved. He wasn't sure she was aware she was home.

"Cyrus? What's wrong?"

He jerked his head in Jennilee's direction. Grandy reached the truck about the same time Jennilee came to life and scrambled out.

"Grandy, you have to help me!" Jennilee threw herself at Grandy and clung.

Del shot a *what happened* glance at Cyrus.

He shrugged. "I found her like this, walking home."

Putting her hands on Jennilee's shoulders, Grandy pushed her back enough to see Jennilee's face. The first thing Grandy noticed was the dirt and bruises, then her eyes flew to Jennilee's hair.

"Jennilee, what…"

"It doesn't matter. You have to cut the other side so it'll match. You have to do it before Charlie gets home, and I have to get cleaned up."

"Jennilee, who did this to you?"

The same mulish look appearing on her face Jennilee had when questioned about what went on at the house across the way, Grandy knew it was useless to try and get any information out of her.

Throwing Cy a grateful look, Del sighed. "Thank you, Cy." Invited, "Won't you come in?"

"Some other time, Del. You got your hands full." Handing Del the package, he got back in his truck.

Grabbing Grandy's hand, Jennilee tugged her toward the steps. "Hurry, please, before Charlie gets home."

Grandy cried as she unpinned the remaining braid and lopped it off. Jennilee didn't make a sound, just clutched both braids in her fists as Grandy undid the French braid against Jennilee's scalp and trimmed the edges even.

Charlie'd braided it tight, and well, so Jennilee had more hair left than she would've if it'd just been braided regularly. What was left came almost to her shoulders.

Thanking Grandy in a bottom of the well voice, Jennilee went upstairs. Came back down a short while later, skin scrubbed pink enough to hide the bruises, hair fluffed out around her face, her eyes like trampled flowers.

Grandy watched silently as Jennilee took her dirty clothes outside to the burn barrel, watched as Jennilee poked and prodded and burned until nothing was left.

∽

Hot, sweaty, and filthy, Charlie dragged in the back door. Practice today'd been especially long and grueling. "What's for supper? I'm starv…" Dropped his helmet and pads where he stood.

Jennilee, sitting at the kitchen table, got slowly to her feet, her eyes glued to his face. Reached up and touched a hesitant hand to her hair.

Charlie stood rigidly, fists clenched, eyes shooting daggers. Stalking slowly across the kitchen, he walked around behind Jennilee, inspected the damage. Kept right on going, was halfway down the hall when he shouted, "How could you?"

Pounding up the stairs, they heard his door slam. Jennilee flinched and swayed, looked through Grandy, her eyes so pain-filled it was like looking into a bottomless well of agony.

~

Jennilee's self imposed exile lasted until Charlie's game. She stayed away from Grandy's, stayed away from Charlie at school. Kept her head down so her newly shorn hair covered the bruise on her cheek and no one could see the one on her forehead.

Bruises gone except for a faint yellow tint Jennilee could conceal by rubbing her forehead and pinching her cheeks, she showed up at the game. Staying off to one side, she watched Charlie with hungry eyes.

As soon as Grandy noticed Jennilee, she walked over and gave Jennilee a hug.

Jennilee melted against Grandy. "I'm sorry I had to involve you in that mess."

"Jennilee…"

Jennilee shook her head, stiffened.

Grandy sighed and pulled her closer. Most kids couldn't keep a secret if their lives depended on it—Jennilee kept entirely too many.

Charlie scored the winning touchdown and Jennilee stared longingly, devouring him with her eyes as the team celebrated jubilantly. Heart-sore, she turned to leave since he was still mad with her. She didn't blame him, didn't know how much longer she could stand to stay away from him.

Felt his eyes on her now, just like she had at school. Careful then not to look up when she sensed his furiously hurt gaze, she didn't turn around now, just kept walking. Couldn't bear to see the hurt condemnation in his eyes.

Jennilee stiffened her spine. Charlie might be furious, might be hurt, but not as hurt as he'd be if he tried to take on Butch and his cronies. She'd done the only thing she could do, under the circumstances.

She'd been right about the other, too. Butch's attack had been deliberate, and planned. Sylvia'd asked her why she *butch*ered her hair like that, laughed like a hyena.

Jennilee swung her head from side to side. Short hair still felt weird.

Hearing Charlie coming at a run, Jennilee knew if he yelled at her again she'd curl up right here and bawl her eyes out, probably blurt out everything.

"Jennilee."

He didn't sound angry. Slowing her steps, Jennilee asked over her shoulder, "Yeah?"

"Grandy's taking me to Dairy Queen in Havelock. Wanna come?"

Jennilee clenched her hands together so tight her knuckles turned white and she could feel every bone in her fingers. "You want me to?"

"I do, Jennilee. I most surely do."

"Okay."

Falling into step, they headed for Grandy's car. "Jennilee, look at me, please."

Jennilee risked a quick glance at Charlie's beloved face.

"I had no right to yell at you or treat you the way I've treated you this week. It's your hair, and you can cut it if you want. It was just such a shock... I'm sorry. Forgive me?"

As long as Charlie blamed it on her, he wouldn't look elsewhere. Jennilee nodded, looking at the ground so he couldn't read her eyes as he was so very adept at doing.

"Jennilee." She risked another glance at Charlie, holding out his hand, patiently waiting.

Taking his hand, she felt the touch resonate all the way to her toes.

Opening the tailgate, Charlie threw his gear in and helped Jennilee into the car, all without letting go of Jennilee's hand.

"Great game, Charlie. You and Jeff were wonderful. As always." Not that Jennilee'd had eyes for anyone but Charlie, but Charlie and Jeff made a top-notch team, on the field and off. Always.

"Jeff insisted you would, but I wasn't sure you'd come."

"I wasn't sure you wanted me to, but I couldn't stay away. Oh, Charlie! My bike."

Getting in on her side, Grandy looked at the two of them in their accustomed spots and heaved a grateful sigh. It had been a miserable week, for all of them. Putting the car in gear, she drove around the field to retrieve Jennilee's bike.

∼

THINGS CALMED DOWN, pretty much returned to normal, at least until report cards came out. Charlie and Jennilee had straight A's. Sylvia didn't.

Celie didn't show the report cards to Mort, just told him her version of events. Jennilee got her butt blistered. Same thing happened next time report cards came out. Jennilee came to dread report cards and expect the punishment.

"If you'd study once in awhile, young lady..." Whack!

"Do your homework instead of spending all your time at Del's..." Whack!

"Stop hanging around that no-good Charlie!" Whack!

Whack! Whack! Whack!

Jennilee never said anything about it, just like she never told about anything else that went on in the Judge's house, but she heard the sound of that belt whistling toward her tender skin in her nightmares.

∼

JENNILEE'S HAIR started growing back out and she once again kept it braided tightly.

Most of the merchants finally said yes to the bike racks. Mr. Donnie and Charlie made them and Jennilee helped set them in place. She looked regretfully at the one in front of the hardware store every time she went by—*if only it'd been there when Butch came after her!*

Not that it would've done any good—he'd have caught her somewhere else.

Christmas came and went. Charlie carved Jennilee an intricate heart-shape and strung it on a gold chain. Jennilee gave Charlie a transistor radio and crocheted him a case for his harmonica.

For Easter Vacation Grandy took them to Kitty Hawk, toured Kill Devil Hills and the Wright Brother's Memorial, climbed the famous sand dune. Camped on the beach and fished all night and half the day.

Starting with the usual Bible school, complete with parables and cookies and kool-aid, their nine year old summer passed in a blur of swimming and playing and riding their bikes. Playing hard, working harder, Charlie and Jennilee's bank account grew by leaps and bounds, just like they did. Grandy swore they grew a foot or more, both of them, said they were growing as fast as time was flying.

Football practice started and shortly after that, school. Grandy'd once again taken them clothes shopping. Things had been fairly peaceful, and Jennilee got careless, took some of her new things back to the Judge's house.

Her favorite new shirt disappeared, reappeared on Sylvia. Jennilee bided her time. Sylvia put it in the laundry, Jennilee reclaimed it with the intention of taking it back to Grandy's and leaving it where it'd be safe.

Sylvia pitched a hissy, told her dad Jennilee'd stolen her favorite shirt.

He looked in Jennilee's room—there it was.

Mort took it back, gave it to Sylvia and blistered Jennilee's butt.

Sylvia wasn't finished.

Charlie was at football practice, Jennilee was working like a mule so she could head to Grandy's as fast as possible.

She froze like cornered prey when Mort walked into the kitchen and pointed up the stairs. Walking ahead of him like a prisoner going to the gallows, upon opening her door, she wished she'd bolted instead of coming up here like a lamb to the slaughter.

Everything in her room, every stitch of clothing, everything made of fabric or paper, was in shreds. Someone had taken a sharp knife, maybe scissors, to the mattress, the sheets and curtains, to Jennilee's clothes, her schoolbooks, her library books, her homework. Her clothes, including the shirt Sylvia coveted, looked like confetti scattered on the floor, along with the report—due tomorrow—she'd spent a week on.

While Mort ranted and swung and connected, she didn't even try to explain or defend, just stared at the nail hole in her dresser where Sylvia'd staked out Goldie. Figured her butt had calluses, and if it didn't by now, it never would.

Jennilee didn't get careless anymore after that. Keeping one old T shirt of Charlie's to sleep in, and an old pair of clothes, she wore the old clothes back and forth to Grandy's, kept her good clothes there and changed before and after school.

Her books and homework—same thing. They stayed in her room at Grandy's.

Too ashamed to ask Grandy for more clothes or to tell Charlie about the books she'd have to pay for, Jennilee only told Charlie she needed to take some money out of their account. He didn't ask any questions, just looked at her shrewdly, told her to go ahead.

Jennilee asked Grandy to teach her to sew, learned how to make a great many of her clothes. Charlie never asked her what happened to the ones Grandy'd bought, or her books. Had a pretty good idea.

Sylvia hadn't gotten all Jennilee's clothes, because they weren't all at the Judge's. Between what Jennilee had left and what she sewed, she had, if not plenty, enough.

CHAPTER 13

The summer they turned ten, the summer of 1974, started out like all the summers they could remember. A few days, maybe a couple weeks of freedom followed by Bible school, then it was back to swimming and playing and exploring to their heart's content.

Mort, doing an expanded sales route, hardly ever came home. Taking full advantage of that fact for her own nefarious purposes, as long as things were clean, Celie didn't much care what Jennilee did.

Charlie and Jennilee rode their bikes farther afield than ever, ranging farther and farther from town. Staying off highway 70 they stuck to the backroads, often staying gone all day.

Grandy'd long ago bought them both boring old-fashioned Schwinn's, baskets on the handlebars and tassels hanging out of the rubber grips. A lot more comfortable and usable than the banana bikes all the other kids had, right now Charlie's basket held a gallon milk jug of kool-aid and a Tupperware container of Dixie cups and plastic utensils.

Jennilee's held a loaf of bread and a jar of Jif peanut butter, another of grape jelly.

Riding aimlessly, no certain destination in mind, they'd been exploring. A different road every day, the sand and gravel tram roads Weyerhauser Timber used for logging.

The variety of wildlife they encountered was staggering. Deer and foxes and raccoons and possums and once, they'd even come up on a mama bear and her cubs. Backing away slowly, they'd been very careful for a long time after that. Birds of every description, box turtles, painted turtles, snapping turtles, snakes—lots of snakes. Copperheads and rattlers and black snakes and chicken snakes and green snakes and water moccasins and king snakes that looked like coral snakes.

Going ghost white pale every time they encountered one of the reptiles, Jennilee wanted nothing to do with anything that slithered and Charlie went out of his way to make sure she didn't.

You could discover a lot riding a bike, way more than you could riding in a car. That's how they discovered the well hidden dirt road leading back into the woods, definitely not a Weyerhauser road. Sharing a grin, they turned their bikes as one and rode carefully down the weedy, pockmarked twin paths. Breaking out of the woods, the road continued between long unused fields.

A mile and a half they rode, and knew they were getting close to the river again. They could smell it, as familiar and welcome as the smell of supper cooking. Another half mile— they were certain because they'd spent some of their hard-earned money on matching odometers. Really cool odometers, with an attached headlight that came on at the flick of a switch and the faster you pedaled, the brighter the light got.

Hitting their brakes, they slid to a simultaneous stop. Stared and stared, stared some more. Looked at each other with wide, matching grins. This was it! This was why they worked so hard and squirreled away their money.

Old, once elegant, and long abandoned, the two story house was straight out of their dreams. They saw it as it could be, as it'd once been—not the weathered, paint stripped off by sun and time outer shell with lopsided shutters, but a beautiful showplace. Even hidden behind a tumultuous explosion of overgrown shrubs and weeds, it was exactly what they wanted.

Dismounting, they set their kickstands and walked forward carefully, weaving through clumps of waist high broom straw and other weeds liberally threaded with ankle shredding catbriars. Ancient live oaks graced the yard, scattered here and there. Circling their house, they discovered camellias and gardenias and azaleas hidden in the weedy undergrowth. Eyes shining, they circled it again, taking in each detail.

Rectangular, huge, wide porches wrapped around both stories like lacy icing on one of Grandy's wedding cakes.

They had no idea who it belonged to, but it wouldn't take them long to ferret out the owner. All they had to do now was come up with the money for the purchase price.

Their headlights were needed that evening, would be needed a great many evenings for most of the rest of the summer.

Grandy greeted them as they tumbled in the kitchen door. "Where in the world have you two been and what on earth were you doing?"

Filthy—and radiant—Charlie and Jennilee shared a quick grin and a lightning game of PSR.

Jennilee headed upstairs, Charlie answered. "Out riding our bikes and playing."

Grandy eyed him curiously, knowing there was more to

the story, knowing she wouldn't be able to pry any more information out of them.

Washing his hands in the kitchen sink, Charlie chattered to Grandy while he rinsed out their kool-aid jug and made a fresh batch for tomorrow, stuck it in the freezer.

Jennilee reappeared, scrubbed and glowing. Sharing a look, they brushed hands in passing and exchanged places.

Grandy got no more out of Jennilee than she had from Charlie.

The next day was Saturday, so they couldn't go to the library or the office of the Ridgerunner. Up with the dawn, they had their chores done and took off. Better prepared this time, they had all the tools they'd need.

Charlie carried a sheathed machete strapped across his back, and their food and drink in his basket. A rake, a hoe, and a shovel were tied beneath his seat and his handlebars and resting on his fenders. Jennilee had the pruning shears, loppers, a small hatchet, several trowels, and gloves in her basket, a couple buckets hanging off her handlebars.

Parking in the shade of one of the wind sculpted live oaks, they unloaded. Putting the koolaid close to the trunk of the tree in the shade and donning their gloves, they got busy.

Clearing all the catbriars and poison ivy and other assorted weeds away from the porch on the river side, they discovered curved flowerbeds outlined in conch shells and buried in creeping grass, a walkway of crushed oyster shells leading from the wide center steps both ways around the house.

Raking and pruning and digging and pulling, stopping only for a rest break and hasty lunch, they worked 'til almost dark.

Refastening their big tools on Charlie's bike and stowing the rest in Jennilee's basket, their headlights glowed like runway lights as they made their way home. Putting the tools back in the shed, they piled in the kitchen door.

Looking at the two of them, Grandy just shook her head. Sunburned, scratched, filthy, blisters all over their hands. "You two building a fort or something?"

Both nodded and grinned.

"Well, be careful."

"Yes ma'am."

Grandy hadn't seen them do PSR but Charlie headed upstairs first tonight. Waiting until she heard water running she asked, "Jennilee, you two aren't doing anything that's going to get you in trouble, are you?"

"No ma'am."

∽

DEFINITELY NOT THEIR usual well-behaved selves in church, they fidgeted and squirmed like a couple antsy toddlers until Grandy finally separated them. Jennilee'd been sitting with Grandy and Charlie ever since Grandy confronted Celie the day she found the horseshoe marks from the flyswatter handle on the backs of Jennilee's legs. Never, not once, had she had to reprimand them for their behavior.

"What has gotten into you two?" Grandy's fierce whisper and her actions got their attention. They behaved the rest of the service.

Brother Anderson greeted them at the door on their way out. He'd seen the little by-play. Most of the time he enjoyed well-behaved children in church, saw too few. For once, he was glad a couple of kids had been acting up. Charlie and Jennilee hadn't done anything bad, and he doubted if anyone else noticed Del's admonishment.

Brother Anderson leaned close to Sister Del and confided quietly, "They are children! I was starting to wonder!"

JENNILEE'S LIGHT

Startling a laugh out of Del, she directed a love-filled look at both of them. "They've got something up their collective sleeve. I've never seen them act like this."

"They're good kids, Del. Whatever it is, it's nothing to worry about."

Charlie and Jennilee waited their turn to speak to Brother Anderson.

"Charlie, Jennilee—so good to see you."

"We want to apologize, sir."

Instead of congratulating them as he wanted to do, Brother Anderson kept his face sober and accepted their apology, gave them a spiritual nudge. "Since you two have so much excess energy, why don't you think about singing during the children's time before the regular service starts? I heard you sing at Bible school. You two harmonize beautifully."

Directing a miserable look at Charlie, Jennilee dropped her gaze as Charlie's eyes darted to Jennilee's aunt and uncle. Brother Anderson watched their hands brush in a fleeting gesture of comfort.

Charlie shook his head decisively. "We can't, sir."

Brother Anderson's eyes followed them out the door as he automatically greeted the next person. When the Johnsons reached him, he pondered discrepancies he'd noticed a long time ago. Jennilee never sat with them, always with Del and Charlie. That in itself wasn't unusual—many of the kids sat with their friends or somewhere besides with their families.

Today was the first time Brother Anderson could remember Jennilee being anything but perfectly obedient. He also couldn't remember one good thing Celie'd ever said about Jennilee. Oh, Celie always made sure she couched her complaints in layers of misdirection, but the gist of it was how terrible Jennilee was. Always bemoaning the fact Jennilee was such a difficult child, how much trouble she got in, what a trial Jennilee was to raise, Celie garnered lots of sympathy for being such a good person and taking in her niece when Jennilee had no one else.

Looking at Sylvia, loudly snapping gum while she picked at the paint on the door frame and chipped a piece off while looking him in the eye and smirking, he mentally compared the two girls. Thought about the gum always found stuck under Sylvia's pew, right about where Sylvia always sat, about the ruined hymnals the cleaning crew complained about, in the same place—and came to a few conclusions of his own.

No wonder Jennilee didn't want to get up in front of the church and sing—it would draw too much attention to herself. Sylvia, despite her mother's loud and frequent claims, couldn't carry a tune in a bucket.

It wasn't nice, but he'd pay the piper later. Brother Anderson smiled. "Sylvia! How'd you like to sing a solo next Sunday?"

Sylvia choked on her wad of bubblegum.

Celie trilled, "Why, thank you, Brother Anderson! She'd be delighted. Sylvie has such a wonderful voice and..."

Pretending to listen to Celie gush on and on, Brother Anderson watched Jennilee get into Grandy's car.

∼

IT TOOK A BIT OF DOING, but Charlie and Jennilee ferreted out who owned their house—Clyde Goodwin. They'd never heard of the man, knew pretty much everybody in town, at least by sight.

Turned out he owned not just their house, but the several hundred acres of waterfront property surrounding it and clear back to the main road.

Already experts at getting their chores done as quick as

possible, they increased their speed. Having helped Grandy in her extensive gardens for as long as they could remember, they were familiar with most of the old plants and shrubs. Many of the treasures in their newfound yard would've been overlooked by others, hacked down or pulled out.

Charlie and Jennilee knew better.

Knew how to prune and propagate, weed and separate and replant, how to save seeds, when to dig bulbs, when to replant them. Grandy had one of the finest gardens in the county, held tours by appointment only, sold a great many of her heirloom bulbs and rooted cuttings.

Familiar with all the plants in Grandy's yard, there were some in their yard they'd never seen before—different varieties of plants they knew. A veritable treasure trove, everything they did uncovered another flower bed or more shrubs, until they were dizzy with discovery.

Scanning Grandy's extensive hoard of plant books, they asked endless questions and researched until their eyes crossed. Regaining its former glory, bit by bit, their yard would take years more to completely restore it.

One of their cleaning forays resulted in finding a totally hidden hand pump. Taking it completely apart, Charlie cleaned it up, replaced the worn out parts, reassembled it, primed it and pumped for all he was worth. Having dumped a couple gallons of Clorox down the pipe while he had the pump off, the first gush came out rusty, muddy, and smelling of bleach. Charlie kept pumping, and pretty soon clear, cold water spewed out.

They stashed a gallon glass pickle jar beside the pump. Putting tea bags in the jar and filling it up partway with water and sugar, then sitting it in the sun resulted in perfect tea. Add some of the cold water from the well and it tasted mighty fine.

A milk jug worked perfect for kool-aid. They just added the kool-aid and sugar and shook until the sugar dissolved.

Quickly tiring of carrying tools back and forth, uncomfortable borrowing Grandy's, they bought their own. Keeping a tarp and WD-40 under one of the porches, every time before they left they sprayed down the tools they'd used that day, wrapped them in the tarp, and stored the whole thing under the porch and out of sight.

The days they weren't pretending to be Stanley hacking his way through the jungle to find Livingstone, they worked to replenish the money they'd spent. Clammed, ran errands, picked up bottles, mowed yards, anything to make a dime or two.

Charlie and Mr. Donnie were getting closer and closer, a situation instigated and encouraged by Jennilee. Going on frequent tow truck runs with Mr. Donnie, Charlie even helped him some in the garage.

Loving that they were spending more and more time together, Jennilee gladly worked her schedule around theirs. Charlie and Mr. Donnie, coming back from a run, swung by Grandy's to pick Jennilee up. Jennilee waved happily to Grandy and Charlie helped her climb up in the cab of the tow truck, climbed in after her.

Back at the garage, Jennilee waited in the office. Whatever the guys were doing didn't take long, and the three of them headed for Mr. Donnie's living quarters to sit for a spell.

Jennilee observed Mr. Donnie while he was getting out tea and pouring them all a glass. He looked better—not so tired and he wasn't drinking near as much. Glanced around with a satisfied smile.

A healthy philodendron lived in the big front window, a lush aloe resided on the kitchen windowsill, everything was spotless. A crocheted afghan covered the well-worn recliner, an oyster basket held Mr. Donnie's magazines, the kitchen table boasted a red and white checked tablecloth.

Framed pictures, mostly of Charlie and Grandy clustered on one wall, a few of Jennilee when someone else'd been there to take pictures. The center shot, one Jennilee'd taken, was of Charlie and Mr. Donnie. Beaming, arms around each other after Charlie'd scored one of many winning touchdowns.

On the drive back to Grandy's, Jennilee listened to them talk excitedly about the old truck they'd just towed in. Rounded a corner to see Butch Jones standing on the side of the road.

Jennilee froze. Just standing, she knew he was up to no good. Butch glared as they drove by and Jennilee shivered.

Charlie, attuned as he was to Jennilee, immediately bristled. "Jennilee, he been bothering you?"

Swallowing past the lump in her throat, Jennilee managed to shake her head.

Charlie put an arm around her and pulled her close. "Jennilee?"

She almost bit her tongue trying not to blurt out just how much she hated and feared Butch. "H...he bothers everybody."

"From now on, I don't want you going anywhere by yourself." Charlie handed out his dictum like a general giving orders.

Jennilee managed a shaky laugh. "How'm I supposed to do that?"

Sounding like he was cussing, Donnie said, "Knot Jones' boy. He's a chip off the old block. His old man's nothing but white trash and that boy's the same. You stay away from him, Jennilee. Meaner'n snakes, nothing but trouble, both of them. The whole family's that way."

Jennilee couldn't have agreed more.

CHAPTER 14

*D*riving carefully down the rutted dirt road, overgrown and nearly reclaimed by weeds, unused by anyone save himself for countless years, Cyrus pulled into the open and slammed on the brakes. Practically crawling anyway, stomping the brakes didn't have much of an effect, except to stir up a huge cloud of dust.

Waiting for the dust to dissipate, he blinked his eyes and looked again. Rubbing them in total disbelief, he let the truck roll slowly closer. Last time he'd swung by to check on things, the yard had been its usual tangled jungle, the way it'd been for more than twenty years. Parking the truck, he stared.

He'd watched, down the long years, sweet gums and pine seedlings spring up, become saplings and then good sized trees, watched as the land reclaimed what had once been extensively landscaped yard.

The yard was once again clear as far as he could see around the house, the shrubs pruned, the crushed shell walkways once again clearly delineated, the grass clipped short. What in the world was going on?

Getting out, he walked around, stepped up on the porch and stopped again. The sagging porches had been swept clean. Checking the doors and windows, he found them all still shut and locked. Peering through the grimy windows, he could see no evidence that whoever was cleaning the yard had been inside.

Careful inspection found the repaired pump and the gallon glass jar, the tarp full of tools under the porch. Shaking his grizzled head, he got back in his truck and left.

∼

NOTICING someone had driven down their road, Charlie and Jennilee paid little attention. Their tools were right where they'd left them. Maybe it'd just been someone curious, like themselves.

Hard at work, hearing a car door slam they headed around the house.

Cyrus stared, slack jawed. Never in a million years would he have suspected Charlie and Jennilee of doing all this work, but it had to have been them. Faces wreathed in matching grins, they waved and called out.

"Mr. Cyrus!"

"What in the world are you two doing way out here? And what are you doing?" Watching the two exchange a look, Cyrus didn't miss the fact that their hands sought each other, clasped.

"Mr. Cyrus, do you know a Mr. Clyde Goodwin? He owns this place. We'd like to talk to him."

"Clyde? Yeah, I know him. I asked you first, and I'm asking again—what are you two doing?"

"This is it, Mr. Cyrus! This is why we work so hard and save our money! Jennilee and I—this is our house!" Charlie swept his free hand out to encompass the house and grounds.

"We want this, Mr. Cyrus." Jennilee added her fervent two cents.

"You two do all this work?"

"Yessir."

"You been inside the house?"

"Nossir. That's trespassing."

Cyrus raised a brow at that. They hadn't hurt anything, had merely cleaned up a neglected yard. And done a fine job, at that. The stumps had even been uprooted, no trace left of any of them. Cyrus remembered this yard, as it had been, years—decades—ago. Charlie and Jennilee were well on their way to restoring it to its former glory.

"Would you like a glass of tea, sir? We don't have any ice, but it's pretty cold."

Charlie looked at Jennilee in surprise. Seldom volunteering anything personal, she was acting as if Mr. Cyrus topped her list of favorite people.

Cyrus had a reputation for being a loner, but he also had a soft spot for these two, especially Jennilee. "I'd love a glass, Jennilee."

"Be right back." Jennilee took off.

Eyeing each other, Cyrus and Charlie stepped up on the porch to wait in the shade. Back in a flash, one arm wrapped around the gallon jar, two pint mason jars and a wet rag clutched tightly in her other hand, Jennilee grinned at Mr. Cyrus' question.

"Makin' sun tea, huh?"

"Yessir."

Charlie looked at them, again puzzled by Jennilee's response to Mr. Cyrus.

Pouring both pint jars full, Jennilee handed one to Mr.

Cyrus and one to Charlie, busied herself wrapping the wet cloth around the gallon jar. Sitting it in the shade where it would catch the most breeze, she dropped down beside Charlie and snagged his jar.

Cyrus eyed them speculatively. "How'd you two find this place?"

Charlie started the explanation. "We were out…"

Jennilee added to. "…riding our bikes…"

Charlie asked earnestly, "You said you know Mr. Clyde Goodwin?"

"Know him, been caretaker of this place since he left. How'd you know about him?"

Charlie and Jennilee shared a gleeful look. "We researched to see who owns this. Do you think he'd sell it to us?"

"It's not on the market."

"We know. We already checked."

"Mr. Cyrus, why'd he leave?" Jennilee, wise beyond her years, sensing tragedy.

"Long story short—his wife and son died and he couldn't bear to live here without them."

"Amelia and Benjamin." At Mr. Cyrus' startled look, Jennilee hastily explained. "We cleaned up the family cemetery. They're the most recent grave stones, and half of Amelia's is blank."

"If you're the caretaker, how come…" Charlie lifted a hand questioningly.

Mr. Cyrus shrugged. "That's the way Clyde wanted it. All he asked me to do was keep an eye on the place, forbade me to do anything to it."

"Where is he now, Mr. Cyrus?" Jennilee, full of compassionate understanding.

"Joined the Merchant Marines. Hasn't been back since."

"He's been gone a long time, huh?"

"More'n twenty years."

"He's still grieving."

Cyrus nodded. It might be a bad thing, to get their hopes up, but he couldn't not show them. "How'd you two like to see the inside?"

Two beaming faces answered him.

Taking a ring of keys out of his pocket, Cyrus hunted until he found an ornate old key, dull with age, inserted it in the front door. It wouldn't budge.

"Hang on, Mr. Cyrus." Charlie's turn, he tore off and came running back, handed the WD-40 to Mr. Cyrus. He and Jennilee waited expectantly while Mr. Cyrus used the little red straw to spray lubricant directly into the keyhole. Trying repeatedly, they all held their breath until the lock gave.

The heavy door squealed and protested. Mr. Cyrus cautioned them, "Mind where you step. This old house has been empty a lot of years. I come in a couple times a year and make sure there aren't any leaks or anything."

Holding hands, Charlie and Jennilee stepped over the threshold as one, faces alight. Inspected their house top to bottom. The inside was dusty and filthy, the kitchen outdated beyond redemption, no indoor plumbing or electrical to be seen anywhere. Nothing that time and elbow grease and a great deal of money couldn't fix.

It was perfect.

Giving them a guided tour, Cyrus kept up a running dialogue. "This house was built in the mid 1700s by one of Clyde's great-greats. A top-notch shipwright, he built this house to last. There's some superficial damage, nothing that can't be fixed."

Stars in their eyes, Charlie and Jennilee imagined what they'd do to each spacious, high-ceilinged room.

JENNILEE'S LIGHT

"Clyde's daddy didn't believe in electricity, said it was a fad and wouldn't be here long. Refused to install it. There's no inside plumbing, no insulation, so you can wire it, plumb it, and insulate it at the same time. The window frames need to be replaced, and the chimneys inspected." Cyrus broke off.

He was talking to the kids like they had a chance of owning the place, like they were adults who knew what he was talking about. "Kids, I shouldn't have let you in, let you get your hopes up. Clyde's never going to sell this place."

Jennilee answered dreamily, certain sure. "He will. Not right now. Later. When the time is right."

Cyrus could only stare.

Charlie, all business, asked, "Do you have an address for Mr. Clyde? We'd like to write him, let him know we're interested."

Cyrus shook himself, reminded himself he was dealing with a couple little kids. "I'm not so sure it's a good idea, but I'll see if I can dig it up. He used to keep a post office box."

Locking the door behind them, Cyrus left the kids to stroll around the yard by himself. Walked, and reminisced. Stopped at the family cemetery. The graves had been lovingly tended, weeds pulled and grass mowed.

Walking back across the yard, early evening shadows beginning to cloak things, he watched as Charlie and Jennilee sprayed down their tools with WD-40, wrapped them in the tarp. Finishing that, Charlie sprayed down an old reel mower.

Cyrus laughed to himself. There was a mystery solved. Maybe, just maybe, they could talk Clyde into selling this old relic to them.

"You two need a ride home?"

"We've got our bikes, but we'd surely appreciate it Mr. Cyrus."

Cyrus threw out, "Del know what you're up to?"

"Nossir. We haven't said anything to anybody."

"Make sure you tell her. I don't like the idea of you two being so far from town and no one knowing where you are."

As he'd done before, Cyrus tooted the horn lightly when he pulled up in Del's driveway. She came out, wiping her hands on a dishtowel. Her eyes flickered uneasily over the kids, settled on Cyrus.

"Cy? Something wrong?"

"Everything's fine, Del. I happened on these two and gave them a ride home."

"Well, thanks. Won't you stay to supper?"

Cyrus' seamed face broke into a wide grin. "I thank you Del, and I accept. Been a long time since I had any of your good cooking."

Hands on her hips, head cocked, Del demanded, "Whose fault is that?"

"Mine. Purely mine. That's what I get for being a stubborn old cuss."

Del laughed as Cyrus helped Charlie unload the bikes and Jennilee headed inside.

"Sir? Whatever you did for Jennilee? I just wanted to say thank you. She needs all the friends and all the help she can get."

"You're surely welcome, son. You keep a sharp eye on her. She's a proud one, and brave."

"I'm well aware of both those things. She's got a good dose of stubborn thrown in as well."

Cyrus threw back his head and laughed. "Don't they all? But what would we do without our women?"

∽

"You say they've cleared the whole yard?"

Supper finished, Del and Cyrus were catching up. Having broken down and sprung for a window unit, the welcome hum of the air conditioner in the living room accompanied their conversation.

Kicked back in the recliner, itching for a chaw but knowing better than to drag out his tobacco and spit cup in Del's house, Cyrus shook his head. "You wouldn't believe what they've accomplished, Del. I would'na believed it if I had'na seen it. Those two have worked like a whole den of beavers, absolutely convinced Clyde will sell to them. They've sure set their hearts on that place."

Hands stilling, knitting needles going slack, Del stared at Cy, bemused. "I'm having a hard time believing they found it in the first place. It must be eight, ten miles out of town, and a couple miles off the main road."

"Ever bit of it. They even asked me for Clyde's address so's they could write and tell him they're interested in buying. I know they're good at saving money—I was at the bank the day they opened their joint account, but I don't know where two younguns think they can come up with that kind of money."

"You don't know my two. Once they make up their minds..." Del laughed.

Cyrus fingered his chin. "Maybe they're figuring on using what the Judge left Jennilee."

"Even if there's a dime left, Jennilee wouldn't touch it if she was starving."

Cyrus looked at an adamant Del. "Kind of figured that's the way the wind blew. Jennilee's gotta lot of pride and guts, and Celie..." Shook his head. "Celie's just the opposite—a completely shameless coward."

~

CHARLIE AND JENNILEE TURNED ELEVEN, then twelve. Still working like dogs on their yard, and Mr. Cyrus had even given them a key to the house. They'd written numerous times to Mr. Clyde Goodwin, detailing their hopes and what they'd accomplished. They'd heard exactly nothing back, but neither had their letters been returned.

CHAPTER 15

Spying Del entering the diner, both arms full of freshly baked goods, Red waved her over as he spoke into the phone. "Yeah, she's here. Del, it's for you. Charlie, and he sounds upset. That's the fourth time he's called in the last ten minutes."

"Charlie?" Dropping her goods on the counter carelessly, Del grabbed the phone.

Talking so fast he was practically incoherent, Charlie begged, "Grandy. You gotta come quick. They sent us home in disgrace. Mrs. Masters said we cheated on a test and Mort's home. He's gonna…"

"I'm on my way. Stay right there." Dropping the phone, she ran for the door.

Red hollered after her. "Hey, Del. Don't you want your money?"

Already half way out the door, Del hollered over her shoulder, "Later. Call Mac and tell him to meet me at my house."

Pulling up in her driveway she found Charlie frantically pouring out his story to Mac.

"He took her. I heard him say he was taking her back to school. He's going to have us put in separate classes."

"Get in." Stepping back into his cruiser, Charlie and Grandy jumped in and Mac took off, lights and sirens going full blast.

Reaching the now empty school, they could hear Mort's angry voice all the way down the hall, blasting out like he had a megaphone.

"Apologize, dammit!" Jennilee's arm clamped in a crushing grip, Mort shook her like a rag doll.

Shaking her head, Jennilee mutely defied him, afraid if she opened her mouth she'd start screaming and never stop. Besides, she had nothing to apologize for.

"Tracy, I don't know what's wrong with her. Cheating, and now refusing to apologize. She won't cheat again, and she will say she's sorry or I'll…"

"Get your hands off her!" Hitting Mort like he was making the game deciding tackle, Charlie shoved Mort away from Jennilee. Placed his own rigid body between them, fists clenched, head lowered like an enraged bull about to charge.

"You little…" Mort raised his fist.

"Touch him and I'll arrest you."

Meeting Mac's cold smile with one of his own, Mort sniped, "Mac. Imagine that. You coming to the defense of these two."

Del stepped around Mac as he moved between Charlie and Mort. The shattered look in Jennilee's eyes nearly broke her heart.

Charlie turned to Jennilee. "Jennilee-honey, are you ok?" Took a step in her direction.

She backed up.

Definitely not.

Mac's no-nonsense official tone cut the air. "Somebody better start explaining."

Mort opened his mouth, Mac raised a hand, turned steely eyes on Tracy Masters. "Would you mind telling me what this is all about?"

"Ahem. I believe I can clear this up." Principal Holmes stepped into the room.

"Please do. Explain to me why I have two absolutely terrified children here." Mac's voice was glacial as his eyes.

Principal Holmes cleared his throat and spoke in the nose-in-the-air tone of a snooty butler. "Mrs. Masters caught Charlie and Jennilee cheating on a test."

"Charlie and Jennilee have no need to cheat. Tracy, what in the world are you thinking, accusing them of such?" Grandy defended her chicks, believed in them unconditionally.

Jennilee's aches subsided, Grandy's belief a welcome balm to Jennilee's battered spirit.

Looking more like she was bar-trolling than teaching with her pancake makeup, teased hair, and too tight and very revealing clothes, Tracy fairly preened. "They had an important test today, one with essay questions. Their answers were nearly identical. They had to have cheated." She wound down smugly.

Grandy wound up. "How about the fact they study together and do their homework together? Did that thought ever cross your mind, or were you so busy lapping up your best friend's poison you didn't even think about that? Just how did they cheat? Were they passing notes, or whispering the answers to each other? What? I demand an answer."

"I don't know how they did it. Charlie sits there and Jennilee sits here." Tracy pointed to opposite sides of the room. "They managed to find a way somehow."

"They managed to find a way. Sign language, maybe? Perhaps they're telepathic." The sneer evident in Grandy's voice, she demanded, "Retest them. We're all right here watching. I demand a retest. They can't possibly cheat with this many adults right here."

Looking to the males in the room, batting her heavily mascara'd eyelashes, Tracy cooed, "What good will a retest do? They've already taken the test and they know the questions."

Unimpressed with Tracy's stalling tactics, Del shrugged. "So make up a new one. It can't be that hard. We'll wait."

"It'll take a bit."

Del crossed her arms, raised her eyebrows, tapped her foot.

Easing steadily closer to Jennilee, Charlie reached out, tentatively touched her arm, winced when she cringed.

Seeing Jennilee's reaction, Del turned her fury on Mort. "Did it even occur to you to ask Jennilee whether she cheated or not, or did you just take someone else's word as gospel?"

"Why would I doubt a teacher's word?"

"Jennilee's grades should speak for themselves."

"They do, quite loudly."

Del stared, completely confused, turned her attention to the kids.

Keeping his eyes on Jennilee's, Charlie whispered, "I'm so sorry Jennilee-love. I couldn't find Grandy."

Jennilee shook her head, not trusting her voice.

"It's my fault. If I'd been quicker…"

Jennilee shook her head again, harder.

Charlie eased a step closer. "I wish we were home. I'd rock you, wrap you in my arms, close to my heart and sing to you."

Tears shimmering in Jennilee's eyes, she nodded jerkily.

The ticking of the clock was the only sound.

New test in hand, Tracy tried to regain control of the situation. "Charlie, you sit over there, and Jennilee, you sit right here."

Making no move to take his seat, Charlie instead watched Jennilee like a hawk. Jennilee stood mutely, unmoving, eyes focused on nothing.

"Jennilee?" Charlie's concern reached her, set her to trembling, set his temper off like a firecracker with a long fuse. "She can't. Sit."

Needing no further explanation, if looks could kill, Mort would've been laid out stiff on the floor as Charlie, Grandy, and Mac pinned him with murderous glares.

Keeping her eyes studiously on her test, on the words dancing and skipping across the blurry page, Jennilee fought for concentration.

One standing at the windowsill and one standing at the teacher's desk, their backs to each other, their thoughts on each other, Charlie and Jennilee finished their tests for the second time. Wrote the last answer down at the same time, turned their papers over at the same time, turned to face each other at the same time.

Jennilee couldn't move, could only wait for Charlie to come to her. As soon as Mac took their tests, Charlie leapt across the room to stand beside Jennilee, careful not to touch her.

Mac handed the papers to Principal Holmes. "Grade these, right here, right now."

The adults watched intently as the answers were read and checked off. Watched sweat pop out on the principal's brow.

"They both got a hundred."

"And?" Mac gave no quarter.

"And, they answered each question almost exactly the same."

"Mort, Tracy, you're hateful. Both of you. Come on, kids."

"Where the hell do you think you're taking my ward, Adele?"

Del's feral smile didn't come anywhere close to her eyes.

"Mac's going to run us by Doc's, then I'm taking both kids home. If you want to argue about it, call Tom. In fact, I'll call Tom. You better call your own lawyer."

Herding the kids outside, towards Mac's patrol car, Mac and Del exchanged worried glances.

Almost to the car, Jennilee's eyes focused and she froze. Swallowed, shuddered. "You're taking me… He s…said…he was going to have me locked up and that I'd n…never get out."

Mac knelt in front of her, kept his voice soft and his hands by his sides when what he really wanted was to wrap Jennilee in his arms and keep her safe. Right after he choked the ever loving snot out of Mort. And Celie. "No, Jennilee. We brought my car so we could get here faster. That's all. We need to take you to Doc's. Can you make it to the car or do you want me to carry you?"

Jennilee lurched back a step, eyes pinwheeling like a terrified wild animal. "Don't touch me."

"I won't, baby. Just a little farther. Come on."

Managing a couple more steps, Jennilee staggered as her knees buckled. Charlie caught her, and the pain of contact sent her into oblivion. When she woke next, she was in Charlie's arms, in their rocking chair, and he was singing softly to her. She felt…foggy. The pain still there, but distant —a dimly remembered nightmare.

"How…" Jennilee struggled to form the one word and get it out.

"Hush, Jennilee-sweet. I've got you. Doc gave you something."

"Doc?"

Body vibrating with suppressed rage, the adults hadn't let Charlie stay in the room while Doc examined Jennilee but he'd taken a long look at her back once they got home. The bruised stripes and defined welts made his blood boil.

He kept his tone low and soothing. Jennilee didn't need any more upset right now. "Doc gave you a shot for the pain. Don't try to move. Just let me hold you. I'll go over the plans for our bedroom again."

Grandy eavesdropped from the hallway, as she had so many times before and would again, tears streaming down her face.

Charlie's voice rolled out smooth as water over boulders in a slow moving creek, the squeak of the rocking chair providing the rhythm to his melody. "We'll take the big suite in the northeast corner, the one on the second floor, so we can see the water and watch the sunrise. We'll breakfast on the porch outside the French doors. I'll get Mose to craft us an extra-large four poster bed, like the one we admired at Hamilton's Furniture in Beaufort. We'll have Mose make us a huge wardrobe, one made of real wood and heavier than a herd of elephants. A couple dressers to match. You can braid one of those rag rugs you adore so much in the colors you like. We'll polish those old wood floors until we can see our reflections. Mose can build us a rocking chair, as close to this one as we can get."

Charlie's voice broke. Silence while he regained his equilibrium, punctuated only by the squeak of the rocking chair.

"We'll convert the dressing room into a huge bathroom. I'll put in the biggest tub I can find and you can take all the bubble baths you want. I'll put in a huge water heater. How 'bout a quilt, Jennilee? A green and white double Irish chain maybe, or a crazy quilt made of silks and velvets in a rainbow of colors. Lacy white curtains that'll make delicate shadow patterns on the floor when the sun shines through them."

On and on, a litany of love.

Listening until she couldn't stand it anymore, until she thought her heart would burst, Grandy eased quietly up the stairs and went face down on her bed, sobbed into her pillow until she had no tears left.

Jennilee floated above the pain, rocked by Charlie, soothed by his promises.

That's where Grandy found them the next morning when she came downstairs, still in the rocking chair. One of the pain pills Doc had prescribed was gone, and Jennilee's glass of water was empty. Both kids were sound asleep, wrapped around each other like trumpet vine on a guy wire.

Jennilee woke long enough for Charlie to feed her a few bites of the breakfast Grandy fixed for her, more from not wanting to hurt Grandy's feelings than because she was hungry. Leaving Charlie long enough to go to the bathroom she took another pill, curled right back up in his lap and passed out again.

Waiting until the most recent pain pill rendered Jennilee unconscious, Charlie gently placed her on the couch, headed for the kitchen where the adults were gathered.

Fist pounding gently, rhythmically, impotently, on the table, daffodil yellow bow tie sporting bright green frogs askew, Tom informed the others, "Del, there's nothing we can do. Don't you think we've exhausted every avenue? Jennilee called it—she stays with them or she goes into foster care. The Judge may be long gone, but his name still carries weight. Celie's already told her lawyer that under no circumstances will she allow you to be Jennilee's guardian. Sobbed and cried, told her lawyer that Jennilee's such a difficult child, Mort just lost his temper, it'll never happen again—blah, blah, blah." Tom spoke bitterly. "I'll say it again—if Cynthia'd just left a will—anything—but there's nothing, and nothing I can do. The Judge's will is unbreakable, and Celie has custody."

Mac snorted. "Mort's been ordered to take anger management classes, which isn't worth—pardon my French—a tinker's damn."

"Doc, can't you document the abuse?" Del pleaded.

Dragging a hand through his hair in frustration, Doc shook his head. "Del, I can document 'til the cows come home. As long as Mort and Celie claim it was just punishment that got out of hand and promise never to do it again, my hands are tied."

"They're going to kill her." Del said it tiredly, aching with sadness.

Stepping into the kitchen, Charlie surveyed the adults sitting at the table, each with a cup of coffee, long since gone cold in front of them. "Celie doesn't want to kill Jennilee—she wants to break her, and she's using Mort to that end. Jennilee's stronger, and we'll win."

"Come here, Charlie Bear." Del held out her arms to her beloved grandson.

Giving her a quick hug and stepping back, Charlie assured the adults, "Jennilee doesn't blame any of you for this, so stop beating yourselves up. She's just glad we have all of you. *We're* glad. We'll get through it. If you could fix it so she doesn't have to go back until she's healed, it would mean a lot."

The assembled adults watched Charlie get a glass of milk, a handful of Grandy's chocolate chip cookies, and head back to Jennilee.

Dropping her head onto her crossed arms, Del let the bitter tears flow while the men looked on helplessly.

CHAPTER 16

Their twelfth summer found Charlie and Jennilee busier than ever. Charlie worked in tobacco, adamantly refused to consider Jennilee doing so. Hot, back-breaking work, he knew she had enough of that at her aunt's.

Jennilee got a job working for Mr. Paul Gillikin at the pharmacy grill, sweeping up, stocking shelves, flipping burgers and making milkshakes.

They added those funds to their account, kept all the side jobs.

Between jobs, riding their bikes side by side on one of the backstreets, they noticed a local realtor pounding a For Sale sign into a neglected lawn. Stopping their bikes as one, they shared a look, grinned and pedaled off.

Didn't say a word as they sped down the long dirt road to Miz Sadie's, their thoughts as in tandem as the two riders themselves. For a long while, they'd been discussing how they were going to come up with enough money to buy their house, should Mr. Clyde Goodwin ever decide to fulfill Jennilee's certainty. Side jobs and chores weren't going to get it.

They needed pots of money. Buying run down properties, fixing them up and reselling them or converting them into rentals would go a long way toward helping them reach their goal. The old Barstow place, the one where they'd just watched Mrs. Jean Lewis putting up a For Sale sign, fit the bill to a T.

Parking their bikes, they headed for Mr. Jubal and Miz Sadie's deep front porch. Knocking politely, Jennilee stepped back to wait.

Face splitting in a contagious grin, swinging the screen door wide, Miz Sadie waved them in. "Why, bless my soul. If it ain't my two favorite younguns. What are you two up to now? Jennilee, I know you didn't come here for more embroidery lessons—you can stitch ever bit as purty as I can. Charlie, you can carve anything and make it look alive. Jubal's taught you all he knows."

Grinning back at the round, midnight dark face of one of their most favorite people in the whole world, they grinned at each other. Miz Sadie didn't see folks in black and white, she only saw whether she liked you or not, and she purely loved Charlie and Jennilee. The feeling was mutual.

Enfolding both of them, one in each strong arm, she kissed them on top their heads. "You two work so much I hardly ever see you anymore. Del need something?"

Charlie and Jennilee returned her hug. "It's good to see you, Miz Sadie. Thanks for asking, but Grandy doesn't need anything."

"What are you two up to? You're grin'n like a couple o' possums."

"We were just wondering if Mose is around. We need to talk to him."

"Mose, huh?" Eyeing them speculatively, Miz Sadie informed them, "He's out back, in his shop. I just made some lemonade. We kin sit in the shade and catch up."

Looking around while Charlie and Miz Sadie were talking, Jennilee loved this full-to-bursting room, crammed with books of every description. Paperbacks, hardcovers, leather bound volumes, all mixed in a glorious hodgepodge. Mr. Jubal'd told them once he'd taught himself to read, couldn't bear to see a book thrown away. Slowly working his way through his ever-expanding collection, Miz Sadie just shook her head and grinned every time he dragged more books home.

Mose had a shop all right—a woodworking shop. Built the most exquisite things from wood, had the ability to restore anything made of wood. Jubal carved, but Mose created.

Charlie and Jennilee headed around back. They needed Mose and his knowledge.

Miz Sadie brought the lemonade out on a museum quality parquetry tray Mose had crafted for her. Her gaze sweeping the three of them, she placed the tray of lemonade and cake on the wrought iron table under the huge old oak, kept her own council. Started pouring, smiling to herself.

Handing Jennilee the green and Charlie the blue left the gold for herself and the red for Mose. How many times had they sat here, just like this, drinking out of these same aluminum tumblers? Charlie and Jennilee always chose the same color, and out of habit Mose and Sadie did the same.

Tracing her fingers over her apron pocket, Sadie fingered the delicate embroidery edging the pockets and the matching hem. Jennilee'd sewn the apron, embellished it and given it to Sadie for her birthday. The child had a rare talent with a needle.

And Charlie—Lord knew that child could carve a piece of wood and make it breathe. Jubal'd shown him the basics, and Charlie'd run with it. Jubal carved decoys, had people comin'

JENNILEE'S LIGHT

from all over just to see, but Charlie'd far outstripped his mentor.

Charlie pulled his harmonica out. An hour later, they were still singing along. Reluctantly, Charlie and Jennilee got to their feet, hugged Miz Sadie and Mose.

Sadie watched them out of sight. "So, you gonna tell me what they're up to?"

Mose regarded his mother thoughtfully. "Not just yet."

Sadie looked at her son with a mother's discerning eye. Mose hadn't been the same since he'd come back from Vietnam. Quiet, plagued by nightmares, haunted by horrors they couldn't imagine, he seemed more than content to work in his woodshop and drift through the days. Didn't care that he lived in their attic like a teenager with no ambition. Didn't spend a dime of his disability checks, banking them all and living off what he made in his shop.

Stopping at all the road signs on the way back, Charlie and Jennilee picked up bottles. Returnables went in one bike basket, non-returnables went in the other. They'd long ago figured out one of the favorite local past-times was throwing bottles at signs from a moving car. All you had to do to get a windfall was check around the signs.

Turning the good ones in for the refund, they trashed the rest. Two bottles of Pepsi and two packs of peanuts later, they were happily dumping their peanuts into their drinks. Finishing their salty-sweet snack, they headed for Miz Ethel's and their weekly chores at her house.

Fireflies were dancing, blinking out their catch-me-if-you-can version of Morse code by the time Charlie and Jennilee ended up back at Grandy's.

Grandy and Mr. Donnie greeted the two as they stepped into the kitchen.

"Hey, kids! Where ya been? Charlie, have I got a surprise for you! Remember that truck of Peter Jenkins' we towed in awhile back? The one with the blown engine? He wants to get rid of it. Whatcha think?"

Jennilee grinned and rolled her eyes at Grandy as Charlie and Mr. Donnie engaged in a rapturous discussion about the 1968 Ford pickup.

～

A FEW DAYS LATER, Mr. Jubal answered their knock this time, finger clamped in a book. Waving them in, he called over his shoulder for Sadie. She appeared instantly, wiping her hands on a dishtowel.

"My stars! Look who's back again!"

"We won't trouble you long Mr. Jubal, Miz Sadie. We just need to talk to Mose again."

"Hush that. You're never any trouble. Sit while I make some lemonade." Grinning from ear to ear, she moved her bulk with surprising grace back toward the kitchen.

"I'll help, Miz Sadie." Jennilee took a step.

Mr. Jubal, tall and thin as Miz Sadie was short and round, spoke. "Jennilee. I need to talk to you." Mr. Jubal outdid Jennilee at her quietest for paucity of words.

Jennilee froze, Charlie shifted closer, Sadie turned around.

"Easy, child. Nothing bad. I found something you need to see." Mr. Jubal reached out for a book on one of his groaning shelves. "You know how I'm always dragging books home, can't stand to see one thrown away?"

Jennilee nodded warily.

"I told you a long time ago I taught myself to read."

Jennilee nodded again.

"I reads—I read slow. I've had these books a long time, found them at the trash dump. They looked important and challenging, so I left them, figured I'd learn to read easier stuff until I built up my skills and confidence. I finally cracked one the other day and…well, take a look." Held it out.

Leatherbound, title in gold leaf, obviously old, part of an expensive set.

It might've been a copperhead he was offering. Jennilee was that loath to take it.

Opening the front cover, turning it so they could see the elaborate bookplate, Mr. Jubal held the book out again.

Charlie took it.

Mr. Jubal encouraged, "Go on, read what it says."

Wide-eyed, Jennilee dropped her eyes to the book. The elegant script difficult to decipher, once her eyes focused there was no doubt about what it said: *This book belongs to and is part of the library of Judge Daniel McRae.*

Jennilee's eyes flew to the loaded shelves, ranks of identical leatherbound tomes filling many of them, locked on Mr. Jubal's.

He waved a hand to indicate the books. "These belong to…"

"You. Finders, keepers, Mr. Jubal. You found them at the dump. They belong to you now. Read them, enjoy them as they were meant to be read and enjoyed."

"But Jennilee…"

Taking a step back, Jennilee tucked her hands behind her. "No buts, Mr. Jubal. They're yours. I'm glad you found them, glad you cared enough to rescue them. Thank you."

"I saved what I could, Jennilee. A pile of 'em were ruined. Near broke my heart."

Jennilee had a pretty accurate idea how the Judge's treasured library had ended up at the dump. "I don't remember the Judge, but I'm sure he'd be tickled to know that someone who loves books as much as you do ended up with them."

Excusing themselves, they went out back to talk to Mose.

An intense discussion and a three-way handshake, and ten minutes later they were riding their bikes back down the dirt road.

One week later the three of them were seated in Mr. Tom Stimpson's waiting room. When it was their turn, they entered his office, outlined exactly what they wanted.

Two weeks later they were back, signing the papers, with Grandy as Charlie and Jennilee's advocate. Charlie, Jennilee, and Mose were now the proud owners of a run down house and half an acre of neglected yard.

~

SIX MONTHS LATER, in March, right around Charlie and Jennilee's thirteenth birthday, the completely refurbished house was put back on the market. It sold, in less than a week, for better than three times what they'd invested in it.

Mose was the brains, but Charlie and Jennilee supplied a great deal of the brawn. They'd sanded and refinished the heart pine floors, patched and repainted the walls, redone the kitchen and bath from stem to stern, helped with the plumbing and rewiring, all under Mose's watchful eye and expert tutelage. Anything that was over their combined heads, they called in outside help.

The first electrician they called came out to the house, took one look and informed them emphatically he weren't workin' for no nigger and two snot-nosed brats.

Jennilee looked accusingly at Mose, linebacker big and black as the Ace of Spades. Eyes innocently wide, she asked in a shocked voice. "Mose—you're…black?"

Charlie added in an aggrieved tone, "Yeah, Mose. You shoulda said something."

"And you two aren't grown-ups?" Shaking his head, Mose tsk'd loudly.

The electrician left in a huff, the sound of their laughter ringing loud in his ears.

After that, they were far more careful in their choices of outside help.

Banking their profits, the threesome kept their eyes open for another property.

Mose found it. Bigger this time, more house, more acreage. Same deal. Combining their resources and their talents, the three repeated their success. That house sold just after their fourteenth birthday.

Mose had no qualms about sharing any and all of his extensive knowledge with the kids, and what Mose didn't know, Charlie hounded the licensed contractors for, soaking up their teachings.

They bought another property in the fall. Charlie and Jennilee found it this time. The biggest house yet, with a couple acres of land and a huge outbuilding.

The two of them came to a sliding stop in Miz Sadie's front yard, dashed around the house to Mose's small, cramped workshop.

"Mose!"

Poking his head out, Mose listened to the two excited teenagers. Well used to them, he had no trouble making sense of their fractured sentences.

"You gotta…"

"…come see! You're gonna…"

"… love it!"

They finished together. "There's a great big outbuilding!" Staring at Mose with shining eyes, they waited for his response.

"Where? Which house?" Their excitement was contagious.

"On the other side of town. The big three story on River Road, just past the sharp curve."

"The old Garner place?"

Both heads nodded in unison.

"That's a pretty big project for just the three of us."

Charlie and Jennilee shared a look. "We don't…" Looked back to Mose.

"…want to resell this one."

"We were thinking…"

"…apartments."

Mose regarded them silently. The Garner place was pretty big. Done right, a bunch of apartments could be made out of the old place, without destroying its integrity. Six, maybe eight.

Charlie and Jennilee shifted impatiently from foot to foot.

"If we're gonna do apartments, we're gonna need a supervisor."

Charlie and Jennilee were fairly dancing. "We thought about that. You."

"Me, what?"

"You. Live there, in one of the apartments, and keep an eye on things."

"And that outbuilding would be perfect for your workshop. You wouldn't have to lose so much time in your shop if you and your shop were in the same place."

Mose chuffed. "Me and my shop are in the same place now."

"Mose…"

"…you can't…"

"…work out of this…"

"…shed forever."

"You're too…"

"…talented. You need…"

"…room to expand."

Mose's head switched back and forth between Charlie and Jennilee like a human metronome.

He thought about it for a solid two weeks before he told them yes.

Work on their most recent house well underway by Christmas, Charlie used his new-found skills and surprised Jennilee with a cedar chest he'd built himself.

"A hope chest, to put your hopes in," he told her as he thumbed the happy tears off her face.

She'd bought him a second-hand Gibson, which he spent all afternoon playing. Some of the older men had taught Charlie in earlier years to play, and he put their teachings to good use. The two of them joined the older folks on the porch, as they did every Christmas, weather permitting. The crowd was listening to Charlie play and harmonize with Jennilee, entranced, when the phone rang.

Del answered it, came back grim faced.

One look and the happiness on Jennilee's face fled. Leaning close to Charlie, she whispered so that only he could hear. "Light my way." Touched him on the shoulder, a butterfly caress. Closing his eyes, Charlie played a haunting melody as Jennilee jumped off the porch and headed back to her aunt's.

CHAPTER 17

The spring of their fifteenth year heralded many changes. Both had taken and passed Driver's Ed, gotten their permits as soon as they celebrated their birthday.

Mr. Donnie let whichever one was with him take turns driving his old wrecker on calls. For years he'd been taking them out on the tram roads, letting them drive up and down. Thanks to his expert tutelage, both kids had become excellent drivers. All they had to do now was get used to driving in traffic.

The new house was closer to being finished, the grounds well on their way. Three stories, brick, and to their delight, Garner House came with a guesthouse. Tucked away behind the larger house, hidden amongst a small copse of live oaks hanging full of Spanish moss, the guesthouse was perfect. Mose claimed it for his own and they'd redone it first thing.

Jennilee helped Mose load his meager personal belongings while Charlie and Mr. Donnie helped load Mose's tools. Miz Sadie watched, tears in her eyes.

Sidling up to the rotund mountain that was Miz Sadie, Jennilee asked, "Are you mad at us, Miz Sadie?"

Sadie hugged Jennilee tight. "Mad? Why would I be mad?"

"For taking Mose away."

"Child, I hate to see him go, but it's past time. If the two of you hadn't dragged him out of his shell, he'd be living in our itty-bitty upstairs like a sick bat for the rest of his life. I'm not mad a bit. I don't know what he would've done without the two of you—you've given him a purpose, a reason to go on living."

Miz Sadie sighed and squeezed Jennilee. "When he came back from Vietnam, he was lost, so lost. I was so afraid he'd never find his way back to us. The only thing he's cared about for years is his woodworking. I'm not sure even that would've held him much longer. He was just slipping away, day by day and nuthin' we did seemed to reach him."

"He's been a blessing to us, too."

Cramming into the front of Charlie's truck, Mr. Donnie, Jennilee, Charlie and Mose drove to Garner House. The four shared matching grins as they turned in the drive and passed the sign. Green letters on a white background—The Garner House Apartments—it was a testament to their success.

Walking toward the guesthouse, Charlie said, "You should be the first one to cross the threshold of your new home, Mose. Go ahead."

Eyeing them curiously, Mose knew them well enough to know they were up to something. Stepping inside, he froze in astonishment. "You two did this for me?" Eyes sweeping the main room, he took in the Welcome Home banner, the cake on the table, the plants on the kitchen windowsill and above the cabinets, the braided rug in front of the sink, the lacy curtains at the windows.

Mose took a couple more steps, turned.

Donnie stood just inside the door, a lopsided smile on his

face. Charlie hugged Jennilee to him, both grinning like possums. "We had help."

Shaking his head, Mose looked past them at the sound of several vehicles pulling up in the driveway.

Mr. Jubal and Miz Sadie, and Grandy got out of their respective vehicles, all carrying bags and boxes.

Sitting in the extra-large and extremely comfortable recliner that had appeared since he'd been here yesterday, dazed with happiness, Mose could only watch as the others set up for a party.

Putting a plate of cake in his hands, Jennilee placed a coaster and then a drink on the table beside his chair. "Well?"

"I don't know what to say, Jennilee. It's…perfect. Thank you, doll."

Charlie slipped an arm around Jennilee's waist. "We wanted to say thank you for all you've done."

Mose smiled widely, took a bite of cake.

Even though they hadn't started renting out any of the apartments yet, Charlie and Jennilee were far from destitute. Hadn't overspent themselves buying the place, and they both kept all their other side jobs. Jennilee'd moved up to being Mr. Gillikin's right hand. The customers adored her, and some of the blue hairs refused to let anyone else wait on them, insisting on Jennilee.

Charlie helped his dad at the garage more and more. The two of them spent countless hours tinkering on Charlie's truck. Dropped a new-used engine in it, reupholstered the bench seat. Repainted the truck a deep metallic blue, put clear coat after clear coat on it until looking at it was like looking into a bottomless pool of blue.

It warmed Jennilee's heart to see how close the two had become. Why, Mr. Donnie was a regular at Grandy's anymore and he'd been at every Thanksgiving dinner and Christmas celebration for the last few years.

∼

FINISHING her shift at the pharmacy, Jennilee started walking home. She'd heard the fire whistle earlier, an air raid siren sounding noise that could be heard all over town and called in all the volunteers. A customer told them there'd been a terrible wreck out on the four-lane. Charlie and Mr. Donnie'd probably gotten tied up at the scene.

Shrugged. She'd walked to Grandy's before, could certainly do it again.

Daydreaming, wishing for her bike, she heard a car coming behind her, instinctively stepped farther off the road. With no sidewalks, she hated to get too close to the deep ditch. The car nearly to her, Jennilee heard the tires leave the pavement, heard the motor rev at the same time the horn blared.

Jennilee leapt. Unable to clear the ditch, she hit the side of the far bank, scrabbled desperately, slid back down into the bottom.

Whirling to face her attacker, some ancient sense told her who it was. As she landed, the car slammed on its brakes, already past her. Fishtailing wildly, the car backed up. Jennilee was stuck.

If she climbed up the road side of the ditch, she was putting herself right back in her attacker's grasp. Climbing up the other side meant turning her back to her attacker.

Jennilee turned and ran down the middle of the ditch back toward town, tall grasses and weeds in the bottom and along the sides catching at her, slowing her down. The car continued to pace her, going backwards on the wrong side of the road.

Jennilee had time for a rueful thought—*Like he's worried about that.* Something hit the back of her head, sending her to her knees in a patch of slimy muck. Fighting her way back to her feet, panting, she turned to face her attacker. The ditch shallower here, she could plainly see the car and its occupant.

Occupants—plural.

She'd been uncannily right. Butch, only this time he wasn't alone. Sylvia sat in the front seat with him, in the middle, his arm around her shoulders. Sylvia must've thrown the bottle, a glass Coke bottle that hadn't been in the bottom of the ditch scant seconds ago. The one that'd hit Jennilee and set her head to throbbing like a toothache on Friday night.

Butch slammed on the brakes again, the open window even with Jennilee. Taunting laughter flowed out, surrounded Jennilee. "Where's your hero now? Or maybe your nigger'll come help you."

Jennilee faced them silently, fighting for breath. The attacks on her she could take, but she would let no one and nothing touch Charlie or Mose. Smiled coldly and forced the words out. "What's a matter? Run out of little kids and helpless animals to torment?"

Sylvia tittered, "Why would we need them when we've got you?"

"And your nigger." Evil laughter came from both of them.

Throwing back a spear of her own, Jennilee felt the satisfaction when it lodged. "Your dad know you're consorting with white trash, Sylvia?"

"You better watch your tongue, or just maybe I'll cut it out for you. It's not like you'll tell Charlie if I touch you. You never have. Maybe, just maybe, some of the real men in town would like to hear just how close you and your nigger are. Only one reason a big buck like that hangs around a little white girl."

Jennilee faced her tormentors, rage pulsing through her, beating down her fear. "Butch Jones, you're as stupid as you look if you think I didn't tell Charlie because I'm afraid of you. I didn't tell him because you're not worth killing." Didn't say a word about Mose, though her heart pounded in terror for him.

"Car, Butch." Clutching Butch's arm, Sylvia looked back down the road toward town.

So she wasn't as complacent as she acted about being seen with Butch. Jennilee stored that nugget away for later.

"I'm not finished with you, or that nigger you think so much of." Putting the car in gear, Butch spun out, showering Jennilee with sand and clumps of grass.

Protecting her eyes with an up-thrown arm, Jennilee scooped up the bottle, gave it a solid heave at the departing car. Had the satisfaction of seeing it hit the back window of Knot Jones' clunker and watching the window shiver into a million pieces. Hollered, "Explain that to your dad, Butch."

She watched Butch's car until it drove out of sight. The one that'd been coming turned off before it reached her. Climbing wearily out of the ditch, Jennilee started for home, changed her mind.

∼

"Jennilee, what in the world?" Chief Mac came out from behind his desk, concern all over his face.

"I'm fine, just filthy. I need to wash up, and then talk to you a minute."

Waving a hand in the direction of the bathroom, Mac waited and fumed. Listened grimly as Jennilee told him what'd just happened, repeating the conversation verbatim. "I know there's nothing you can do. It's my word against theirs, and Sylvia will deny she was even with Butch. I didn't come here to tattle and whine. Someone needs to know. I need a written record somewhere. I won't have Charlie and Mose blindsided by scum like Butch."

"Jennilee, you know how deep prejudices in this town run. You be careful."

Temper snapping, Jennilee raged. "Chief Mac, we haven't done anything wrong. Mose is a wonderful, talented human being and a decorated Vietnam vet and if he wants to repair houses and re-sell them…"

"Jennilee! Whoa. I'm not arguing with you. I personally happen to think Mose and his parents are salt of the earth. Everybody doesn't feel that way. As tight as the three of you are… Well, it was bound to cause trouble."

Jennilee swallowed, gritting her teeth against the inherent stupidity of some people, reminded herself Chief Mac was on her side. "I didn't come here to lecture you. I came here so… I need help, before Charlie or Mose find out and decide to take matters into their own hands. Butch might be white trash, might live to fight, but he doesn't stand a chance against either Charlie or Mose and he's not worth one drop of their blood."

"Easy, girl. I agree completely. How're you going to keep Charlie from finding out about this?"

Jennilee blurted out, "I've never told…" Clammed up as Chief Mac narrowed his eyes. He might look and act easy-going, but underneath, he was all cop, and he'd done a stint in the Marines before coming back to Chinquapin Ridge.

"Never told what, Jennilee?"

Jennilee shook her head stubbornly, mutely. The run-in with Butch and Sylvia'd rattled her more than she'd realized.

"Butch is the one who beat you up and cut your hair, isn't he? How many other times has he hurt you?"

Aggravated more at herself than the Chief, Jennilee sniped, "You want dates and times?"

Mac reprimanded her gently. "You should've said something before now, Jennilee."

Jennilee met his gaze squarely, her eyes deep and shadowed with bitter knowledge. "To what end, Chief? You'd've been honor bound to confront him, and we both know Charlie would've found out. Besides that, if you confront Butch, Knot's going to take up for him, and then I'll have the whole clan after me. I wouldn't be surprised if Knot doesn't come bustin' in here and press charges over his broken window."

Mac eyed Jennilee thoughtfully. She held entirely too many secrets. If Butch and Sylvia'd joined forces, it would add another dimension to the hell that was already Jennilee's life. "Let's get you home."

Jennilee didn't say another word until they were almost to Grandy's. "Thanks, Chief. I appreciate everything you do for me, for us."

Taking his eyes off the road for a sec, Mac prompted gently, "Jennilee, you're not doing Charlie any favors by not telling him about this."

"Chief, you know how protective he is. If he finds out about this, I'm not sure I can stop him at merely beating Butch into a bloody pile. I can live without a lot of things, but Charlie isn't one of them."

Shaking his head, muttering under his breath, Mac conceded grudgingly. "I don't want you walking anywhere by yourself anymore. If Charlie's late, you call me."

Jennilee burst out laughing. "You sound just like Charlie. You're not a taxi, Chief."

Just getting out of the patrol car as Charlie and Donnie came flying down Grandy's driveway, Jennilee watched as Charlie brought the wrecker to a sliding halt in a cloud of dust. Erupting out of the truck like a bat out of a cave, her name already flying off his lips, he looked frantic. "Jennilee?"

"I'm fine, Charlie."

Mac watched her play Charlie like a Stradivarius in the hands of a master.

"Jennilee? If you're fine why…" Charlie headed for Jennilee like a heat-seeking missile, his eyes missing nothing, taking in the muddy clothes and her disheveled state, Chief Mac and the patrol car behind her.

Walking up to him and placing a hand over his heart, she looked into his eyes. "Charlie! A car was driving too fast and ran off the road behind me. I heard it and jumped into the ditch to get away and got all muddy. Chief Mac gave me a ride home."

"Who…"

"Charlie, everything happened so fast. By the time I got my wits back, the car was long gone."

Mac shook his head and left them to it as he greeted Donnie and they headed inside. Jennilee told just enough truth to make it plausible, and he had to admit, it did sound good. If she hadn't told him what really happened, he never would've guessed anything was wrong.

"Sorry, Mac. That wreck out on 70 highway—it was a doozie." Donnie offered that tidbit as they climbed the steps.

"Yeah, I was listening on the scanner. Highway patrol had to take that one. Out of my jurisdiction."

"Wish it'd been out of mine." Donnie smiled ruefully.

Smiling in commiseration, Mac locked gazes with Del as he and Donnie entered the kitchen. Watched her tighten her lips and nod slightly as she picked up on his unspoken message.

Still in the driveway, Charlie forced Jennilee to look at him. "Are you sure you're ok?"

"Fine, Charlie. Just filthy."

Charlie kept at her. "Why were you walking on the wrong side of the road?"

"Charlie, I'm not a two year old. I know to face traffic. It was that little stretch on Harper Street, the one that only has one decent spot to walk."

Charlie's ire was growing. "Why didn't you wait? I told you I'd come pick you up."

"Charlie..."

"No buts, Jennilee. I won't have it. You either wait for me, or you call Grandy or Chief Mac or..."

"Charlie! I will not! I am perfectly capable..."

"Jennilee..." Charlie stopped her at the top of the steps, running his hands over her, verifying for himself she was fine. He *had* to touch her. She scared him to death.

"Charlie, I'm fine! Now leave it!"

Charlie was still sputtering, Jennilee still insisting as they entered the kitchen. Jennilee caught the Chief's eye and quirked a brow in an *I told you so*.

Grandy picked up on it, tried to dispel the tension. "Jennilee, why don't you go get washed up and changed. You've got time before supper."

Throwing Grandy a grateful look, Jennilee started to do just that. Snagging her, Charlie cupped her face and rested his forehead against hers. Sliding his hands around her head to let her braids down, he encountered the lump directly behind one ear.

He tensed and Jennilee braced herself for the storm. It broke quickly and viciously.

"If you're so *fine*, you wanna tell me why you have a goose-egg the size of my fist—on the back of your head?" His voice was low and threatening. Not threatening to her—never to her.

"Something must've hit my head. There's all kinds of trash in the bottom of that ditch."

"Un uh, Jennilee. All the mud's on the front of you. You fell forward."

"Charlie, I'm not sure exactly what happened. When I realized the car was too close, I didn't turn around. That ditch is too wide to jump from a standstill and I didn't have time to run. I just bailed. I hit the other bank and fell back down into the bottom."

Mac's estimation of Jennilee went up another notch as she faced Charlie, soothed him without lying, without looking to anyone else for help. If she'd so much as blinked, Charlie would've been on it like white on rice. Mac just hoped the fine line Jennilee was walking didn't catch up with her.

CHAPTER 18

"Jennilee, you wanna tell me what's wrong, or you gonna let me think you finally realized I'm a big black man and you're a pretty little white girl? A black man that's an escaped convict maybe, or a just released parolee with a prison record for assaulting pretty white girls." Mose didn't look up, just kept sanding.

Throwing a quick glance in Charlie's direction, Jennilee kept her voice low. "Mose Freeman, the only things you have a record for are distinguished service in the military and being a wizard with wood. I trust you with my life."

"Then tell me why all of a sudden you tense up every time I get within three feet of you, or I'm walkin' right now, and I'll never so much as speak to you again."

Fierce now, a mama bear defending her cub, "You haven't done a thing."

Mose didn't bat an eye. "Who's talkin', Jennilee, and what'd they say that has you so spooked?"

"Doesn't matter, Mose. You just watch your back. I'll keep my distance."

"Jennilee, you can't keep an eye on me and Charlie all the

time, and we can't work together and stay far apart. Let us help. Talk to me. Ignorance can get you killed."

"If Charlie finds out, I'm afraid someone will get killed, and it won't be Charlie. I won't have either of you hurt because of me."

"You think I'm gonna let some skinny little white girl put herself in the line of fire for me? I've dealt with bigots and idiots all my life. I kin handle it."

"Mose..."

"Hey! What are you two whispering about?"

Blinking rapidly, Jennilee swallowed several times. "You. How slow you are. I asked you ten minutes ago to..."

Coming up behind her, Charlie wrapped an arm around her waist and lifted her off her feet. "What was that? Complaints? Whining? Bellyaching? What do you say, Mose? We could..."

Jennilee elbowed Charlie. It had no effect, other than to cause him to shift his grip and hold her closer. Burying his face in her neck, nuzzling gently, he teased, "Mmm. I think I found the honey pot."

"Jennilee." Mose's implacable tone set Charlie's radar off.

Jennilee threw their friend and partner a fulminating glare.

"Jennilee?" Setting her on her feet, Charlie loosened his hold enough to turn her to face him. "What is it?"

"Somebody said somethin' that's upset our girl."

Rigid, avoiding their eyes, Jennilee informed them, "I already told Chief Mac."

Charlie and Mose shared a look. If she'd told Chief Mac, it was way more serious than she was letting on. "Then tell us."

"Why? So you can go all macho on me and get yourselves hurt? No thank you!" Jennilee tried to pull away.

Without hurting her, Charlie kept her where she was,

shook her lightly. "Tell me, Jennilee. I have a right to know. It's my responsibility to protect you."

"I can take care of myself, so back off." Jennilee clamped her lips, turned her head.

Charlie and Mose knew she wasn't denying Charlie was her protector as much as she was trying to protect him, divert his attention to herself instead of her tormentor.

"Somebody that's a bigot and a bully." Mose tapped his chin thoughtfully with one sausage-like finger.

Charlie speculated, "Someone who knows our routines, keeps a close eye on all of us."

"Somebody that knows Jennilee well."

"Someone jealous and hateful."

"What's your guess, Charlie?"

Charlie narrowed his eyes thoughtfully. "Best guess? Butch Jones." Knew he'd struck a nerve when the slightest tremor betrayed Jennilee.

"That was mine, too."

Charlie's tone went low and cold. "He threatened you, Jennilee?"

When Jennilee didn't answer, Mose answered for her. "The scumbag didn't threaten her, did he, baby? You wouldn't take that from him."

Charlie's tone switched from righteous anger to puzzled disbelief. "He can't possibly think he could take me on and win."

Mose's was certain. "He didn't threaten you, Charlie. He said somethin' agin me, 'cause he knows an adult black man, especially one with a military background, would find it hard to retaliate against a teen-aged white boy without major repercussions. Somethin' along the lines of a white girl associating with a nigger."

"Don't you dare say that about yourself, Mose!" Jennilee looked as outraged as she sounded.

"I've heard worse, missy."

"That's not all of it. Is it, Jennilee?" Charlie tipped her chin up so he could see her face. "Look at me, Jennilee. I'm not mad at you. Furious with him, and hurt that you didn't trust me enough to tell me, but I'm not mad at you. Never that, Jennilee-sweet."

"I trust you, so don't go there!"

"Not enough to tell me..."

"Charlie..."

"No buts, Jennilee."

"Charlie, you can't let anything happen to you. I won't survive losing you." Perilously close to full-blown panic, Jennilee threw her arms around his waist and clung.

"Jennilee-baby, I'm right here and I'm not going anywhere." Tucking her head under his chin, Charlie ran one hand up and down the length of her back, massaged her nape with the other. Exchanged a long look with Mose.

Jennilee wouldn't be going anywhere by herself, not if Charlie had anything to say about it, and he did.

～

"Mr. Tom, I appreciate your time. I know you're busy." Jennilee came around Tom's desk and hugged him, rested a hip against his desk. "I can't stay long. My current babysitter'll be here in a minute."

"Watchdog, Jennilee, watchdog." Tom corrected her gently. Practically the whole town knew about Charlie's lifelong obsession with protecting Jennilee, just not why. An obsession that'd kicked up a notch in intensity in the last little while. Tom joked, "Who's babysitting today?"

"Grandy. She's next door, agreed to let me come visit you if I promised not to go anywhere else. I don't want anyone knowing what we talk about today. You have to promise me, or I'll leave without saying a word." Jennilee waited until Mr. Tom gave his solemn oath before handing him two envelopes. "I want you to have this, and I made a copy for Chief Mac."

Opening the envelope with his name on it in Jennilee's distinctively graceful script, more than print and slightly less than calligraphy, Tom scanned the contents. His blood pressure rising rapidly, he knew why Charlie was so adamant Jennilee not go anywhere by herself. Charlie might not know, but he suspected.

Tom held a detailed list of everything that'd ever happened between Jennilee and Butch Jones. Every bit of bad blood, every conflict, every playground scuffle. Jennilee hadn't just detailed what Butch had said and done to her, she'd noted every blow she struck for herself.

"I know how he is—Butch will twist everything so it makes me look like the bad guy. I have never, ever, instigated any contact between us. I have, however, defended myself when warranted."

Tom scanned the first page again. Butch definitely had the makings of a fine criminal, and a good head start on prison life. From trying to extort lunch money, to attempting to bully Jennilee into doing his homework, right on up to attempted blackmail and soliciting crude sexual favors—oh, yeah. Jennilee hadn't caved to him, not once, and she'd paid a heavy price for every stubborn refusal. "Jennilee…"

Her musical voice—as distinctive as her writing and just as special—reminding Tom of wind chimes and creek water flowing and early morning birdsong, Jennilee admitted ruefully, "Don't *Jennilee* me. I know how that reads. I'm not stupid, but I won't trade anyone else's safety for mine. Not now, not ever. I just want you and Chief Mac to know this has been going on a long time."

Tom's admiration for Jennilee grew by leaps and bounds

as he perused the list of injuries she'd dealt Butch. A black eye, a bloody nose, various scratches and bites, once even a swift, hard kick to Butch's groin that put him out of commission for a couple days.

His contempt for Butch grew as he looked at the list of hurts she'd born silently. Her braid being cut off, assorted bruises and scrapes. She'd even stood between Butch and some of the smaller kids repeatedly. Perusing further, he glowered. "Jennilee, some of this... This is attempted murder. You should've said something a lot sooner."

"No disrespect Mr. Tom, but what could you or anyone else have done? I can't prove any of it and the judicial system seldom takes an active interest in playground bullying, which is exactly what they'd call any of these incidents. I've given as good as I got for the most part. He's taken it to a whole different level, threatening Charlie and Mose. I won't have it."

"You should've at least told Charlie."

"Why? He's upset enough about the latest threat, and he doesn't even know the particulars. What do you think would've happened to Charlie if I'd told him sooner?" Jennilee waited a beat. "I can tell you exactly. Charlie would've gone after Butch, beaten Butch to a pulp for any one of the things on that list. Butch's whole sorry family would've ambushed Charlie somewhere, probably killed him, at the very least put Charlie in the hospital. I can deal with Butch. I can't live without my Charlie."

Tom looked at Jennilee. Pretty as a picture, slender and curvy, weighed about 120, mostly muscle, mostly alone. Thought of Butch. Dark haired, heavy browed with coarse features, well over 200 pounds, a lot of flab, and a family like a nest of human cockroaches. She was right. There was nothing any of the adults in her life could've done—just like the situation at her aunt's. Interference would only have made it worse, if such a thing was possible. Jennilee had more burdens to bear than any one person should have to.

"Mr. Tom…" Jennilee's words dried up at the sound of the bell jangling over the door in the outer office, followed by Grandy's voice. "Good seeing you, sir. Have a nice day."

Just that quick, she was gone. Tom shook his head and tucked Mac's envelope into a desk drawer, made a mental note to take it to him later.

∼

JENNILEE GAVE up her freedom without complaint. If having an adult around meant Charlie wouldn't go after Butch, she'd do it. No more slipping off by herself, no more independence. She'd gotten around Charlie's dictate before, smiled and nodded and done what she wanted, but no more. She adhered strictly to his orders, made sure one of her babysitters was with her at all times, stayed away from Garner House and Mose for awhile.

Waiting for one of her babysitters to pick her up or drop her off or escort her somewhere was hard. She had so much to do, kept to a tight schedule to fit it all in.

Giving up her freedom kept Charlie alive. Any sacrifice was worth that.

And yet, clenching her hands nervously, Jennilee eyed the clock. "Mr. Donnie…"

"Just a minute more, Jennilee. Almost finished." His voice was muffled, accompanied by metallic clinks and clangs and mumbles from under the hood.

Jennilee threw another panicked glance at the clock. The clock whose hands seemed to be spinning like a top. That's what he'd said five minutes ago, fifteen minutes ago, half an hour ago. "Mr. Donnie, I have to go. *Now.*"

They'd been right on schedule to leave when someone

pulled up to the garage with an *It's making a weird noise. Have you got a minute?* The best mechanic around, Mr. Donnie couldn't pass up the opportunity to help someone figure out what was wrong with their vehicle.

"Mr. Donnie, I gotta go." Jennilee's terror of her aunt's retaliation warred with her word to Charlie.

Something in her tone finally got through. Donnie raised his head, took in Jennilee's white face and tense body.

"I'll be back in a bit, Herb. I promised to see Jennilee home."

Pulling up in Grandy's driveway, Mr. Donnie shut the truck off. "I'll come over and tell Celie why you're late."

"Thanks, but don't bother, Mr. Donnie. It won't do any good." Jennilee sounded hopeless. Mort hadn't touched her since the fiasco at school, but there were worse punishments than a whippin'.

CHAPTER 19

*J*ennilee slipped through the gap in the privet hedge and sideways into Charlie's waiting embrace. Didn't have to open her mouth for him to know something was bad wrong. He held her, stroked a hand soothingly up and down her back, waited. She'd tell him, or not.

Jennilee clung to Charlie, face pressed into the hard muscles over his heart. Mumbled against his chest. "I can't go."

Charlie's heart skipped a beat, slammed into double time. Easing back, he tried to read her face in the faint starlight.

"What do you mean you can't go?"

"Just what I said, Charlie. I can't go."

"We've been planning this trip for months."

"I know that. Go, have a good time." Jennilee was numb, but as always, her first instinct was to protect Charlie. Two weeks without Charlie, without Grandy. Jennilee'd never survive it. And that was the least of it.

"Let Grandy…"

Jennilee shook her head emphatically. "No. Don't drag Grandy into this. It won't do any good."

"Fine."

Jennilee eyed Charlie suspiciously. He'd given in way too easily.

"Fine?"

"If you can't go right now, we'll go later. Reservations can be changed. No biggie."

"I can't, Charlie."

"You can't go, or you can't go later?" Narrowing his eyes, Charlie pinned Jennilee beneath his fierce stare.

"I can't go to Washington DC with you. Not now, not later."

"Why?"

"They said…" Jennilee choked, unable to continue.

"Said what, Jennilee? Tell me." *They* didn't have to be specified. Celie and Mort. Charlie used every bit of his charm to coax an answer out of Jennilee. When she got this upset, she'd just as likely clam up and nothing could make her talk. Rubbing his hands up and down her arms, Charlie gave it his best shot.

Frozen to the core, Jennilee'd known two weeks ago getting supper on the table late was going to cost her. "They said…" Shaking now, she dropped her head, buried her face in her hands.

Charlie gathered her close. "Ah, Jennilee-baby." Wanted to tell her, *whatever it is can't be too bad*, but knowing Jennilee's aunt and uncle as he did, it could. "I'm right here. Tell me." Leaning close, he still couldn't make out her muffled words, tried to lift her head.

"I can't go anywhere with you and Grandy anymore. Not if it's an overnight trip."

Pulling her hands away from her face, Charlie bracketed

her face with a palm on either cheek. Practically nose to nose, he ground out, "What do you mean?"

"They said I'm too old to be spending days at a time away from home with you. They think we're..." Jennilee clamped her lips shut tight to keep Celie's venom from spilling out and contaminating Charlie with its foulness.

"You're just like your mother—a whore. You think I don't know what goes on when you go away with them? Well, I won't have it! You're not going to go away with them anymore. You're getting too old to be sharing a motel room with Charlie. I know what you're like! You needn't think when you get knocked up, you can continue to stay here and raise your bastard."

On and on, until Jennilee wanted to scream. A river of poison, threatening to drown her. Of course, Celie hadn't let Mort hear her vicious diatribes.

She'd merely suggested, in a worried tone, that perhaps Jennilee was getting a little too old to be spending nights in close proximity to a horny teenager. Like Jennilee and Charlie didn't live next door to each other, didn't spend nearly every waking moment, mostly unsupervised, in each other's company anyway. Mort didn't spare a thought to that —just got outraged and fell right in with Celie's evil machinations.

Picking up on her unspoken thought, Charlie didn't state the obvious—if he and Jennilee wanted to have sex, they could do it just as well, probably better, here. The fact they hadn't certainly wasn't for lack of opportunity. On a trip, they stayed as close as skin to Grandy, hadn't shared a room for years. Grandy always got adjoining rooms. She and Jennilee shared one, Charlie took the other.

"Don't say anything to Grandy just yet. Maybe I can figure a way out of this." Jennilee didn't want to involve Grandy, didn't want anyone else to know how humiliated and ashamed she felt. Hadn't wanted to tell Charlie, couldn't figure any way not to.

"Hush, Jennilee-honey. It's not like Grandy won't notice if you don't go. We'll figure something out. We've got a week."

Drawing a deep, shuddering breath, then another, Jennilee leaned into Charlie to absorb some of his strength.

∼

BREAKFAST AND SUPPER were on time, whether burnt or raw, at the Judge's house. Few clothes were washed and those that were, the dark clothes ended up with bleach spots, delicate fabrics ended up too wrinkled to wear. Beds went unmade and the sink overflowed with dirty dishes. Things came to a head when Mort poured a glass of milk, took a sip, and immediately spit it back out.

Hearing his bellow all the way upstairs, Jennilee smiled grimly. Let the games begin.

"What the hell is going on around here? First, I have to wash out a glass, then the milk's sour."

Sylvia appeared at Jennilee's door, gloating. "Dad wants to see you downstairs. Now!"

Long past time to make a stand, Jennilee took her own sweet time answering the summons.

Called downstairs like a red-handed inmate, Jennilee regarded her aunt silently. Any animal, backed into a corner, would eventually fight back. Jennilee'd been in a corner most of her life.

Clamping a hand around Jennilee's upper arm, Mort marched her to the filthy kitchen. "What's the meaning of this?"

"What?"

Mort gestured. "Celie says it's your turn this week to

clean up in here. I want it done, pronto, or you're going to be in big trouble, young lady."

Jennilee shook her head.

Mort's face turned beet-red and his eyes bulged like a strangling frog. "Are you defying me?"

"Merely trying to discern the truth. If it's my turn to do the kitchen, ask her whose turn it is to do the laundry. While you're at it, ask her whose turn it is to make the beds? Or do the grocery shopping? Or cook? Or mow the yard? Or check the mail even? I don't believe the mail's been brought in all week." Lobbing her attack, Jennilee waited to see what came back.

Mort looked dumbfounded, as if the thought of someone actually having to do the chores had never crossed his mind. Jennilee'd bet every dime in her and Charlie's joint account it hadn't, figured he assumed diminutive helper elves came out at night to cook and clean out of the goodness of their little pea-pickin' hearts.

"Celie? Is it Jennilee's turn to do the kitchen or not? And what about the rest of the house?" A puzzled Mort looked to his wife.

Skinning her lips back in a feral grin, Jennilee watched her aunt's eyes dart around the disaster of a kitchen. Celie couldn't blame the kitchen, the laundry, the house, the meals, the lack of groceries—everything that hadn't been done and needed to be—on Jennilee without telling on herself.

Celie's eyes darted from Jennilee, to Mort, to Sylvie. Darted around the kitchen. Mort liked—insisted on—a well kept, orderly house, clean laundry, meals on time. Jennilee's unspoken threat came through loud and clear.

"Maybe I was hasty. Might even have been wrong about whose turn it is. I've been so upset about this latest thing with her wanting to go off with Del, I just haven't felt like…"

"So, whose turn is it? And why hasn't anything else been

done this week? And why are my meals suddenly unpalatable? I won't have it, I tell you!"

Predictably, Celie covered her face and burst into loud sobs.

Just as predictably, gathering Celie close, Mort tried to hush her. His attempts only made her wail louder. Around Mort's arm, Celie moved her hands aside and glared, dry-eyed and furious, at Jennilee.

Jennilee rolled her eyes and went back upstairs.

The sound of Mort's car driving away heralded Celie's arrival in Jennilee's doorway, hurling vitriol. "You sneaky brat! I suppose you think this is funny. You think I'll cave and let you have your way."

Jennilee eyed her aunt cooly. "What I think is, you've had your way for far too long. Things are going to change around here, or Mort's going to find out the truth—in a hurry. I can promise you, he won't like it."

Weighing her options, Celie conceded with one last dig. "Fine, then. You can go this time, but I don't want to hear it when you turn up…"

"I go with Grandy and Charlie, anywhere, any time they ask with no extra chores when I get back."

"Who's going to…do stuff while you're gone?"

"Hire someone. It's not like you're going to lift a manicured finger. Why don't you try your daughter? She just might be capable of doing something besides her hair and her nails."

A furious squeal, and Sylvia stepped into Jennilee's room to stand shoulder to shoulder with her mother. "I am not doing any of *her* disgusting chores!"

"Your mother know what company you're keeping?" Flicking a desultory glance at her cousin, Jennilee decided right then and there…*Might as well be hanged for a sheep as a lamb.*

"Don't change the subject, *Jenny*. We're talking about your responsibilities."

"*My responsibilities?* You want to lecture *me* on responsibility? Go right ahead." Crossing her arms, Jennilee leaned back against her dresser, right against the spot where Goldie'd breathed his last. Thinking of his senseless death, of all the indignities she'd suffered at the hands of her relatives, she kept her rage uppermost so she wouldn't chicken out and back down.

"I'm waiting, *Aunt Celie*. Well? Talk to me—tell me all about shirking responsibility. Just remember what's going to happen when *Uncle Mort* doesn't have any clean clothes and there's nothing fit to eat in this filthy house. How are you going to convince him all of it's my fault without clueing him into the fact that you don't do diddly-squat around here? Nothing except spend money that's rightfully mine?"

Celie spat, "You ungrateful bitch!"

Jennilee parried, skillfully lobbed a counterattack. "You're the ungrateful bitch. You're living in my house, squandering my inheritance. And, while you're doing an excellent job at both of those, you've always done a piss-poor job of taking care of me, which is the sole reason you're here in the first place."

"What makes you think this is yours? That's utterly ridiculous!" Going from the shade of a ripe plum to something putrid and rotting in a heartbeat, Celie's return salvo lacked any weight whatsoever.

Jennilee's calm reply deflated Celie right into silence. "Is it?"

Shock plain on her face, Sylvia demanded, "What's she talking about, Mom? Mom? Answer me! You said this would someday be my house, that your dad left everything to us."

"That's not the only lie she's spoon-fed you, Sylvia. Might as well get used to it. Isn't that right, *Aunt Celie?*"

"Shut up! Just shut up!"

"Afraid hubby will finally see you for the conniving bitch you really are?"

Regaining a semblance of her catty self, Celie smiled evilly, formed her hands into claws, complete with long, dangerous nails. "He'll never believe you over me."

"You just keep thinking that. Like cream rising to the top, the truth will eventually come out. What do you think you'll have left when it does? You're going to lose everything you've schemed your whole life for."

Celie took a deep breath, her world on the verge of crumbling. If she couldn't intimidate her niece any more, how was she going to get her to do anything? Celie'd long assumed her niece was too cowed, too beaten down to ever fight back. This new persona struck terror into her heart, shivered the foundations of Celie's secure little kingdom.

Syrupy sweet, Celie urged, "Sylvie, honey, go downstairs."

"Why bother to send her away? She's just going to eavesdrop. She took your teachings to heart. Might as well let her stay. She just might find out something she needs to know." Jennilee didn't dare gloat just yet, but she could feel elation bubbling up inside herself like a pure stream of water coming from deep underground.

∽

JUST AS PLANNED, Jennilee took her accustomed place in the middle of the front seat, secure between Charlie and Grandy as they headed to DC, right on schedule.

Slanting a look in Jennilee's direction, Charlie wondered at the slightly smug smile touching the corners of her mouth. Feeling his gaze, Jennilee turned to him. Charlie blinked at the light beaming from her as she smiled fully. It was like staring into the sun.

CHAPTER 20

Garner House opened a year to the day after they'd purchased it. Pricey apartments, close to town and yet quietly urban, set in elegantly landscaped grounds. One or two bedroom units with spacious rooms, each with their own kitchen and bath. Within two weeks all eight were snapped up, with a lengthy waiting list.

Thanksgiving came and went once again, and Christmas arrived in due time.

Jennilee's gift to Charlie was two identical packages. Very large packages. Charlie took his own sweet time opening them. Jennilee sat on the floor at his feet, her eyes never straying from his face. Opening the first one, Charlie felt his heart clench.

Jennilee might've been out of her mind with pain and painkillers, but she'd heard every word Charlie said to her the night he held her after her last beating. Soaked up his promises and held them close to her heart, returned them ten-fold.

An over-large double Irish chain quilt, done in white and exquisite shades of aquamarine. Charlie spread it out, bunched it up, brought it to his face, stroked the soft, quilted fabric over his cheek. "You made this for us?"

"Grandy and Miz Sadie helped—a lot."

"It's…beautiful."

Smiling, Jennilee nudged the other package. Charlie opened it, felt his heart stop, his breath catch in his throat. A crazy quilt, done in velvets of every shade and hue, fancy stitching along the edges of each piece. Didn't have to ask to know that while Jennilee might've had help with the piecing, she'd done every stitch of the decorative trim herself. He'd seen enough of her work to know that for a certainty.

"Jennilee…I don't know what to say. These…these belong in a museum somewhere."

Bright laughter silvered the air. "I hope our home's going to be warmer and more inviting than some stuffy old museum."

Feeling like she should get up and leave, Grandy shot a half embarrassed look at Donnie, avidly watching the kids with a hungry look on his face. The look of a man who'd eaten his last morsel of food and knew there wouldn't be any more. Ever.

Charlie sat with both quilts spread out over his lap, admiring them with hands and eyes for a long time. Setting the quilts aside reverently, he reached for his gifts to her.

Jennilee opened the first one and words failed her. A cutting board, made of alternating strips of dark and light wood, oiled to a high shine. "Charlie…" She looked at him, her heart in her eyes. He knew how much she enjoyed cooking, could testify to just how good a cook she was.

Reaching out, Charlie cupped her cheek, stroked a thumb over her cheekbone. "Open your other one."

Swallowing past the lump in her throat, Jennilee held the package, turned it over and over before she started unwrapping. Lifted the contents out with a breathless gasp. "A bread bowl! Charlie! It's perfect! I'll start using it today!"

Charlie'd carved her bread bowl, sometimes called a dough bowl, out of a single piece of spalted pecan. More of a rectangular oval than a round shape, oiled and taken care of, such bowls could last for generations. Grandy still made biscuits and bread and rolls in the very one that had belonged to her great-grandmother, made by the same ancestor who'd crafted the rocking chair.

"When did you find time?" Questioning each other at the same time using the same words, they burst out laughing.

Talking over each other, telling their tales, they didn't even notice when Grandy and Donnie got up and left them to it.

Charlie carrying one quilt and Jennilee the other, their first stop was the linen closet where they hunted up some old sheets. Wrapping the quilts in the sheets, Charlie placed them reverently in Jennilee's cedar chest, nestled at the foot of her bed.

"Jennilee, I never expected..." Caught himself looking around Jennilee's bedroom. Neat as a pin, he never came any farther than the doorway. His sense of honor wouldn't let him overstep that boundary.

Jennilee regarded him solemnly. "Why not? I expect you to get Mose to build us the furniture you promised me. I'll make the rugs. Everything in our bedroom, in our whole house, will be there to reflect our love."

Charlie blinked and swallowed. Didn't have any idea why he'd been so blessed, wasn't about to argue.

Taking his hand, tugging him over to her closet, Jennilee opened the door to show him a box of material scraps. "Look! I've already started saving material for the rugs. I'll get it cut and braided and then..."

"Jennilee."

Looking up at the purity of his tone, she was caught unaware. The look of absolute love on Charlie's face was so...so everything. Jennilee melted, her body becoming a puddle of lava. Charlie was the sun, and her world revolved around him.

Giving a light tug, Charlie brought their bodies into close contact. Always touching each other, this... This was...different. Jennilee watched wide-eyed as Charlie slowly lowered his face to hers. Her hands slipped up his hard chest and her arms, of their own volition, fastened around his neck.

Charlie's strong arms molded Jennilee to him, his callused hands tracing the contours of her back, her waist, her hips, her sweet little derriere. Wrapping one hand around the nape of her neck, he held her exactly where he wanted her. Tilting her head for better access, his lips brushed softly across hers, a butterfly touch. Came back for another sip, settled. Like a fledgling butterfly drawing life-giving nectar from a flower for the first time, Charlie drew Jennilee's sweet taste into his own mouth. Knew he'd never get enough.

Jennilee's world had flown off its axis, gotten too close to the sun. She was burning up, would never survive. Like a moth drawn to a flame, she wanted to get closer and closer still, uncaring if she went out in a scorching burst of heat and light. It would be worth it.

Charlie broke off first, rested his forehead against hers while his heart thundered and he tried to remember how to breathe.

Finally managed to gasp out, "I think a meteor just struck."

"Un huh."

Still cradling her head, Charlie whispered softly against her lips, "Merry Christmas, Jennilee."

Jennilee's reply was just as soft. "Merry Christmas to you."

"We gotta go downstairs."

"Un huh."

"Just one more kiss, sweeting."

"Un huh."

Another meteor struck, making a bigger impact than the first. Gouging out an unmistakable, well defined crater, sending out pulsating shock waves, the heat and impact fusing everything into a single blended mass. Melding their hearts together irrevocably.

They broke the kiss, breathing like a couple racehorses coming down the home stretch. Backing away slowly, never taking his eyes off Jennilee's, Charlie eased toward the door, pinballing blindly into Jennilee's dresser and then the wall before finding the doorway.

Jennilee watched him, the fingers of one hand pressed to her tingling lips.

∼

Looking up as Charlie and Jennilee came into the kitchen, Del looked closer. Shook her head.

There was…a light, shining around them. Charlie and Jennilee were positively glowing. They'd only been upstairs a few minutes. What in the world could possibly have happened in that short a time?

Shrugging, Del got back to work, throwing out orders like a general. Upwards of thirty people were coming for Christmas dinner.

Looking at Charlie speculatively, Donnie switched his thoughtful gaze to Jennilee. Mentally promised himself a serious heart to heart about the birds and the bees, pronto. He and Charlie'd discussed such things more than once, but it definitely looked like Charlie needed a refresher.

Del got used to seeing that aura around the kids. Donnie finally pointed out what it was, and Del had her own talk, definitely not the first, with Jennilee. The latest opportunity came as they were working together in the kitchen, decorating a cake for a special order.

Head down, helping put the finishing touches on an exquisite wedding cake, Jennilee focused on the portion she was icing. "We want you to do our wedding cake, Grandy."

A beat, and Del asked, "Planning one soon?" Here was a door, wide open.

Jennilee's laughter filled the air around them like the rice that would soon shower today's wedding couple. "Been planning it a long time, but we're not getting married until after Charlie graduates from college."

"Jennilee, I've seen how you and Charlie look at each other. It's changed drastically since Christmas. You and Charlie—please be careful. You know I adore babies, but..."

Jennilee stopped, looked Grandy in the eye. "Grandy. I thank you for your concern, but Charlie and I are not having sex, won't until we're married. I would never put any child of mine..." Jennilee shivered.

Grandy finished in her head. *"...through what I've been through."* Could plainly see the hurt in Jennilee's eyes and posture as remembered accusations and insults rang in Jennilee's head.

Bastard. Unwanted. Nuisance. Pest.

Grandy didn't know the half of it. Jennilee couldn't count how many times her aunt had told her Cynthia should've had an abortion, given Jennilee up for adoption, left her in a dumpster, drowned her in the river and left her body for the crabs—anything except kept her.

Donnie met the same adamant brick wall every time he talked to Charlie, which was frequently. Working on the wrecker this time, maintenance stuff, both peering into the engine, wrenches in both their hands and greasy rags in their back pockets, Donnie caught Charlie off guard. He'd witnessed a scorching kiss the evening before.

"Charlie, you know I think the world of Jennilee, but you keep your pants zipped until after the two of you are married. I mean it. I've never laid a hand on you, but…"

Charlie laughed, the sound bouncing and echoing off the raised hood, then the confines of the garage. "I told Jennilee you saw us last night. If all I wanted was sex, I could get that any time. I think more of Jennilee than that. I won't touch her until after we've said our vows, and you don't have to worry about me going out and getting some somewhere else. I would no more cheat on Jennilee than I'd get her pregnant without a ring on her finger. She's suffered too much because of what her aunt thinks of her mom."

Donnie looked, really looked at his son. Tall, handsome, muscular, confident. Star of the high school football and baseball teams, Donnie knew Charlie wouldn't have any more trouble coaxing a girl into a figurative backseat than snapping his fingers. With his killer good looks and personality, not to mention his highly visible profile, girls hounded him all the time. Always unfailingly polite, Charlie never let it go any farther, had eyes for none of them except Jennilee.

Mose even said something. It got quiet, too quiet, in the latest house they were working on. Mose went to see what the kids were doing. Knew what they were *supposed* to be doing, was pretty sure he knew what they were *actually* doing. He was right.

"You two gonna catch on fire if you keep that up." His quiet words made a vivid contrast to the toolbox he'd deliberately dropped.

Both of them jumped, but they didn't break apart guiltily, merely finished their kiss, turned their heads as one to look in his direction.

"We've already…"

"…had this lecture…"

"…several times…"

"…from Dad…"

"…and Grandy."

Mose huffed, "You've had the lectures, but were you listening?"

"Mose, the lectures were…"

"…unnecessary…"

"…but we…"

"…appreciate…"

"…your concern."

Charlie pulled Jennilee closer, pressed a kiss to the top of her head.

Slipping both arms around his waist, Jennilee nestled her head directly over Charlie's heart. "We want you and Mr. Jubal and Miz Sadie to come to our wedding."

Mose nodded, a grim look on his face. "Let's just make sure it ain't a shotgun wedding."

Jennilee laughed. "You gonna wield the shotgun for me, Mose?"

"You think I need a maniac holding a shotgun to talk me into marrying you?" Charlie started tickling Jennilee.

Jennilee's laughter filled the empty house they were redoing, spilled out the open windows and doors like light in the windows of home after a long journey.

Mose shook his head. There'd always been a definite spark in the air around these two, but now it was like standing beneath a high voltage power line just before a storm. Humming, crackling, popping and hissing—downright makin' the hair on your arms stand up.

CHAPTER 21

Jennilee'd always admired Charlie's strength, his handsome good looks, his sunny disposition. Since Christmas day and their first kiss, she'd caught herself over and over fantasizing, staring at him when he wasn't looking. Practically drooling right now, Charlie seemed oblivious, working on moving lumber.

Charlie managed to keep a tan year-round, and with his white blond hair and dark chocolate eyes, he was a big ol' piece of eye candy. Every time he smiled, Jennilee's heart went into meltdown. When he played his guitar or sang for her, she was a goner. Just looking at him sent her heart into spasms.

Like right now. He wasn't wearing anything special—just old, faded blue jeans and a white T shirt. It was the way he filled them that had her tongue hanging out. The jeans molded themselves to his narrow hips and long legs, and that was just the front view. The way he made the rear of those jeans look should've been illegal.

And that old white T shirt—well washed and well worn, it clung snugly, outlining Charlie's bulging biceps, his washboard abs. Slipping up just a little every time he bent it revealed the delectable strip of tanned skin across his back.

Licking her lips, Jennilee swiped the back of one hand across her forehead. She'd swear the temp had gone up a hundred degrees in the last few seconds. Staring as Charlie bent once more, she swallowed hard as he squatted, balanced a stack of boards on his shoulder, flexed his muscles and hefted it. Followed him with her eyes until he disappeared.

"You gonna make that boy hurt hisself."

Jennilee sucked in a breath that exploded outward in a laugh. "That obvious, Mose?"

Mose appeared to consider her question. "You could probably post it on a lighted billboard just to make sure."

Sharing a grin, Jennilee resolutely stopped ogling Charlie and got back to doing her part.

Charlie watched her the same way. Coming out for another load of lumber, he stopped in the doorway, feasted his eyes. Jennilee was angled forward, measuring and marking boards for cutting. He hated her hair being up, but she insisted on tight braids and keeping it in a coronet tight against her head. Probably safer that way, given all the things they did—power tools and paints and varnishes and caulking and stuff. Jennilee's hair was part of her sexy attraction and just like her feminine curves and her mega-watt smile, Charlie couldn't get enough.

She'd let her hair down for him when they were alone, at their house or Grandy's. They no longer needed to pin it in place—instead, they'd worked out a method of weaving it back into itself, splicing it like a piece of rope. Unless you knew where the end was, it was almost impossible to undo. He still brushed and braided it, but even that pleasure couldn't compare to seeing it cling to the curve of her waist or drape over her shoulder to mold the fullness of her breast. Or the way it swayed and rippled like something alive when she walked. Hardly anyone outside their close circle realized her hair was long again, falling all the way past the back pockets of her jeans.

He'd lain awake many a sleepless night fantasizing about just her hair. Knew exactly how he wanted her to look when they got married—traditional white dress, long and lacy, a circlet of flowers around her head, her hair a river of gold flowing down her back.

Charlie's eyes dropped from Jennilee's bright hair to her body. And what a body! Curves in all the right places, dips and hollows just where they should be. All of that wrapped in an unbelievably soft package, and Jennilee's softness fit his hardness perfectly. Muscular, but in a girly way, all those muscles wrapped in skin softer than rose petals.

The vision in front of him wavered, superimposed by a vivid mental picture he carried of Jennilee from last summer. The two of them had been out in the river, anchored and lazily fishing for supper. Jennilee, attired in nothing more than a few scraps of strategically placed material and tired of fishing, stretched out on the bow cap and dozed. Charlie didn't say a word, knowing she needed every bit of rest she could glean. Hearing him reel in another fish, Jennilee came out of her doze. Looking at him with proud eyes, she flashed him a smile and rolled over.

Her back view just as delectable as her front, he hadn't protested a bit. Jennilee, trailing a hand in the water, watching it drift past, called his attention to it. Stretching out on the bow cap beside her, Charlie watched the tide coming in.

Almost but not quite high tide, they watched together, enchanted, as the incoming water slowed, slowed, stopped for an infinitesimal beat, then switched directions, heading back out.

Having grown up on the river and close to the ocean,

they'd seen the tide change hundreds, thousands of times. After all, it was high twice a day and low twice a day. That was the first time they'd ever seen it exactly at zero hour, a thing of magic and mystery. As if the ocean had exhaled, then inhaled—a giant taking a long, slow breath.

"Better watch what you're doing 'stead of watchin' her." Mose handed out that bit of advice the same way he did every other bit. Completely patient, in his quiet rumble. "Our girl's not gonna like it if you bruise that purty face of your'n or damage those muscles she keeps eyeballin', not to mention what she's gonna do to you if we have to buy more lumber."

Charlie laughed. Jennilee looked up, flashed Charlie and Mose a knowing grin. That was one of the things he loved best about his Jennilee. Just like her noticing the exact moment the tide changed, she could find magic anywhere, make anything mundane seem like a miracle, just by her presence.

~

MOSE WAS dead on about Jennilee's reaction to Charlie getting hurt. Two weeks after his little lecture, they celebrated their sixteenth birthdays with a big cookout at Grandy's. The back yard filled with people, the only ones conspicuously absent, as always, were Celie, Mort, and Sylvia.

The proud owners of two brand spanking new licenses, both had passed the written and driving tests with ease, Grandy having taken them right after school.

Suddenly realizing Charlie was nowhere around, Jennilee looked everywhere, walked around the house to see if maybe he'd moved their truck. Not just moved, gone. Beginning to panic, she heard it coming down the driveway.

Standing on the front porch, one arm around a porch

post, the other shading her eyes, she waited impatiently. Heart thudding slowly, heavily, as the truck came to a jerky halt, sun in her face, she couldn't make out a thing. Didn't have to see Charlie to know it was bad.

The truck door slamming galvanized her. Leaping off the porch, she bolted for Charlie like an arrow loosed at a bulls-eye.

"Go back in the house, Jennilee." Charlie's quiet command flew right past her.

Jennilee came to a sliding halt, breath burning in her lungs, eyes huge in her paper-white face. There was blood on Charlie's face, on his torn shirt, dripping off the backs of his lacerated hands. One eye was swelling shut. No need to ask who Charlie'd been fighting and why didn't much matter.

"Charlie…"

"Don't ask, Jennilee. Just go back to the party." Dabbing his knuckles on his shirt, Charlie dropped his hands back to his sides.

"No." Slipping her arm around his waist, Jennilee helped him inside and up the stairs into the bathroom.

He tried to close the door in her face. "Go on, Jennilee."

"Try it! I'll have Grandy and Doc up here so fast your head will spin!"

Conceding defeat, Charlie sat gratefully on the lid of the toilet. Wrapping a wet washcloth around the knuckles of each hand to keep the blood from dripping all over, Jennilee eased his T shirt over his head. Barely managing to keep from crying out at the livid bruises blossoming over his shoulders and torso, his upper arms and ribs having taken quite a beating, Jennilee didn't realize she was crying until the drops spattered on his jeans, adding to the dark splotches already there.

Jennilee set to washing the blood off, needing to see just how bad the damage was. Charlie's nose was swelling to match his eye, but it didn't appear to be broken. Both lips were split in several places, one cheekbone was laid wide open. Now that she could breathe again, Jennilee wondered just how bad Butch looked. Wondered what new torment he'd think up for her. And not just him, now—his whole horrible pack of nearest and dearest.

Charlie captured one of her ministering hands in his least battered one. "He won't ever bother you again, Jennilee. His kin won't either." *Not after he'd bearded the lion in his own den.*

Jennilee dropped her eyes, fearful of what else he might see. *How'd he do that? How did Charlie know what she was thinking, sometimes before she did?* "What about you? And Mose? I can't bear you getting hurt on my account."

"The way you hurt me by not telling me he's been bullying you all these years?"

Like the braggart he was, Butch had boasted of countless torments—before Charlie beat him into the ground. Charlie's gentle reproof stung like a whiplash. "You have so little faith in me you think he could best me?"

Tear-drenched eyes met his. "In a fair fight? He doesn't stand a chance. But he doesn't fight fair. He's a sneaky, manipulative, backstabbing…"

"Okay. I get the picture. I know how he is. You can't be putting yourself in harm's way for me. I'm bigger and stronger. You're the woman I love. It's my right to protect you."

"I can love you but I'm not allowed to protect you?" Eyes flashing, Jennilee made her displeasure known.

"He's a bully, Jennilee. They never stop if you back down to them—they just keep escalating their attacks."

Jennilee faced Charlie, hands fisted at her sides, body rigid. "You think I don't know that? I've never, ever, backed down to him."

"You never told anyone, either. You let him have the

upper hand. He hurt you, time after time. Beat you up and cut your hair off, and all this time you let me think you were the one that cut it. You never said a word."

"None of the pain and humiliation he dealt me hurt half as much as seeing you like this. Now I'll be worried to death every time you get out of my sight."

"Like I worry about you?"

"Charlie…"

"No buts, Jennilee. You think it hurts me any less to know he's been torturing you for years and you never said a word? How do you think I feel each and every time you walk back through the gap in that damn hedge? Just like what goes on over there—you never say a word. You just suck it up and keep it inside. You've got to stop doing that. Let it out, Jennilee. You can't keep it bottled up. Share your pain with me. *For better or worse, Jennilee.* We're in this together."

Averting her eyes, Jennilee shook her head. "I don't want that to touch you."

"It does, Jennilee. Whether you want it to or not. You think it…diminishes you to admit that someone's abusing you? That if you tell me, it somehow means I'll think you deserve whatever they do to you? You don't deserve any of it and I can't do a damn thing about it." Frustrated, running on an adrenalin induced high, his tone was sharp.

"You're here, Charlie. That's enough. I need you to light my way. If I didn't have you…" Covering her face with her hands, Jennilee rocked on her heels, a tortured moan coming from deep in her soul.

On his feet instantly, arms around her, Charlie soothed, "I'm here, Jennilee-baby, right here. I'm not mad at you, just hurting for you."

Pausing outside the closed bathroom door, hand raised to knock, Mac heard both voices. His first thought was that Jennilee'd been hurt again. Opening the door, he stuck his head in. Taking in Charlie's bruised and battered body, his raw knuckles, the possessive way he held Jennilee, Mac understood at a glance. "You two okay?"

Charlie met his eyes squarely. "Yessir."

"You look like you got hit by a freight train."

"I'm aware of that, sir. I tried to slip up here, get cleaned up before anyone saw me, but..." He shrugged and winced at the same time, gave Jennilee a gentle squeeze.

"Jennilee, go get Doc." Mac's tone brooked no nonsense.

Charlie bent his head, murmured something Mac couldn't catch. A bit louder, he added his soft command to Chief Mac's. "Go, Jennilee-honey. I promise I'll stay right here."

Tilting her head back, Jennilee gave Charlie a look that nearly broke his heart. Her face was wet with tears, her eyes drenched with unshed tears waiting their turn.

Mac had to look away, nearly blushed as Charlie picked up a clean washcloth, ran it under the tap, wrung it out as best he could between his least sore hand and the side of the sink. Gentle as a mother with a newborn babe, he ran the cloth over her cheeks and chin, pressed his split lips to her forehead. "Sorry I ruined our birthday."

Opening her eyes, lashes spiky, Jennilee shook her head. "You didn't ruin anything. I'll be right back."

Mac moved aside and Jennilee was gone like a puff of smoke. Waiting until he was certain she was out of hearing, he addressed Charlie again. "What's going on?"

Meeting Chief Mac's gaze in the mirror, Charlie held his knuckles under the faucet on the off chance that maybe he'd be able to move his hands tomorrow. The cold water stung, focused him. "A little unfinished business, sir."

"I can see that. Tell me you didn't put Butch in the hospital."

"He'll live. He won't bother Jennilee again—not in this

lifetime." Charlie grimaced. "Jennilee obviously told you everything."

"Charlie—she didn't want to tell anyone. Jennilee came to me awhile back and told me what was going on because she didn't want anything coming back on you later. If anything happens to you... I'm not sure she could take it."

"Jennilee's got no business keeping stuff like that from me."

"That's what I told her, but it's how she protects you. What in particular set you off today?"

Charlie tensed.

Looking out the door, making sure Jennilee wasn't back yet, Mac nodded.

Charlie spat blood into the sink, rinsed his mouth, ran more water. "Jeff told me Butch's been running his mouth."

Not waiting for more details, Mac guessed shrewdly. "About Jennilee and what she's supposedly been doing—for him and to him, what he wants her to do, what he's going to do to her."

Charlie burst out, "Anyone that knows Jennilee knows it's a passel of lies, but still. I won't have it. She's got enough to deal with."

Amen to that. Mac stepped back and let Doc into the bathroom.

CHAPTER 22

Spring and summer flew by faster than ever, what with the new house and all the other things they were involved in. A summer of fun and freedom. A driver's license made all the difference in the world, and they took full advantage of it.

Charlie and Jennilee and the gang of kids they hung around with made the most of it—the same herd of kids they'd been playing with since they could all walk. Someone always had a couple bucks for gas, they'd all pile into a couple of vehicles and do something.

The movie theater in downtown Morehead. Lazy days perfecting their water skiing. Driving around the Circle at Atlantic Beach checking out the tourists and the amusement park. Ongoing tournaments at the arcade in Havelock. Long days at the beach, beach parties that included cookouts and lasted well into the evening.

One such beach day, the whole gang congregated, trickling in a few at a time all afternoon. Someone had brought a huge pot, someone else potatoes and onions and salt and pepper, someone else bowls and utensils, a cooler full of soft drinks and ice. The guys got a driftwood fire going, fashioned a tripod from their trusty stash of emergency equipment. The pot was now hanging over the fire, the potatoes and onions joined by fresh caught fish and shrimp and clams, whatever bounty the ocean held and they could scrounge.

The day'd been hot, the evening breeze was cool, and the chill on top of their sunburns would make the chowder extremely welcome.

A day of fun and sun, topped off by an impromptu concert by Charlie and Jennilee.

Even a run-in by some of the kids with Butch and Sylvia earlier over a supposed slight couldn't dim their happiness. Butch might still torment others, but he gave Jennilee, and especially Charlie, a wide berth.

Butch and Sylvia banished from sight and memory, the kids all gathered round as Charlie played his guitar and he and Jennilee sang. The rest of the kids sang along.

Sweet Home Alabama. American Pie. Traveling Man. Margaritaville. Cheeseburger In Paradise. Seasons In The Sun. Brown-eyed Girl. Time In A Bottle. Brandy. Billy, Don't Be a Hero. You're So Vain.

The crowd dancing and swaying to Meatloaf's *You Took The Words Right out Of My Mouth*, Jeff held Charlie's guitar. Every time Charlie sang his part of the vocals, Jennilee leaned backwards while Charlie leaned over her. When it was her turn, Jennilee did the same to him.

Backlit by the fire, Charlie wearing cut-offs, Jennilee in a bikini with a towel knotted around her hips, the two of them were unmistakable. Charlie's white-blond hair shone like a beacon and Jennilee's hair was down, flowing around her like a cloak of gold, reflecting the firelight, accentuating her every curve.

Ending the song in a blazing kiss with Jennilee bent backwards and cradled in his arms, amid thunderous applause and hooting and hollering from the assembled crowd, none of them noticed a lone adult coming out of the dunes. Charlie, upright once more, holding Jennilee tight against himself, took the soda Jeff thrust into his hand. Let Jennilee have a long swallow before taking a drink himself.

Charlie told everyone, "That's it for awhile, guys. We gotta take a break."

The sounds of disappointment were just starting when a ripple of silence started at the back of the crowd. Working its way forward the wave crested, spewing Mort out onto the fire-lit sand. Everyone froze, as if they'd been playing statues and someone yelled out *Freeze!*

Mort's fury as palpable as heat shimmers on hot pavement, Charlie automatically stepped in front of Jennilee.

"I should've known! Can't trust the lot of you! In the car, Jenny. You are going straight home right now!"

Charlie tried to reason with him, politely. "We're not doing anything and we're not late. Curfew's an hour and a half from now."

"I can see exactly what you're *not doing* and curfew's been moved up to right this minute!"

Charlie's words freed the others from their frozen poses.

"Just a cookout."

"Just singing."

"Please..."

Mort roared, "No begging and no excuses! I've got eyes. Sex and drinking and probably drugs as well. Get in the car, girl, or you'll be grounded for the summer."

Sweeping his arm back, Charlie sensed more than felt Jennilee's movement, knew she was doing something with her hair. "Nossir. If you insist on Jennilee leaving right now, then she will. I brought her, I'll take her home. You're welcome to follow us."

"You've always been a smart-ass. Your daddy should've

taken a belt to you a long time ago, but the only thing he pays any attention to is the bottom of a bottle."

Jennilee touched a hand to Charlie's back.

For her sake, Charlie fisted his hands at his side. Bit his tongue, kept his angry retort to himself.

"Right now, Jenny!" Turning around, Mort stomped back the way he'd come. To the edge of the dunes, he whirled to face them, roared once more. "And get some clothes on!"

His words fell into the night like a lead sinker knocked off a pier. Charlie was just finishing pulling his T shirt down around Jennilee's hips. Mort shook his head in confusion. Must've been a trick of the firelight. Just a few moments ago he'd have sworn Jenny's hair was long again.

Sounding apologetic, Charlie offered, "Guys, we hate to leave y'all to clean up this mess…"

Handing Charlie his beloved guitar, Jeff thrust his chin in the direction of their vehicles, hidden behind the dunes. "Don't worry about it. Go—before he gets any madder and thinks up some hideous punishment for Jennilee."

Charlie only made one comment the whole ride. Jennilee didn't say anything. "Threatening you and putting you down—that's the way he talks to you all the time, isn't it, Jennilee?"

Jennilee's silence was assent enough.

∽

CHARLIE HAD no clue what her punishment was and Jennilee wouldn't say, but her curfew was drastically foreshortened. Charlie even set his watch fifteen minutes fast, just in case.

After that, more often than not, the whole gang ended up at Grandy's, just like when they were younger. Grandy's house rang with laughter and shouts. Fierce mock battles were waged over intense games of Monopoly and Risk, Battleship and Yahtzee.

Enough people, and a game of touch football or an impromptu baseball game sprang to life like toadstools after a summer rain.

Grandy loved the kids, all of them, loved having them. Loved listening to them fill her house and bring it to full life. Loved watching Charlie and Jennilee interact with the others. Besides, if they were at her house, she didn't have to worry about what they were doing somewhere else. They'd promised, but they were teenagers, with a full complement of hormones running amuck.

Because of that, right after their birthdays, Grandy'd taken Jennilee to Doc for a complete gynecological, had him talk to both Charlie and Jennilee about the birds and the bees and methods of birth control. She trusted them, but she hadn't forgotten what it was like to be young and in love.

She and Forrest hadn't been much older when they'd gotten married. Donnie'd come along quick, right after their first anniversary. WWII had happened, Forrest had volunteered, and for thirty-five years now he'd lain under a white cross in a field of red poppies. It didn't seem possible he'd been dead fifteen years longer than he'd lived and breathed.

∽

SUMMER FLEW BY, school started again. Almost ready to put their latest house on the market, football practice was in full swing. Life had been too easy for Jennilee for a couple months—far too long.

Life threw her a definite curve, and the pitch struck her full on, knocked her for a loop.

When they didn't show by 10:00, Grandy called Mac. Met him at her front door, panic-stricken as the moths battering at the porch light. "Mac, you've got to find them. I've called all their friends, everyone and everywhere. You know Charlie'd never do anything like this. He and Jennilee are more responsible than most adults. He'd never chance her getting in trouble like this."

Mac could see the terror in Del's eyes—fear that something had happened to Charlie and Jennilee like what'd happened to Iris or Cynthia. "Calm down, Del. I'm sure they've got a reasonable explanation. I'll go look. You stay here in case they show up, and call dispatch to let me know. I'll have dispatch call you as soon as I find them."

An hour later, the interior light was what gave them away. Having driven down this old dirt road on an off chance, Mac could plainly see them, Charlie on the driver's side and Jennilee against the passenger door, both sound asleep. Had a quick thought—*that's the first time I've ever seen them in the truck when Jennilee wasn't seated right beside Charlie.*

Peering in Charlie's window showed school books and papers spread all over their laps, the dash, the seat between them. A cassette was in the tape player, playing the Eagles Greatest Hits, barely audible.

Mac's flashlight plainly showed Charlie's football gear in the bed of the truck, along with cans of paint, a toolbox, various power tools, scraps of lumber. It didn't take a genius to add it up. Worn out from a combination of practice, working on their latest house, and school and jobs, they'd both succumbed to exhaustion.

Mac would bet anything Jennilee'd nodded off first. Charlie, knowing how much she needed the rest, let her sleep. He'd inadvertently followed, and now there was going to be hell to pay.

The sharp rap on the window instantly woke them. Seeing who it was, Charlie didn't bother to check his watch.

Throwing Jennilee an *oh, shit* look, books and papers hit the floor in a muddle as Charlie tried to start the truck and roll down his window at the same time. "Chief Mac—I am so sorry. Please let Grandy know we're fine and we'll be home in ten minutes."

Jennilee's face was ghost white, her eyes huge, her white-knuckled hands crushing the notes she held.

Mort wasn't waiting when they pulled into Grandy's driveway—not like Jennilee expected and feared. She sat, numb, until Charlie opened her door. Hadn't even moved back across the seat to sit beside him. Stumbling out, she let him comfort her for just a blink before pushing resolutely away, her eyes glued to the gap in the hedge.

Bursting out the back door as soon as she saw the headlights, Grandy flew to the truck. Running her eyes all over Charlie and Jennilee, she looked gratefully to Mac, right behind them, all three spotlit by Mac's headlights.

Charlie caught her in a tight hug. "Grandy—I am so sorry. We were studying and I fell asleep. This is all my fault."

The outside light came on and the kitchen screen door slammed at the Judge's. They turned as one to face the dark gap, like some B horror movie. Stupid kids hear a noise and even though all their instincts are screaming danger, instead of fleeing for their lives, they investigate the source.

Charlie clasped Jennilee's icy hand in an unbreakable grip.

Surrounded by supporters, Jennilee watched mesmerized as Mort stalked through the gap. Knew exactly how those stupid kids felt when they finally confronted the monster. Too late to run now, death was imminent and would be painful beyond belief.

Jennilee braced herself, could sense the guillotine hanging over her head. The heavy weight over her wouldn't deliver a clean, swift justice—more like a mangled strangulation, punctuated by protrusions and painfully sharp points designed to deal a slow, agonizing death.

Charlie stepped forward. "This is my fault, and I apologize, sir. We were studying and I fell asleep."

They could plainly see the mottled color of Mort's livid face as he lit into them. "*Studying?* Is that what they call it now? I know exactly what you were doing! She's a—she's just like her mother." Turning his wrath on Mac, he spit out, "If I thought it'd do one damn bit of good, I'd press charges. Knowing you, you'd get him off, take his side once more. I ought to…"

Mac stepped in front of both kids, his reply deceptively soft. "Threatening an officer of the law will get you some serious jail time, Mort."

Mort spluttered incoherently.

Mac drawled in the same silky tone, knowing it would infuriate Mort even more, "You could at least listen to the kids before you go jumping to the wrong conclusion."

Mort sneered. "Studying? Yeah, right. Like I'd believe that. Just like they were *studying* at Radio Island that night I went after her. I didn't believe Sylvie when she told me what was going on so I went to see for myself. Boy, did I ever get an eyeful!" Shot out even more venom. "Like she's ever studied in her life! If ever anybody needed to, it's her, but she's so wrapped up in that damn boy…"

Del found her voice. "Mort. Calm down. They're home now and nothing happened. If the kids said they fell asleep studying, then that's what happened. And if you were so concerned, why weren't you out looking, or at least calling around?"

"How do you know I wasn't?"

Del shot back, "The same way I know the kids were studying."

"Regardless of what they were doing, she's late. Hours past her curfew, and she'll have to take her medicine."

"Sir, I told you it was my fault. I accept her punishment."

"Oh, you'll feel it as well, I promise you. She's grounded. For a month. Nothing but school. No job at the pharmacy, no nothing. She's not leaving my house for anything except school, and if she's not in the house by quarter after 3:00 every single school day, for every minute she's late I'll add another day. I'm staying in town the whole time, so don't even think about trying to get around me."

Charlie chose his words and tone carefully. "A month? Sir, that's hardly fair. This is the first time we've ever…"

"Six weeks, now. Wanna keep adding time? Not only that, she's to have absolutely no contact with you. No phone, no riding to and from school with you, no contact at school because I'll know. When I find out about it, I'll just keep adding days. I'd prefer it if she never had any contact with you again."

A month without Charlie'd loomed like an eternity. *Six weeks? No contact?* Her knees buckling, Jennilee found strength enough somewhere to stand. If she went down now, she'd never get back up. Touching Charlie on his forearm, a butterfly caress that conveyed every iota of what she was feeling, she slid her hand down to cover their clasped ones.

Squeezing their interwoven hands in empathy and apology, Charlie brought his other hand to cover hers.

Jennilee flexed her fingers, a subtle reminder to Charlie to let go.

Mort pointed toward the Judge's. Glared at Charlie. "None of that damned caterwauling from you either. If I hear your guitar or your harmonica or so much as your voice…"

Jennilee struggled to breathe air that had suddenly acquired the consistency of cold molasses. Her very light had just been cut off, and she was trapped in a pitch black cave littered with bottomless crevasses.

CHAPTER 23

Terrified Mort would just keep adding days until the end of her life, Jennilee held to the strictest letter of Mort's law, wouldn't even read the notes Charlie left in their shared locker. Wouldn't eat the breakfast and lunch he left there.

Charlie was beyond careful not to be anywhere close when Jennilee needed anything out of it. Mac or Doc or Tom picked her up and dropped her off before and after school, made sure she wasn't late.

All of them watched her fading before their very eyes.

Jennilee lost weight, dark circles ringed her dull eyes, her hair, usually so bright, took on the color of unpolished antique gold. Every slightest noise or movement made her flinch. Her grades plummeted. Withdrawing into herself, there was nothing they could do about it except pray she made it until the six weeks was up.

She didn't.

Charlie used his lunch hour for extra football practice—unofficially, of course. Running through some strenuous exercises with Jeff, hoping the additional physical activity would merit him some sleep this night, Charlie felt Jennilee's eyes on him. Stopped right in the middle of what they were doing.

Between classes, Jennilee stood motionless, her eyes fixed on Charlie, soaking up his beloved form. Even across the width of the field and the distance separating them, he could feel her gaze burning him. Felt plainly her desolation. Hurrying students coming between them, he lost sight of her. A break in the stream, and he could see her once more. Without warning, she collapsed in a heap.

Bolting across the field, pushing his way through the crowd gathered around her limp form, Charlie came to a sliding halt on his knees. "Jennilee-baby."

Her eyelids flickered, opened. Her starving gaze focused on his face, drank in his beloved form. "No! You. Can't. Touch. Me." Tried to push away from him, didn't have the strength.

Sylvia's gloating voice taunted, "Wait'll Dad hears about this."

Jennilee's eyes rolled back in her head and she lost consciousness.

Charlie scooped her up, Sylvia's taunts following. Completely ignoring Sylvia, he slowed only long enough to inform a nearby teacher where he was taking Jennilee.

Jeff opened the passenger door of Charlie's truck and Charlie slid in, cradling Jennilee's slight form. "Hurry, Jeff."

That was all Charlie said to Jeff, but he kept up a ceaseless murmuring to Jennilee.

Bursting through the front door of Doc's office, Charlie was bellowing for Doc before Jeff even got the door all the way open.

Half an hour later, Charlie prowled the waiting room like a caged wolf separated from his wounded mate, just waiting for his chance to fight his way out and go to her.

Having been apprised of the situation and more than willing to offer support, Chief Mac, Mr. Tom, Jeff, Mose, Mr. Jubal and Miz Sadie filled the waiting room and watched him. Grandy was in the back with Jennilee and Doc.

The office door opened and Mort's strident voice filled the room.

If Jeff hadn't been quick, and Mose quicker still, no telling what Charlie would've done. Each grabbed an arm and held him back. Charlie almost fought free. Locking both huge arms under Charlie's and back over his shoulders, Mose laced sausage-like fingers behind Charlie's head.

"You bastard! You did this to her."

Mac stepped between them, facing Charlie. "Easy, son. You're only making it worse."

"How? He's trying to kill her, and he's almost succeeded."

"I'm not the one who knocked her up."

Silence—absolute, total, glacial silence met Mort's statement.

Trusting Mose to keep hold of Charlie, Mac faced Mort. "What the hell are you talking about?"

"The school called and told me Jenny passed out at school. Celie said she's been throwing up every bite she eats and it's obvious she's losing weight for a reason."

Giving an inarticulate growl, Charlie struggled harder.

Stepping out of the back in time to catch Mort's accusations, Doc took the wind out of Mort's sails. "Mort, you're one sadistic son of a bitch. Normally I wouldn't tell you this, because it's none of your damn business. Everyone else here's as close as family to Jennilee and knows it anyway. Not only is Jennilee not pregnant, she's untouched."

"You're lying. What'd she promise you?"

Lifting a ferociously struggling Charlie off his feet, Mose whirled him in the opposite direction, their backs to Mort.

Spoke in a low rumble like distant thunder. "Calm down. Jennilee needs you, now more than ever."

Doc's voice was warm as a mid-winter blizzard in Siberia. "The only thing wrong with Jennilee is she's malnourished and dehydrated and her nerves are completely shot from living with you and Celie."

Grandy appeared. "Charlie. Jennilee's awake."

Charlie stopped fighting Mose, breathing hard, his face anguished. "Jennilee doesn't want me to go back there, does she? She's terrified he'll add more time to her sentence."

"I will, too. I told you six weeks with no contact and I meant it. The count starts over again today." Mort's tone was as hard and ugly as his expression.

Mac intervened. "Enough, Mort. They've adhered to your punishment for a month. That's more than long enough, especially considering they were only late the one time. Go on back, Charlie, and tell Jennilee it's over. You have my word."

Mort threatened, "If you go back there, I'll send her away —to boarding school or something. You'll never see her again."

Maybe Charlie was stronger than Mose thought, or maybe Mose was as tired of Mort's bullshit as Charlie. Whatever the reason, Mose lost his grip. Charlie attacked like an avenging angel.

Dodging around Mose, then Jeff and Chief Mac like he was in the most intense football game of his life and the stakes were not mere points but his very life, Charlie's fist connected with Mort's face. The crashing blow knocked Mort off his feet and sent him sliding across the polished floor of the waiting room. Charlie went after him like an enraged bull.

It took the combined efforts of all the men in the room to pull him off.

Still struggling, Miz Sadie walked up to Charlie, cupped his face in her strong, work-worn hands. "Go to her, Charlie. Don't worry about this. Jennilee needs you."

Throwing one more look at the blubbering piece of trash bleeding on the floor, Charlie shrugged his friends off, turned his back.

∼

Gripping the doorframe of the small exam room, shaking with suppressed emotion, Charlie looked his fill. Jennilee's slight form barely made a bump under the blanket covering her, her face was the color of the sheets, her golden eyelashes glittering crescents against the bruised skin beneath her eyes.

Sensing him, blinking several times, rapidly, Jennilee managed to open her eyes and keep them open. He saw the panic flare, heard the monitors go crazy.

"I can't go."

Jennilee swallowed, completely confused. Drifting in and out like she was, she wasn't sure any more what was real and what wasn't. Voice rusty with disuse, she croaked, "Go where?"

"College. I can't go. I can't bear to be away from you that long."

A half-laugh bubbled out. "Of course you can."

Charlie shook his head. "No way."

"Yes, way. We've been planning this for years. You'll be fine."

How could Jennilee be encouraging him to leave her after what she'd just gone through? "You won't be fine."

"I'll be fine, truly I will. It won't be like this. I'll be able to call you, and write, and come see you on weekends."

"I'll still be gone."

"You will. But after that, we'll spend the rest of our lives together, just like we've planned all along. You can't give up now. We're so close. You have to go."

Charlie stepped into the room. Jennilee almost came off the bed. "You can't!"

His turn to buoy her, softly, his words punctuated by his steps, he said, "Oh, yes I can."

"Mort…"

"…is in no position to argue."

"Oh, Charlie. What have you done?"

Charlie sat on the edge of the bed. "What I should've done a long time ago." Catching her hand, the one that wasn't connected to the IV, he brought it to his lips.

Seeing the evidence plain on his knuckles, her eyes flew to Charlie's face. "Tell me you didn't…"

"I did, and I don't regret it one bit. I just wish you'd been there to see it."

Paling even more, Jennilee's monitors went crazy again.

"He's a bully, Jennilee. What'd I tell you about bullies?" Strained to catch her reply.

"A bully I have to live with."

"Say the word. We can be in South Carolina in a couple hours. All we need is the license fee. He can't touch you if we're married."

"Not until you finish college, and we won't need to go to South Carolina then."

"Jennilee…"

"No, Charlie. We've had this conversation a thousand times. I'm not going to change my mind. You need to go to college and you can't do it with me hanging around your neck like a dead albatross. I'll marry you, and gladly, as soon as you graduate."

Charlie teased, "So you think you're an albatross, huh? You sure smell better than a dumb old dead bird."

Nuzzling her neck gently, mindful of her fragility, he

inhaled her scent, and instantly his teasing took on a serious tone. His arms slipped beneath her, cradling her to him. "You can't scare me like that again. My heart almost stopped when I saw you go down."

"I'm s…sorry."

"Don't you dare apologize to me, Jennilee. Ah, God. I've missed you so much." Charlie buried his face in the crook of her neck.

Wrapping her arms around him, Jennilee stroked his hair, rubbed the nape of his neck soothingly.

Hearing Doc and Grandy come in, Charlie turned, kept his place beside Jennilee. Kept her hand firmly in his. "How soon can I take her home, Doc?"

Doc eyed them. Jennilee really needed to stay in the hospital overnight, did not need any more stress right now. The best place for her was Grandy's, in Charlie's arms, being rocked by him. "Let this IV empty out and I think it'll be okay to take her home. Jennilee, you've lost a tremendous amount of weight. If I release you, you have to promise me you'll get lots of rest and eat properly."

"I'll see that she does." Charlie's word was good as gold.

"I also want you back here in a week for a follow-up. I'll come by the house before then. If I have any doubts about whether you're eating right and resting lots, I will put you in the hospital."

"Thanks for sticking up for me, Doc."

"Any time, Jennilee. Any time."

CHAPTER 24

Taking the map out of her desk at Grandy's, Jennilee spread it out. Rechecked the mileage. She'd rather crawl on her hands and knees over sandspurs and through fireants all the way to South Carolina than walk back across the yard.

She'd been here a week and a half tomorrow, knew she had to go. Any longer and she'd give in to Charlie's constant badgering to head south for a quick civil ceremony. That wasn't what she wanted, and she wouldn't settle for less—not for herself and not for Charlie.

Stood slowly, still weak and shaky, although not like she had been. Charlie and Grandy'd coddled her to no end.

Laughing to herself, she slowly made her way to her bedroom door. Didn't even know for certain the age of consent was lower in South Carolina. One of those rumors that floated around and everyone took for gospel, she wasn't going to find out for sure. If it wasn't... It made a nice safety net, just the same.

As she'd known he would be, Charlie was right outside

her door. She held up a hand, palm out. "Let me walk, Charlie."

Charlie grinned, a slow sexy grin that lit his handsome face and made Jennilee think of long, hot kisses—and other things. "I like carrying you."

"Show-off!"

"For you, Jennilee-sweet, anytime." Pinning her against the wall, he kissed her until her world was spinning. Pulled back with a satisfied smirk. "Still think you can walk?"

Jennilee lifted heavy eyes, both hands fisted in Charlie's T shirt. "Right now, I could probably float downstairs."

Charlie threw back his head and laughed. "Do you have any idea what you do to my ego when you say things like that?"

Going to go up in flames if she didn't get some distance between them, Jennilee pushed futilely against his chest. Might as well've shoved on the side of the house.

Charlie eased back reluctantly. The last ten days had been… Charlie'd needed it as much as Jennilee. He paced her going down the stairs, sandwiched her between himself and the rail. She said she felt better, Doc said she was, but Charlie could hardly stand to have her out of his sight.

Knew as soon as they finished breakfast, maybe lunch, hopefully supper, she'd ask for two things: him to braid her hair, then for him to leave.

Jennilee hadn't been out of the house except to sit on the porch, the one that couldn't be seen from the Judge's, and she'd left her hair down the whole time she'd been here. Hadn't left the house because she'd spent most of her days sleeping, only rousing when Charlie got home from school. Left her hair down, well, because.

Stroking a hand down its glorious length, Charlie tangled his fingers in the waterfall of gold silk ever so gently. Tipping her face up at his possessive touch, Charlie just had to kiss her again. Had to. Like he had to take his next breath.

Jennilee cupped his face. "Don't look so sad, Charlie. You know I have to go back."

"Someday…"

"Someday *soon*."

That promise merited another kiss, then another.

Entering the kitchen hand in hand, Jennilee's lips were swollen, eyes bright, color good, looking a far sight better than she had when Charlie'd carried her into the house.

Walking over to Grandy, Jennilee wrapped her arms around the older woman, buried her face in Grandy's shoulder. Inhaling Grandy's familiar, beloved scent, she stood there, just soaking up love as Grandy returned the gesture.

Throwing a muscled arm around both women, Charlie pulled them close. Both slipped an arm around his waist, drawing him into the circle.

∾

"How could you?"

Jennilee calmly met Celie's rage. "How could I what?"

"You know very well. How could you let Charlie attack Mort like that?"

"Me? You lied to Mort, led him to believe something that wasn't true. Your lie tripped you up. It's only going to get worse. You've built your life around lies, and like a house of cards, the slightest touch is going to bring it all crashing down."

Celie sniffled, "He's gone, for weeks this time. He's so embarrassed."

Jennilee shrugged. "You set him up, got no one but yourself to blame. If he had any sense at all, he'd keep right on going, never come back."

Right on cue, Celie burst into tears. "I heard you. I heard you throwing up."

"You didn't hear me." Searching within herself for calm, Jennilee focused on the picture Charlie'd slipped under her bedroom door at Grandy's last night. Thought about nothing but the picture while she made a stab at catching up on over a week's worth of chores.

Jennilee'd spotted it first thing this morning. A detailed illustration of a medieval bride from some ancient text, it depicted a fair maiden about to be wed to a handsome knight. Agreed totally and completely, knew exactly what Charlie was pointing out—the dress the woman was wearing.

White, long and flowing, molded to her every curve. Wide bell sleeves with delicate embroidery around the edges of the sleeves and the scoop neckline, a golden girdle accentuating the curve of waist and hips, Jennilee could bring the dress into the twentieth century with no problem.

A white satin bodice and gown. Floral ribbon garters just above her elbows to pouf the upper sleeves and match the trim around the neckline, laces up the back to ensure a perfect fit and add a sexy touch. Ribbon roses to tuck the diaphanous overskirt into scallops so the embroidered underskirt would show.

Jennilee'd widen the neckline so the edges of it just caught on the tops of her shoulders, topped by a petite bouquet of ribbon roses and loose ribbons so the ribbons flowed down her arms. She'd wear a circlet of fresh flowers with ribbons trailing down the back of her head, leave her hair unbound, the way Charlie liked it best.

Planning the details got her through a mountain of laundry, and dishes, and dusting. The rest would have to wait. Exhausted, Jennilee dragged herself upstairs to her room, fell asleep dreaming of the look on Charlie's face when he saw her in her wedding dress.

Watching anxiously, his heart in his throat, terrified she'd overdo and end up in the hospital, Charlie relaxed when Jennilee's light came on, not too late, went back off almost immediately.

Charlie'd gotten all her homework assignments, turned them in as she finished them, so she only had a few tests to make up. Jennilee couldn't do anything about the grades she'd let slip. Try as she might, she couldn't remember much about the previous month. All she could recall was an aching sense of loss and bitterly cold darkness.

Mort was still gone when report cards came out, and for once, Jennilee's grades merited the undeserved beating he'd dished out for so many years.

~

CHARLIE AND MOSE hardly let her lift a finger on the new house they purchased close to Christmas. Allowing her to come and watch them, talk to them, if they thought she was overdoing they took her home.

Jennilee went back to work at the pharmacy, part-time, part of the time, all Mr. Paul would allow. He was as adamant as Charlie about Jennilee doing too much.

He'd known she was a valuable employee, hadn't realized just how valuable. Half the blue-hairs in town threw a hissy when Jennilee hadn't come to work for well over a month, and Mr. Paul found out a lot of things he hadn't known about his customers or his store.

Hardly bigger than Tinkerbelle and just as insubstantial, Mrs. Ginny Watson had pitched a fit when he rung up her medicine, swore he'd overcharged her. Outraged, she let him have the sharp side of her temper, ending with, "*Jennilee never overcharges me!*"

Politely asking what Jennilee charged, Mr. Paul kept his surprise to himself at the low figure Mrs. Watson named. Choked when she said that's all she'd been paying for a couple years. Curiosity aroused, he went back through the old cash register tapes, ever since Jennilee'd started ringing up customers.

There it was, in faded blue ink, faithfully recording the same amount every time. Checked a little further on the tapes—every time Jennilee'd rung up Mrs. Watson's ridiculously low charge, whether it was a half hour or an hour or two later, the rest had been rung up. Jennilee had to have been paying the extra, because the till had never been short, not that much.

The second day she was back, business slow, no customers in the store, Mr. Paul fixed them both a milkshake. Jennilee was still far too thin.

"Jennilee, there's a discrepancy I want to talk to you about, involving Mrs. Watson."

"Mr. Paul, I never shortchanged you. The amount due was paid."

"I'm not accusing you of stealing. I just want to know why?"

Idly playing with her straw, twisting it, picking it up and watching the thick shake slide down to plop back into the glass, Jennilee raised her eyes to his. "Did you know Mrs. Watson lost her husband and both her brothers in WWII? Lost her son in Korea and her grandson in Vietnam? All her other family is dead, her grandson never married before he was killed. She has no one left to take care of her. Miz Ginny never worked outside the home, so her Social Security check isn't worth the stamp to mail it. Medicines and taxes eat up most of her savings. She's too proud to accept charity and too old to work."

"You should've told me, Jennilee."

"I didn't see any reason to."

The blue hairs came in just then, en masse. Surrounding Jennilee, she greeted each and everyone, gratefully inhaling their little old lady perfume of talcum powder and mildew.

Donnie was next. Cornering Jennilee, he quietly let her know just what he thought.

"Jennilee, I appreciate everything you've done for me, but it has to stop. You have enough on you without taking care of me as well. All this time, I guess I just thought Mom..." Donnie trailed off for a moment, shook his head decisively. "No more, Jennilee."

Donnie's apartment, which had been so magically cleaned for years, had suddenly once again become dusty, things out of place, magazines and old papers scattered here and there, the lush plants withered and drooping. Suddenly as in not too long after Mort grounded Jennilee.

Jennilee averted her head, but Donnie caught the gleam in her eye. Raised his voice without meaning to. "I'll start locking the door, Jennilee. I mean it."

"Dad? You're gonna start locking your door?" Always overprotective where Jennilee was concerned, Charlie caught the warning tone in Donnie's voice. "What's up?"

"Nothing. Just trying to convince Jennilee not to overdo."

"Good luck. What're you doing now you're not supposed to be doing, Jennilee?"

All those years and Charlie hadn't known either!

Jennilee didn't answer.

∼

THANKSGIVING CAME AND WENT, Celie and Sylvia joined Mort

for the week, where ever he was. Pretending they weren't coming back, Jennilee reveled in staying at Grandy's.

Christmas, same thing.

Jennilee bought Charlie a new, much better guitar and gave him two big braided rugs for their bedroom. Charlie bought Jennilee a brand spanking new, top of the line Pfaff sewing machine, gave her a jewelry box he'd commissioned from Mose. Charlie'd carved exquisite flowering vines into the top and sides. A new heart pendant nestled inside, fashioned out of an acorn sized burl. Polished to a high shine, it looked like two hearts joined together.

Opening the box that held the sewing machine, Jennilee shot Charlie a blazing look. Knew exactly why he'd bought it —he might as well've included another picture of her wedding dress. She'd do the embroidery herself, by hand, but the delicate satin and diaphanous material required a far better machine than the old second hand Singer Jennilee currently used.

Taking the heart pendant out of its velvet nest, hands shaking, Jennilee admired it, held it out to Charlie. Stepping behind her, unfastening the chain she wore and only took off to bathe or swim, he replaced his original heart shape with the new one. Jennilee reverently placed the old one in her new jewelry box.

Grandy felt like she'd just watched an old movie, a silent picture with facial expressions and body language the only clues to what was going on. You'd have to be blind and deaf not to catch the messages flowing back and forth between her two chicks.

∽

CHARLIE WON the school's spring talent contest hands down. Looking like a GQ model wearing a dress shirt, tie, sport coat, and tailored slacks Jennilee'd sewn for him on her Christmas present, playing the guitar she'd bought him. Dedicated the song he'd written and composed to Jennilee, not that there was any doubt in anyone's mind who the song was about or for.

Finishing to a standing ovation, Charlie had eyes for no one but his Jennilee. Front and center as he'd requested, in an exquisitely embroidered and perfectly tailored homemade dress the color of her eyes, hands clasped to her heart, tears streaming unchecked down her face.

All the whole town talked about for days, the older folks remembered what it was like to be young and in love, the young folks wished they had Charlie's courage and talent.

For their seventeenth birthday, Grandy and Mr. Donnie surprised Charlie and Jennilee with a weekend trip to Raleigh. Saturday they took in the sights, ended up at Crabtree Valley Mall.

At the Kanki, a Japanese Steak House famous for its food as well as the show its chefs put on.

Like nothing they'd ever seen, Charlie and Jennilee watched enthralled. Their chef cooked on the grill right at their table, knives flashing and food flying in an orchestrated drama rivaling any magician's act. They applauded their chef's performance loud and long.

Donnie drove home the next day, Grandy beside him. Kept sneaking glances in his rearview at the two in the back seat. Charlie had his arm around Jennilee and she was snuggled close to his side.

He'd watched them all weekend, holding hands, laughing, hardly ever more than a step apart. Watched as complete strangers stopped to stare at the two young people, so obviously in love.

Catching him looking, Grandy squeezed Donnie's thigh

consolingly. Laying his hand over hers, Donnie resolutely pushed his grief away.

If he just knew what'd happened to Iris—had a grave to finalize her death... The pain was still there, a raw, gaping wound that would never heal properly without some form of closure. Wished briefly for a drink, mentally shook his head. He'd been years without one.

Catching Donnie's expression in the rearview, Jennilee nudged Charlie, started singing *Seven Bridges Road*.

Donnie drove and listened, wondered if there were any songs they didn't know the words to. All the words, not just a line or two or the chorus. The last of *Reminiscing* faded as they pulled up at Grandy's.

Total silence at the sight of Mort's car next door. Another look in his rearview showed both kids, faces pale, Jennilee's hair once again tightly braided. She made a small sound, buried her face in Charlie's shoulder. Cupping the back of her head, he pressed her closer.

CHAPTER 25

Mort stayed around a good while this time.
Jennilee got more nervous by the day. Something was about to happen, something she was going to get blamed for sure as the world. Noticing Jennilee's unease, Charlie questioned her repeatedly. She swore there wasn't anything specific, and there wasn't.

Just the same, he kept a close eye on her, made sure if he wasn't with her, she knew exactly where he was, made sure she could get ahold of him.

Dropping her off at the Judge's after school, Charlie headed to the garage. If he hadn't been so edgy, he never would've heard the phone over the air wrench taking lug nuts off a rim.

Tapping his dad on the shoulder, holding his hand to his ear with his thumb and pinkie extended in a *phone* gesture, Charlie sprinted for the office. One word. One beseeching word struck terror into his heart, had him bellowing her name.

"Charlie…"

"Dad! I gotta go. Call Grandy and Chief Mac. Something's wrong at the Judge's."

Pelting out the open bay door, Charlie headed for his truck at a dead run.

Bringing the truck to a sliding halt, Charlie bailed so fast he forgot to shut it off, already yelling her name as he flew up the front steps. He'd lived next door to this house all his seventeen years, and other than the time he'd sneaked in to spy on Grandy's confrontation with Celie, he couldn't remember being inside.

Terrified of what he might see, more terrified for Jennilee, he didn't bother to knock. Slamming the front door open, skidding to a stop, he bellowed her name.

No answer. Some extra sense tuned him to her whereabouts, his personal lodestone calling out to him.

Charlie charged to his right. Mort stood across the room from Jennilee, his furious countenance as red as it'd been in Doc's office. Charlie only had eyes for Jennilee. Ghost-white pale, he couldn't see any marks on her, not that that meant anything.

"I've got you this time, you bastard." Mort waved a letter as he snarled at Charlie.

Hearing rapid footsteps behind him, Charlie paid no attention to that or Mort, slowly made his way to Jennilee.

Frozen, one hand still on the cradled phone, her eyes dominated her face.

"What is it, Jennilee-honey? Talk to me."

"Mort, what in the Sam Hill is going on here?" Grandy distracted Mort, allowing Charlie to get a little closer.

He hated that spooky look in her eyes, like she was going to bolt any second and never stop running until her heart burst.

"I'll tell you. That lying bastard right there..." Mort pointed the crumpled paper at Charlie.

Grandy interrupted, "Mac's on his way."

"Good. He won't have far to go to arrest your grandson."

"Mort—have you lost your mind?"

Completely focused on her, Charlie coaxed, "Jennilee-love, what's wrong? Talk to me. I'm right here."

"He said…" Jennilee was trembling so hard Charlie expected her to fly apart before his very eyes.

"Tell me, Jennilee." Encouraging her, grounding her, Charlie moved slowly closer and closer.

The sound of sirens filled the air, froze the room's occupants.

Might've been minutes, could've been seconds. Mac and one of his deputies pounded up the front steps, announced themselves and entered the living room.

"What's going on here?" Mac's authoritative voice filled the room.

Grandy shrugged. "That's what I'm trying to find out."

Mort, a triumphant grin on his face, pointed at Charlie again and demanded, "Arrest him. I'm swearing out charges of statutory rape. Not even you will be able to get him out of this one. I've got proof." Rattled the paper in his hand.

Charlie made contact, the barest brush of his hand against hers.

"He said…" Jennilee swayed and Charlie caught her slight weight as her body went boneless. Tipping her face up, she turned distraught eyes to Charlie's face. "He thinks we… murdered our baby."

Charlie would've gone after Mort, but it would've meant dropping Jennilee.

A concerted indrawn breath, and all eyes turned to Mort.

Mort announced, smugly confident in his accusation. "She had an abortion. I'm holding the proof. All of you always side with the two of them, but you can't refute this."

Charlie's voice was low, dangerous. "Jennilee and I would

never consider murdering our baby. If we'd made love, much less a baby, you'd know it. We'd be married and she'd be out from under this roof and out from under your thumb."

"Oh, she's had an abortion, alright." Mort was gloating now, certain of victory.

Charlie's growl was echoed by Jennilee's moan of distress.

Mac stepped between them. "Mort, let me see that letter you keep harping on." Making Mort walk to him and put the damning evidence in his hand, Mac scanned the letter, read it again. "This letter's from an abortion clinic in Virginia. Says here that said patient—Lee, Jenny had an abortion on November 12th of last year. This is a follow-up."

"See, I told you." Mort was fairly dancing with glee.

Holding Jennilee tightly, Charlie gritted out, "He's lying."

"What about the letter?" Mort fired back like an attorney going for the death penalty.

Charlie shrugged, held his ground. "It's a mistake."

"Maybe it wasn't your...*mistake*."

Coming close to dropping Jennilee, Charlie couldn't see for the red haze obscuring his vision, couldn't hear over the roaring in his ears. Turning away from Mort's arrogant certainty of Jennilee's guilt, he used Jennilee to anchor himself.

With Mort badgering Mac to arrest Charlie, Grandy saying something scathing to Mort, Mac focused on Charlie and Jennilee's quiet whispers.

"Jennilee, he needs to know."

"Not from us."

"Jennilee..."

"No!"

"Fine then. Let's go. We can be in South Carolina in a couple hours."

"Charlie..."

"Jennilee. I can't take this anymore. He's going to kill you or put you in an insane asylum. Don't let him do this to us."

Grandy's voice rang out. "Charlie, Jennilee, get in the truck."

Buttons about to pop off his shirt, eyes about to bug out of his head, Mort squalled. "You're not taking her anywhere."

No one paid Mort any mind.

Charlie scooped Jennilee up, Mac ran interference.

Refusing to relinquish his hold on Jennilee, Charlie climbed into the passenger side of his still running truck, Jennilee in his lap. Donnie helped Grandy in, gunned it.

Charlie spared a thought—where'd his dad come from? Realized he must've made the calls Charlie asked him to and followed Charlie to the Judge's. Forgot it, focused all his attention on the woman-child in his arms, the woman he loved more than life itself. Going limp, breathing becoming shallower and shallower. "Hold on, Jennilee. Hold on. We're almost to Doc's."

Charlie refused to leave Jennilee, even in the exam room.

"I'll close my eyes. Put up a curtain, do what you have to do, Doc. I'm not leaving her."

Doc looked to Grandy. She shrugged. Charlie rested a hip against the edge of the exam table and leaned over Jennilee, holding both Jennilee's limp hands in one of his, stroking her hair back with the other. Eyes unfocused, becoming more and more unresponsive, she paid no mind as Grandy and the nurse slid her jeans off.

Charlie murmured, soft and low, breaking their hearts. "Nobody believes his lies, Jennilee. Don't you worry about a thing, Jennilee-sweet."

"Charlie, Jennilee. This is Dr. Hartsog. He's joining my practice. If you don't mind, I'll let him examine Jennilee. He doesn't know anything about…your situation."

Jennilee was too far withdrawn to answer and if the new

doctor didn't know about them, Mort might accept his verdict better than Doc's. Charlie nodded. "Do it."

Finishing his exam swiftly, Dr. Hartsog left. Doc lingered. "She needs to be in the hospital, Charlie. Just overnight."

Charlie shook his head. "It won't do any good. You can't do anything to help her. I'm taking her home."

Dropping his hand on Charlie's shoulder, Doc squeezed. "I'll come by after we close."

"I appreciate that, sir."

~

Doc, Mac, Dr. Hartsog and Mort crowded into Doc's office.

"Well? I'm waiting." Mort repeatedly smacked the rolled up letter against his open palm.

Clearing his throat, Dr. Hartsog began. "I'm not sure what's going on here, or what you want me to tell you."

Mac ordered, "Just tell us what you found."

Mort sneered, "Say what they told you to say like a good little stooge, so we can get on with this."

Dr. Hartsog stiffened, narrowing his eyes at the unpleasant man with the equally unpleasant agenda. "I haven't spoken to Dr. Mason about this case, other than to examine the patient, per his request."

Mac persisted. "Tell us about it."

Shrugging, Dr. Hartsog complied. "It was a routine pelvic. I don't know what you're looking for. The female seemed… out of it, but otherwise healthy. If you're asking about sexual activity, her hymen's still intact."

Mort came to his feet, roaring, hands fisted at his sides. "That's impossible! You're lying for them!"

Dr. Hartsog faced him squarely. "I have no reason to."

Mort clutched the paper in his hand like a lifeline. "She's had an abortion!"

Dr. Hartsog fired back, "Not unless it was an immaculate conception!"

"Give it up, Mort. You heard what he said." Mac's was voice deceptively quiet.

"But…but…"

"No buts, Mort. Lay off Jennilee. That's an order!"

The paper Mort held moved feebly, like a flag in the stillness of a heat wave. "What about this?"

"What about it? There are two other females in your house. I suggest you have a serious talk with both of them."

"How could you think that my wife or my daughter—Sylvie's just a child!"

Mac fired back, all his protective instincts leaping to the fore. "How could you think that of Jennilee? And Sylvia's no more a child than Jennilee. They're the same age, give or take a couple months."

Charlie ignored the raised voices as he carried Jennilee out. There'd been no doubt in his mind what Doc would find, but this vindicated Jennilee. Maybe it'd get Mort off her back for awhile. Charlie snorted to himself. *Yeah, right. And maybe his mom and Jennilee's would come back and they'd all live happily ever after.*

Unresponsive, Charlie figured it was too much to hope Jennilee was beyond hearing. Every single time she got like this it made his blood run cold. What if she went so far away she couldn't get back? Cradling her, he anchored her to him with whispered love words and promises.

Charlie's tormented eyes met those of his father and Grandy. They'd all heard the venom spewing from Mort. A silent crowd rode back to Grandy's.

Donnie held the door for Charlie with his precious burden, Grandy followed them to the living room and the rocking chair. Charlie gave them both a tip of his head and forgot them. All his attention was focused on Jennilee. All his formidable will dedicated to protecting her, bringing her back from where ever she went when she hurt this bad.

Charlie rocked her for what seemed an interminable length of time, rocked and crooned old love songs.

Jennilee didn't move, didn't speak, but he felt it the instant she came back. Cradling her closer, he let out a relieved sigh, kept singing.

Doc showed up, spoke to Charlie, rested a hand on Jennilee's bright head.

Thanking him again, Charlie assured him, "Doc, we're indebted to you. Jennilee'll be alright. We just need to rock for awhile." *All night, and maybe tomorrow.*

Still rocking, Charlie singing softly, the distant voices of the adults talking in the kitchen making a harmonious background, Jennilee moved. Curling tighter into Charlie's chest, her tears started soaking his shirt.

A sharply indrawn breath and then, "They killed a baby." Pressing her face against his hard heat, Jennilee fisted a hand in his shirt.

"I know, Jennilee-love. I know." Charlie's heart felt like it was being squeezed in a vise.

"He blamed it on us."

Jennilee's pain tearing him apart from the inside out, Charlie felt rage take its place. Not only had Mort accused them of murder, he'd accused Jennilee of infidelity.

"I'm tired, Charlie. So tired."

"I know, sweeting. Rest. I've got you, safe in my arms, close to my heart. Rest, and think only good thoughts." There'd be no sleep this night, not for either of them.

Pausing in the doorway, Mac heard the low murmurs coming from the rocking chair.

This time, Jennilee was cocooned in a faded old quilt. One that had belonged to Grandy's mother, made probably in the thirties or forties out of feed sacks. One with heavy cotton batting and quilted in rainbows—rainbows made by wrapping a string around a pencil, holding the end of the string in place and marking a line, then turning the pencil a bit to loosen the string and so mark the next line for quilting.

Mac knew it wasn't for the warmth, knew Charlie was sweltering beneath Jennilee and the heavy old quilt. Smelling of Grandy's cedar chest, it was as much a comfort to Jennilee as Charlie's arms. Mac just could make out Jennilee's hand clutching the edge, her restless fingers stroking the time-softened fabric and grooved lines of quilting.

The blanket from Doc's office lay abandoned in a heap on the couch.

CHAPTER 26

Mort left early the next morning. Still awake, still rocking, Charlie and Jennilee heard his car start. A deep, heartfelt sigh and Jennilee was asleep, just like that. Rocking her a bit more to make sure, Charlie carried her upstairs, tucked her in her bed.

Leaving the door open a crack, heading back downstairs, he met Grandy on the landing. Gave her a quick hug. "Call me when she wakes up. I'll be at the new house."

Del leaned against the wall and tried not to cry, knowing he'd go work himself to the point of exhaustion.

Hitting the screen door with the flat of one hand hard enough to send it crashing back against the wall of the house, Charlie threw a seething glance at the house across the yard. Leapt off the porch and over the steps, landed on the walkway. Hands fisted at his sides, he strode to his truck, yanked the door open, got in and slammed it. Clenching the steering wheel, gritting his teeth, he gripped until his hands went numb. Pressing his forehead against the top of the steering wheel, he resisted the urge to bang his head like a toddler throwing a tantrum.

A mere hairsbreadth from kidnapping Jennilee and dragging her to South Carolina, or even to the courthouse in Beaufort. *Bo*-fort, not *Bu*-fort as they pronounced it in South Carolina. The old dispute over the pronunciation focused him, calmed him enough he felt capable of driving.

Charlie'd changed shirts, had on one of the soft white cotton tees Jennilee loved so. The one he'd worn was soaked —soaked with his sweat and Jennilee's tears. She'd cried all night—huge, silent tears from a bottomless well of pain. Feeling each and everyone of them to the depths of his soul, he felt like he still had that tear-soaked shirt on.

∼

THEIR LATEST PURCHASE, a beautiful old brick house with tongue and groove floors and bead-board ceilings and wainscoting, was spacious, gracious, and needed a lot of work thanks to previous owners' *renovations.*

Charlie set to.

Watching while dust and sheetrock and splinters of lumber filled the air, Mose could've sworn they'd decided to leave this wall 'til later. Shrugged philosophically.

Charlie finally looked up, sweat dripping, breath heaving. Leaning on the handle of the sledgehammer he'd been wielding, he shoved his goggles to the top of his head.

Uncrossing his arms and shouldering himself off the wall Mose asked, "Jennilee alright?"

Hefting the sledgehammer, Charlie took another swing at the offending wall, gave the sledgehammer a toss that landed it on top of the pile of debris. "As alright as she'll ever be as long as she's still under their roof."

Mose made a sound of assent. "What about school?"

"What about it, Mose? Do I look like I could sit still and pay attention today? Besides, my grades'll stand it."

Retrieving the sledgehammer, Charlie attacked what was left of the wall.

"What's up this time?" Looking Charlie up and down—bloodshot, red-rimmed eyes, fury emanating from every pore—Mose waited patiently while Charlie worked out more frustration. Already in the loop, Mose felt like destroying something himself, but one of them had to keep a cool head. Miz Del'd called his mom, filled her in. Charlie needed to vent, to work off some of the poison, and Mose was perfectly content to let him.

"Mort accused us..."

Wham!

"...of..."

Wham!

"...murder."

Wham!

"He thinks..."

Wham!

"...I got Jennilee..."

Wham! Wham!

"...pregnant..."

Wham!

"...and we..."

Wham—wham—wham—wham.

A spate of blows and the remainder of the wall collapsed in a shower of dust. Charlie shot Mose a pain filled look.

"He accused Jennilee of having an abortion, I insisted I hadn't touched her. Son of a bitch had the gall to suggest the baby wasn't mine."

"And he's still alive?" Mose's dry humor dragged Charlie out of his anger as all the beating and banging hadn't been able to.

Hours later, the first pile of debris cleaned up and another one created—this one of hideous burnt orange shag carpet and padding they'd pulled off the wide pine floors, they stopped for a break.

"I'm scared, Mose."

"You, scared?"

There was just enough sarcasm in Mose's voice to make Charlie grin. "Not like that. Scared of leaving Jennilee while I go to college. I can finish in about two years, with all the extra classes I've taken, and if I take classes during summer semesters as well."

"Two years isn't that long."

"Too long. I hate not being around her for five minutes— two years is a lifetime."

"So don't go."

"I thought about it, considered it. There's nothing here, Mose. Other than the Base, there's nothing that pays a decent wage. I love it here, can't imagine living anywhere else, but I'll not let Jennilee work herself to death or do without. She's had a bellyful of that her whole life."

"So take her with you. Lots of folks get married and still go to college."

"She won't. I've asked her and asked her. Jennilee says I won't be able to concentrate on school if she's around."

Mose laughed. "I 'spect Jennilee's got the rights of that. When she's around, you wouldn't notice a herd of flying elephants if they landed on your head."

"I love her so much it hurts, Mose. Jennilee's my everything."

"I know, Charlie. I know."

Mose shook his head. Knew it wouldn't do any good to mention that most adults, much less seventeen year olds didn't own an apartment building, free and clear. Hadn't bought and redone and resold house after house.

Finished for the day, Charlie headed home. Grandy

hadn't called, so Jennilee was still sleeping, needing it after yesterday and last night.

Checking on her when he got home, he eased her bedroom door closed, headed for the shower. Jennilee didn't look as if she'd moved since he tucked her in this morning. Probably hadn't. The long hours were starting to catch up with Charlie, too.

Revived somewhat from the shower, he checked on Jennilee again. On her side this time, slowly coming awake. Kneeling beside the bed, Charlie waited, wanting his face to be the first thing Jennilee saw when she opened her eyes.

Her eyelids fluttered, warm ocean eyes met melted dark chocolate. Lips curving in a wide smile, Jennilee stroked a soft caress across Charlie's jaw. Turning his face, he pressed a kiss into the center of her palm, never taking his eyes off hers.

"Thank you."

Charlie knew Jennilee wasn't thanking him for holding her but for believing in her. Mort's accusations had hurt, but a single moment of doubt from Charlie would've destroyed her. "Better?"

Jennilee nodded. "I need to get up."

"Come on, Jennilee-love. I'll run you a bubble bath." Tugging her to her feet, he pressed a kiss to her forehead. "Stay in as long as you want. I'll leave the door cracked. Call me if you need me."

Jennilee's lopsided grin made his heart stutter, lurch into overtime. "I always need you."

"Keep that up and you won't be alone in that tub."

Jennilee laughed—a low, sultry sound that heated his blood and promised long, hot nights filled with passion. Stumbling down the hall together, Jennilee sat on the toilet seat. Charlie turned on the taps, poured in a healthy dose of bubble bath and some bath salts. On his knees, he swirled the water with his hand, dissolved the salts and stirred the bubbles to a froth.

She squeezed his shoulder, Charlie turned and kissed her with everything he was feeling. "Get in, Jennilee. I gotta go."

Glancing at the tub, filled nearly to overflowing with hot water and bubbles, Jennilee trailed a fingertip over Charlie's lips. "Someday."

Charlie backed out, Jennilee's promise ringing in his ears and heart.

∽

GRANDY MADE homemade chicken noodle soup and grilled cheese on homemade bread for an early supper. Shooed them away when they started to help clean up. "Go on, you two." Gave them both a hard hug, waved them off. "Go rock her some more, Charlie. You both look like you've been dragged through a knothole backwards."

That got a small laugh out of Jennilee. "Reckon we do."

Joining them, Grandy let out a chuckle at the stack of LP records on the record player. Like the cabinets that held the games, the order of the records made sense to the kids if not to her.

Working on a puzzle, Grandy listened to the squeak of the rocking chair and songs that ranged from the soundtrack of *Dumbo* right on through Don Williams, Johnny Horton, Johnny Cash, Marty Robbins, Gordon Lightfoot, and a host of others.

A couple records into the stack, Jennilee unfolded herself. She and Charlie sat beside Grandy, the three of them working the puzzle in companionable silence.

A knock on the front door had Jennilee paling instantly and Charlie moving protectively closer. Del didn't realize she was holding her breath until Doc called out.

"Anybody home?"

Del answered. "Back here."

"How's..." Doc trailed off as he came into the living room. "How're you doing, Jennilee?"

"Much better, thanks."

"Charlie, you look kind of rough yourself."

"Yessir."

"Either one of you get any sleep last night?"

"Jennilee slept a good part of the day."

"I want both of you to rest tomorrow as well. Doctor's orders. "I'll call the school and let them know. Jeff can pick up your homework. Tomorrow's Friday, so that'll give you a couple more days to rest." Doc didn't say *get over it.* There wasn't any getting over what'd been done to them.

∼

IN THE SKIFF and out on the river while the pearly light of pre-dawn cloaked the world, they headed to their favorite fishing hole. Easily avoiding all the oyster rocks and sand bars, net stakes and crab pots, Charlie knew the river as well as he knew the layout of his bedroom.

Anchoring, they watched the world come to life. Charlie sat on the cooler, Jennilee in his lap. The river was—as the old folks would say, slick cam—nary a ripple to be seen except the ones they'd caused and those quickly faded to nothing.

Shore birds were calling, high overhead gulls screamed and wheeled, flashes of light winking as the sun struck the gulls' wings. A solitary pelican flew by, water level and making no more noise than a painting of one. A mullet jumped, splashed back into the water and was gone. The tang of salt air filled their lungs, peace seeped into their souls.

The sun rose and flushed the world with color, chasing the gray away as if it'd never been.

Fishing half-heartedly, Charlie watched Jennilee, stretched out on the bow cap, face down, watching the water. The wind picked up with the sunrise and a gentle breeze riffled the water. It hit the hull repetitively with soft smacking sounds, lulling Jennilee into a half doze.

Fishing and dozing, watching the river life, they spent most of the morning relaxing and restoring their souls.

The distant drone of a boat motor reminded them they weren't alone. Probably some fisherman checking his nets or crab pots. Someone they knew, someone who knew them. Someone who'd want to stop and make small talk. Polite inanities they had no stomach for right now.

A shared look, and Jennilee pulled up the anchor, rinsed the mud off and stowed it. Besides, they were starving, and the tide was going out. A Pepsi and a pack of nabs only went so far.

Charlie cut the motor as the skiff slid along side Grandy's dock. Jennilee stepped out, tied the bow rope around a post, quick as a wink while Charlie got the stern. Collecting their things, they crossed the yard hand in hand.

A note propped on the table, written on the back of a bill envelope, told them Grandy'd gone to Morehead to deliver a wedding cake. Had some errands to run. Not to expect her back 'til close to supper time.

Scribbling his own message below Grandy's, Charlie went outside while Jennilee heated some leftovers. Dragging their bikes out of the shed, he dusted them off, oiled them, made sure the tires had plenty of air.

Leaving the kitchen as spotless as they'd found it, Charlie tugged Jennilee outside. She hadn't paid any attention when he went out, figured he was putting up the life jackets and fishing poles, setting the boat to rights. At the sight of their well-used bikes, she smiled. Once an integral part of their lives, the bikes had fallen by the wayside since they'd gotten their driver's licenses.

"Let's go ride."

Jennilee's smile was all the answer he needed.

Riding aimlessly, they shared a grin and took off, pedaling steadily. Wound up at their house. It didn't quite look lived in, but neither did it look abandoned. It looked like it was…waiting.

Bee-lining for the cemetery, they paid their respects.

Charlie and Jennilee didn't go inside very often—it wasn't fully theirs yet. Their hearts had claimed it, their hands and sweat had wrested the yard back from oblivion. No word from Mr. Clyde Gillikin to date, but they hadn't lost hope, and Jennilee still wrote faithfully.

Unlocking the door, they wandered. Ending up in their bedroom, they looked around, just absorbing…everything. Standing behind Jennilee, Charlie wrapped his arms around her, inhaled her sweet scent.

Leaning back into him, Jennilee let his love surround her. Doc had wrested a promise from both of them not to work any this weekend. They wouldn't break their word, but a promise not to work couldn't stop them dreaming.

They could see this house, restored, as clearly as if they'd seen the future. Their bedroom, especially. The bed would go here, the dressers on that wall and that wall, the wardrobe there. Jennilee's cedar chest at the foot of the king size bed, one of Jennilee's quilts covering the bed, her braided rug on the polished floor beneath their rocker.

The ride back to town was slow, leisurely, filled with the scent of turpentine from the just logged pine forest bordering the paved road. In no hurry for the first time in forever, they stopped at the school playground. Pushing Jennilee on the merry-go-round, Charlie jumped on, spun until they were deliciously dizzy. Racing to the tall metal slide, they slid down over and over, chased each other back to the top.

Took a turn on the see-saw, up and down, up and down.

Holding hands, they moved to the monkey bars.

Saved the best for last—swings. The tall, metal A-frame kind with u-shaped rubber seats suspended on chains. Pumping hard, harder, to see who could get the highest, swinging so high there was a pause and then a thump at the apex of each arc they left their seats for an infinitesimal moment and crashed back. Sharing a look, they swung as high as they could. Bailed at the same time. Free-fall! Landed and rolled head over heels to a tumbling stop, laughing like hyenas.

CHAPTER 27

*G*randy looked out the kitchen window just in time to see the two of them get off their bikes. Happy, smiling, sunburnt and relaxed as she hadn't seen them in…so long she couldn't remember.

Giving them both a hug as they stepped into the kitchen, she didn't say a word about the grass stains on their knees and the backs of their shirts or the bits of grass in their hair. "Hamburgers and hotdogs sound good?"

Jennilee kissed Grandy's cheek. "Perfect."

"Oh, Charlie. Jeff called. Said to call him back, please."

Listening to Jennilee chatter while Charlie dialed, Grandy noted the shadows still lurking deep in Jennilee's eyes.

Pressing the handset against his shirt, tipping his head up, Charlie inquired, "Jennilee-love, feel like company?"

"Jeff?"

"Yeah, and Michelle."

Jennilee smiled. "Sure."

Grinning to herself, Grandy put more burgers and dogs on. It didn't matter if Jeff had just finished eating supper at his parents'—the boy ate like there was no tomorrow. And if Jeff and his sometime girlfriend could lift the shadows a bit more, Grandy was all for it.

A quick flash of PSR and Jennilee headed upstairs. Charlie snagged her hand. Grinned. "Wash your hair good—it's full of grass."

Jennilee snickered. Leaned up and brushed her lips across his. "So's yours."

Out on the back steps, Charlie bent at the waist, riffled his hands through his hair. Straightening, he looked directly at the house across the way.

Celie glared back at him out the kitchen window, so much hate on her face Charlie felt it like a physical blow.

Face set and hard, Charlie stomped back in and headed upstairs, stomping all the way.

What in the world? Something had upset Charlie. Looking out the kitchen window, Grandy saw nothing out of the ordinary, just the yard between the houses, the path between the hedges, the Judge's house.

Funny thing, that. The house had belonged to Jennilee for years, years in which Celie'd claimed it, and it was still the Judge's house to everyone in town.

Charlie didn't give Jennilee a chance to get all the way out the bathroom door before enfolding her in a tight embrace. "Tonight, Jennilee. Let's go tonight."

"What happened, Charlie?" No answer sent her voice escalating. "Charlie?"

Charlie shook his head against her towel turban. "Nothing. I just…"

Smoothing a hand up and down his back, Jennilee curled one in the hair on the back of his head. Nearly crushing her with his strength, Jennilee didn't let out a peep, didn't let on, stayed relaxed against him.

"I don't see how you can bear to go back over there. Just the thought is killing me."

"I can go because I know you're here, lighting my way. Not much longer, Charlie, then I'll be free."

"If they don't manage to kill you between now and then."

Doing the only thing she knew for certain sure would distract him, she tugged his head up with the hand latched in his hair, found his lips. Let hers, and her fresh from the bath body, do the talking.

"Ten minutes." Grandy's call interrupted their tryst.

Stroking his hands up and down Jennilee's back, Charlie tried to calm himself. Inhaled her scent—some kind of floral soap and the sweet, sweet essence that was Jennilee. The towel wrapped around her head had fallen to the floor. Keeping his eyes locked on hers, he tangled a hand in her long hair, brought the mass to his face and inhaled.

"Get your shower, Charlie, and after we eat…"

Charlie growled, his voice guttural with suppressed arousal. "…after we eat, I'm brushing your hair, and I want it left down."

Jennilee nodded.

By the time Charlie showered, dressed and made it back downstairs, Jeff and Michelle had arrived. Flicking him a quick glance and a heated smile, Jennilee turned back to helping Grandy.

Donnie showed up just as they were getting supper on the table. Setting another place, they welcomed him into their circle.

The women shared knowing grins as the men tore into the food like it was all that was left on the planet.

Making short work of the cleanup, the women joined the menfolk in the living room, the soft sounds of Charlie's guitar guiding them in like a homing beacon. In a melancholy mood, old love songs and sad, bluesy instrumentals flowed from his fingertips.

Making a quick detour upstairs, Jennilee snagged her brush. The music followed her, letting her know in no uncertain terms Charlie was upset about something.

In the living room doorway, she stood and stared. Charlie was so good looking, so special. Jennilee couldn't imagine life without him.

Feeling her gaze, Charlie ended his playing with a discordant crash. Locking eyes, Jennilee correctly read his misery. Whatever had unsettled him this evening had to do with her —not just her, but her going back to the Judge's.

Stiffening her spine, she was *not* giving in to him and taking the quick way out. As soon as Charlie graduated, she'd say yes, marry him anywhere in the world he wanted her to, as many times as he wanted her to. Right now, one of them had to be strong and sensible.

Reading the resolve in her posture, Charlie closed his eyes, took a deep breath. Badgering her only tormented them both, and Jennilee did not need any more aggravation in her life.

Opening his eyes, resolutely banishing his fear and anger, he smiled winningly.

She smiled back, the sun breaking out from behind a dark cloud.

Setting his guitar aside, Charlie held out his hand. Handing him her brush, Jennilee caressed his fingers with hers. Dropping to the floor, she settled in the open vee of his knees.

Unwinding the bun she'd wound her wet hair in, running his fingers through her tresses, Charlie began stroking the brush gently, wary of tangles.

The others in the living room might not be privy to the

details but they knew there'd been an entire conversation between Charlie and Jennilee. Whatever it was, they'd worked it out.

Rousing themselves out of their fascinated silence, conversation picked up. Donnie watched Charlie and Jennilee, hunger plain on his face. That could have been, *should have been,* Iris and himself. Would this ache never go away? He still missed her so much—if he just knew what'd happened, it would go a long way toward healing.

Picking up the TV remote, Jeff restlessly flipped channels. Charlie brushed, long, slow strokes, Jennilee fairly hummed with pleasure, words and half sentences were idly batted around.

"Took the skiff out this morning…"

"…dolphins. Beautiful."

"…missed a test."

"Cake turned out perfect."

"Mrs. Dodson…another fender-bender."

"Again?"

All of them relaxed, lost in the simple pleasure of good company. Jeff sat up excitedly as a car commercial came on. "Hey! That reminds me. Guess what I found?" He stood, dug in the front pocket of his jeans, came up with something metal, something that jangled and clinked.

The horror movie that was the main attraction came back on. The spooky music just reaching its crescendo, Jeff held out his hand, palm flat, treasured find in the middle.

"Look! I was out in Bernie Gray's back pasture with my dad's metal detector. Sometimes you can find really cool Civil War stuff out that way. There was an encampment there and…"

"Give me that." Donnie's emotionless voice stopped Jeff's excited narration.

All eyes swung from Jeff's find to Donnie, froze at the anguished look on his face. Taking a faltering step toward Jeff, Donnie stood like a statue, never taking his eyes off the object in Jeff's outstretched hand.

"Mr. Donnie, take it easy. I didn't steal this or anything. It's just a key ring with a couple keys and an old Marine Corps ring on it. I figure some Marine lost it while he was out hunting, or parking with his girl."

In the same flat tone, Donnie said, "The inside of the ring bears the initials DFM and a date of 1962."

Jeff stared, open-mouthed. "How'd you know that?"

"Because that's my ring and those are my keys."

A puzzled look on his face, still not sure why Mr. Donnie seemed so outdone but willing to hand his find over to the rightful owner, Jeff offered, "You must've lost them a long time ago. They were pretty deep and caked with dirt. Took me awhile to clean them up. I'm sure glad I found them for you. Here." Giving them a toss, they winked and flashed through the air.

Catching them in both cupped palms, Donnie stared at what he held as if Jeff had tossed him a jeweled spider. A poisonous one that might come to life at any second.

Grandy, hands covering her mouth, couldn't hide the pasty shade of dirty dishwater her face had taken on.

"Grandy? What's up?" Charlie and Jennilee flanked her, afraid she was going to collapse.

"What's the big deal? You lost them, I found them and gave them back." Jeff looked as bewildered as Charlie and Jennilee.

Dropping her hands from her mouth, Grandy reached out to her only son. "Oh, Sweet Jesus. He didn't lose them. That's Iris' set of keys to Donnie's Buick."

JENNILEE'S LIGHT

"Tell me again, son. Exactly where did you find them?" Mac had come running at Grandy's distraught call.

Donnie sat on the couch, clutching the keys like a lifeline, his unblinking stare fixed on Jeff.

Jeff stammered, "I…I was looking for Civil War relics—you know—buttons and bullets, stuff like that. Out in Bernie Gray's back pasture. I've found cool stuff out that way before."

"Can you take us to the spot?"

"Sure. I mean, I guess I can. Those keys were way down. The dirt's been disturbed pretty deep there."

Donnie lurched to his feet, face gray, eyes burning holes in his head. "I have to go."

Mac tried to reason with him. "Not right now, Donnie. I'll get a team out there first thing tomorrow, soon as I can get them together and it's light enough to see."

"Now! What if…" Donnie's voice broke and he stumbled.

Jennilee closed the distance between them. Chief Mac wasn't getting through. "Mr. Donnie." Face wet with tears, Jennilee implored, "You can't go out there. I know it's been a long time, but if there's any shred of evidence, you don't want to destroy it. We'll go with you, first thing in the morning, stay as long as we need to. Please, Mr. Donnie." Wrapping her arms around his waist, Jennilee buried her face against his chest.

That night was the longest one Grandy could remember since the night Iris disappeared.

Sending Jeff and Michelle home with a strict warning not to say a word to anyone, Mac didn't want or need a bunch of thrill seekers traipsing all over the site. Thirteen years made the likelihood of any evidence still being there almost nil, but stranger things had happened.

Leaving the foursome sitting in the living room like a

bunch of zombies, Mac got to work. Went back to his office, started making calls, lining things up.

Charlie and Jennilee dozed fitfully in the rocking chair, Grandy sat on the couch. Donnie alternated pacing and staring out the windows into the dark with sitting and staring at the keys. None of them offered him false words of comfort. There wasn't any possible good reason for Iris' keys to have been where they were.

The sky was just beginning to lighten around the edges when the phone rang. Donnie grabbed it, nodded, remembered to make an audible reply, gave a terse *hello*.

Grandy and Jennilee headed to the kitchen, both of them feeling this was going to be an all day thing. Calling Miz Sadie from the kitchen, Jennilee explained quickly.

By the time Miz Sadie showed up a few minutes later, Grandy and Jennilee were well on their way to having a cooler filled with sandwiches. The coffee pot had been going non-stop, filling thermos after thermos. Gallons of tea filled a big thermos, the kind with the side spigot. A cooler holding nothing but ice sat ready and waiting.

Sadie enveloped Del in a tight hug. "You go on out there with your boy. I'll take care of things on this end."

Stepping into Miz Sadie's embrace, Jennilee soaked up Miz Sadie's love like a dry sponge. "I'm sorry to bother you but thanks for coming."

"Hush that talk and get out o' my way befo' I swat yo' behind." Giving Jennilee another squeeze, Sadie put her apron on and set to. "Y'all got to eat sompin' afore you go. You jest keep doin' what you doin' and I'll whip you up some breakfast."

The more emotional Miz Sadie got, the more her accent deepened. Right now it was as pronounced as Jennilee'd ever heard it.

JENNILEE'S LIGHT

True to her word, Sadie had ham and eggs and hot biscuits on the table in a matter of minutes.

A glum crew staring at the bounty, Sadie crossed her arms. "Sompin' wrong with my cookin'?"

Four pairs of apologetic eyes met hers.

"I know y'all are upset. You got to eat to keep up your strength."

Donnie pushed his mostly untouched plate away. "I can't eat. It feels…like I'm betraying…" Swallowed hard. "Iris."

"Hush that. You been eatin' every day since she's been miss'n. No betrayal to it. It jest hurts worse now you got a chance of findin' out what happened."

Taking a couple bites, Donnie stood and Sadie gave him one of her should-be-patented hugs, a hard squeeze and a pat-pat-pat followed by a middle of the back rub, as if making sure the love sank in. "Bring her home, Donnie."

Charlie and Donnie carried the full coolers out to Charlie's truck. It seemed the day should be half-gone, and yet the sun was just peeping over the horizon. Grandy and Jennilee were right on their heels with paper sacks full of plastic and Styrofoam cups, paper plates and napkins. A bag of sugar, stirring sticks, powdered creamer for the coffee.

They drove, without a word spoken, to the end of the long dirt road that led to the back of Bernie Gray's back pasture. A cloud of dust hung in the air from the procession of trucks already there.

Chief Mac had everyone stopped way back, Jeff having already shown Chief Mac exactly where he found the keys. Now that they knew where to look, there was a huge area where the soil had been dug up and smoothed back over. Not much would grow in that old orangey clay. The disturbed area was plainly delineated, just a few scrubby weeds growing here and there.

They'd all seen it before when someone did some serious

digging in their yard or had a septic tank put in. If the dirt was carelessly pushed back into the hole so that the clay remained on top, the yard would always be brown and bare in that spot, no matter how much water and fertilizer and grass seed you invested in it.

Spotting them, Chief Mac finished with the person he was talking to, walked over. "Mornin' folks."

"Chief Mac, who are all these people?" Charlie and Jennilee gazed at the multitudes swarming over the site.

"I called in some favors. Some are FBI, most are from other law enforcement agencies. A lead like this in an old case…" He didn't tell them he'd come out here last night with a powerful flashlight, Jeff in tow. Once he'd seen the size of the disturbed area, he'd gotten a sick, certain feeling in his gut, decided to pull out all the stops.

"Mac, we've got sandwiches and coffee and tea."

"I appreciate that, Del. I surely do, and I'll pass the word. I need y'all to stay back, out of the way."

Charlie turned the truck so they could sit on the tailgate and watch, easily hand out food and drinks.

"Doesn't look like they're doing much." Donnie leaned against the tailgate, one hand visibly clenched in the front pocket of his jeans, face taut with strain. Grandy stayed close on one side, Jennilee crowded up next to him on the other. Winding her fingers through his, she did the same to Charlie on her other side.

All kinds of strange looking equipment appeared and was put to use. The hole slowly got wider and deeper. Slowly, because they didn't want to miss anything, no matter how small.

Mr. Jubal, Miz Sadie, and Mose showed up around noon with baskets full of fried chicken, bowls of potato salad and green beans, and rolls. More ice and sweet tea, less coffee this time. Styrofoam plates and plastic utensils.

Diving gratefully into the plate Miz Sadie handed him, Mac wondered how much more of a reprieve they'd have before people started showing up. Not much, or he'd eat his hat. You couldn't hide much in a small town. Grimaced to himself. Somebody had damn sure hidden something big here, for a lot of years.

A distinctive thunk, metal on metal, had all their eyes locking on the pit.

Coming to life, Donnie leapt forward and tried to push past Mac, scattering chicken bones and plastic utensils every which way as Mac dropped his plate and caught him, held him steady. "Wait, Donnie."

"They found something. I have to…"

Face set, eyes full of pity, Mac shook his head. "Donnie. Trust me a bit longer, will you?"

Charlie and Mose flanked Donnie, each ready to grab an arm. Charlie nodded. "He'll wait, sir."

As the sound of shovels scraping on metal increased, Jennilee slipped up behind Mr. Donnie. Wrapping her arms around his waist, she pressed her head to his back.

Easing to the edge of the hole, Mac peered in. Not an old hunk of scrap metal as he'd hoped. Definitely a car. An older model car. Mac's gut roiled, tied itself in knots around Sadie's most excellent repast.

Bad news never got any easier to deliver, no matter how many times you did it.

Waiting until the windshield and back window were cleared of dirt, Mac jumped down in the ever-deepening pit and rubbed a hand over both, one at a time. Shone a flashlight around the interior. There was nothing in the car—nothing big enough to be the remains of a body.

The crew digging at the rear of the car got down to the bumper, lower, down enough to uncover the license plate. Looked to Mac.

Rubbing the dirt off the rusty plate, Mac closed his eyes, nodded his head in confirmation, that particular plate number seared into his brain. He'd seen it enough in the missing person report, searched for those numbers for years, seen them in his nightmares. Well, one of his nightmares had just come to life.

A deep breath, and, "Pop the trunk, boys."

CHAPTER 28

A squealing groan rose into the air, a pregnant silence followed.

What was left of Iris Meyers hadn't driven herself into this pit, put herself in the trunk, and then covered the car with dirt.

Face the color of putty, Mac's eyes locked on Donnie as he climbed out of the pit and headed in their direction.

Donnie's knees gave way and he hit the ground. Lunging back to his feet, he fought like a berserker as Charlie and Mose held him.

"Let me go to her. Let me go." Donnie's anguished cry shredded their hearts.

Grandy and Jennilee and Miz Sadie were crying, arms around each other.

Mac paced toward them, compassion written all over his face. "Donnie, listen to me. The teams have to do their work. It's the only way we have a chance of catching whoever's responsible."

"All these years—she was right here! I have to…" Struggled futilely as Charlie and Mose tightened their hold.

Donnie might feel compelled to go to his wife's remains, but it wouldn't do any good. Let him keep his memories of her intact. He did not need to see what Mac had just seen.

Iris' bones, bits of hair and clothing still clinging to them, tumbled in an ignominious heap.

Donnie went to his knees again, keening pitifully. Charlie and Mose kept their grips tight, offering comfort as well as restraint.

When Donnie showed no further signs of trying to get to the pit, Charlie and Mose let go, stayed close. Flashes from the investigators' cameras went off like strobe lights as they recorded each detail.

Donnie, quiet now, arms wrapped tight around his ribs, rocked back and forth ceaselessly. His eyes never wavered off what he could see of the pit.

Leaving the older women, Jennilee knelt in front of Donnie. Her lashes spiky, a hitch in her voice, she cupped his cheeks. "No matter how bad this is, it's better to know. Now you can lay her to rest. No more nightmares of *what if*. They'll find the person who did this. Stay with us, Mr. Donnie. We need you. Charlie, Grandy, me. We all need you."

Donnie slowly focused on Jennilee, his pain mirrored in her eyes.

Charlie and Mose kept a wary eye on Donnie. Making no effort to jump and run, he merely reached out and enfolded Jennilee in a tight hug. She returned it and they stayed that way, attempting to comfort each other for soul deep wounds that had no solace.

Charlie hit his knees beside his dad. Jennilee stirred and they both looked at Charlie. Donnie reached out and pulled Charlie close, as close as Jennilee. The three of them remained on their knees, locked in a tight embrace.

As she'd promised, Jennilee and the others stayed. Stayed

until the investigative teams were finished and the recovery teams took over.

Mac approached their little huddle, face as colorless as unpainted porcelain, harsh lines of strain and worry etched deep. "Donnie, go home and take the kids. This is going to be..."

Donnie shook his head. Hadn't said anything since his outburst at the discovery of Iris' remains.

Jennilee countered, "Chief Mac, he needs to see this out. Not seeing it won't make it any less heartbreaking."

"Have it your way." Mac gave a loud whistle. They watched as the black body bag, hardly thicker with Iris' remains in it than it had been empty, was handed reverently up to the crew waiting at the edge of the pit.

A bulldozer, recruited from a local construction company, took no time at all grading a ramp, hooking to the car and towing it up and out. Loading it on a flatbed wrecker with a tilt loading ramp took a few more minutes. Everyone disappeared as if a magician had waved his wand.

"Where are they taking her?"

"I pulled some strings, Donnie. She'll be taken to one of the best investigative facilities in the world—the Forensic Science and Research Training Facility at Quantico. It might take awhile, but when the results come back, it'll be worth it. If there's anything to find, they'll find it. Now go home. Shoo. All of you. It's been a long day. A long week. Go. And that's an order."

Leaving Mr. Donnie's side long enough to slip her arms around Chief Mac's waist Jennilee rested her head against his chest, over his heart. "Thanks, Chief, for everything."

Taking off as quickly as she'd come, Mac watched her return to Donnie's side. Wrapping an arm around his waist, taking Charlie's hand in her free one with Del on the other side of Donnie, they headed for Charlie's truck.

Mac shook his head, a common reaction around Jennilee. She'd just experienced what had to be the worst few days of her life, and yet… She radiated love and comfort like the sun threw out light and heat.

CHAPTER 29

The rest of the spring of 1981 passed in a blur, well into summer.

Charlie stuck closer than ever to Jennilee. Both of them stuck to Mr. Donnie like cockleburs to a long haired dog.

Things were coming to a head at the Judge's. If Celie or Mort punished Jennilee for anything, she either completely stopped doing her chores, or did a half-assed job on the ones she did do. Celie backed off considerably. Mort still hadn't connected the dots.

Iris' remains were returned. They held a memorial service, buried her at Oak Grove beside Cynthia. Nothing was determined except that she'd been murdered, her car and body dumped where they'd been found. Someone had gone to a great deal of trouble to hide both.

Jennilee drifted through the days, and everyone who loved her kept close tabs. Deep shadows filled her eyes, her seldom heard laughter had a hollow ring. Mort's last attack had struck deep, inflicting wounds that refused to heal.

Abnormally tired, content to do little, Charlie figured her body was telling her it needed a break from the grueling pace she set herself. He kept a sharp eye out, sharper than a momma hen on her chicks with a hawk circling overhead.

When she was at Grandy's, Charlie rocked her and rocked her and rocked her. Jennilee lay passive in his arms, her face tucked into his neck. The only thing she responded to with any fervor was Charlie's kisses.

At their house, Charlie was mowing the lawn with an old clunker of a riding mower. Normally, Jennilee'd be doing the trim or weeding flowerbeds. Not today.

Sprawled motionless in the hammock Charlie'd strung up beneath a big live oak, he knew she wasn't sleeping, checked on her every time he made a pass. Made another pass only to find the hammock empty, Jennilee nowhere in sight. Cutting the mower off and bailing, twisting this way and that frantically, he bellowed her name.

Found her in the family cemetery, on her knees beside Amelia's grave.

Jennilee turned a tear-stained face up to his. "She's so sad, Charlie."

Looking around, seeing nothing but headstones, Charlie asked cautiously, "Who's sad?"

Jennilee indicated the grave in front of her with a wave of her hand.

"Amelia?"

Jennilee nodded. "Clyde's been utterly alone since she and Benjamin died, and it's breaking her heart. She misses him so much."

Charlie tried to quell his panic. "Jennilee? You're scaring me. Come on, honey. Let's go home. I think you've been out in the sun too long."

Shaking her head, Jennilee disagreed. "I'm not crazy and I don't have heat stroke. I can hear her crying for him, for them. Promise me something."

Not trusting this fey mood covering Jennilee like a

mantle, Charlie wasn't about to give his word without knowing what he was promising. "Maybe."

"If something happens to me, promise me you'll find someone else. I don't want you suffering alone for the rest of your life. Not like Grandy and your dad and Mr. Clyde. I can't bear the thought."

Charlie shook his head. "That's a copout and you know it. You think I'll give you a promise like that so you have an excuse to give up? No way. You said you loved me, and I hold you to that. You're it, Jennilee. There is no other for me."

A fresh round of tears coursed down her face.

"Answer me this—if something happened to me, would you go find another man?" Charlie nearly laughed at the shocked look on Jennilee's face. "So, what's good for the gander isn't good for the goose? You can't have it both ways, Jennilee."

Charlie knelt, cupped his hands on her shoulders. "What brought this on? Talk to me, Jennilee. You're breaking my heart. I've watched you, ever since Mort accused us of murder and infidelity. You've been…holding back, keeping something from me."

Jennilee slumped, let her head loll back, her eyes drift shut. Raised her head back up, shook it as she opened her eyes. "It's just…everything. I'm so tired, Charlie. I sleep and sleep and sleep and I'm still exhausted."

"You take too much on yourself. You are not responsible for everyone."

"How can she live with herself?"

Ah, now they were getting somewhere. Charlie didn't have to ask who. Sylvia. "Jennilee, listen to me. There's something wrong with Celie and Sylvia. Besides that, they're cruel and shallow and selfish. Everything you're not. That's how. Doing what she did would destroy you because you're a good person, through and through. Just like you're upset about

Amelia. Do you think anyone else can hear her, or hearing, would make the effort to be concerned?"

"You believe me?"

"When have I ever doubted you?"

"How come I can hear her?"

Jennilee's plaintive cry scraped a fresh wound in his already scored and bleeding heart. "I don't know, baby. Maybe because you lost someone you loved, who loved you. Maybe because you've had a raw deal and you're more sensitive to the pain of others. There's a word for it. Empath."

He could see the doubt in her eyes. "Listen to me, Jennilee. We're surrounded by people who've loved and lost, or suffered great tragedies in their lives. Grandy lost her husband and raised my dad by herself. My mom disappeared under horrible circumstances and my dad's grieved about it for years. Your mom was brutally murdered and you've been raised by a bunch of sadistic whackos. That much grief and negativity is bound to have an effect on someone as sensitive as you are. Let it go, Jennilee. We're almost there. Soon we'll be here, in our house. Married with children of our own. Surrounded by love. That's what you need. To be surrounded with love."

A watery smile flickered across her face. "I am, Charlie. I am. You surround me with love just by being."

Cupping her cheek, he stroked her cheekbone with his thumb.

"There are others like us, Charlie. I feel it. They need us as much as we need them. The brothers and sisters we should've had. I hear them calling to me, like souls lost in a dark cavern."

"I don't doubt you, love, but I can't stand this fey mood of yours. Come on, Jennilee. Let's get away from here."

"You're not done."

Charlie shrugged. "The grass'll still be here next week."

"Not South Carolina."

Charlie shook his head. "No more teasing about South Carolina, I promise."

Scooping her up, he deposited Jennilee back in the hammock. "You stay right there until I get our stuff put up." He hustled to get the mower in the barn, what had been an outbuilding for the construction of boats at one time. A nice building, constructed of cypress, built to last, no expenses spared, just like the house.

Stowing their personal stuff in the truck, he came back for Jennilee.

"Charlie, I can walk. I'm not an invalid."

"Never said you were. I like carrying you. It makes me feel all strong and macho."

"It makes me feel useless."

"Never that, Jennilee. Cherished. That's a better word. Cherished."

Giving in, too tired to argue, Jennilee barely noticed as Charlie deposited her in the driver's seat and urged her to slide over. Sliding just enough for him to get behind the wheel, she curled against him and closed her eyes. Dozed, and when she woke, they were at the end of a long dirt road in the middle of nowhere.

"Where are we?"

"It's a surprise. I found this when I was out hunting last fall. I've been saving it for a special occasion."

"Found what?"

"Come see."

Intrigued, taking Charlie's hand, Jennilee followed him willingly down an overgrown path.

"Close your eyes and walk 'til I tell you."

At Charlie's, "Now, Jennilee," she caught her breath.

"Charlie, it's beautiful!" Jennilee opened her eyes to see a little slice of Heaven in the form of a good sized pond, rimmed by scrubby growth and patches of knee high grass. Water lilies and lily pads floated at one end.

"It's just like the Mill Pond."

"Yeah, Jennilee, just like, only way smaller. Local legend has it the Mill Pond formed due to a long ago fire, likely from a lightning strike. The peat bog burnt out, and over time filled with water. This probably formed the same way."

"The Mill Pond must've burnt out a long, long time ago, judging from the towering cypress trees dotted all over its surface."

"Ours isn't that old. You don't have to worry about stumps or anything here. The bottom's pretty even. Just stay away from that end—those lily pads have extensive roots. The rest of it's clean and about eight feet deep."

Summertime, swimsuits were required wear. Tugging her shirt off, Jennilee shimmied out of her shorts. Pulling his shirt over his head, Charlie held out a hand to Jennilee. They made a mad dash for the water, leapt off the bank, landed with a splash.

Swimming, relaxing, shadows dispelled for a little, Jennilee floated. Arms and legs spread, her golden hair formed a shimmery halo around her, shining even through the tannin stained, tea colored water.

Charlie tread water right beside her. "Are you ready to..."

Jennilee's stomach growled. Both of them dissolved into laughter. Jennilee collapsed to tread water herself.

"I was going to ask if you were ready to get out, but I think you're ready for lunch."

Laughing again, Jennilee answered. "Yes, to both."

Matching lazy strokes, they swam to shore, climbed out. Leaning to one side, Jennilee wrung the water out of her hair.

Charlie'd been right—both to bring her here and to save

this place for something special. Jennilee's laughter contained none of the sadness it'd held all summer.

Hand in hand, they walked back to the truck. Reaching over the side, Charlie hauled out the ever present cooler, opened the driver's side door and reached behind the seat. Retrieving a blanket, making sure Jennilee wasn't watching, he slipped his hand under the seat. Fumbled a moment, slipped something into his front pocket.

Back at the pond, Charlie shook the blanket out, set the cooler on the edge. With a half bow and a sweep of his arm, he indicated for Jennilee to sit. She sat, reached for the cooler.

Deflecting her hand, he brought it to his lips.

"Let me. Let me spoil you the way you should be spoiled every moment of your life."

Giving in Jennilee simply watched as Charlie, with all the fanfare of a magician pulling things out of his hat, pulled things from the cooler—sliced, cooked, and ready to go. "Bread! Mayo! Lettuce! Tomato! Bacon!"

Clapping enthusiastically, she egged him on. He made the sandwich with the same flourish, cut it in half and mushed it down so it'd hold together.

"You're only making one?"

"Hold your horses! You're going to ruin my show! Now, behold! With a little cooperation from my beautiful and talented audience, I can make this sandwich...disappear!"

Grinning, he held half the BLT out to Jennilee. Taking a big bite, she raised a hand to wipe off the tomato juice and mayo oozing down her chin. Charlie forestalled her again, leaned close and licked it off. Backed up long enough to take a bite and let Jennilee finish chewing and swallowing her bite.

"Good?"

"Umhmm."

"More?"

Jennilee nodded.

"I don't know. I gave you the first bite. I think you should earn the next."

"Earn how?" Jennilee grinned and batted her eyelashes suggestively.

"A kiss! A kiss from yonder fair lady will earn another bite of this magic food!"

Bantering back and forth, in between kisses, Jennilee ate two whole sandwiches—the most she'd eaten at one time in a good while.

"I am stuffed!" Jennilee flopped back on the blanket, threw an arm over her eyes.

"Too stuffed for dessert?"

"Dessert?"

Charlie laughed at her interest. "How 'bout a drink first?"

"Umm. I am thirsty." Jennilee heard the hiss of a carbonated drink being opened.

Before she had a chance to sit up, she felt a trickle of cold drops on her stomach. She squealed, Charlie laughed.

"That's cold!"

"Be still and I'll get it off."

About the time Jennilee realized he hadn't said *wipe it off*, she felt a shadow on her heated skin, then Charlie's warm lips and tongue lapping the liquid off her flat stomach, following the drops as they slid off her ribcage.

Pouring a little into her bellybutton, he sipped again. "This is the best cream soda I've ever…"

"Cream soda? Gimmee." Tilting her face to his, Jennilee puckered her lips.

"Ah, ah, ah. I've upped the ante. I demand more than a kiss this time."

"More? How much more?"

Charlie was quiet for a moment. "I want to touch you."

"Have I ever told you no? You touch me all the time."

"I want to touch you the way a man touches the woman he loves, the woman he wants to make love to. I want to look at all of you."

Jennilee's eyes snapped open, met his. "Charlie. Are you sure? I'm not going to Sou…"

Putting a finger on her lips, he hushed her. "I'm sure, and I promise I won't make love to you until you're my wife. I just want to touch you, look at you, dream a little, pleasure us both. We deserve that much."

"Give me a minute. I need a drink first."

Helping her sit up, Charlie held the bottle to her lips. Jennilee took a long swallow, then another.

Told him shakily, "If we start this, I don't know if I have enough strength to let you stop. As long as I just think about it and you don't actually touch me, I can be strong. Once you touch me… I want you—want to be your wife so much it hurts. I need—*crave*—the closeness that physical intimacy brings."

"Ah, Jennilee-sweet. Never mind. I don't want to add to your burdens."

Both quiet for more than a few heartbeats, they watched iridescent dragonflies skim low over the pond, watched one light on one of the beautiful lilies.

"Can you be strong enough for both of us? Because I can't." Meeting his gaze, Jennilee let all her longings and insecurities show.

"Have I ever broken my word to you?"

Shaking her head, Jennilee leaned into him with a tortured moan. "Whatever you want, Charlie. I'm yours. Body, heart, and soul."

Burying his face against her neck, he tangled one hand in her hair. "How do you manage to always smell so good? Sweet, like that cream soda you like so much. Even just coming out of that old pond—you don't smell like pond water, you smell of flowers and…" Nuzzling her neck, he tasted, nibbled, absorbed.

Jennilee moved and he thought she'd changed her mind. His heart stopped, then took up a mad pounding as her arms twisted up behind her back, undid the clip holding her bikini top together. Reaching her hands up behind her neck she undid the clip there.

Watching the bikini top fall to the blanket out of the corner of his eye, he dragged in a deep breath, reached out a shaking hand. "Sweet. You are so sweet, just like your scent. Perfect, Jennilee. You're absolutely perfect."

Jennilee closed her eyes and arched her back in ecstasy as his calloused hands touched the naked skin she bared to him for the first time.

"Soft. I've never felt anything so soft." He traced her nipples with his fingertips, cupped her, hefted her breasts in his palms. Thumbed her nipples and drew another tortured moan from her.

"Charlie…"

"I'm right here, Jennilee-love. Right here. I'm not going anywhere." He continued to stroke and caress her, delighted in the revelation of her passionate nature. Just like her hair, normally kept bundled up all tight and neat. Just like she let her hair down for him, she let her passion out for him, and only him.

Charlie followed as Jennilee stretched out on the blanket, lifted her hips and wriggled out of her bikini bottoms. Kissing her long and deep, Charlie finally leaned back on one elbow, skimmed admiring eyes down her torso, followed that with his hand.

Jennilee's hips came off the blanket, thrust into his hand as he covered her mound.

"This is the way it's going to be on our wedding night,

Jennilee, only I won't stop. I want plenty of light so I can see every expression that crosses your face. I want to please you until you come again and again, screaming out my name."

Caught in a sensory overload, Jennilee couldn't make out his words, only Charlie's beloved voice. Deep and sweet like his kisses, it'd never cracked like so many teenagers' did, merely changed overnight. He went to bed, just like always and woke up one morning sounding like an angel.

Jennilee's blood turned to molten lava, her skin felt like it was going to burst into flame any second. Every time, every where Charlie touched her set off detonations—repeated explosions of colors and shapes until she was nothing but a hot, tight knot of feeling.

Leaning over Jennilee, Charlie started kissing. Beginning at her mouth he worked his tortuous way down. Nibbled on her chin, her neck, her perfect breasts. Traced her ribs, outlined her bellybutton, almost drove her insane when he nipped and licked his way down the outline of both hip bones. Worked his way back up and started over.

Moaning incoherently, thrashing her head from side to side, Jennilee begged non stop. "Charlie, please. Please. Charlie." Didn't know whether she was begging him to stop or to never stop.

Grabbing his biceps, she tried futilely to pull him closer. Pulling herself up against his hard chest, she rubbed her aching nipples on his crisp chest hair, like a cat pacing back and forth under a caressing hand.

Giving up on that, wrapping both arms around his neck and a leg around his thigh, she plastered her body to his. She could feel the hard length of his arousal pressing against her naked hip, one thin layer of denim and a thinner layer of cotton all that separated them.

Trembling beneath him, straining against him, Jennilee was driving him crazy with her actions and those sexy little whimpers. He could feel her heart, thundering against his own. Sweeping a possessive hand from her shoulder down her back to her hip, he pulled her closer, fitted her body perfectly to his. Claimed her mouth with his own.

Focused on kissing, drowning in the sensations they were creating, he didn't notice her hands trailing down his chest, worming between them. Jennilee had his cutoffs unfastened, well on her way to pushing them and his underwear off his hips when he realized what she was doing. She closed one hand around his shaft, and Charlie swore he saw stars. Whole planets and galaxies burst to life before his eyes.

Heaving off her, rolling to his side, he caught both her hands in his. They lay staring at each other, both gasping. Jennilee closed her eyes, but not before he saw the flash of pain.

"Sorry."

Charlie brought their joined hands to his lips. "Why, baby? You were upfront with me. You told me if I started this you wouldn't want to stop. I should've listened. But, Jennilee —I wouldn't trade what we just experienced for anything."

Jennilee shuddered.

"Do you want me to...finish you?" He moved a hand to cup the tight golden curls on her mound, antique gold instead of new gold.

A twitch, a heavy sigh, and Jennilee opened her eyes. "No. I want to save that for our wedding night."

"I can see what this cost you, baby, and I'm sorry. Not sorry enough to wish we hadn't done it. This is what's going to get me through two years of being away from you. I'll carry this memory with me the rest of my life and beyond."

They stared into each other's eyes while their breathing slowed and their heart rates returned to a semblance of normal.

"Charlie? I want to see you."

Still right on the verge, a hairsbreadth from detonating, Charlie considered refusing. Took a deep breath—for her, he could do this. Hadn't she just let him look his fill, touch to his heart's content? Another deep breath and he rolled to his back, shoved his shorts and underwear off as far as he could, kicked them off the rest of the way.

Jennilee sat up, her gaze on his throbbing shaft like a magnifying glass focusing sunlight. Leaning forward, she reached out to touch his glistening tip.

Charlie caught her hand, shook his head desperately. "Hanging on by a thread here."

Swallowing her disappointment, Jennilee complied. Flashed him a wicked grin. Licked her lips—slowly. "I could…"

"No way, Jennilee. Don't even think about doing that. I'm already aroused enough. What you've done is… When you wrapped your hand around me…"

Their eyes met and held. Jennilee made a soft sound of agreement.

His voice nothing like his usual melodious tones, Charlie informed her, "I'm going for a swim."

Lying back on the blanket, Jennilee listened to the frantic thrashing as Charlie swam back and forth. Let the sexual tension seep away, let the sun and the sounds of nature sooth her. That had been…breathtaking, literally. She didn't regret it, not a single moment.

Drip drying, Charlie watched Jennilee sleep. On her side, one hip cocked and one knee drawn up, she looked like a mermaid sunbathing in her human form. Following the sweet curve of her derriere, Charlie stifled the urge to throttle Celie as he looked closer. Close enough to see the silvery horseshoe shaped scars left by the metal handle of Celie's flyswatter. Wished he'd hit Mort harder, more, when he saw the long silvery lines that could only have come from a belt or a switch.

Rage beat back the last remnants of arousal. Dragging his shorts on, he remembered what he had in his pocket. Went to his knees beside Jennilee. "Hey, sleepyhead. Wake up. Thought you wanted dessert?"

Stretching like a contented cat, Jennilee slitted her eyes, purred, "I thought that was dessert."

"Be hard to top that, but I've got something else for you."

"So feed me. I don't feel like moving."

"Sit up, Jennilee."

Opening her eyes, Jennilee reached for her swimsuit, suddenly shy.

"No, don't. Stay just like you are. Please."

"You put your shorts back on."

"Better for both of us that way."

Jennilee rose to her knees. Smiled. "Someday."

"Someday," Charlie affirmed. He looked her up and down, kneeling naked in front of him. "If I live a thousand years, I'll never see anything as beautiful as you are right this moment."

"Charlie—why so serious?"

"Jennilee, we've always talked about getting married, but I've never asked you properly." Charlie rose to one knee. "I'm asking now. Jennilee, will you marry me?"

Jennilee looked from his beloved face to the hand he was holding out and the ring he held up to her. Exquisite—there was no other word for what he was offering.

Jennilee's hand shook as much as Charlie's had when he reached out to touch her for the first time. "Charlie…I…yes. Yes. *Yes!* "

"Give me your hand."

Laying her hand across his outstretched palm, Jennilee watched as he slid the ring on her finger. "With this ring, Jennilee, with this ring."

"Charlie—it's beautiful." She examined the ring, a visible sign of their love for each other. Two narrow bands of white gold bordered by yellow gold on the outside edges, and down the middle, between the twin strips of white gold, aquamarines inset in white gold filigree. Aquamarines that went all the way around the band in a never ending circle.

"Not as beautiful as you."

"Where..."

"I had it commissioned. The yellow gold is for your hair, the white gold and aquamarines for your eyes. Legend has it aquamarines originated in a mermaid's treasure chest, tradition states a woman who wears them will have a happy marriage filled with joy and wealth. They're the perfect stones for you."

As much as it meant to her, as beautiful as the ring was, it struck terror into her heart. "Charlie, I love it, but..."

"I know, and I don't expect you to wear it just yet. I just... needed to give it to you."

"I'll wear it back to Grandy's, then I'm going to have to keep it hidden for awhile longer."

"I understand."

"Charlie, it's going to break my heart to take this off."

"I know, Jennilee, I know."

Reaching out, Charlie palmed the nape of her neck and pulled her to him for a long, scorching kiss.

CHAPTER 30

Grandy and Donnie eyed them as they entered the kitchen, hand in hand.

"What've you two been up to all day?"

"We worked at our house some, mowing and stuff."

Laughing, Jennilee corrected, "Charlie worked. I lazed in the hammock."

"Then we went swimming."

"We had a picnic."

That wasn't all, but whatever they'd been doing, the shadows were gone from Jennilee's eyes and her laugh no longer sounded fake and tinny.

Instead of the usual PSR, both headed upstairs at the same time.

Donnie heaved a sigh. "Looks like I better have another serious talk with Charlie."

Grandy nodded, turned back to what she was doing. From the looks of those two, it was way past time for a talk to do any good.

Stopping outside Jennilee's bedroom door, bringing their joined hands to his lips, Charlie pressed a kiss over the exact spot where his ring belonged. Opening Jennilee's hand, he tucked her ring into it, closed her fingers around it. "I'll put it back where it belongs as soon as it's safe."

Wrapping her arms around Charlie's waist Jennilee clung, her head over his heart.

～

For Christmas, Charlie gave Jennilee a lily pad and water lily complete with dragonfly, all of it life-size. Carved all of wood, the dragonfly perched on the flower, its wings cleverly inlaid with mother of pearl.

A set of antique dresser scarves was her other present.

"I found those at a flea mall."

Looking at the water lily and dragonfly he'd carved and embellished, then the intricately embroidered water lilies and lily pads and dragonflies on the scarves, Jennilee smiled at Charlie like he'd given her the world.

Jennilee gave him a set of cufflinks, white gold banded in gold with a delicate dragonfly etched into the aquamarine stone set in each one, and a handmade kaleidoscope with dragonflies and water lilies engraved around the brass tube. A kaleidoscope she'd designed and implemented.

Charlie read the note in the box with the kaleidoscope and almost came unglued right then and there.

I want you to see what I saw.

The scorching look he gave Jennilee turned her to jelly. Rising slowly, he stalked her, hauled her to her feet and gave her a Christmas kiss that almost knocked her socks off.

Grandy and Donnie exchanged a look.

"Cool it guys, or I'm gonna go get the water hose."

"Yessir." Charlie moved back away from Jennilee far enough to get a piece of paper between them—maybe.

THEY PURCHASED another house and counted down months. Worked on it and counted down weeks. Down to counting days—hours—minutes, they each laid their plans and waited impatiently.

The morning of their eighteenth birthday, Jennilee rose before dawn, as usual. Went downstairs, as usual.

First Celie, and then right behind her, Mort, entered the kitchen at their normal time to find Jennilee motionless, one hip propped on the counter, staring out the window toward Grandy's.

No coffee brewed, no breakfast cooked, no table set, no nothing. The fact there was no bounty of food was astonishing enough. The fact Jennilee was in the kitchen brought them both up short.

Celie couldn't believe Jennilee'd ignored her long standing dictate to be nowhere in sight when she herself entered the kitchen.

Mort couldn't remember the last time Jennilee'd joined them for a meal, Celie having tearfully told him long ago Jennilee refused to eat with them. Preferred instead to eat at Del's. Hadn't he seen Jennilee, with his own eyes, refuse to eat at their table? How many times had he seen Celie sit right beside Jennilee, trying to coax her to eat? Watched as Jennilee adamantly refused. How many times had he punished Jennilee, to no avail? No matter what he or Celie did, Jennilee wouldn't touch a bite.

Furious, Mort demanded, "Where's my breakfast? I've got to go."

Mort liked a big, traditional breakfast. Little did he know he'd probably seen his last one in this kitchen. Jennilee came to life at his question and her cheering thought.

Wringing her hands, Celie threw a hate filled look at Jennilee. What was the brat up to now? "It's...it's Jennilee's turn to cook."

Mort rounded on her. "Jennilee, is it your turn to cook?"

"Not any more." Jennilee's answer rang like rain-bells, drawing a snarl from Mort.

"What the hell does that mean? Don't be giving me any of your lip."

"It means things are going to change around here."

"You think you're suddenly too good to help out around here?"

Jennilee watched with detached interest as Mort's face took on the unhealthy shade of a ripe plum. "You really should get your blood pressure checked."

"Blood pressure? If not for you, I wouldn't have a problem."

"Well, then." Jennilee smiled, a fierce smile that came nowhere near her eyes. "You shouldn't have any problems after today."

"Will you stop talking in riddles?"

"You have no idea what today is, do you?"

"Friday. So what? I have an important meeting this morning."

Jennilee shrugged.

Mort fisted both hands and took a threatening step.

Moving away from the counter a step—toward him—Jennilee pulled her lips back in a grim parody of a smile. "You really, really want to keep your hands to yourself."

"Why, I oughta..."

Jennilee fought down the urge to do her best Three Stooges response. "Ought to what? Take your belt off and beat me bloody?" Turned to Celie. "Maybe you'd like to try locking me in the closet or in my room?"

Mort roared, "What's gotten in to you? You've always been mouthy and disrespectful, but this…this takes the cake."

Jennilee's smile, genuine this time, lit her face all the way to her eyes. "Chocolate—Grandy's homemade three layer with fudge icing and chopped pecans sprinkled on top."

"Have you completely lost your mind?"

"Last chance to come clean, Celie. No? The only ones losing anything today will be you three." Jennilee included Sylvia, since she'd just walked into the kitchen.

Celie finally found her tongue. "No! You can't have it! I won't let you take what I've worked so hard to…"

"Steal? Funny thing is—I never wanted any of it. Not the money, not the house, not the name or the prestige. All I ever wanted was family."

"We're your family." Mort sounded like he really believed it.

Jennilee felt no pity, no remorse at what she was about to do. She'd paid her dues—in blood, sweat, and tears. "Maybe your definition of family—not mine." Switched her gaze to Celie. "Whatever money's left, you're welcome to it, though I seriously doubt there can be very much. The house and land are mine to do with as I wish."

"You can't throw me out! This is my house. Tell her, Mort." Celie turned to Mort, prepared to throw a raging fit.

"Dry it up, Celie. Your lies have caught up with you. You can continue to live here—under one condition. This house stays as clean and well kept as it is right now. Inside and out."

"But…but…"

Jennilee shook her head, grinned as she handed out her ultimatum. "No buts. You've got a couple of choices—do it yourself or hire someone. I really don't care."

Cocked her head, remarked thoughtfully. "Of course, a full time cook, housekeeper, and yard man is gonna cost you a pretty penny. That's really gonna cut into what you've got left. Whittle it right down. No more fancy clothes, no more new car every year, no more of those trips to the spa you enjoy so much and so frequently."

Eyeing her cousin, Jennilee told Celie. "It'd go a lot easier on you if you could persuade Sylvia to help, but then again, she's made her views on menial labor perfectly clear. She's about as amenable to chores as I am to her bosom buddy Butch."

Mort looked from Jennilee to Celie, completely befuddled. "Celie, what's she babbling about?"

Celie cranked up the wailing.

Jennilee smiled. "She's crying because she missed her last chance to throw me a birthday party."

"Today's your birthday?"

Jennilee's smile widened in direct proportion to Celie's noise. "Yes it is. My eighteenth. Good-bye."

"You're leaving? Just like that?"

"Yes I am."

Hand on the doorknob, Mort's next question stopped her. For an instant. "Aren't you even going to take any of your things?"

Not bothering to turn around, Jennilee threw over her shoulder, "What things would those be? There is nothing—not one single thing in this house I care for enough to take with me." A low chuckle escaped her as she pushed open the screen door and stepped out, deliberately making no effort to keep it from slamming. A couple quick steps and a flying leap and she by-passed the steps, landed on the walk.

There he stood—her Charlie, in the gap between the hedges, a welcoming smile on his face, arms open wide.

Jennilee skipped a few steps, broke into a run, joyous laughter pouring from her.

Mort watched, dumbfounded. Realized with a shock he couldn't remember ever hearing Jennilee laugh before. It trailed behind her, each golden note floating in the air like iridescent soap bubbles.

Catching her in a bear hug as soon as she stepped through the hedge, Charlie whirled her around until they were dizzy. Kissed her until they were breathless. Letting her slide down the front of him, he framed her face. Casually reached up, loosened the splice and let her hair fall around her, a waterfall of gold silk. Gazed deep into her eyes, all the way to her heart.

Captured her hand and brought it to his lips. "Jennilee, my one true love, will you do me the very great honor of agreeing to become my wife?"

"Yes!" Her hand rock steady this time, Jennilee held it out for Charlie to slip her ring back on, right where it belonged.

Walking up the dirt path toward Grandy's kitchen door, hand in hand, reaching the brick walkway bordering the flowerbeds, Charlie told her, "Close your eyes."

"Charlie! Another present? You'll spoil me."

"I intend to, to no end."

Charlie guided her down to sit sideways on the top step. "Whistle, Jennilee."

Jennilee did, almost immediately heard scrabbling, felt something warm wriggling against her. Looking down, she saw the most adorable white puppy with black and tan markings.

"She's a Feist, Jennilee, eight weeks old. She's housebroken and doing as well as can be expected with her obedience training. I just picked her up—she doesn't have a name yet."

Cradling the puppy, getting her face washed in response, Jennilee snuggled her and loved on her. "She's such a jewel!"

They broke out laughing. "Jewel it is."

Jennilee stepped into the kitchen, holding the ecstatic puppy. Stepped into a welcoming party/ birthday celebration.

"Everyone, I officially asked Jennilee to marry me." Charlie held up their joined hands so they could all see her ring.

"I officially said yes!"

Amidst the squeals and hoots and hollering that followed their announcement, Grandy got ahold of her, passed her to Mr. Donnie, then to Chief Mac, then to Doc, on around the room until Mr. Jubal and Miz Sadie and Mose and Mr. Tom and Jeff all got their turn. Grandy brought the birthday cake out of the pantry—chocolate, with fudge icing and chopped pecans sprinkled on top *and* between the layers.

"Birthday cake for breakfast? Woohoo!"

Jennilee oohed and ahhed over the cake, the rest of them oohed and ahhed over her ring and Charlie's announcement.

Slices of cake later, most of the party-goers pleaded work or school and disappeared. Following Mr. Tom to the door so they could speak privately, Jennilee hugged him and Charlie shook his hand. Mr. Tom laid a hand on both their shoulders.

"When you're finished here, I'll be expecting you. Everything's ready. All that's needed is your John Hancock's."

"Thanks for everything, Mr. Tom."

"We really appreciate it."

"Glad to do it."

"And the other?"

"Taken care of, Jennilee. As we speak."

As soon as the door closed behind Mr. Tom, Charlie caught Jennilee in another bear hug, kissed her long and well.

"We made it, Charlie! We really did it!"

"You did it, baby."

"I never would've survived without you and everyone that was here this morning. I wish you could've seen their faces! When Celie stepped into the kitchen and breakfast wasn't ready, Mort right on her heels…"

"Jennilee, know what I want for my birthday present?"

"Yeah, but you're not getting that until our wedding night."

Charlie laughed, low and sexy, pulled her tighter against his hard body. "That too, but I'm willing to wait. I never want to hear their names spoken in this house again."

"That is one present I give you freely, right now and forever." Standing on tiptoe, Jennilee pulled his head down and sealed her promise with a kiss.

"Speaking of presents…"

"Charlie, not another one!"

"I told you, I intend to spoil you every chance I get. I can never make up for what's been done to you, but I'm going to give it my best shot."

Charlie headed up the stairs, tugging her along. "You know how I asked you not to go into the room beside yours because I was working on something in there?"

"I haven't, Charlie."

Wrapping an arm around her head, pretending to give her a noogie, he told her, "I know that. I'm not doubting you. That's where your other present is."

Kissing her down the hallway, Charlie backed her into her bedroom, gave her another kiss that rocked her world. "Close your eyes."

"You like saying that to me, don't you?"

"Oh, yeah." Charlie brushed his lips over hers, and she complied with a smile. He spun her, kept his hands on her shoulders and propelled her forward.

Jennilee heard a door open—*what door?*—smelled the

distinctive scent of new lumber and new construction. Charlie walked her in. "Open, Sezme."

Jennilee blinked, blinked again. Scanned from left to right and back. Grandy's house had always, as long as Jennilee could remember, only had the one full bath upstairs with a half bath downstairs. Now it had another full bathroom—and what a bath.

Once a sewing room, this room had long been used as an extra closet. Deep and narrow, with a window at the far end opposite the old door, it'd contained nothing but shelves and boxes. Had. Now it was transformed.

A huge old clawfoot tub nestled against the wall beneath what'd once been a narrow window, now a wider space made up entirely of glass blocks. A vanity and beveled mirror lined the wall in front of her, the commode and the linen closet were tucked in the corner behind the new door. Done in soft colors to match Jennilee's eyes, the bathroom was a work of art and a labor of love. Soothing ocean colors—greens and blues and hints of grays set against a creamy background melded and blended in a tranquil mix. Gold-toned fixtures completed it.

Not just an empty bathroom, Charlie'd filled the glass étagère beside the tub with an array of bubble baths and bath salts. Huge, fluffy, supremely soft towels and washcloths hung on the towel racks and filled the linen closet. A new bathrobe hung on the back of the door, silk.

And not a bathroom for everyone. Charlie'd blocked off the old door so you couldn't even tell it'd ever existed, at least from the inside, and he'd do the same to the outside, now that Jennilee knew about her bathroom. The only entrance was through Jennilee's bedroom.

Charlie watched in the mirror as expressions flitted across Jennilee's face. All the late nights had been well worth it.

Catching Charlie watching her reflection, Jennilee turned and flung her arms around his neck, burst into tears.

Holding her tight, Charlie stroked his hands down her hair and back while she sobbed. "Let it out, baby. You've held it in long enough. They can't touch you anymore." Crooned to her until her tears slowed and dried.

"Charlie, I don't know what to say. I'm…overwhelmed."

"And I intend to see you stay that way the rest of your life. How 'bout, ooh, Charlie? This is so wonderful. I can't wait to try it out."

Laughter dispelling the last of her tears, Jennilee agreed. "I can't wait. Thank you, thank you, thank you!"

"Well, what are you waiting for? You can use as much hot water as you like. I put a hot water heater just for this bathroom in the closet next door."

"Charlie, I can't believe you did all this for me."

"Why? You think you don't deserve every bit of it and more?"

"It's not that. It's just…so wonderful. When did you have time?"

"I had lots of help. Now quit worrying and try out your tub. We told Mr. Tom we'd be at his office shortly." Attempting to sound stern, Jennilee's happiness was contagious. Charlie personally didn't care if she spent all day in the tub, and Mr. Tom would wait.

As excited as any child on Christmas morning, she opened jars and bottles and sniffed the various bubble soaps and salts, rubbed the towels against her face, touched every surface. Picked up and held the little seashell shaped soaps on the vanity one by one, admired the swirly blue-green-purple Depression ware bowl that held them. Cradled the antique perfume bottles lined up on the counter in front of the mirror one by one, sniffed the contents. Brushed a finger in a loving caress over her lily pad and dragonfly, now resting in a place of honor on the top shelf of the étagère.

Jennilee turned to Charlie, eyes shining. "Do you want your present now?"

Looking her up and down, Charlie leered suggestively.

Laughter spilled from her lips like water from a broken water main. "Not that one, not yet." Brushing past him, giving him a quick kiss in passing, Charlie turned to watch her cross her bedroom and pull the covers back on her bed.

"Jennilee?"

"Will you get your mind out of the gutter for five seconds?" Trying to sound serious, she ended up laughing. Reaching under her pillow, Jennilee crossed her arms over her chest, held something white clutched to her heart when she turned back to him.

Taking the envelope she held out, Charlie ran it slowly through his hands before flipping it over to read the return address. His heart stuttered at the name in the top left-hand corner.

Clyde Goodwin.

His eyes flew to hers. She nodded.

"The house. Our house? He's going to sell it to us?"

Jennilee nodded. "Happy Birthday to us."

"But...you haven't opened it."

"It's addressed to both of us."

"He might be telling us to stop pestering him."

Jennilee shook her head, supremely confident. "Go ahead, open it."

Wearing the same fey look she'd worn when she told him Amelia was crying for Clyde, Charlie had no doubt she was right. She'd told Mr. Cyrus long ago Clyde Goodwin would sell them the house when the time was right.

"It came yesterday. It was all I could do not to show it to you then."

Charlie sat slowly on the edge of the bed. Jennilee sat beside him, thigh to thigh and a little behind. Resting her chin on his shoulder, she waited.

Slipping his finger under the edge of the envelope like Charlie Bucket opening his first Wonka Bar to see if there was a Golden Ticket inside, he slowly broke the seal. Unfolded the single sheet of paper.

CHARLIE AND JENNILEE—

I've received, and ignored, your letters for years. Why should I let anyone have our house? Spiteful, I wanted to let it crumble and decay into nothingness, like my life. I couldn't stand the thought of another couple filling it with love and laughter and children when I was so alone, lost without my wife and son. My beloved Amelia came to me in a dream, insisted you're to have our house for that very reason—so you can fill it full of love and laughter and children. She told me your love for each other was true, that closing up the house and closing off my heart was no way to live. Jennilee, Amelia also told me you heard her crying and you cried for her. She heard what Charlie told you and repeated it to me. We are both at peace now. I am no longer so bitter, and she understands I cannot love another. I am content to wait until we can be together again. May you have a long and happy life together. Thank you, for everything.

Clyde Goodwin

A FIGURE FOLLOWED THE MESSAGE, high enough not to be insulting to either party, not high enough to be out of their range.

They read the missive, read it again. Charlie slipped his arm around Jennilee and held her close, pressed a kiss to her temple. "We'll have Mr. Tom draw up the papers and we'll cut Mr. Clyde a check. We'll have plenty left to start working on our house right away. *Our house!* "

"Those words have a nice ring to them. Almost as nice as a few other words I know." Holding her hand out, Jennilee wiggled her fingers so that her ring winked and shone.

Tackling her to the bed, Charlie tickled her breathless. "I'm sure glad you heard Amelia."

Jennilee pulled him down for a kiss. "Me, too."

Hand in hand, they went back to her bathroom. Jennilee picked out a bubble bath while Charlie turned the taps on. "Take your time, Jennilee. Enjoy, love."

"I will."

"Happy Birthday, Jennilee."

"Happy Birthday, Charlie. This is the best birthday ever."

"They're only going to get better from here on out, Jennilee. I promise." Charlie winked and closed the door behind him, whistling *Zippity Doo Dah* as he left her bedroom.

Jennilee smiled and started undressing, all the while singing *I'm The Happiest Girl In The Whole USA*.

∼

WHILE JENNILEE TOOK her time soaking and dreaming and reveled in the ability to do both, Charlie finished his last birthday present. This one was for both of them.

The first thing he did was dig a large hole in the gap between the hedges. A trip around behind the shed garnered a privet in a ten gallon container. Large—not quite as big as the ones that'd been there longer than he could remember, it'd fill the gap and catch up quickly.

Whistling, he backfilled the hole, watered it well, tamped the dirt down. Getting the tiller out, he tore up the dirt path from hedge to walkway. Raked it smooth and made another trip to his stash. Sod, this time. Dormant, but warm weather would bring it to life, green it up. Laid it so tight and well, no one who didn't know would ever suspect there'd ever been a path, or a gap between the hedges.

Went inside and hit the shower, still whistling. Couldn't wait to see Jennilee's face when she saw that.

CHAPTER 31

Next door at the Judge's house, it was a bad time. Mort had his hands full with Celie, bawling at the top of her lungs.

Jennilee hadn't been gone five minutes when a car full of strangers in suits pulled up, opened the front door without knocking, came right on in. Spread out, some going upstairs, some remaining downstairs, all with video recorders and cameras and notepads. All videoing, snapping pictures and scribbling furiously.

Mort bellowed to be heard over Celie. "What the hell do you think you're doing? Get out of my house! I'm calling the cops."

One of the suits handed Mort an envelope. "We have the owner's full and complete permission to be here. It is at the owner's behest that we video and photograph every room, take notes on the condition of said rooms, and document everything we find. When you read your contract, the one you're holding, you will find the owner's terms set forth therein. We are required to make routine and unannounced inspections at our discretion. If we, at any time, find the condition of this house to be less than satisfactory, your contract is terminated. This is your only warning, and once said contract has been terminated, you have twenty-four hours to vacate the premises or you will be forcibly removed."

"We're the owners. You can't do this. I'm calling my lawyer."

"If that's what you think, then I suggest you make that call." Turning his back, the suit began panning with his video camera.

Mort called his lawyer, got a recorded message that said he was on vacation—for several weeks. A message he could barely hear over Celie's caterwauling. Hanging up the phone, for the first time in their married life, he yelled at Celie. "Knock it off!"

Opening the envelope, he started reading, choked at the first words. So it was true—Jennilee did own the Judge's house. Mort got a sinking feeling in the pit of his stomach. Surely there was some misunderstanding.

His stomach bottomed out somewhere south of his ankles as he and Celie followed the suits around, listened to the comments flash back and forth, especially when they reached Jennilee's room.

"The padlock and hasp are on the outside of the door?"

"Affirmative."

"She sneaks out at night."

A cold trickle of sweat trailed down the middle of Mort's back at Celie's whine, a protest completely ignored by the suits.

"The windows are nailed shut."

"Affirmative."

"I told you—she sneaks out at night."

The trickle became a flood.

"This room is in the attic."

"Affirmative."

"We put her up here so…"

"There is no apparent heat source in this room, nor is there any sign of air conditioning or a fan of any sort. There are no personal possessions."

Mort's shirt was soaked. "Wait. You have to listen to our side."

～

CHARLIE, Jennilee, and Grandy piled into his truck and headed for Mr. Tom's office. Spent a good hour signing here and there, making everything right. All the accounts and paperwork were legally in Charlie and Jennilee's names, all the properties, including Clyde Goodwin's house—theirs as soon as the paperwork was complete—were in both names. No co-signers, no advocates.

Mr. Tom sat back, steepled his fingers. "Congratulations, you two."

"We never could have…"

"…done it without you and Grandy."

"You know Celie's going to fight this."

Reaching for a thick ledger beside her chair, Jennilee flashed Charlie a quick grin. Another tangible reminder, like the non-existent gap in the hedges, that Celie's reign of terror was over.

"She can fight all she wants. I'm sure she's going to try and convince everyone she spent all that money on me, that somehow I owe her for every little thing so she should get the house. She'll try to get her hands on our accounts, claim that what we have I stole from her over the years. I think you'll find this useful."

Handing the ledger to Mr. Tom, she and Charlie stood,

ready to go. They had things to do today that didn't include anyone else.

Grandy started to stand.

Tom cleared his throat. "Sit, Del. There's one more thing I need to discuss with you."

Charlie and Jennilee grinned. Radiant grins that made Del wonder what they were up to. "Thanks, Mr. Tom. See you later, Grandy."

"Wait…"

"Mr. Tom's gonna…"

"…give you a ride."

"Love you."

The door closed behind them. Tom started laughing at the expression on Del's face. "Give it up, Del. They have their own agenda. As their friend and lawyer, I advise you to go along with it." Laughed harder as he flipped the ledger open to the first page. Even as a child, Jennilee's handwriting had been beautiful, and distinctive. There, from just after their seventh birthday, noted in her childish script, was every penny earned, every purchase made, written down and documented.

With receipts.

"I need you to sign one more paper Del, and then I've got something to show you before I take you home."

Del read the deed he pushed across the desk to her, shook her head. "Tom, I can't…"

"Here. They said you'd react this way." Handing her a sealed envelope, turning to the sideboard and giving Del his back, he afforded her a moment of privacy.

Del opened the envelope to find a beautiful handmade card with one word on the front, surrounded by a wreath of flowers drawn in a heart shape. The word was Grandy.

The message inside read, in Jennilee's beautiful script:

Grandy,

We can never repay you for all the things you've done for us over the years, for all that you are to us. You taught us to follow our dreams—it's time for you to do the same. Please accept this token of our love in the spirit in which it was given.

Love,

Charlie and Jennilee

Eyes wide and disbelieving, a shocked Del looked at Tom. "Tom. A restaurant? They can't just give me a restaurant."

"They already have."

Del continued to stare, her gaze slipping back and forth between the card in her hand and the deed on the desk. "They can't—it's too much. They can't do this. It's just…too much money. Too much…everything."

"Del—how many contracts have you signed off on for them? Think back on how many houses they've bought and sold, how many projects they have going. And that's just what we know about. On top of that, Charlie's a shrewd investor. Allow them do this for you."

"Tom…how in the world?"

"Everything they've done, every dime they've earned, they've set aside a portion of it, invested it for this very reason.

"I knew they had money—they work like dogs and they haven't let me pay for their school clothes or anything for years and years—but this—I had no idea."

"Close your mouth before you start catching flies, sign the papers, and let's go see your restaurant."

CHARLIE AND JENNILEE drove back to Grandy's, picked up Jewel, grabbed picnic stuff and headed for their house.

Pulling up beneath the big live oak that shaded the drive, Charlie turned off the truck.

"I keep thinking I'm dreaming and I'll wake up any minute."

"Me too."

"Cemetery first?"

"Yeah."

Snapping off a few azalea blooms and some daffodils, kneeling beside Amelia's headstone, Jennilee laid the impromptu bouquet on the grave. "Thank you, Amelia. You contacted Clyde at the perfect time. He wasn't ready to listen before. He sold us your house, and we'll do our best to fill it with love and laughter, and I hope, children. You're always welcome, inside or out. I hope you find peace. Clyde seems to have found his."

Charlie swore he heard a soft *thank you* float by in a sudden breeze that came out of nowhere, fluttered Jennilee's hair like a soft caress.

Jewel barked once, wagged her whip of a tail ecstatically.

Spending a long time just wandering around inside their house, finally, at last, it was truly theirs! All their dreaming and scheming had borne fruit. Charlie'd been plotting and figuring for years, knew almost to a T how much plumbing and electrical stuff they'd need, how much insulation, how much of this and that. Old houses were money pits, especially old houses that'd been empty and neglected for the length of time theirs had been.

This one had been extremely well built, but not *that* well built. Puzzled, Charlie said so. "Some of this stuff, Jennilee—I just don't know. The house is dusty and filthy, but there's really not much damage. Not like there should be as long as it's been empty. None of the windows are even broken—not that I'm complaining. You know yourself how fast houses deteriorate in this climate. It's as if the house has only been empty a year or two instead of decades. The outside needs more work than the inside, and it's mostly cosmetic."

Jennilee gave him a brilliant smile and a one word answer. "Amelia."

∼

THE SUITS POKED and prodded until nearly lunchtime. Mort had a raging headache, he'd missed his meeting, and he still hadn't had any breakfast. Like the Cat In The Hat, packing up Thing One and Thing Two and disappearing, everything looked the same when the suits left, would never be the same again.

Heading for the kitchen to get a drink of water and a couple aspirin, Mort leaned against the counter, looked out the window. Choked as his eyes automatically followed the dirt path across the yard to the gap in the hedge—only, there was no gap. A solid line of shrubs, unbroken from end to end, met his disbelieving gaze.

Loud snuffling and whimpering came from behind him. "How…how could she do…that to me?"

Trying to coax Celie out of her mood, knowing she'd get a migraine and end up in bed for days if he didn't, Mort said, "Honey, why don't you fix us some lunch? Something simple —you know—like that egg and cheese stuff I like so much with some of your hot biscuits. You know how much I love your biscuits."

"How can you expect me to cook after the morning I've had?" Bursting into loud wails, Celie headed upstairs. He could hear her stomping all the way up, could still hear her muffled noise when their bedroom door slammed.

Switched his gaze to Sylvie.

"Don't even think about it. I am not a servant." Flouncing out, Sylvie left Mort staring at an empty doorway.

Giving up on either one of them fixing his lunch, Mort opened the frig, decided the Family Diner was his best choice.

Always crowded at lunch time, he managed to find a booth in the back corner. Slid in with his back to the room, placed his order, and stared unseeingly at the wall. His food had just arrived when a commotion at the front of the restaurant caught his attention.

Bertha, complaining loudly and vocally to Chief Mac. "I want you to arrest her! Do you know what I caught her doing this time? I don't suppose you care. You've always taken up for her, no matter what she does."

"Bertha, calm down. Better yet, let's take this outside."

"No! I'm staying right here. Everyone in this room, in this town, should see her for the lying, conniving…"

"Enough!" Mac's voice boomed out.

Mort got a sinking feeling in the pit of his stomach. His food, which had looked and smelled so appetizing now had all the appeal of rotten scallop guts.

Bertha pressed on. "Stealing flowers out of the barrels along the main street—in broad daylight, no less! I caught her red-handed. When I confronted her, she admitted she was taking them. There—now what are you going to do about it?"

"Bertha… By *she* I assume you mean Jennilee."

"You know that's who I'm talking about. Who else do you protect no matter what they do? Her, and that grandson of Del's. You act like they're…"

The restaurant was as silently attentive as any theater crowd.

Mac leaned back in his chair. "Who do you think

furnished and placed those half barrels and takes care of the flowers?"

Bertha gaped at him like a landed fish. "W...who? The Garden Club, or the women of the Rotary or...or..."

Shaking his head, Mac resisted the urge to laugh out loud at the expression on her florid-gone-suddenly-pasty face. "Charlie and Jennilee put those barrels out years ago. They keep flowers in them, take care of them year-round, at their own expense. Jennilee wasn't picking flowers, she was deadheading."

Charlie and Jennilee might not want any recognition for themselves, for the things they did, but they were by-golly going to get some today.

Mac crossed his arms and grinned at Bertha as the audience began showing their approval by tossing figurative bouquets onto the stage.

"Charlie and Jennilee do most of the maintenance work at Oak Grove cemetery."

"Charlie and Jennilee are always doing stuff at the nursing home. Singing, bringing magazines and helping the residents. Picking up prescriptions, dropping them off, running errands."

"Charlie and Jennilee help the Scouts with their projects. Just last month, both of them helped the Scouts build a bridge on the Neusiok hiking trail through Croatan National Forest. And they donated the materials."

On and on, coming from nearly every table at the restaurant. Nothing but compliments and praises for Charlie and Jennilee.

Rising slowly, Mac put his hands on his table and leaned into Bertha, forcing her to bend backward. "They also... placed the bike racks up and down the main street, again at their own expense. They help the veterans put up and take down the flags that fly from each light pole for Veteran's Day and other holidays. Not only that, they help put flags on all the veteran's graves on Memorial Day. Who do you think organizes the annual Easter Egg hunt in the Park? For that matter, who do you think donated most of the new playground equipment at the park?"

Mac spoke louder, covering Bertha's outraged hisses and moans, saving the one he knew would irk her to no end for last. "Who do you think donated…"

A breathless moan of denial came from her at the gleam in his eye.

"…all those new children's books to the library?"

Bertha let out a wail and ran out, to the sound of loud applause.

Mort clenched his jaw in an effort not to stand up and yell out the truth. Jenny sure had all these people snowed. Just wait'll the truth came out.

CHAPTER 32

Charlie watched Jennilee's eyes flick over the newly laid sod and newly planted privet, squeezed her hand.

"You really surprised me with that."

"No more than you surprised me this morning, putting the Judge's house in both our names. Jennilee—are you sure? That's yours—the only thing you have left of your mom."

"Charlie Meyers! Everything else we have is in both our names. Why shouldn't that be? Unless you don't want it?"

Charlie stopped her for a lengthy kiss. "It's yours to do with as you wish. If it was up to me, I'd raze the damn thing —with them in it."

Jennilee's laughter rang out, pure and sweet. "Before this is over, they may wish you had."

Still laughing, hand in hand, they entered the kitchen to find Grandy clenching a kitchen towel like she was wringing a chicken's neck.

One look at them and Grandy burst into tears.

"She loves it."

"Yep."

Slinging an arm around Jennilee, the two of them stood there grinning.

More wringing. "You...can't."

More grinning. "We already did."

"It's too much money. I can't let you...can't accept..."

Charlie gave a careless shrug. "The restaurant's yours. Do what you want with it."

"Grandy, I'm going to be living here until Charlie graduates from college, and you won't accept a dime from me."

"That's different."

"How, Grandy?"

Looking from one to the other, Del gave in and hugged Jennilee tight, held out her other arm to Charlie.

"Okay. You guys win, but nothing else, do you hear me?"

"So you don't want the..."

"Charlie!"

Grinning, Charlie squeezed Grandy and laughed out loud. "We wouldn't dream of refurbishing your restaurant. On the other hand, we know a couple good construction people and plumbers and electricians."

"Who? I'll need some, and you two know who to trust."

It was Jennilee's turn to laugh. "He's being silly, Grandy. He's talking about us."

"You guys..."

Charlie put both arms around Jennilee. "Who'd you think?"

"You two have been doing all your own stuff?"

"For years, Grandy. Mose got his contractor's license and electrician's license and plumber's license after we started doing houses together and we help him with everything. I'll get my own licenses as soon as I take a couple of courses and get certified. You gonna change?"

"What?" Del was in mild shock with all the day's revelations.

"Did you forget? Dad wants to take us all out tonight for our birthday."

Hours later, bellies filled and hearts content, the four of them and Jewel sat on the front porch. Charlie played his guitar and he and Jennilee sang, ballads this evening. Donnie listened, amazed again at the scope of their talent and knowledge.

Civil War ballads, WWI and WWII, stuff from the roaring twenties right on up to the present. Older ballads, songs that'd come across the ocean with the earliest settlers. Some he knew, some he'd never heard, some he'd heard only once or twice.

Ending *Three Bells*, they segued into *Danny Boy* and without missing a beat, did an awe inspiring rendition of Roger Whittaker's *The Last Farewell*.

Donnie had tears in his eyes and his throat was thick when they finished.

Headlights coming down the driveway caught their attention.

"That's Jeff and Michelle. I'll have Jennilee home by midnight, Grandy, and I'll be quiet when I come in, Dad."

Donnie couldn't answer. His son was eighteen and this would be the first night Charlie'd spent under his roof in more years than he cared to count.

Donnie slept in his recliner or on the couch most of the time anyway, if you could call his tossing and turning *sleep*. Charlie could have Donnie's bedroom. It wasn't like Donnie used it enough to matter.

Jennilee headed inside to put Jewel in her crate, Charlie headed for his truck to put his guitar inside.

Bounding back down the stairs, Jennilee gave Grandy and Mr. Donnie a hug and a peck each, and they were gone in a flash of taillights and loud music.

Del and Donnie looked at each other, burst out laughing

and went inside. "Our chicks have grown up. Doesn't seem possible. Seems like just yesterday that was you heading off for a hot date, Donnie, and a day or two before that it was me."

~

EVERYONE ADJUSTED EASILY to the change in living conditions. Ecstatic, Jennilee sang all the time, her face wreathed in smiles, the shadows gone from her eyes.

No matter how much Grandy fussed, Jennilee was up every morning before dawn, quietly doing something, Jewel at her heels. No slouch as a housekeeper, it was a big house and sometimes it took Del a day or two to figure out what Jennilee'd done, something different every day.

All the curtains downstairs had been taken down and washed, hung back up, the windows sparkling. The pantry cleaned and re-organized from top to bottom, outdated stuff thrown out and replaced with new. The frig and freezer and deep freeze cleaned out. The floors mopped and waxed. On and on.

Del got a sick feeling deep in her gut, one that refused to go away. You didn't learn how to work that silently and efficiently overnight. It took practice—loads of practice. Years of practice.

Had a flashback of the Judge's house being unbelievably filthy the first time she'd reamed Celie. Another flashback from the time she'd confronted Celie about locking Jennilee in a closet. The house had been spotless that time. Not for a million dollars would Grandy believe Celie'd suddenly developed an urge to be Suzy Homemaker. All these years, and the child had never said a word, other than *chores*.

Chores, ha!

Slavery hit closer to the mark.

Donnie took them all out to a restaurant on the anniversary of finding Iris' body.

While they were waiting for their food, he told them, voice quavering, "You probably think this is a sick way to commemorate something so gruesome, but… Finding Iris' body…hurt. But at least now I know. I know she's not out there somewhere, still alive, trapped somewhere in unimaginable pain, at the mercy of some sicko. I can't tell you how much it means to me to finally know."

Jennilee covered his trembling hand with hers. "You don't have to apologize Mr. Donnie. Not to us. We understand."

"Excuse me a minute." He shoved back from the table and walked off.

Following his dad with his eyes, Charlie took a sip of his tea. "Dad's quit drinking."

"When?" Grandy was breathless with joy, giddy with disbelief. He'd been sober for a long time, but after they'd found Iris' body, he'd fallen off the wagon, gone on a binge that lasted for weeks.

Charlie shrugged. "I don't know exactly, but I don't think he's touched a drop since that spell last year. There's nothing in his apartment, not even empties. Not that I was snooping or anything. I was looking for things, trying to figure out where he keeps everything. He could sure use your organizing talents, Jennilee. I know where you put everything."

"Are you belittling my housekeeping skills?" Donnie came back in just in time to catch Charlie's last words.

"I wouldn't call them…skills, exactly."

They all burst into laughter.

"Two men in an apartment… I don't know." Jennilee's comment brought another round of laughter.

Grandy said, "Didn't you used to have a housekeeper, Donnie? So hire someone again."

"It...um...didn't work out and I told her not to come back to clean anymore." Donnie shot Jennilee a look, one Charlie intercepted.

"Jennilee? Look at me." Charlie reached out a hand and cupped her face.

Grandy's gaze flew from Donnie to Charlie to Jennilee. "You did that? You cleaned his place for years! Jennilee, what are we going to do with you? You take too much on yourself."

"I've been telling her that for years." Right there in the restaurant, in front of Grandy and his dad, Charlie kissed her. A light kiss, butterfly wings across her lips. "Thank you, for taking care of Dad. That's not all, is it?" Kissed her again, deeper. "You're like Scheherazade, Jennilee. Only instead of you telling a different story every night, we find out a new secret about you."

The waitress arrived with their dinners and good food halted the conversation for a bit. Over dessert, Donnie cleared his throat.

"I appreciate all of you coming, despite the occasion. Charlie...I can't think of a better time to give this to you. It's from your Mom and me. She'd be proud of you, Charlie. You've grown into a fine young man. I've told you before, but I'm telling you again—I'm proud of you."

Donnie slid a dog-eared manila envelope across the table to Charlie.

Charlie stared at the envelope, raised his eyes to his father. "Dad..."

"Open it, son."

Jennilee put her hand on Charlie's thigh, under the table, squeezed reassuringly.

Charlie untucked the flap of the envelope and shook the contents out. A bankbook fell into his hand. He opened the bankbook, perused it slowly, turned to the last page. Shock registered on his features. "Dad, I can't..." Shook his head and held the bankbook out to his Dad.

"Yes, you can. It's yours. Your Mom and I started a college fund for you before you were even born. I kept adding, even after... It's what your Mom wanted, Charlie. It was her dream that you go to college. You always said you planned to anyway, so I never made a big deal out of it."

Charlie and Jennilee exchanged a long look. They already had money set aside for tuition, and Charlie planned to work while he was in college, but it would be petty to refuse his dad's gift.

"Thank you, Dad. And Mom, too."

Jennilee looked from one to the other and grinned like the cat that got the cream.

"Don't look so smug, Jennilee. I don't have money for you, but I do have an early graduation present. Now seems like a good time to give it to you." Mr. Donnie leaned back and pulled something from the front pocket of his slacks. Held out his fist to Jennilee. "Hold out your hand."

It was Jennilee's turn to look like a deer in the headlights. "Mr. Donnie..."

Charlie put a hand on her shoulder, leaned close and whispered, "What's good for the gander..."

Taking a deep breath, Jennilee held out her hand.

Mr. Donnie dropped a set of keys onto her open palm.

Jennilee looked at the keys, looked back up at Mr. Donnie's face. "Mr. Donnie...I...thank you."

Donnie leaned over and placed a kiss on Jennilee's cheek. "I figured with Charlie at college, you'd be doing a lot of driving back and forth, especially since freshmen aren't allowed to have a vehicle on campus. I don't want you out there in that old rattletrap truck. The car's not brand new, but it's a good one. I'll feel much better knowing you've got a decent vehicle."

"Dad, thanks again. I never expected this."

"Me, either."

Grandy laughed. "Just like my restaurant. You two look as shocked as I did that morning in Tom's office. Other people are capable of keeping secrets and giving gifts, you know."

"Mr. Donnie? You start third shift tomorrow?"

"Yeah, Jennilee, so I'm off all day.

"Would you come out to our house with us tomorrow? There's something we want to show you. It won't take long, I promise."

Charlie added, "You too, Grandy."

∽

EARLY THE NEXT morning found Jennilee in her accustomed spot in the truck, right beside Charlie, Jewel on the seat beside her. Jennilee glanced in the rearview at Mr. Donnie's car, right behind them. This was the first time Mr. Donnie or Grandy had been out to their house since it had officially become theirs.

Charlie and Jennilee and Jewel gave them a tour of the house first, then walked around the yard. Jennilee took Mr. Donnie's hand in hers and swinging their joined hands, all but skipping, told him. "The grounds are wonderful, but we think you'll particularly appreciate this."

They walked across the yard, out towards a gazebo situated on a small rise. Climbing the steps, Jennilee let go Mr. Donnie's hand and sat on one of the benches that lined the inside of the gazebo. Donnie stepped up beside her and looked out the other side.

Irises. A huge, huge bed of them in full bloom in a rainbow of colors. Yellows, blues, pinks, whites, purples, bronzes. Their heady scent wafted to the humans in the gazebo, wrapped them in memories.

Donnie stood speechless for a bit, then shuffled slowly across the gazebo and down the steps. Charlie and Jennilee and Grandy watched in silence as he walked back and forth, up and down the bed for a long while. Finally stopping, he bowed his head and stood motionless for uncounted minutes before snapping off a single cobalt bloom.

Coming back to the gazebo, he sat down heavily and stared at the bloom he held. "This is where you get all the irises you've been putting on her grave."

"Yessir."

"Thank you, for that and for all the other flowers you keep putting there."

Jennilee leaned over and kissed him on the cheek. "Sit here as long as you like. We've got some stuff to do." Charlie and Jennilee rose, linked hands. "And Mr. Donnie? You're welcome here anytime."

Grandy walked off with the kids and Donnie never noticed. Sitting, staring at the bounty of irises, he felt peace seep into his soul. It had been a long time coming.

Finishing the jobs they'd set for themselves for the day, they found Mr. Donnie in the hammock, fast asleep with the iris across his chest, on top of his heart, a peaceful smile on his face.

Charlie, Jennilee, Grandy, and Jewel got in Charlie's truck and went back to Grandy's. Mr. Donnie's car was right there whenever he was ready to leave, and he needed the rest.

~

Charlie threw himself and Jennilee into a whirlwind of social activities, Senior picnic and all the other events happening so close to graduation. Charlie and Jennilee, along with Jeff and Michelle, made a spectacular foursome at Prom.

Prom King, Charlie looked every inch a king in his tux. Dancing the obligatory dance with the Prom Queen, he returned to Jennilee's side, stayed shadow close.

Sylvia came in, dressed to the nines and hanging on Butch's arm. Wearing an expensive cocktail dress, one far too revealing and ostentatious for a high school prom, one she wrongly assumed would make her look suave and sophisticated, she looked like a high priced call girl fallen on hard times.

Butch dressed up was even scarier. A thug was still a thug, no matter what he wore, and Butch looked like a scummy drug dealer doubling as Sylvia's even scummier pimp.

Jennilee couldn't suppress a shudder at the sight of the other couple. Charlie pulled her closer and whispered, "Easy, love. I'm right here."

Jennilee took comfort from that, refused to think about what would happen when Charlie left for college. Caught her breath as everything clicked into place. "Charlie—that's why you're doing all of this! That's why you got me Jewel. That's why we're suddenly going to every event and why you're surrounding me with people. You want me to get used to being around other people so when you're off to college I won't miss you so much, won't be by myself. I appreciate what you're trying to do, but you have to stop. *You have to stop.* I'll be fine."

Pulling her into a secluded corner, Charlie pinned her between the wall and his body. "You listen to me, Jennilee. I love you more than life itself. Being away from you for two years is going to destroy me if I know you're here all alone. I have to know that you'll be safe, that you won't retreat into your shell without me here to rock you, to anchor you. Do this for me, Jennilee-baby. It's the only way I can go and leave you."

Jennilee pressed her forehead to his chest. "Charlie—what am I going to do with you? I'm not fragile—I won't shatter if someone touches me or says something ugly. I'll be too busy after you leave to worry about it. I've got so much to do, and I'll drive up every weekend. I'll call you every night, I promise. I'll write you every day."

"You can't..." Charlie tucked her close and rocked her. "Jennilee, you can't work yourself to a frazzle. I won't be here to keep an eye on you and make sure you don't."

"That's why you're recruiting every single soul in town to babysit me?"

"Not every single one."

CHAPTER 33

Celie screamed and threw a vase at the retreating back of the latest housekeeper she'd hired. It shattered against the wall and showered glass and water and flowers all over the floor. This housekeeper hadn't lasted two days. She'd seemed eager enough to take the job when Celie interviewed her.

The wretched woman had come to the house, looked over the list of chores Celie wanted done, and agreed to it. When she found out Celie expected them all done, and yesterday, she'd quit. Told Celie in no uncertain terms that it wasn't humanly possible to get all that done, and definitely not for the pittance Celie was offering.

What now? None of the agencies in three counties would send anyone else out here. Celie had been blacklisted. Word having gotten around, none of the small, privately owned housecleaning services would have anything to do with her either.

Celie stomped into the kitchen. Same thing in here. The last woman she'd hired to cook had laughed in her face, had been laughing still when she went out the door and got into her car.

What was she supposed to do? Mort was due home anytime now. The house was a wreck, the yard was sorely in need of mowing, there weren't any clean clothes left in the house, and the pantry and the frig both resembled nothing so much as Mother Hubbard's cupboard.

Celie did what Celie did best. Placed the blame exactly where it belonged. This was Jennilee's fault—all of it. With that thought, Celie did another thing she did well—she went upstairs to her bedroom to take a nap. She felt a migraine coming on. Definitely. As soon as she woke up, she'd call and book a full body massage and a facial, spend the whole day, maybe two, at her favorite spa. After that she'd go shopping.

Why, she felt better already.

∽

MORT MISSED the prom due to a misunderstanding on his part, so he failed to see his little girl all dressed up and to meet the boy who escorted her. He'd written down the wrong date—he could have sworn he wrote down exactly what Celie told him—but he made it home in time for Sylvie's graduation. Came home to an overgrown yard and an absolutely filthy house. A house devoid of edible food in any size, shape, or form. One look at his face and Celie burst into tears.

"I tried, Mort. I'm so upset about what she did, I can't get anything done. I've had migraine after migraine. None of the housekeepers or cooks I hired would stay. She's done something, poisoned them all against me."

Mort knew there wasn't any use in reminding Celie that if the guys in suits came by and found the house in this kind of shape, they'd be out on their asses. Unable to get ahold of his own lawyer after the first go-round with the suits, Mort had contacted Tom, who set him straight in no uncertain terms on who really owned the Judge's house. Celie had assured him, through copious tears, that it had just been a misconception on her part.

Going into his study, he closed the door and started making calls. A couple of the cleaning agencies laughed in his ear and hung up, most of them just hung up on him. Finally, a call to a cleaning service in Wilmington, two and a half hours away, netted results.

Mort figured the exorbitant fee they demanded up front was still cheaper than losing the house. He needed a drink, even if water was the only thing left in the house. Washing a glass out, he drank deeply and let his eyes wander around the kitchen. This was all Jennilee's fault. She'd had no call to upset Celie this way.

Noticing the overflowing mailbox when he turned into the drive, Mort had stopped and picked up the mail. He'd thrown the stack on the kitchen table in a helter-skelter pile when Celie started crying, added it to the debris already covering the table. Mort began going through it. A great deal of junk mail and tons of bills.

Frowning, wondering why the bills were being sent here when usually all Celie's bills were sent to the accountant and paid out of her trust fund, Mort sat down at the kitchen table, shoved a space clear, and started opening in earnest. All of these bills were past due and none of them had been paid. Credit card after credit card, maxed out. Must be some mistake. He'd have to make some calls. Something was dreadfully wrong here.

Couldn't help but notice that it looked like Celie had had plenty of time between her migraines for shopping and massages and getting her nails done.

Mort got on the phone, made some calls, and got a nasty

shock. The bills were coming to the house because Celie had fired the accountant, who refused to speak to Mort about Celie's trust fund. They were past due because she'd made no effort to pay them. He got the same story everywhere he called—all efforts had been made to be nice about collecting with no response on Celie's part. Assuring the creditors he would make good on the bills Mort got busy writing checks.

The next day, Mort attended graduation, like most everybody else in town, where he got several more nasty shocks. Attended by himself because Celie was in bed with another migraine. She'd wanted to come, practically begged him. Mort had had to put his foot down and insist that she stay home.

Trying to locate Sylvie in the identical crowd of caps and gowns was like trying to single out one specific penguin on an ice floe. So busy looking he hadn't even opened his program yet, Mort was still searching when the Valedictorian's speech was announced. He didn't pay much attention to that announcement—at least not until he heard who the Valedictorian was.

Charlie Meyers? Impossible!

It couldn't be Charlie. There was just no way. Hadn't Celie told him over and over what a no-good troublemaker Charlie was, how he only got passed to the next grade because of Del's influence? Hadn't he seen it for himself? That's how he'd known Charlie and Jennilee were lying when they got caught out after curfew. Poor Del—she'd believe anything those two spoon fed her. They hadn't been studying. Neither one of them ever studied—he'd never even seen Jennilee crack a book. Hadn't he punished Jennilee time after time for her poor grades? Not that it had made any difference.

Having watched Twilight Zone religiously, Mort felt like he'd stepped into an unseen episode. A bizarre world where everything seemed all right—no one else seemed to notice anything unusual in the fact that Charlie—and Jennilee—were being given award after award and honor after honor. Charlie had even won several scholarships.

None of this could be happening. It couldn't be real. Mort scanned the crowd again, looking for Sylvie. Sylvie was the one who should be up there on that stage, garnering all those awards and accolades. She'd had straight A's all through school. Hunted furiously through his program. If he could find her name, he could probably figure out exactly where she was.

Scanned his program. Scanned it again. What a crock! They'd left his daughter's name off. In search of someone to ream, Mort was making a bee-line for the edge of the platform serving as a stage. He just could see Principal Bestwick when Tracy Masters intercepted him.

Her obnoxious trill grated on already strained nerves. "Mort, whatever are you doing here? I can't believe you came to watch Jennilee walk across the stage. I don't know how you can stand to be here when Sylvie didn't even graduate."

Mort grabbed both her upper arms in a painful grip and shook her, got right in her face. "What are you babbling about?" Had the satisfaction of seeing Tracy go pale beneath her heavy makeup.

Eyes glittering with malice, she zealously informed him. "I told Celie months ago. Tried to tell her. She didn't want to hear it. I heard through the grapevine that Sylvie wasn't doing well in school, not that she ever has. Sylvie's almost at the very bottom of her class. Her grades were borderline then and they've gotten worse. Personally, I think it's that Jones boy she hangs around with. Butch is nothing but troub…"

Mort was sweating heavily, his face the color of puce, his

voice just below a shout. "What do you mean? Just what are you insinuating?"

Several people in the crowd turned and frowned at Mort, shushed him.

His voice rose a notch and he bellowed, "Explain yourself, Tracy! What exactly are you talking about?"

Three of the biggest male teachers and the football coach headed his way. He was still yelling as they escorted him off the field and to his car, ordered him off school property.

"You can't do this! I have every right to be here! I'm calling the…" Fat lot of good it would do to call Chief Mac. "I'm calling my lawyer."

Coach laughed heartily as he opened Mort's car door, waved him in. "Go ahead, Mort. That's probably a real good thing for you to do, if you can still afford one. I hear the public defender is booked up solid for the next couple of months at least."

Mort snarled, more confused than ever. "What the hell are you talking about? If I can afford one?"

"You better go talk to Celie. It's not my place to tell you anything."

Mac, having been at the other end of the field, showed up while Mort was standing beside his car, undecided whether to leave or try to bluff his way back in to the ceremonies. "Go home, Mort, and talk to your wife. Don't let her tears or her headaches or her tantrums distract you this time. Have a real heart to heart. When you're done with that, call Tom. It might not be too late to salvage a little something. Oh, and Mort, you might better go by Doc's office for a checkup. You don't look so good." Mac almost felt sorry for Mort.

Almost. After the hell he'd made Jennilee's life, Mort deserved pretty much anything he got.

Mort looked back and forth, from the Coach to Mac. He'd loved Twilight Zone, could have sworn he'd seen every episode. He must have missed this one somehow. It just kept getting more and more bizarre. Maybe that's why it had never made it to a TV screen. This was too bizarre, even for Rod Serling.

Mort got in his car, slammed the door and left, tires squealing.

Coach shook his head, echoed Mac's unspoken sentiments. "Poor guy. If I didn't know how he's treated Charlie and especially Jennilee all these years, I'd almost feel sorry for him." Shook his head again. "Nope. No can do."

"Ah, the joys and miseries of living in a small town."

"Yeah, I expect he's gotten all the joy out of this one he's going to get."

Mort sped back home. A nasty little voice in his head kept asking, *Home for how much longer?* The first thing he noticed was a van from the cleaning company parked in the driveway —right beside where Celie's car was normally parked. Getting out, he walked around the van, toward the house. Where was Celie's car?

Stepped in the door to find an industrious crew hard at work. The place already looked better, more like its old self. One of the cleaning crew walked over to him.

"Are you Mort Johnson?"

"Yes. I'd like to thank you for coming on such short notice."

"Yeah, well. I already talked to your wife." *Bitch. Not just a bitch, a disgusting slob of a bitch. No wonder they'd had to call a company from Wilmington to come clean this place.* "We're going to have to up our fee considerably. She okayed it before she left."

"What? But the person I talked to told me..."

Trying to keep her tone polite, the cleaner couldn't keep the smug gleam out of her eyes. "That was before we got here and saw the place. It's going to take us at least two more trips, maybe three to…"

Mort sighed. "Do it. Did my wife say where she was going?"

Boy, did she. Said a lot more, too. None of it nice. "Something about going to Jacksonville for a massage and shopping because we were making too much noise and stirring up too much dust."

"I'll be in my den if you need me." Mort retreated.

"Oh, Mr. Johnson—this came special delivery and I signed for it. It looks important and your wife had already left."

Mort turned around, icy dread gripping his heart. Took the registered letter from the hand that held it. Staggered to his den and closed the door. The crew had already been through here, and it hadn't been that bad anyway. No one used his den when he wasn't home. Crossed to his desk and sat down heavily. Stared at the envelope like it was Pandora's Box. Stared for a long time. Stared at the logo in the return address corner. A woman's boutique—a very high priced, all inclusive, woman's boutique. Swallowed and tried to ignore the heavy, queasy lump in his stomach. Opened it slowly and ignored the letter, scanned the enclosed bill.

Almost had a cow when he saw that it was the exorbitant bill for Sylvie's prom dress—past due. And the jewelry. And her hairdo and makeup. And her nails. And her shoes.

Shoes couldn't really cost that much, could they?

And speaking of Sylvie—where was she? Mort slipped out of his den and upstairs. Maybe Sylvie was in her bedroom. She wasn't at graduation, for sure. Mort opened her bedroom door—as far as he could.

So much junk on the floor that the door would only open a crack, Mort shoved harder, like a bulldozer pushing against a boulder imbedded in the earth. The door gave way and he stared in disgust. He'd heard that teenager's rooms were always messy, but this was beyond messy and well into disaster. What had gotten into Sylvie? She'd always kept her room clean, even if it had tended to be cluttered.

Pizza boxes with half-eaten, moldering remnants still in them, fast food wrappers from McDonald's, take out boxes from every restaurant around littered the floor. No, not the floor. The piles. The floor was completely hidden beneath piles. Clothes and jewelry and magazines and shoes vied for space. The bed was unmade and piled high as well. The whole room looked like a mall that had been hit by a tornado and all the leftover debris pushed into a pile.

A pharmacy bag from a drugstore in Havelock caught his eye. Mort waded through the piles to Sylvie's dresser, picked up the bag. Sylvie had been sick and Celie hadn't told him?

Mort felt even more confusion when he picked up the bag. The tag stapled to the outside of the bag had Jenny's name on it. Why would Jenny need medicine? Maybe she'd left it when she stomped out. No, because it was dated last week, and she'd left in March.

Mort finished reading the tag, staggered back a step and dropped the bag. *Birth control pills!* He could understand Jenny having those—the way she and Charlie carried on, she probably needed a double dose. He still wasn't convinced Jenny hadn't had an abortion. Doc and Mac and Del had lied for her, just like always.

But why would Jenny's birth control pills be in Sylvie's bedroom?

Head pounding, rubbing his chest, Mort couldn't take anymore right now. His overloaded brain begged for mercy and he backed out of the room, practically ran over one of the cleaning crew. He hastily pulled the door shut and stammered, "L...leave this room. It's my daughter's and she'll take care of it."

Having gotten a good view of the bedroom in question, the woman just smiled and agreed.

∽

GRADUATION CEREMONIES WERE HELD OUTSIDE, on the football field. The crowd of parents and siblings, grandparents and aunts and uncles and friends of the family spread out to line both sides of the chain link fence around the field when they ran out of space on the bleachers.

Wild hoots and hollers greeted the last students' walk across the stage. Tossing their caps in the air along with the others, making their way to the bleachers, Charlie and Jennilee found Grandy and Donnie. Hugs all around, lots of back patting and congratulations.

Grandy wiped tears off her face. "I can't believe how many awards the two of you got. I'm so proud of you."

"One more and Jeff would've beaten me, and he was only a couple points behind me, almost got Valedictorian." Charlie grinned, kept one arm wrapped around Jennilee.

Grandy urged, "Let's go home. I know you've got plans to go out with Jeff and Michelle later tonight."

"We have to find Mr. Jubal and Miz Sadie and Mose first. I saw them earlier."

Charlie and Jennilee scanned the milling crowd. Head and shoulders above the crowd, Mose was hard to hide. Like fish swimming upstream, they wiggled and wriggled until they reached their goal.

Mindful of where they were and the large crowd of small minds surrounding them, Charlie and Jennilee let Miz Sadie hug them, simply shook hands with Mr. Jubal and Mose.

Mr. Jubal's grin was ear to ear. "You two..." Shook his head and grinned more. "If I finish every book I own, I won't be half as smart as the two of you."

Laughing and joking, the families wove their way through the crowd and back to their vehicles.

It took them awhile, because it seemed every single person attending graduation wanted to congratulate Charlie and Jennilee.

CHAPTER 34

Mort left the house right after the cleaners did and drove around aimlessly for awhile. Celie was in Jacksonville and there was no point in driving all the way there, at least an hour's drive both ways, to confront her. Tonight, or tomorrow, would be soon enough. Sylvie was a different matter.

Different comments from varied sources kept replaying in his head.

Tracy, telling him Sylvie was hanging around with that Jones boy—what was his name? Butch? Why on Earth would Tracy think that? All the Joneses were trash—fight at the drop of a hat, meaner than a snake, steal from their own mommas—trash. Mort tried to recall more about this…Butch.

One of the younger Joneses, still—a couple years older than Sylvie. Something about a car, and constantly being in trouble. A fairly distinctive car. Mort drummed his fingers on the steering wheel and tried to remember. Black. Butch drove a black car with heavily tinted windows, barely legal. Car or tinting. A black Trans Am with a gold bird, wings spread wide, painted on the hood around the spoiler, from the edge of the grill to the windshield.

No way. There was just no way Celie would let Sylvie hang around with scum like that. Now, Jenny—Mort could easily see Jenny hanging around with Butch. She fit the picture much better. Jenny was the one always in trouble, the one that had had an abortion, the lazy one with bad grades. She was practically glued to Charlie, and Charlie was nearly as bad as Butch.

Something else Tracy said rattled and called for attention, like a slimy drug dealer banging on the bars of his cell. Sylvie was failing? Had failed. Again, no way. Sylvie had always been the one with straight A's—all the way through school. Jenny must have paid off plenty of people to get the recognition she'd falsely claimed today.

Speaking of paying people—what was that crack the Coach made? Something along the lines of *if he could afford a lawyer?* Mort had plenty of money in the bank, besides Celie's trust fund. Checking account, savings account, CDs, and he owned a sizable portfolio of stocks and bonds. It had hurt to find out that the Judge's house wasn't theirs, but they still owned the smaller house in town that the Judge had given him and Celie for a wedding present. They'd been renting it out for years and investing the rent money.

Mort thought about going by the diner for supper, changed his mind and headed to the grocery store instead. He'd restock the pantry and frig, grab a pizza on the way home. Went to the Winn-Dixie in Morehead because he didn't want to be seen in the Red and White in the middle of downtown Chinquapin Ridge. Everybody and their brother would be there, and he just didn't feel like making small talk.

Passed, coming and going, a newly renovated restaurant out on the four-lane but on the town side and still within the city limits. Somebody had done a lot of work to the place and there was a big sign out front—UNDER NEW OWNERSHIP—GRAND RE-OPENING NEXT WEEK!

Pulling into his driveway, he noticed cars parked all the way down Del's long driveway, and the yard was full as well. Looked like they were having a celebration. Shaking his head as he unloaded the groceries from the car, he thought to himself—*Go ahead and have fun while you can. The truth about Jenny will come out sooner or later. You'll all be sorry. How could that many people be so blind to what was right in front of them?*

Mort had to rest twice before he got all the groceries inside. Mac's crack about seeing Doc rang in his head, even over his huffing and puffing. Jenny didn't even live here anymore and she was still affecting their lives. He wouldn't have high blood pressure or an ulcer if it wasn't for her.

Struggling with the last bags, something else Mac had said repeated itself. *Salvage something*. What had Mac meant by that comment? Salvage meant to…save what was left.

Mort put the groceries away and resolutely pushed it all aside. He'd talk to Celie as soon as she got home and get everything straightened out. Breathing hard, he headed upstairs to see if Sylvie was home yet. She wasn't.

Making his way back downstairs, he ate half the pizza, standing at the kitchen sink, all by his lonesome.

Not even the music and lights and laughter from next door could keep Mort awake long enough to wait for his girls to get home. His and Celie's bedroom was in the middle of the house, the AC was running wide open, all the windows closed, and still he could hear the party next door until all hours of the night.

∽

DEL LAUGHED and tried to catch her breath as her latest dance partner guided her to the edge of the whirling crowd and toward the refreshments. Charlie and Jennilee took a break from their music making and headed her way, reached the punch at the same time.

Handing Grandy a cup and then Jennilee before taking one for himself, Charlie and Jennilee raised their plastic cups to Grandy before taking a drink.

Grandy returned the gesture. "How did you two do all this? I thought you were going out with Jeff and Michelle?"

Laughter, followed by explanations. Jennilee shook her head and her face lit. "All we said was…"

"…we were going to a party with Jeff and Michelle.

"Yeah, but you didn't say the party was here!" Del looked around at the twinkling lights strung in the live oaks and shrubbery, at the brighter lights shining on the area they'd designated as the dance floor, at the food and fun and all the guests.

"You didn't…"

"…ask!"

"Charlie, Jennilee—this is supposed to be your time."

"It is."

"And we wanted to share it with you."

"We wouldn't be here…"

"…without you."

Shaking her head, town between laughter and tears, Grandy admonished affectionately, "You two are incorrigible!"

"We had good teachers." Charlie hugged Jennilee close and both of them looked at Grandy with shining eyes.

"Besides, everyone wanted to celebrate…"

"… your restaurant opening next week."

"There's no where we'd…"

"…rather be than right here."

"I'm all aflutter." Grandy patted her cheeks. "I can't believe it's really happening."

"Believe…"

"…it!"

"Everything's…"

"…ready."

Del eyed her two thoughtfully. "Ready thanks to you two. You've worked like dogs."

Laughter filled the air. "We wouldn't have done it…"

"…if we hadn't wanted to."

"Don't forget…"

"…Mose helped, too."

"Neither one of you is going to be able to speak intelligibly for two years. No one's going to know but half of what you're saying." Mose came up behind them, his deep laughter filling in the spaces left by their higher pitched tones.

More laughter.

"Mose…"

"…you know…"

"…how we are."

"That's what I said. Both of you are so used to finishing the other one's sentences—with Charlie going to college and you staying here—we're going to have to wait until you get together again before we find out what you're saying. You two are worse than listening to one end of a phone conversation."

Laughter wrapped around them, filled the air, wafted up into the trees and farther, up into the star-sprinkled velvety sky.

Later, much later, most of the guests gone home and most of the party mess cleaned up, a happy but tired crew collapsed on the porch.

Mr. Jubal and Miz Sadie sat together on the porch swing, Grandy and Donnie sat on the glider and Mose and Charlie sat sideways on the top step, leaning back against the posts of the porch railing. Jennilee sprawled contentedly, bonelessly, between them and against Charlie, his arms around her, Jewel asleep beside her.

Jeff and Michelle were the last to leave, with a wave and a *see you in the morning.*

"Y'all got plans?" Grandy stirred herself to ask.

Charlie nuzzled Jennilee's hair. "A bunch of us are heading to Shackleford in the morning. We'll finish the last bit on your restaurant next week. We're taking the weekend off, right guys?"

Jennilee murmured her assent and Mose grumbled, " 'Bout time you let us have a day off."

"Me? Jennilee's the one in charge."

Jennilee, her voice heavy with sleep and teasing, said, "Better enjoy it, because our next day off is 4th of July." Laughing, Jennilee held a hand out to Mose. He enfolded her much smaller hand, squeezed gently.

Charlie snorted, "See? What'd I tell you?"

A round of laughter spilled from everyone on the porch.

The soft smack of flesh hitting flesh and Donnie said, "That's the first mosquito I've seen all night."

"Charlie's spray must be wearing off."

"You sprayed?"

"The trees and shrubs and flowerbeds, what I could reach. It lasted for awhile. Long enough to have a good time."

"Speaking of time…"

"Time we all headed to bed."

"Got that right."

All the various parties got to their feet slowly, reluctant to end the wonderful evening.

As the round of good-nights started, Charlie and Jennilee snickered, then laughed out right. "We sound like…"

"…the Waltons'."

Another burst of laughter and everyone drifted off.

Charlie and Jennilee stood just outside the circle of light

cast by the porch light. A long kiss later, and then another and another, and Charlie whispered against Jennilee's lips, "Dream of me."

"Always. G'night."

Charlie backed away bit by bit, 'til nothing but their fingertips were touching, unwilling to lose contact with Jennilee until the last possible second. Jennilee stood and watched him until he reached his truck. Hand on the truck, Charlie encouraged her. "Go on in, Jennilee."

"I'm going."

" 'Night, Mary Ellen."

Jennilee was still laughing as she went inside and Charlie drove off.

∽

BOAT LOADED at the crack of dawn, they were long gone before the sun peeped over the edge of the world. Not Mr. Donnie's wooden skiff, but a sleek fiberglass boat—a twenty footer designed for speed, and all theirs.

Heading out Newport River to the Intracoastal waterway and then to Beaufort, they slipped out by Duke Marine Lab and Radio Island, headed across the Middle Marshes to Shackleford. An uninhabited island, Shackleford Banks was part of the Cape Lookout National Seashore. Once home to Diamond City and whalers and fishermen, with a population of around 600 people, severe hurricanes in the late 1800s had decimated the island. The people'd moved elsewhere and now the wild ponies and other wild creatures were the only permanent inhabitants.

Around nine miles long and varying from less than a quarter mile to somewhere around a half mile wide, it was a prime spot for picnicking and camping, fishing and shell hunting. Charlie and Jennilee, along with the rest of their gang had explored it from one end to the other.

The first to reach their designated meeting spot, Charlie and Jennilee didn't care, not in the least. The others would show up eventually. Saturday after graduation, most of the kids were going to sleep late after a night of partying.

Until then, they had the island to themselves. Running the boat close to shore, Charlie anchored. Clambering overboard, they waded in. Heading across the island, coming out on the ocean side, they wandered up and down the beach hand in hand, collecting shells.

Sitting, they watched the waves and the birds. The Garden of Eden must've felt like this, before the fall. Utterly peaceful, no sense of other people—just sand and water as far as the eye could see. Charlie and Jennilee might've been Adam and Eve, so isolated were they, and perfectly content to be so, needing no one else. Nothing but each other.

Charlie sat with his knees up, Jennilee between them, his arms around her. Jennilee nestled comfortably, her forearms and hands covering Charlie's, their fingers linked. Nuzzling his face into her hair, he murmured, "I think you're a mermaid."

"What?" Laughing, Jennilee turned her face to his over her shoulder, shared a quick kiss.

"You love water, and you swim like you've got gills."

"That makes me a mermaid?"

"Your eyes are the color of the ocean in summer—right there where the shallow water meets the deeper and the color changes from greeny-blue to a darker blue. Your eyes are that same color—greeny-blue in the middle and darker around the edges."

Jennilee smiled and shook her head. "You'll have to do better than that."

Bringing their joined hands to his lips, Charlie kissed her

ring finger right over her engagement ring. "Aquamarines are your signature stone, and they did originally come from a mermaid's treasure chest."

Jennilee shook her head again, bemused by Charlie's gentle teasing.

Burying his face in her hair, he told her, "Mermaids have beautiful, long hair—and yours is that. They can bewitch a mortal man with their beauty and their hair and their..."

"Charlie..." Jennilee protested laughingly.

"...voices. Their singing. You sing like an angel—or a mermaid. Maybe mermaids are angels with tails instead of wings."

Jennilee laughed harder. "Last I looked, I didn't have a tail, and I know I don't have wings."

" 'Tis said a mermaid can shed her tail and become human when she seeks her true love."

Sobering, Jennilee told him, "Were I a mermaid, I would forsake my underwater castle and all my jewels and my tail—forever, with no regrets—for just one kiss, one touch, from you."

Charlie cradled her, kissed her long and slow and deep. Melded their mouths together while one hand held her still and one hand roamed. Wearing nothing but her swimsuit with a T shirt over it, Charlie traced the outlines of her bikini bottoms, across her belly and thighs and hips, slid his hand up under the edge of her shirt and rubbed his knuckles across the sensitive undersides of her breasts.

Jennilee wound her arms around his neck. Moaning low in her throat, pressing her body to his, she held nothing back.

"Sweet, Jennilee. You are so sweet." Charlie kept up a ceaseless murmuring, praises and love words flowing from his lips. Kissed the side of her neck and reveled in Jennilee's passion as she angled her neck to give him better access, both of them so lost in their love for each other nothing else existed.

Crowing like a rooster, Jeff exulted, "Told you! Where's the five you owe me?"

"Sucker bet, Jeff. We all knew what they'd be doing."

Distinct laughter flowed from a crowd of people.

Tightening his hold for a moment, Charlie withdrew his hand from under her shirt, kissed her again for good measure. "Guess maybe you're not a mermaid."

"Oh?"

"Mermaids are supposed to be extremely shy and skittish, able to disappear in a blink, and you're still here—despite the arrival of the gawkers."

"Maybe if we just ignore them, they'll go away."

Jeff crowed again. "Not a chance, Jennilee. We're here to stay!"

"Oh, well, then." Leaning her head back on Charlie's arm, Jennilee grinned at the circle of friends ringing them, close enough to block the sunlight.

Disentangling their limbs, Charlie rose gracefully, tugged Jennilee up. Pulled her close and kissed her thoroughly, ignoring the cries of *knock it off* and *get a room.*

∽

DEL HEARD the boat motor long before they showed up at the dock. The kids tied up, collected their stuff. Heading to the house, sunburnt, tired and happy, they spotted her coming across the yard and broke into wide grins.

"Hey guys! Guess I don't need to ask if you had a good time."

Jennilee hugged Grandy, one armed, kissed her on the cheek. "We had a great time! I brought you loads of shells.

We found a bunch of unbroken conchs and sand dollars and…"

"Can we talk about geegaws later? I'm…"

"Starving!" Jennilee and Grandy finished for him, punctuated by laughter.

Charlie indignantly informed them, "I was going to say *famished*, but…"

"Figured you would be. Supper's ready and waiting."

"Sounds good to me, cause lunch was about three days ago."

"Good thing we don't set the clocks by your stomach!"

Jennilee chattered excitedly as they washed up at the kitchen sink. "Grandy, you should've seen the sand dollars! Not the ones we brought home, but live ones! All over the bottom in this one spot at Shackleford, they're covered with pinkish…hair—almost like a crew cut. I guess that's how they move. There were tons of them. I've never seen live ones before. They were so neat. So beautiful. I…"

Looking from Jennilee's animated face to Charlie's, watching her, Del almost wept at the love she could so plainly see. Catching Grandy's expression, Jennilee turned to Charlie. Broke off, returned his look.

Charlie took several deep breaths, bent his head to her. "Not half as beautiful as you."

Jennilee tilted her face up, expecting a kiss.

Charlie didn't kiss her and he didn't move back, kept his eyes locked with hers. "Grandy—guess what I saw at Shackleford."

"I have no idea."

"A mermaid. A real, live mermaid. She was the most beautiful thing I've ever seen."

Jennilee laughed and laughed as she threw her arms around his neck.

∼

CHARLIE PICKED Jennilee up early every morning, dropped her off late. If they'd been close before, now they were practically attached at the hip.

Del's Diner was a smashing success from day one. All the locals knew just what a fantastic cook Del was, and she'd recruited Sadie to help. Between the two of them, if you couldn't find something on the menu you liked to eat, you weren't breathing.

Featuring good old fashioned home cooking, word spread, even among the tourists, and Del's quickly became *the* place to eat. Charlie and Jennilee bussed and waited tables, washed dishes, helped out any way they could.

A homey atmosphere, one that made you feel like a kid again going to Grandma's for Sunday dinner, was evident in everything from the butter yellow walls of the dining room to the overflowing plates and bottomless glasses of iced tea. From the tables and chairs Mose'd built to look like they belonged in some old farmhouse kitchen, to the old fashioned looking salt and pepper shakers and hot pepper vinegar bottles on every table, to the light fixtures and wide wooden floorboards, it radiated cheer and goodwill.

A couple antique hutches with glass doors graced either side of the main room. One was filled with Depressionware glass—the swirly blue-purple-green kind. Bowls, platters, vases—you name it. The other was filled with old bottles—medicine bottles of every shape and size, perfume bottles in exquisite shapes, brown glass Clorox bottles from pint size right on up to gallon. Milk bottles, Pepsi bottles, whiskey bottles—lots of whiskey bottles, some with the original corks still in them.

Charlie and Jennilee'd been collecting bottles for years, picking them up where ever they found them, mostly out in the marsh, or in the river. Early travel had been mostly by boat—finish with a bottle, toss it over the side. Nothing more than trash to the people of earlier centuries, they were treasures now.

Charlie and Jennilee surprised Grandy again and did the landscaping. Flowerbeds bordered the front walkway, overflowing half barrels dotted the parking lot. Two more half barrels flanked the steps, full of fragrant, welcoming rosemary. Hanging baskets and planter boxes on the porch rails added more color. Rocking chairs on the porch provided some extra seating and a bit of waiting room—they needed it.

Mose and Charlie and Jennilee built a long, L-shaped, glass fronted counter near the entrance, Grandy filled it with her cakes and pies and baked goods. Coming and going, patrons could peruse what they wanted for dessert. Or if they had something that particularly pleased them for dessert, they could buy a whole cake or pie, one cookie or a couple dozen cookies to take with them when they left. A great many people came in just for the desserts, and Del still took special orders.

Good thing they were all used to hard work, because a week into it, they'd already had to hire more help—twice.

CHAPTER 35

As busy and happy as Charlie and Jennilee and Grandy were with the restaurant, Mort was even busier and unhappier.

All the checks he'd written to pay Celie's bills started coming back—they all bounced. Every single one of them. Mort stomped into the bank, reamed out the young clerk who dared to wait on him, the one who told him there was no mistake—there was no money. None in his checking account, a mere pittance in his savings, and the automatic overdraft on his checking account was maxed out. Mort tried to cash in his CDs only to be informed that he no longer had any CDs.

The new bank manager, Mr. Whipple having retired, came out of his office and politely escorted Mort back into his office, closed the door.

"Mr. Johnson, calm down."

"I will not! I demand to know what is going on! Where is all my money?" Wild-eyed, fists clenched, spittle flying with each word, Mort stomped back and forth.

Keeping a close eye on the deranged looking man, Mr.

Hepler kept a hand close to the buzzer that would alert the clerks to a possible situation. "Mr. Johnson! You have—had—joint accounts, on everything, with your wife. Mrs. Johnson withdrew the money from the savings account and cashed in the CDs months ago. We have tried repeatedly to contact you about your checking account, to no avail. I suggest you go talk to her. And I suggest, you find another bank. This kind of behavior will not be tolerated."

Mort kicked the corner of the expensive desk and the manager pressed the panic button. This was getting way out of hand.

"I also suggest you leave. Now. Before you have to be escorted out."

"I'll be back and you'll be sorry. You're new here and you don't have a clue what's going on. There's been some kind of mistake. I demand…"

The manager heaved a sigh of relief as the obnoxious customer left, slamming the office door behind him and cutting off the rest of his tirade.

Mort drove straight back home, intending to drag the truth from Celie. He gave the mailbox a leery glance as he drove past it and kept going. Sylvie's car was in the drive, a hot red Mustang convertible, but Celie's Caddy was gone. Where the hell was she now?

Since he'd been home this time, she'd been gone more than she'd been home. He'd tried to talk to her when she came back from Jacksonville after staying gone two days. Mort had asked her sarcastically how long it took to get to Jacksonville and back and Celie had airily informed him she'd changed her mind. Gone to Myrtle Beach instead.

He pressed, she started crying, and that was the end of that. Celie'd claimed a migraine and gone to bed. Disappeared the next day before he had a chance to question her anymore, and pretty much stayed gone.

Well, Sylvie was home, for a change. He'd talk to her.

Sylvie met her father at the front door. "It is miserably hot in here! Do something about it! Call the repairman or something. I can't live like this!" She tried to brush past him and Mort grabbed her arm.

"You're not going anywhere, young lady, except my office. We need to talk."

Too shocked to protest, Sylvie let him propel her down the hall. What had gotten into him? He never spoke to her in that tone of voice. Jennilee, when she was in trouble, which was always, but never her.

"Where's your mother?"

"How should I know? She's your wife."

At her insolent tone, Mort felt his blood pressure shoot up another notch. "Sylvie, don't push me. I have had a bad day, a bad couple of weeks. First things first—how come you didn't tell me that you weren't going to graduate?"

Right on cue, Sylvie burst into tears.

"Dry it up, Sylvie. I want some answers, and I want them now. How come your room is a disaster? And the rest of the house? You're grounded until your room is spotless and you've done your share around the rest of the house. And why are there birth control pills on your dresser?"

Sylvie looked at her father, really looked. What she saw scared her. He'd never been like this with her, never treated her like this. "It's all her fault. She did this."

"Your mother?"

"No! Jennilee!"

"Jenny hasn't been here for months. How can any of this be her fault?"

"It…it just is. I'm not doing…any of those things. I'm not cleaning or…"

"Fine. You're grounded until I say so. Give me the keys to

your car and go to your room." Mort held out his hand, palm up.

"I will not! I'm going out. I've already made plans." Sylvie whirled and started out the door.

"If you take off in your car, I'll report it as stolen."

"You can't do that! It's mine!"

Mort shook his head. "You're not eighteen yet, and the title is still in my name. Get upstairs, and when you're finished with your room, you can come help me with the kitchen."

Sylvie slammed the door behind her. He could hear her stomping up the stairs and heard the distinct sounds of objects being thrown and crashing against the wall.

She was right about one thing—it was miserably hot in here. Mort got up and went to check the panel box. None of the breakers were tripped. That meant either the heat pump was shot or… He stopped dead in the middle of the kitchen. A totally silent kitchen. No hum from the frig, no lights on on the microwave. The kitchen clock was still, the hands frozen. The power was off. That explained it.

Took a step and froze again as the truth sank in. The power was off, alright.

Picked up the phone to see if he could wheedle the power company into turning the power back on 'til he could get his hands on some funds. No dial tone. Mort carefully replaced the handset, picked it up again just as carefully. Still nothing.

Numbly, he sat at the kitchen table and tried to figure a way out of this mess. A long while later, he heard the front door slam and a car gun its engine as it took off. If Sylvie had defied him and taken her car…

Mort looked out the front door in time to see the back of a dark car flying down the driveway. He didn't have to see the whole car to know it was a black Trans Am. A black Trans Am with a gold fire-bird painted on the hood.

CHARLIE'S BIGGEST FEAR, other than how Jennilee'd take their separation while he was at college, was Butch. To that end, he bought Jennilee a handgun. Deferring to Mose and Chief Mac's knowledge and training, Charlie got them to teach her how to use her weapon. Practiced until Charlie was satisfied and Jennilee was an expert shot.

Taught her more, at Charlie's insistence, about self defense. Again, Mose and Chief Mac knew a lot of little tricks that weren't in any manual. Things they'd learned the hard way, in combat. Dirty, nasty tricks—tricks that just might save your life.

Installed a CB radio in the new-used car Mr. Donnie'd given Jennilee for graduation so if she broke down on her weekend drives to and from State she could call for help.

Watching, Jennilee laughingly protested, "Charlie, I already feel conspicuous enough. Do you know how redneck a CB in a Crown Vic looks?"

Charlie hadn't even looked up from what he was doing. "Ask me if I care."

"Charlie…"

"Don't *Charlie* me. I'm antsy enough about you driving back and forth to Raleigh by yourself. That long straight stretch between New Bern and Kinston—there's nothing for miles and miles. If you break down… You've got two choices: I install this and you learn how to use it, or I'll hire someone to drive you."

"Don't you dare."

"Jennilee…"

Mr. Donnie caught their little exchange. "Jennilee, don't argue, or I'll drive you myself."

One look at Mr. Donnie's anguished face and Jennilee gave in, tears in her eyes.

Mr. Donnie tried to make light of his fears. "A Crown Vic is not conspicuous. Ostentatious, maybe." Took a deep, calming breath. "It's also one of the best cars out there—built heavy and built to last. That's why I got it for you, but things happen. You know how to change tires and stuff. Something happens you can't fix, you get on that CB, stay tight until the Highway Patrol gets there. You make sure you keep your doors locked, young lady."

Looking up, Charlie didn't say anything out loud, but Jennilee heard him loud and clear. *"Make sure your gun is in your hand, and be prepared to use it."*

Jennilee didn't bother to protest anymore. Lots of people, lots of women, drove that highway everyday—by themselves, and they were perfectly fine. They weren't her, didn't come with her overwhelming baggage.

∞

SUMMER PASSED in a blink and Charlie was off to college.

Charlie doing what he had to do so they could get married, Jennilee worked on her part of the bargain. Didn't tell Charlie, but the day they'd dropped him off at the NC State campus, she'd taken advantage of his absence and the multitude of shops.

It'd felt beyond strange to shop without him. Normally, the only time she did was the brief time they separated to buy each other's birthday and Christmas presents. Jennilee pretended that's what she was doing as she looked through material.

Knew exactly what she wanted. Grandy and Mr. Donnie watched knowingly as Jennilee picked out fabric in one store, pastel silk embroidery thread and ribbons in another. Since Charlie'd given her the picture of the wedding dress he wanted, they both wanted, she'd been planning. Planning that had gotten her through a lot of chores and unpleasantness.

Jennilee'd drawn out the dress pattern to suit her, had the patterns for the delicate embroidery done as well. Both were in her cedar chest. Now she had everything she needed to get started.

Making a mock-up out of muslin, she played with it until she was satisfied with the fit and flow. Decided in a hurry wide bell sleeves were only for women who did nothing but sit around and look pretty.

Working on her dress was how Jennilee got through the interminable first week Charlie was at college. Dark and cloudy that whole week, or so it seemed to Jennilee, like an endless gray day, a heavy fog settled in, blanketed everything so colors and sounds were muted, distorted.

Friday afternoon it started brightening up, and by the time she got to Raleigh, it was more sun than clouds. By the time she picked Charlie up, the sun was shining brightly.

Charlie drove home, one hand on the wheel and one arm around Jennilee. Going to their house first, they parked and got in some serious necking with a lot of heavy petting thrown in.

Jennilee didn't cry when they drove back to Raleigh late Sunday afternoon, didn't cry as she drove back home alone because she'd promised she wouldn't. Came in late and went straight to her room, called Charlie to let him know she'd made it safe and sound, went face down on her bed. Buried her face in her pillow and let the tears come. Jewel plastered herself against Jennilee and whimpered in sympathy.

Giving up on getting any sleep, she took her remaining, still dry pillow and headed downstairs, Jewel at her heels. Held it, and Jewel, and rocked.

Del stood in the living room doorway, as she had so many

times before. Felt her heart clench. Stubborn! Without a word, she headed for the kitchen.

Setting down the tray that held cocoa and cookies, Del turned on a lamp, still had to call Jennilee twice.

Jennilee looked up all hollow eyed, completely devastated, tears running a river. Closing her eyes, she buried her face in her now soaked pillow.

"Sweetie, you can't keep this up for two years. Even if you think you can, I can't stand it. You're breaking my heart."

"You can't tell Charlie." Jennilee's voice was raspy with tears.

"Then you'll have to. I don't know why the two of you have to be so stubborn about this. This...separation is tearing you apart. Go ahead and get married. He can still go to college."

"Grandy. Charlie's spent his whole life looking out for me, protecting me. He's always, *always,* been there for me. He needs this time away, needs time to himself. I'll be okay. I just have to...cry a bit. I think all those years of not letting it out have caught up with me."

"Hogwash."

Jennilee shook her head, tears glittering on her face and lashes. "They couldn't make me cry, Grandy, not for years and years. No matter what punishment they dished out. I got so used to holding it in, bottling it up, I only cried a few times. I'll be alright, I swear. If it bothers you that much, I can move out, go to one of the apartments at Garner House."

"Jennilee! Don't you dare even suggest such a thing! I never said it bothered me—I said it was breaking my heart, and it is."

"Grandy, if I can't convince Charlie I'll be okay without him hovering every second, he's only going to get worse. It'll get so bad, he won't let me out of his sight. I'll be as trapped with him as I ever was with them. I can take being separated for awhile if it means he won't end up resenting me later for being so needy and dependent."

Staring at Jennilee, Del patted the couch. "Come sit beside me. I'm not Charlie, but maybe I can comfort you a little."

Giving a watery laugh, Jennilee got up and resettled beside Grandy. Took a mug of cocoa and blew on it. "You're always a comfort to me, Grandy. I wouldn't have made it without you."

Sipping, dipping her cookies in her cocoa, Jennilee tried to explain. "Charlie thinks he needs college so he can provide a good life for me, for us. I've never said anything, and I've never cared about the money. He's never stopped to think we already have way more than most people ever will. If we never sold another house, never hit another lick, we wouldn't starve. Charlie needs the extra security of a degree, needs it for me—thinks he does. I'm willing to wait—what's a couple more years compared to the rest of our lives?"

"You two..."

"He doesn't want to have to go to work every day and leave me. I'm good with that. I enjoy helping him fix up houses but he... He is stubborn. Charlie doesn't want me to *have* to work. Ever. At all. He wants to wrap me up and put me on a shelf. If you tell him what a time I'm having, that's exactly what he'll do."

Finishing her cocoa, Del set her mug down and enfolded Jennilee in a tight hug. "What am I gonna do with you?"

"Love me, Grandy. Just like you've always done."

"Ah, sweetie, what would I do without you?"

Jennilee choked on a laugh. "You've got it backwards."

Melting against Grandy, she slipped an arm around Grandy's waist. Soft, so soft Grandy almost couldn't hear the words, Jennilee told her, "I need this, too Grandy. It sounds stupid, and I know I'm not handling this very well, but I need this time away from Charlie. I've leeched off him, and you—

emotionally—long enough. It's time I learned to stand on my own two feet."

There wasn't any response Del could make that Jennilee would hear. Besides, what would she tell Jennilee? That Jennilee was braver and tougher than most adults? That most adults would've caved under the work load and the psychological terror that had been Jennilee's entire life so far? Del hugged her close and stroked her bright hair, wished for the millionth time things had turned out different.

Wish in one hand and spit in the other—see which one fills up faster.

If only—if only Iris hadn't disappeared, if only Cynthia hadn't been murdered, if only Cynthia'd left a will, if only… Take it back farther than that. If only Cynthia's husband hadn't vanished, if the Judge hadn't been such a self righteous prick, if only Celie hadn't been just like him but worse, if only, if only, if only.

You could spout if onlies 'til the cows came home and it wouldn't make one damn bit of difference.

∽

JENNILEE WORKED AT THE DINER, worked on her wedding dress and anticipated Charlie's return. Older and smarter now, she had the time figured out down to the seconds. Every time she looked at a clock and despaired, she consoled herself with the thought it was that many less years/months/weeks/days/minutes/seconds until Charlie was home for good.

The Diner was packed, one of the waitresses left early, sick, and Jennilee was scrambling non-stop. Being Jennilee—running the dessert counter, waiting two stations, and carrying on a running conversation with one of her favorite customers—she made it look easy.

"The sides this evening are squash, fried okra, corn on the cob, or..."

"What's fried okra?"

Jennilee regarded the adorable five year old in front of her, wearing his favorite Superman T shirt, scrunched her face and shook her head. "Okra? It's nasty. Really nasty. You don't want any of that. Why don't you try..."

Ricky shook his head stubbornly. "That's what you said about pickled beets and 'sparagus and 'shrooms. They were all yummy. I wanna try the okra."

"Are you sure? You know if you ask for something and you don't eat it, Miz Del won't let me give you a cookie for dessert."

Ricky wavered—a sure cookie or an unknown vegetable? Considered. Jennilee liked to tease. If he told her he didn't like something, she didn't try to make him eat it, just grinned and smacked her lips and said, "Good! More for me!"

Nodding decidedly, Ricky affirmed, "Okra."

"Okra it is!" Jennilee finished taking their orders, winked at Ricky's grinning parents.

Hearing a commotion, Jennilee looked up. Her heart plummeted. *Butch and Sylvia.* Not just Butch and Sylvia, but what looked to be a loud, drunkenly belligerent Butch, a smirking Sylvia by his side.

Slapping her latest order on the counter so it could take its place in line, Jennilee bee-lined for the front door. The petite teenager hostessing didn't stand a chance against Butch sober. Drunk, there was no way.

Face and voice flat, eyes hard, Jennilee jerked her head. "Take my tables, Angie." Grateful for the reprieve, Angie slipped away like a ghost.

Weaving in place, exuding Mad Dog from his very pores, Butch gloated evilly, "Pershonal servish. What a nicsh touch. Maybe I'll have you for deshert."

"You'll get no service here. Leave, now."

"Who's gonna make me? Charlie-boy isn't here to protect his little slut. Where's your nigger? Maybe you're getting too old and he's found hisself another white girl." Butch looked around, whistled. "Here, boy. Come out, come out. How 'bout a threeshome?"

"You're a disgusting piece of human trash, Butch. Leave."

"Thish is a restra…restar…reshrant, ain't it? I wanna eat!"

"You're not eating here. Go home. Sylvia, take your drunken buddy and… Never mind, you're drunk, too. Just leave."

Sylvia smiled and snarked, "Leave, or you'll what? Call Chief Mac? He's eating at the Family Diner. Oops, maybe I shouldn't have said that."

"You never change, Sylvia. Too bad for you."

"Hey, all you cushtomers! This bitch won't let me have a table. Are you shure you wanna eat here? I heard they…"

"Enough, Butch. Get out. Now." Jennilee rolled up on her toes, flexed her fingers.

"You think you can take me? You little…" Butch raised his voice, raised his fist, leered. Instead of hitting Jennilee, he stumbled, deliberately smashing the side of his fist through the front of the glass display counter.

"D'jou see that? She shoved me into 'at counter! Somebody call the Sheriff."

Jennilee froze, hands clenched at her side.

No reaction wasn't what Butch wanted. Gripping a shard of glass, he swiped at Jennilee. He might be way bigger and meaner, but Jennilee had a lifetime of abuse and crawling bottled up inside her.

Without thought, running purely on instinct, Jennilee used some of the moves Mose and Chief had taught her, insisted she practice until they became second nature. Butch ended up on the floor, one hand cupping his balls and one covering his nose. Curled in a tight ball, bleeding like a stuck pig, writhing and moaning.

Sylvia dropped to her knees beside him, screaming. "Bitch! We'll sue! You can't attack customers like this!"

Jennilee stared coldly at them. "You forget yourself, Sylvia. The law's on my side. There's a whole room full of customers who saw Butch swing at me, saw me defend myself. This is our establishment, and there's no law that says we have to serve rude, abusive drunks. Speaking of which, you're not legal drinking age yet—you won't be eighteen for a couple weeks."

Mumbling from the heap on the floor.

The bell over the front door rang sweetly. Keeping her eyes on Sylvia and Butch, Jennilee asked, "What was that, Butch? I couldn't hear you."

Butch squirmed and panted, "I'll get you for this! I'll kill you! I'll burn this place down around you!"

"That's what I thought you said. Thank you for clarifying."

"Trouble, Jennilee?"

Jennilee shook her head. "Nothing I couldn't handle. Good to see you, Chief. I was just getting ready to call you."

"I was going to get some supper, but it looks like it'll have to wait. Time I take these two to Beaufort and get the paperwork done…"

Sylvia jumped to her feet, screaming shrilly. "I am not going to jail!" Lunged, long red nails aiming for Chief Mac's eyes.

Chief Mac spun Sylvia around, pinned her against the counter and slapped cuffs on her.

"Wanna bet? I'm still Chief of Police here, you're in my jurisdiction, you're still underage, and you're drunk. Not to mention aiding and abetting a criminal and assaulting a police officer. Sylvia Johnson, you are under arrest. You, too, Butch."

A stunned Sylvia leaned on the ruined dessert counter while Mac knelt and rolled a swearing and thrashing Butch over, handcuffed him as well. Read them their rights while Butch spat swear words and curses, still in too much pain to do more than curl into himself.

Jennilee jumped as a voice spoke and two young Marines flanked her. The one on Jennilee's left introduced them. "Sir, ma'am. I'm Josh and this is Will. My apologies for not stepping in quicker. We heard the raised voices, but by the time we realized just how bad it was and got over here, it was over. Not that you needed our help, ma'am."

Will held out a hand. "Congratulations, ma'am. That was…beautiful. Textbook take down."

Jennilee went red to the roots of her hair. "Jennilee, and thank you."

"Sir, if we can be of assistance?"

Chief Mac grinned and indicated Butch with a lift of his chin. "Name's Mac, and thanks. I could use some help taking out the trash. I'll get Sylvia if you two will take Butch here."

Sylvia attacked Chief Mac again, kicking and swearing at the top of her lungs. One swift move and Mac was behind her, escorting a squirming, squealing Sylvia out. Josh and Will each grabbed one of Butch's arms and muscled him up and out, still screaming threats.

By the time Josh and Will came back, Jennilee had most of the broken glass cleaned up, the customers settled back down and eating, and everything running smoothly once more.

Before Del and Sadie realized anything was amiss, it was over except for the cleanup. The two older women came out and hovered over Jennilee, cooking forgotten.

Jennilee shooed them back to the kitchen. "I'm fine. The

only thing hurt is the dessert counter and the contents. Doesn't look like anyone's taking any extras home this evening. Let me get this finished and…" Threw a desperate glance around the filled to capacity dining room and the equally filled porch full of people waiting their turn.

"Jennilee, we'll clean this up."

"Let you get back to waiting tables."

Looking from Josh and Will to the mess, then to the dining room and the waiting customers—back and forth—Jennilee gave in. "If you don't mind, I'd sure appreciate it."

Scurrying away, she left them to it. The tone inside the restaurant was subdued, the happy chatter muted. Keeping Angie taking orders and filling drink orders for a few minutes got Jennilee just about caught up.

"Here's your okra!" Delivering the order to Ricky's table, Jennilee took one look at Ricky's distraught face and came to a complete standstill. Unloading their plates, she crouched beside him.

"Ricky, honey, everything's okay."

Ricky sobbed and threw his arms around her neck. "He s…scared me. I th…thought he was going to h…hurt you."

Patting his back consolingly, Jennilee hugged Ricky to her. "Shh, baby. He's a bully. You have to stand up to bullies or they just get worse. I'm fine."

Ricky's high pitched tones permeated every corner. "Y…you protected all of us. You're like…like Superman. You look just like us, but you're brave and you fought the monster and won. You kicked butt!"

Somebody said, "Hear, hear!" and the whole room erupted into cheers and whistles. Standing up with Ricky in her arms, they could see Jennilee's beet red face—just before she buried it in Ricky's neck.

Later, much later, restaurant closed, customers gone, Jennilee collapsed into a chair in the kitchen. Laughed until she couldn't catch her breath. Del and Sadie eyed her, wondered briefly if they should call Doc. Caught her malady and started laughing themselves.

Mac and Mose, coming in the back door of the kitchen, found the women laughing like a pack of hyenas. Mose, having been apprised of the night's going's on by Mac, was in no mood to be placated.

Jumping out of her chair to fix them a plate, Mose laid a hand on Jennilee's arm. "Girl, what were you thinking?"

"Mose. Stop worrying so much. I wasn't thinking anything, and I didn't go looking for trouble. It came to me, and I handled it, just like y'all taught me. I'm probably safer right now than I've ever been."

Irate, Mose glowered. "And just how do you figure that?"

"Everyone in the diner, including Chief Mac, heard Butch threaten me. If any little thing happens to me now, the first person on the suspect list will be Butch. Maybe now he'll... leave me alone."

Mose and Mac snorted their disbelief as Jennilee dished up. She'd just set the plates in front of them when they heard a knock at the front door. Del went to see who it was, shadowed closely by Mac.

"We're closed. Y'all come again tomorrow and..." Getting a good look at the two on the porch, Del started laughing again, reached out, flipped the lock. "Come in, come in. I didn't get a chance to thank you properly."

Not even in the door good, Del hugged first one and then the other, making the tips of their ears pinken.

Del urged Josh and Will back to the kitchen with her. "We're back here, closing up for the night, but if you boys want..."

"No, ma'am. We didn't come back for more food, though it was the best we've ever eaten."

"We just wanted to make sure you ladies got home safe, but it looks like you've got it covered."

Josh and Will eyed Mose, shared a look.

"Mose, these are the gentlemen who helped me earlier—Josh and Will. Josh, Will, this is Mose."

Two retired Marines and two active duty Marines eyed each other, and no words were necessary.

Surrounded by warriors, extremely overprotective ones, Jennilee told them, a tad desperately, "Thanks again, and if there's ever anything…"

Sensing her tension and sure of the cause, Josh said slowly, "There is one small thing."

Jennilee nodded encouragingly, hoping he'd ask for…a cake or a pie…free meals for the rest of his life. Something simple.

Taking his turn at teasing, Will stated, "We couldn't help but notice your engagement ring."

Jennilee blinked, raised a brow. "Sorry guys, I'm taken."

Josh quipped, "We don't know the lucky guy, but if he ever changes his mind, we'd like to put our names at the top of the list."

Silence, followed by Jennilee's laughter ringing out. "Not a chance—of Charlie changing his mind, that is. Seriously, I appreciate what you did, and I'd like to repay you."

"You already gave us our supper."

"Little enough in light of what you did for me. A bunch of other customers offered to pick up your tab as well."

"We didn't have a chance to do much—you beat us to it." Shifting his gaze to Mose and Mac, Josh stated, "You two taught her."

Nods from both the older men.

Mac, all business, asked Josh and Will, "Where y'all stayin' in case I need further statements?"

"Right now, the barracks on base. We've been looking at

houses and apartments, but we haven't found anything yet. We'd like to stay together, split the rent."

Sharing a look, Mose and Mac grinned at each other like the cat that got the cream. Mose smirked at Jennilee. "We just might be able to help you with that."

Jennilee stuck her tongue out at him.

"It just so happens I know of a two bedroom apartment coming up empty here shortly."

Two more babysitters! Jennilee gave a mock groan that garnered laughter from all the other adults in the kitchen.

CHAPTER 36

Celie's screeches rang and echoed inside Mort's aching skull. "You have to do something! You have to! You can't leave my baby in jail all night—she's locked up with *criminals. Do something!*"

Mort watched Celie pitching a serious hissy, and realized he didn't much care anymore. "What would you like me to do?"

"Get her out! Are you deaf? Pay her bail, hire a lawyer. Do something for once in your useless life! Grow a spine!"

"We have no money, remember?" Sighing tiredly, Mort looked around and shook his head. How could Celie forget something like that?

"You don't need money to get her out. Just go do it." Celie tried wheedling now, and Mort found it every bit as distasteful as her diatribe.

"It's more than just underage drinking. Sylvia's also being charged with drunk and disorderly, aiding and abetting, DUI, assaulting an officer, and a couple of other things I can't remember. There's no way we can come up with bail money.

We don't have a blessed thing to put up as security. She'll just have to spend the night."

Mort watched, detached, as completely detached as if he was watching a particularly bad movie and the TV remote was broken. Celie's theatrics didn't move him anymore—and when had that happened? They'd fallen into a pattern early in their marriage—Celie threw a fit and Mort soothed her and did what she wanted. No more.

When tears didn't work, Celie threw another temper tantrum and stormed out. "This is all Mac's fault! Trumping up the charges to make Sylvie look bad. He's always hated my Sylvie! If you won't help, I know someone who will. I hate this dump!" Her words rang out loud and clear right before the door slammed behind her.

Mort sat down heavily on the lumpy couch, careful to avoid the broken spring. He didn't much like this place either, but it was the best he could do. Two months, and this place looked as bad, if not worse, than the Judge's house before the cleaners. Since they'd been evicted, they'd already had to move twice.

Leaning his head back and closing his eyes, Mort faced some truths. Unpleasant ones. His daughter was far from the paragon she'd always appeared, and her mother was worse —far worse.

When confronted with the fact that they were broke, practically destitute, Celie had cried and told him there must be some mistake—they couldn't be broke. When he'd assured her they were—totally—she'd pitched a hissy then, too, and disappeared for a couple of days. To some spa, no doubt. Mort wondered tiredly how she'd paid for it.

Celie had avoided as long as possible the fact that the Judge's house didn't belong to her, had never belonged to her and that the house could be taken away any time. Avoided it right up to the day the men in suits came back, took one quick look around, and served Mort and Celie with their eviction notice.

They'd been allowed to take what they could load up in twenty-four hours. Mort had done most of the loading while Celie sat and boohooed. Mort had thought to stay at a motel until he could evict the tenants of their small house, the one the Judge had given him and Celie for a wedding present.

It shouldn't have come as any surprise, wasn't really, to find that the house was no longer theirs, hadn't been for years. Celie had sold it, without a word to Mort. That money was gone, with no record or recollection of how or where. He'd found them a cheap room in a sleazy motel on the outskirts of Havelock for a couple of nights, until they could find something to rent—a couple of nights that had turned into a couple of weeks.

Then he'd found this 10' x 50' trailer on the edge of town in a seedy trailer park. The tantrum Celie had pitched when she laid eyes on it should have gotten them arrested for shooting off illegal fireworks. They'd moved in, if you could call it that, and things had gone downhill from there. Those fireworks were nothing compared to the show when Mort suggested Celie quit whining and get a job.

Mort's stomach growled and he thought about going to the Family Diner, thought about the pocket change that was all he had left to get him to his next payday. Oh, well. His doctor had been after him for years to shed a few pounds.

∼

JENNILEE'D CALLED Charlie from the Diner as soon things calmed down sufficiently, again as soon as she got home. Might as well get it over with. He'd find out anyway—if he didn't already know. Heaving a sigh, listening to the phone ring on the other end, she couldn't find it in her heart to be angry with anyone for caring.

Laid back on her pillows and stroked Jewel. Listened to the phone ring. And ring. And ring. No answer meant one of two things—the simple explanation, the one she hoped was the right one—was Charlie was working late or studying elsewhere. The one that was probably correct—the one Jennilee dreaded—was Charlie wasn't answering because someone else had already called and he was headed home.

Rolling off the bed, Jewel at her heels, Jennilee sighed and quietly headed downstairs.

∽

STANDING in the living room doorway as Grandy was wont to do, Charlie drank Jennilee in. Curled in their rocker, fast asleep, Jewel in her lap. Raising her head and thumping her tail, Jewel didn't bark, didn't get up.

Jennilee dragged heavy eyelids up to find Charlie sitting on the couch, staring.

"How long have you been here?"

"A while."

Jennilee struggled to wake fully. "Silly man. You've got a big test tomorrow. You can't…"

"Don't tell me what I can't do! Nothing—*nothing*—is more important than you."

"Charlie. I'm fine. He never laid a finger on me—I swear. I did just what you had Mose and Chief Mac teach me, and it worked."

"Jennilee… What were you going to do? Not tell me about this, just like all the other times he came after you?"

She explained patiently, "Charlie, I called before I left the Diner, again as soon as I got home, and I've been calling. When you didn't answer, I came down here to wait for you."

"You were that sure I'd come home?"

"As sure as I was that someone would tattle."

That startled a grudging laugh out of him, dispersed most of his temper and a bit of the worry.

"Hey! Guess what? Or do you already know?"

"That you've got two more bodyguards?"

Jennilee rolled her eyes. "Josh and Will are every bit as overprotective as you are."

Charlie snorted.

"Mose offered them one of our apartments."

"That's good enough for me."

Jennilee made a rude noise. "Figured it would be." Nudging Jewel to the floor, she stood. Closing the distance between them, Charlie crushed her to him. Holding her tight, too tight, he stroked a hand down her hair.

"Woman, you scare me to death."

"Never. Just keeping you on your toes."

Charlie muttered, "If that's the case, I should be a world class ballerina by now." Sinking into the rocking chair with a laughing Jennilee in his arms, in his lap, Jennilee melted contentedly into Charlie's familiar warmth.

"So, how'd you get here?"

"Borrowed a car."

Rocking until almost five, by the time Grandy got downstairs a scant half hour later, Jennilee had a full breakfast on the table. Eggs, fried potatoes, grits, bacon, ham, red-eye gravy, biscuits, and a big pot of coffee.

"Mornin' Charlie. Figured you'd be here."

Charlie gave Grandy a hug, leaned in so she could buss his cheek. "You figured right."

"Thought you had a big test today?"

"Not 'til 10:00. I've got time to make it back."

"Cuttin' it close, Charlie Bear."

Charlie grumbled, "I'm going. I wanted to say hi to you before I left. You two act like you can't wait to get rid of me."

Jennilee shivered and moved to the sink, hiding her expression from Charlie. Stepping up behind her, he wrapped her in a hug. Jennilee turned, melted into him. Holding her, Charlie rested his chin on her head and stared at what he could see of the empty house across the yards.

It might as well be invisible for all the attention Jennilee paid to it. Hadn't given it a second glance since the day she walked out. Hadn't paid any attention while her relatives still lived there, didn't pay any attention when they were evicted. Charlie couldn't blame her—that house held nothing but bad memories for Jennilee.

"You better get going." Muffled against his chest, Jennilee's voice sounded teary. She looked up, eyes dry.

"See you Friday."

Jennilee nodded. "Here. I made some biscuits for you to take back. Ham, ham and egg, ham and egg and cheese."

"Are you trying to founder me?"

That got the barest of smiles from her and a sassy reply.

"If you eat all that, you've got no one to blame but yourself. Give some to whoever you borrowed the car from."

∼

A WEEK after Charlie's middle of the night jaunt, finished with classes for the day, he spotted Jennilee.

The classmates walking with him stared as Charlie stopped in mid-word and mid-stride, their eyes following his gaze to the beautiful young lady leaning against the hood of an old blue truck.

Never taking his eyes off Jennilee, Charlie handed the books he was carrying back to their owner. Rather, held them out, waited a beat and let go. Didn't even notice when the books thudded to the sidewalk, scattering papers everywhere.

Watching Charlie arrow straight to the woman, Tony started laughing at the petulant look on Marlee's face. "Charlie told you up front he was engaged."

"So what? He's not married yet."

"And you wouldn't care if he was. I tried to tell you he's just being polite. You might as well quit chasing him. He can't even see you."

Tony looked from the girl beside him to the one Charlie was heading for. Marlee might have beauty and money and brains, but Charlie hadn't given her a second look, had completely ignored her endless invitations and innuendos.

Lots of young couples, supposedly in love, were all over the campus. Usually no one paid any attention to the lovebirds. Everyone within range stopped and watched the interaction between these two.

Stopping a couple steps away from Jennilee, Charlie absorbed the sight of her like a dry sponge sucking up water. Jennilee remained still, leaning back against the truck, eyeing him every bit as intently.

Charlie swept his eyes from top to bottom and back up. Jennilee wore a new dress, one she'd sewn, and her hair was down, just the way he liked it. Charlie's eyes followed the spray of embroidered flowers that splashed up the mid-calf skirt and across the fitted bodice. Jennilee did love to embroider on things.

Giving a passing thought to how her wedding dress was coming along, he knew better than to ask. He'd see it on their wedding day and not a second before.

Closing the distance, Charlie stood thigh to thigh with her. Neither spoke. Reaching over her shoulder, gathering her hair in one hand, Charlie brought the mass to his face. Inhaling deeply without taking his eyes off hers, keeping his hand fisted in her hair, he touched his forehead to hers, wrapped his arms around her and tucked her close.

Hands on his waist, Jennilee dropped her head, pressed her face against him.

The entire crowd around them let out a breath they hadn't known they'd been holding.

Feeling the fine tremors running through her whole body, Charlie tightened his arms and waited. Jennilee'd just been here Friday, spent the weekend. Driving the truck today instead of the car, and obviously upset.

Taking a deep breath, Jennilee pulled back enough to see his face. Hated to give him this bit of bad news, dreaded it with every fiber of her being. "It's started."

"Oh, baby. I'm so sorry."

Jennilee shuddered, clutched his shirt. "I wanted to tell you face to face. I didn't want someone…"

"Easy Jennilee-love. Nobody's called. Let's go somewhere and you can catch me up." Charlie kept an arm around her, kept her close, escorted her to the driver's side door.

"It's bad."

"Worse than we expected?"

Jennilee sighed. "No, but still…"

"Bad enough."

"Hey, Charlie!" Tony grinned. Charlie'd told him his girl was beautiful, but every guy said that.

"Tony. Sorry to walk off like that." Drawing Jennilee closer, Charlie said proudly, "Tony, this is my Jennilee. Jennilee, meet Tony Marcellini. I told you about him. We just met a week or so ago, and he's already the best friend I've got here."

Dredging up her manners, Jennilee held out her hand. "Pleased to meet…" Froze as a light came on, let her smile light her face. "Thank you for letting Charlie use your car."

"You're more than welcome. Thank you for the breakfast." Tony held Jennilee's hand longer than necessary, Jennilee's smile making him lose all his good sense.

A sultry female voice intruded. "Aren't you going to introduce me, Charlie? I thought I was your best friend here."

Charlie gave Jennilee a reassuring squeeze. They'd both been through this a thousand times. Charlie'd been chased all through school by other females, hadn't so much as been tempted. Marlee was no different, no matter how highly she thought of herself.

"Go away, Marlee. Charlie's busy, and taken." Tony winked conspiratorially at Jennilee.

Tossing her head so her hair swung just so, Marlee pouted, "I'm sure I don't know what you're talking about. I'm just trying to be friendly."

"Yeah, like a viper."

"Tony! Was that nice?"

"No, but true."

Jennilee made an impatient movement, needing to be alone with Charlie. He picked up on it immediately. "Jennilee, this is Marlee. We have some classes together. Marlee, this is Jennilee."

"Classes together? We're lab partners. I thought…"

"You thought wrong, Marlee, and I've told you that over and over. I'll be your classmate and friend. That's it."

Marlee stared. She'd figured Jennilee, being from Charlie's hick town, would be a backwoods pushover. The look Jennilee was giving her said she'd been down this road, more than once. Told Marlee plainer than words Jennilee was bored to tears with the scenery.

"Not to be rude, but we've gotta go. Family emergency." Charlie edged Jennilee a step closer to the driver's side door.

Marlee smiled brightly, falsely. "What? She's ditching you for a new guy?"

Charlie pinned Marlee with an icy glare. Jennilee sighed

and turned her face into Charlie's shoulder, dismissing Marlee like a pesky bug.

Marlee protested, "It was a joke. You know—ha, ha."

"Nothing funny about it, Marlee. Excuse us." Opening the door, Charlie held it for Jennilee.

"Charlie, you want me to tell dad you'll be late, or you won't be in at all?"

"Tell him... Never mind, Tony. We'll ride by there." Handing Jennilee in, Charlie got in, cranked the window down as he regained some of his composure. "You need a ride?"

Marlee struck a pose, breasts out, hip cocked, head tilted. "I'd love a ride. I'm going to..."

Charlie dismissed her as fast as Jennilee had. "Give it up, Marlee, unless you wanna ride in the back. Tony?"

"Yeah, since you're going that way. I'd appreciate it. Gino drove today and he's got late classes."

Tony got in just in time to hear Charlie question Jennilee.

"How come you're driving the truck?"

Sounding far away and dazed, Jennilee answered slowly. "What? Oh. I was using the truck, running errands for Grandy and I stopped by Mr. Tom's office. He was just getting ready to call me, and...and well, here I am."

"Jennilee, I've gotta go by Mr. Carlo's. I told you about him—just started working for him. Won't take but just a minute."

Jennilee nodded, her mind a million miles away.

Driving one-handed, lacing the other through Jennilee's, Charlie squeezed reassuringly. "Stay with me, Jennilee."

They'd get through this, no matter how bad it seemed right now.

"Guess what, Jennilee?" Didn't get an answer, wasn't expecting one. "Guess how many brothers and sisters Tony has?"

A groan from Tony and Charlie continued. "Nine, Jennilee. *Nine.* Can you believe it? You don't even want to know how many cousins and aunts and uncles there are."

Jennilee looked at Tony as if he'd just admitted to being a three-headed, eight-legged, purple and green alien from another galaxy. "Nine?"

"Yep. 'Fraid so."

"Nine?"

Tony started ticking off names on his fingers. "My oldest brother is Carlo Jr. Then there's Frank, and Isabella, and Sophia, and Gino, then me. After me there's Alessandro and Angelina—they're twins—then Russo and the baby, Nicoletta." Waggled the fingers he was holding up. "Yep, that's nine."

"You have…" Jennilee took a moment to tally. "…five brothers and four sisters?"

"Guilty."

"Wow. I can't imagine."

Charlie listened gratefully as Tony regaled Jennilee with tales of his brothers' and sisters' exploits and escapades. Pulling up, trying to figure out how to persuade Jennilee to come inside instead of sitting in the truck and brooding, Charlie was even more grateful when Tony beat him to it.

Tony took one look at the vehicles parked in the driveway and down the street. "You gotta come in, Jennilee—looks like most of the family's here. Come in and meet them. The rest will probably show up."

Waiting for her to say no, Charlie just about fell out of the truck when she asked tentatively, "You sure it's okay? I don't want to intrude."

Tony grinned. "Trust me, Jennilee. In a family as big as ours, one more person doesn't make any difference."

"It's like...Thanksgiving." Holding tight to Charlie's hand, Jennilee stared in amazement at the people everywhere. Old people, young people, middle aged people, babies. And food. Lots and lots of food. "Tony, if you're celebrating something, we'll come back another time."

Charlie watched Jennilee like she was watching Tony's family. She hadn't taken to any one like this since Mr. Cyrus, and he still didn't know why she adored Mr. Cyrus the way she did.

"Celebrating?" Tony looked around quizzically. "Oh, because of all the food and stuff? Nah—it's always like this. A madhouse."

"Always?"

"Oh, yeah." Smiling widely, Tony dragged them deeper into the melee, right into the heart of it—his mama's kitchen. "Mama, someone I want you to meet."

The round-figured woman stirring something at the stove turned and beamed at them. "Who is this?"

"Mama, this is Charlie's girl, Jennilee."

From the look on Jennilee's face, she was no longer in any hurry to get him alone. All for anything that got her mind off their troubles, leaning close, Charlie whispered, "Be right back."

Jennilee nodded, unable to take her eyes off Tony's mother. *Ten kids?*

"I am so glad my Antonio brought you here."

"Pleased to meet you, ma'am."

"Teresa."

"Yes ma'am. I mean...Miz Teresa. Anything I can do to help?"

Smiling broadly, Teresa gave Tony a motherly look he had no trouble interpreting. *See? See! This is the kind of girl you need to bring home.* "Not in that dress. It is exquisite—the stitching is so fine."

Jennilee confided, where normally she wouldn't have admitted anything. "It's mine. Dress and embroidery."

A horde of people swept in, surrounded them. Finding herself in the middle of a laughing, chattering crowd, Jennilee struggled to keep names and faces together. In constant movement, like a school of fish—noisy fish with black, curly hair and black, laughing eyes.

Jennilee absorbed sights and sounds and tried to stay out of the way. Tried to comprehend a permanent family this large and loving, if the jokes and teasing and nicknames streaming back and forth were any indication.

A toddler fell and bumped his head, almost at Jennilee's feet. Fast as Jennilee was, before she could reach him, a woman she assumed was the boy's mother thrust a squirming baby into Jennilee's arms and scooped up the squalling toddler.

Jennilee's face softened and went all dreamy. The baby reached out a chubby hand to Jennilee. Catching the baby's wrist, Jennilee kissed the sweet fingers, lost herself in the magic. Looked up to find Charlie standing right in front of her.

For the second time that day, a large crowd of people stopped what they were doing to observe Charlie crossing a space to stand with Jennilee. The love and longing on her face was as visible as airport beacons guiding in a plane.

Charlie held out a finger to the baby. She gripped it, her wrist still in Jennilee's loose clasp.

Desire was written all over Jennilee's face in great big neon letters. *I want this.*

Charlie knew she didn't mean just the baby, although she wanted that, too. Jennilee wanted the whole shebang—the huge family, the overflowing home, the loving chaos.

The raw emotions on her face instantly and forever won the undying loyalty of Tony's big, noisy, Italian family.

"Hey!"

Looking down at the imperative tone, Charlie and Jennilee saw a gorgeous little girl with a kool-aid mustache and a gap toothed grin.

"I'm Bella." Ebony eyes framed by lush lashes glanced at Charlie, focused consideringly on Jennilee. "Are you a princess?"

Meeting Charlie's amused gaze, Jennilee looked back to the little girl, shook her head solemnly. "Not that I know of, Bella, but Charlie here thinks I'm a mermaid."

The little girl's eyes widened and her mouth formed an *o* of surprise. "Really? A mermaid's way cooler than a princess."

The little girl raised her arms in silent demand and Charlie obligingly picked her up. Both of them took in Jennilee's ocean eyes and bright gold hair as Charlie speculated. "Maybe Jennilee's a mermaid-princess. What do you think?"

Tilting her head, the child nodded vigorously. "Will you..." Her face fell. "You can't go out and play, 'cause you got your good clothes on. Will you come back someday, maybe play in the pool with us?" Bella cast a speculative glance at Jennilee's sandaled feet, and everyone in the room knew what the child was wondering. *If she gets wet, will her mermaid tail appear?*

"I'd love to."

"Hey, Princess! We're about the same size—would you like to borrow some clothes?"

The whole crowd laughed uproariously at Jennilee's instant nickname as Angelina—Angel—made her offer.

Jennilee blushed and grinned, handed the baby back. "If it's not too much trouble."

Bella latched onto Jennilee's hand and the trio headed upstairs.

Charlie heaved a sigh of relief. "Miz Teresa, may I use the phone? I'll pay you for the calls—they're long distance."

"You'll do no such thing! Tonio, show him the phone in your father's office, and don't take any money from him. Charlie, your money is no good here, so don't even try!"

Tony showed Charlie to his father's office.

"Tony, stay. This won't take long."

Grinning, Tony agreed. " 'Sides, if I stay, I can make sure you don't accidentally drop some money or something. You better not disobey mama."

Tony tried not to eavesdrop, but it was hard not to hear Charlie's side of the conversation.

"Grandy, hey." A pause as Charlie listened. "Yeah, that's what I was calling to tell you. She's here." Pause. "Seems to be, as well as can be expected." Pause. "I know. We knew this was coming. I'm not sure what she—we—are doing about coming home today. We haven't had a chance to talk. I'll call you as soon as we decide. Don't wait up for us, in any case." Pause. "Go on, it sounds busy. Love you, too. Bye."

Charlie hung up and dialed another number. "Hi, Miz Emma. This is Charlie. Is Mr. Tom available?"

Tony didn't have a clue who Mr. Tom was, but he must have been expecting Charlie's call.

Charlie started talking again almost immediately. "Mr. Tom." Pause. "Pretty hard, although it wasn't unexpected." Pause. "Jennilee wants to what? Nossir. She's just panicking. Sink or swim, we're in this together. We've got the utmost faith in you, if not the legal system." Pause. "Thank you, and we'll be in touch." Hanging up, Charlie scrubbed a hand over his face.

Looked up to find Tony and Mr. Carlo, concerned looks on their faces. "I appreciate the use of your phone, Mr. Carlo. I made one call to Del's Diner and one to Tom Stimpson's

Law Office. Miz Teresa already told me I wasn't allowed to pay for the calls, but I will repay you."

Carlo waved him off, well aware it was a futile gesture. "No need." Prompted by concern, he asked, "Jennilee is embroiled in some legal trouble?" Her actions in the kitchen had endeared her to all of them, and they'd taken her into their hearts instantly.

Charlie eyed them. He and Jennilee weren't normally wont to air their dirty laundry in public, but as fast and hard as she'd taken to Tony's family, she wouldn't care. She'd need all the friends she could get to make it through this.

Sucking in a deep breath, Charlie blew it back out and raked his hands through his hair. "Long story short—Jennilee's mom died when Jennilee was little. Her aunt and uncle got custody—of Jennilee and her trust fund. They did a lousy job of raising Jennilee and they've blown all the money. They're greedy, sanctimonious SOBs and they want more. Want what we've worked all our lives to earn and build. They're taking her to court, to try and prove that what we have we stole from them. I don't think they have a snowball's chance—we've kept all our receipts and we have detailed ledgers—but I hate for Jennilee to go through this. She doesn't deserve this—not any of it."

"If there's anything we can do…"

"Not that I know of, Mr. Carlo. Either this will work out or it won't. It's not even the money so much. I'd give it to them if I thought for one second they'd take it and go away. They won't. They're leeches—sadistic leeches—and they'll never leave her alone until they bleed her dry, body and soul. If it was up to me, I'd spend every last penny we have to shut them down, once and for all. Jennilee can't take much more, so I'm not going to push it."

"We're here if you need us."

"Thank you, Mr. Carlo. You have no idea how much that

means to both Jennilee and myself. Jennilee's the most important thing in my life. I may have to be gone—a lot. If you need to hire someone else, I understand."

"Take care of your lady, Charlie. We'll worry about the catering and the remodeling later."

CHAPTER 37

"Grandy! Tony has the most marvelous family! Five brothers and four sisters. I can't even count how many aunts and uncles and cousins and nieces and nephews. I told them about you and they all want to meet you. You have to come to Raleigh and meet them. Please?"

Del listened to Jennilee rattle on.

"Grandy—the Marcellini's own and operate a catering business. Miz Teresa—that's Tony's mama—gave me some great ideas I'd really like to try at the Diner." Jennilee wound down at Grandy's silence. "If you want to, that is. It's your place."

"Jennilee! Don't be silly. It's as much yours as mine. If you want to try something, we will. I'm just enjoying listening to you. It's a rare treat to see you this excited."

Running to the door and back, Jewel danced in a circle, hurrying Jennilee.

"Okay, okay. I'm coming." Jennilee went out, still talking to her little mutt.

Charlie and Grandy watched them disappear. "How's she doing, Charlie? Really?"

"Breaking my heart, Grandy. Mr. Tom told me she asked him about putting everything solely in my name. No dice—we sink or swim together. Jennilee's terrified they're going to lie their way into our money, just like they've lied about so many other things. Did she say anything to you?"

"Not a peep, Charlie. Jennilee found out and took off without a word. I wouldn't have known at all if Tom hadn't called, and then you."

"That's what I figured. We're going to have to keep a close eye on her. I've got a feeling this is going to get real ugly, real fast."

"Rock her, Charlie. See if she'll sleep a bit. Jennilee barely sleeps anyway—she's up all hours of the night working on her 'projects'. She helps me at the Diner, and Lord only know what other pies she's got her fingers in."

~

DEL STOOD in the hallway and listened. Not right maybe, but how else could she find out anything? Jennilee was as close-mouthed as a clam. The soothing squeak of the rocker punctuated their words.

"Jennilee, I don't want you to worry about this. I'm not going to lie to you and tell you they don't have a snowball's chance, because we both know that just because something is right doesn't mean right always wins. If they do, and I'm not saying I think they will, we'll start over. We worked hard before to get where we are, and we can do it again."

"No, Charlie! I won't let them do this to you, to us."

"Jennilee-honey. We both know what a conniving, back-stabbing bitch she is, and there are enough people still around that remember your grandfather and will side with her just because of who she is. I just don't want you to worry about something neither of us has any control over. We've got each other, and that's all that really matters."

"Prepare for the worst and hope for the best?"

"Ke sera sera."

"Do I look like Doris Day to you?"

Charlie eyed Jennilee thoughtfully. "No, you're much more beautiful."

Jennilee's laughter spilled out, wrapped around both of them, flowed out into the hallway and lightened the shadows surrounding Del. "I think you're just a tad prejudiced."

"Beauty is in the eye of the beholder."

"What is this—cliché night?"

"I can spout them all night long."

"A wise guy, eh?"

"Sure, Moe."

"Why, I oughta…"

Del shook her head and headed upstairs, glad her two chicks could indulge in a little silliness. Even if it was only for a couple of hours before Charlie headed back to college. Jennilee had been adamant about that. There wasn't anything he could do here right now, and he didn't need to miss any classes.

Charlie was driving the truck back and parking it at the Marcellini's. He'd been adamant about that.

∽

"HOUSE? YOU CALL THIS A HOUSE?" Tony stared, whistled, stared some more. "You could lose my whole family in this place."

"Yeah, well…" A rare day off from classes, Charlie'd bee-lined for Jennilee and the coast, dragging a willing Tony along.

"If we ever get it fixed up, you're all welcome, anytime."

Jennilee didn't say it out loud, but they heard her unspoken, *if we don't lose it.*

Tony wandered around. Their *house* was unbelievable. They'd said they were restoring an old house, and he'd assumed a normal size place. This was a mansion. He walked all the way around the house and never left the porch. At least twelve feet wide and encompassing both stories, the porches wrapped around the house like a lacy bow on a package. Most of the rooms had French doors that opened out onto the porch.

And not just ordinary French doors—these were huge, obviously custom built, with sidelights on both sides and fanlights over the tops. The windows were the originals, that old wavy glass from centuries ago.

Inside, he found the same grand and gracious proportions. No expert, it didn't take much of one to see the beauty beneath the dust and neglect. Eighteen foot ceilings, wide planked hardwood floors, wide crown molding, solid wood doors and the kind of attention to detail seldom seen anymore. He got to the kitchen and stopped, mouth hanging open.

"What do you think?"

Charlie and Jennilee stood behind him, Jennilee in front of Charlie, his arms tight around her, both grinning like monkeys.

"I think my folks could run their catering business out of this kitchen and still have room left for the restaurant they're opening. What army are you two planning on feeding?"

"Ours, of course!" Jennilee laughed. "We promised..." *...Amelia...* "...when we bought this place we'd fill it with children and love and laughter."

"Better get started."

"Already have."

Tony's eyes flew to Jennilee's belly, flat beneath her shirt.

Charlie burst into laughter. "Not like that. Jennilee's not pregnant, won't be until she wears my ring on her finger. She meant your family, along with all our other friends. We'll fill this place with adopted families until we can make our own."

Tony groaned, half serious. "All of them? You want all of them to come here?"

Following Charlie around, watching him work, Tony didn't notice exactly when Jennilee disappeared.

"Hey! Where'd Jennilee get off to?"

Looking up with a grin, Charlie shrugged. "She's around somewhere, out talking to…" …*Amelia*… "…her plants or something. I can grow stuff, but I swear the plants perk up and do a song and dance routine when she walks by—like a Disney movie. Let's go find her, before she gets in trouble."

"Trouble?"

"Not what you're thinking. She'll work herself to death if you don't watch her like a hawk."

Stepping out on the porch, Charlie let out a shrill whistle. There, coming from the outbuilding—Jewel's distinct, high pitched bark.

Jennilee smiled but didn't look up as the guys came in. "Go back to your playing and leave me to mine."

"What are you *playing* with now, Jennilee-love?"

Stepping back, she waved her hand at the work bench in front of her. A sign, like the one at Garner House. Charlie read the words Jennilee'd just finished painting.

- Amelia's Echoes
- *Give your garden a little history*
- *with heirloom plants from the past.*

"Jennilee, what's this?"

Glancing at Charlie, Jennilee explained. "All those cuttings we rooted? I've got enough starts with some size to them to put some up for sale. And enough bulbs and seeds."

"Who's Amelia?" Tony caught the look that passed between Charlie and Jennilee. Half the time he felt like a whole other conversation was going on between them—one out of the hearing range of anyone but the two of them.

A long beat, and then, "The previous owner's wife. Amelia died a long time ago. I want to do this in her memory."

"Grandy's annual?"

"Yeah, next week."

Not only did Charlie and Jennilee hear things other people couldn't, they spoke in shorthand.

"Explain, please." Tony looked from one to the other.

Laughter exploded around them like quail coming up under their feet.

"Grandy always holds…"

"…an open house…"

"…for her garden…"

"One in the spring…"

"…and one in the fall."

"She sells…"

"…plants and stuff."

"So you're going to sell some of your plants and call them Amelia's Echoes because they're old plants and they belonged to some woman named Amelia?"

"Not just Amelia's, but all the previous gardeners who lived here and created these wonderful gardens. Amelia's Echoes are a gift from the past—plants that've been handed down for generations, should be handed down for generations more. These plants are…"

Charlie plastered his lips to Jennilee's. Both came up for air, grinning. "Tony, don't get her started. You have no idea.

Jennilee can spout names and histories like she's a Bedouin and they're pedigreed Arabians."

Eyes alight, lips swollen, Jennilee smiled. "Pay no attention to him, Tony. He loves these gardens as much as I do."

∼

Weekends Jennilee spent in Raleigh, she now spent at the Marcellini's. Once they found out she'd been spending her time at a hotel, they wouldn't take no for an answer.

Except for that first day, Jennilee never showed up without bringing something. Fresh caught seafood, jars of preserves, cakes and pies, on and on. Fit into their family as if she'd been born into it. If Miz Teresa shooed her out of the kitchen, she could most often be found playing with the children.

They surrounded her, adored her, and she returned the adoration. *Jennilee says* became a common byword with the Marcellini's rambunctious brood.

Charlie came in from class today to find Jennilee already at the Marcellini's. Seated cross-legged on the sun-dappled patio, a baby in her arms, a toddler in her lap. Playing some kind of singing game with the kids, upturned faces seated around her riveted on Jennilee's radiant face, the kids were eating it up.

He stood and watched, feeling such a rush of love he couldn't contain it.

One of Tony's uncles moved around unobtrusively, snapping pictures. He had his own photography studio, he was fantastic at what he did, and he was always taking pictures. No one paid him any mind.

Charlie couldn't wait 'til the game was finished. He had to kiss Jennilee—now. Like he needed air to breathe. Going down on one knee, he palmed her head. The younger kids giggled, the older ones made gagging noises and protested the interruption.

"Hey, Jennilee-princess."

"Hey, yourself, gorgeous."

"Missed you."

"Missed you more."

Touching his forehead to hers, Charlie was instantly thrown into a sensory recall of dragonflies and kaleidoscopes. Pulling back, he looked at Jennilee and saw the same memories in her eyes. Her jubilant laughter silvered the air and he kissed her again.

Taking the baby, he waited while Jennilee set the toddler on his feet. Rising, Charlie held out a hand and helped her up, wrapped an arm around her and inhaled her scent.

They stood in the midst of a ring of children, their love shimmering the air around them. Staring deep into each other's eyes, the baby cradled in Charlie's arm and the toddler standing by Jennilee's side, one hand reaching up to hold hers, the other children were utterly silent, motionless, basking in the magic moment.

A distant horn blared, and the spell was broken.

CHAPTER 38

Charlie made it home the weekend they were having Homecoming at church, Tony and Angel in tow.

Tradition was to have dinner on the grounds after Sunday services, and every family brought plenty. The foods were placed outside, weather permitting, on long pieces of hog-wire stretched between trees. Picnic style, everyone helped themselves to a bit of everyone else's favorite dishes and secret recipes. Quite a bit of friendly competition ensued, and the dinner garnered a great deal of compliments and bragging rights, as such events always did.

Guest speaker for the day was Brother Anderson. One look and he knew he'd soon be performing the ceremony he'd promised Charlie and Jennilee so long ago. They'd kept in touch, but this was the first time he'd seen them in years. More in love than ever, there was positively a light shining around the two of them. "Charlie, Jennilee. It's so good to see you!"

Both hugged him. "And you, sir. Another year and a bit…"

"…and we'll hold you to your promise."

"I'll be here, Lord willing."

Service over, food laid out, everyone was merely waiting for Brother Anderson's blessing so they could dig in. Making it brief, soon plates were being filled, oohs and ahhs already echoing before the food was even sampled, known favorites avidly being sought out.

A bit of so-and-so's fried chicken, somebody else's crab cakes, chicken and dumplings, fried shrimp, potato salad, deviled eggs, green beans and ham, sweet potato casserole, melt in your mouth light rolls. Plates filled to overflowing, most people set theirs down at whatever table they planned to eat at and headed out again, for the dessert table this time.

Another tempting array—cakes and pies and desserts of every description and flavor. Again, pretty much knowing who brought what, everyone searched out their favorites.

Charlie and Jennilee were helping, filling cups with ice, then tea or sodas.

Filling their plates, setting them down to claim seats, Tony and Angel made for the desserts. Jennilee'd laughingly warned them to get some early or all the really good stuff would be gone.

Taking his place in line, Tony unknowingly stirred up a hornet's nest. "I want a piece of Jennilee's coconut cake, please."

The woman serving the desserts, a complete stranger to Tony, lit into him. *"Jennilee's?* Don't you mean Celie's?"

Taken aback at the venom in her tone, he took a deep breath and unknowingly whacked the nest another time. "I don't know any Celie. I want some of Jennilee's cake, please. That one right there." Pointed it out so there was no mistake.

Face all pruned up, Bertha spat, "How dare you? Did she put you up to this?"

Well on his way to exchanging momentary shock for righteous rebuttal, Tony glanced in Jennilee's direction and held his tongue. "I'm not sure what you think I've done, but…"

A crowd gathering, Brother Patterson, the regular preacher, tried to soothe her. "Sister Bertha, calm down."

"I will not! She's still telling lies, spreading hate. Celie's been through enough. Losing her house and everything she owns, after all she did for Jennilee—that ungrateful b…brat. And now Jennilee's trying to lay claim to this cake. Why, everyone knows Celie's brought this cake to every Homecoming for the last ten years or better." Bertha's voice rose with every accusation.

Jennilee froze in mid-motion. Bertha's voice carried, reaching every table, shutting down the hum and buzz of conversation. All eyes locked on Bertha before switching to Jennilee.

Brother Patterson tried again. "Sister Bertha, this is supposed to be a time of rejoicing and fellowship. This is not the place, nor the time to…"

"Then when is? No one wants to talk about the horrible things Jennilee's done to Celie. How could she? All the family she has left in the world and you see how she treats them. What kind of person treats their only family like that? Refuses to speak to them? Evicts them from their home?"

Charlie stiffened and reached for Jennilee even as she lifted a hand in a gesture to him to hold back from retaliating. Not here, not now. Pressing a light touch low on her back, letting her know he supported whatever decision she made, he watched as Jennilee took a deep breath, prepared to let it slide. Anyone who mattered knew the truth.

Sick inside, Jennilee was trembling, inside and out. Hadn't done this intentionally—just fixed what she normally fixed for Homecoming. Hadn't given it a thought.

Tony gave another whack, deliberate this time, not backing down in the face of the harpy's misguided wrath. If she wanted to have this out here and now, he was all for it. "I have no idea what you're talking about, but I watched Jennilee make that cake and I'm the one who carried it here."

"I suppose next you're going to tell me she brought that and that and that!" Each *that* was punctuated with a jab of Bertha's finger toward some item of food on the main tables.

Tony smiled, eyes cold. "Actually, she did."

"Liar!" Bertha flung that at Tony like a poisoned spear.

While Jennilee might take Bertha's venom herself without a word of defense, no way would she let it spill over on Tony. "Bertha! Enough. Don't take out your hate for me on an innocent guest."

"How'd you get him to lie for you?" Bertha's oily implication rang plainer than words. "Are you going to deny Celie's been bringing that coconut cake to Homecoming for years? And all the other stuff you're claiming?"

A rumble ran through Celie's most ardent supporters.

"Are you?" Fairly screaming now, face mottled and spittle flying, Bertha reminded Jennilee of years earlier.

Too bad—for Bertha. Jennilee was no longer a child to be intimidated by an adult in a position of authority. Replied evenly, "I'm not denying she brought it all these years."

"There! See! How can you all just stand there and and believe the bulls…she dishes out. Sure, she looks all sweet and angelic, but…"

Fastening her gaze on Celie, standing beside a much thinner, older looking Mort, Jennilee calmly stopped the tirade. "I agreed she brought it—I never said she cooked it—any of it."

"Well, she could hardly bring it if she didn't cook it."

Jennilee tossed back mildly, eyes still on Celie. "Then ask her for the recipes. Better yet, ask her what she brought today."

"I have asked for the recipes—Celie said…she said she didn't have anything written down."

"I'm sure she did—and she didn't. Would you like me to write them down for you?" Jennilee cooly switched her gaze back to Bertha, but not before seeing the light go on in Mort's eyes. Jennilee snorted to herself. Took him long enough.

Picking up on the rest of Jennilee's question, Bertha asked, "What do you mean—ask Celie what she brought today? The same things she always brings."

"We've already established that I brought all those things. So what did she bring?"

Looking around for support, all Bertha saw was shock and disbelief, a dawning understanding on many faces that had for so many years stood staunchly by poor Celie while soundly condemning Jennilee.

"Ladies. Ladies, please." Brother Patterson was wringing his hands, completely at a loss as to how to stop this catfight. Young, this was his first church—he didn't have a chance. Looking to Brother Anderson—arms crossed, smile beaming—for help, he knew he'd get none from that quarter.

A strained silence fell over the whole crowd. Bertha burst into tears and fled. Jennilee calmly went back to filling drink cups as Mort turned and stalked off, Celie running after him.

And like the tide changing, the pendulum swung.

∼

"She's lying, Mort. You know what a liar she is."

"Is she? Do I? Do I know anything? What did you bring today? You didn't bring a damn thing, did you? I'd know, because we rode together. I would've noticed food in the car, Celie. You haven't cooked, not once since she moved out. If…

Jennilee…is such a liar, write down some of my favorite recipes. Cook…something."

Celie struggled to keep up with a furious and fast walking Mort, her high heels sinking into the soft ground with each step. "Mort, please."

Whirling, he confronted his wife. "Please what? You can't, can you? You…*used*…that child—for years. Like…like a slave. Did you ever do *anything*?"

"Of course I did. I…"

"Don't lie to me anymore, Celie. Just don't." Mort got in, slammed the door without bothering to help his *wife* get in. Not his Mercedes, not Celie's Caddy, but an old clunker on its last legs—all they'd been able to afford after both of theirs had been repo'd. Wondered just what else his *wife* had lied to him about.

∼

CHARLIE AND JENNILEE, Tony and Angel stayed for the afternoon sing. Sitting in Grandy's usual spot, right beside Grandy, Jennilee sat between Charlie and Grandy, like always. Both clasping one of her hands in one of theirs, sitting or standing, silently giving her their support.

Doing something else out of character for her—Jennilee sang—loud and clear. She'd been quiet long enough.

A lot of surprised heads turned as her sweet voice rang out for the first time in church, and accompanied by Charlie's, swelled above the crowd and soared joyfully.

Brother Anderson smiled wider. The quiet little girl he'd known had turned into quite a woman.

∼

CHARLIE WAITED until they got home, waited until they got

changed and drove out to their house before cutting loose. Tony and Angel watched, open-mouthed as Charlie picked Jennilee up and spun her around and around.

Laughing like a maniac, kissing her over and over, Charlie told her. "I am so proud of you, Jennilee-baby. That was…perfect! You never raised your voice, didn't lose your temper, didn't snipe. You just took everything she threw at you and let it explode right back in her face. Perfect, Jennilee-sweet…perfect. Absolutely magnificent. Perfect, perfect, perfect!"

Jennilee blushed. "Thank you for…giving me a chance… for not…rushing to my defense." *For letting me do this on my own.* Blushed harder as she looked at Tony. "Tony, I am so sorry…"

"Don't be. That was worth it. I take it that biddy was one of your aunt's friends. How come she hates you so much?"

"Her daughter is…"

"…my aunt's best friend."

"She used to be…"

"…the head librarian, recently retired."

"We, uh, asked her…"

"…for some information once."

Tony and Angel could do nothing but stare as Charlie and Jennilee laughed until they fell down.

~

PAPERS WERE SERVED two weeks before Thanksgiving, with a court date of December tenth.

Jennilee began steadily losing weight, gained bruised circles under her eyes. Charlie worried, worried more, threatened to quit school and come home.

Jennilee vetoed that. "You'll do no such thing. You'll be

out for Thanksgiving, then Christmas break soon enough. I'll be fine until then."

There were a few bright spots in the unrelieved gloom. People who'd snubbed Jennilee forever started speaking to her, a few even apologized. Bertha wasn't one of them. They heard through the grapevine Mort filed for a divorce.

Despite those tidbits, as the court date got closer, Jennilee got quieter and quieter, sank deeper and deeper into herself. Slept less and less, ate sporadically.

Charlie called her several times a day just to touch base, usually first thing, then at lunch, then again in the afternoon and again before bed.

Letting Jennilee's phone ring and ring, as he'd been doing since before classes started and between every class since early morning, it was lunch time now, and still no answer. Heading home this afternoon as soon as classes let out, he knew Jennilee wasn't on her way to Raleigh.

Grandy answered at the diner. No, Jennilee wasn't working today, but Charlie knew that. He knew her schedule as well as she knew his. Called Mose. Called Miz Sadie. Called Mr. Tom. Called Chief Mac. Called his dad on the off chance she was at the garage.

Headed for the Marcellini's and his truck.

All of them were keeping close tabs on her, so where could she be? Charlie's panicky calls had half the town actively looking for her. Frantic by the time he got to Grandy's, she met him at the door, having given up on cooking. Jewel was gone, so where ever Jennilee was, at least Jewel was with her.

Checking their pond first—sometimes Jennilee came out here when she was troubled, he headed for their house next, even though Grandy told him several people had already checked there. Pulling up in the driveway, he felt his heart do a slow roll before settling. Jennilee's car was in its usual spot. So where was she?

Heading for the cemetery first, Charlie then went through the house, room by room. Checked all the vast porch, both stories, the outbuilding, the dock, everywhere he could think of. Ended up back where he started, in the family cemetery—and there she was.

His heart stopped, then melted. He must've missed Jennilee the first time, didn't see any way possible he could have. Curled up beside Amelia's grave, on a bed of flowers, surrounded by great drifts of them like a puffy, colorful comforter. Sleeping like a baby.

Jewel, lying off to one side, head on her paws, whined and moved her tail lightly when Charlie whistled. She refused to move, her attention riveted on Jennilee.

Careful not to so much as nudge the flowers, Charlie knelt and called to Jennilee, watched the flowers slowly fade with each syllable that fell from his lips.

Amelia! Another message from Amelia. It had to be—but what? Good news, if he had to make a guess.

Waiting 'til the flowers faded completely, loath to crush any of them, he scooted closer, brushed a hand across her cheek. "Jennilee-honey. Wake up. I was worried about you. Everybody was."

Jennilee's eyes fluttered, focused on Charlie. "Everything's going to work out, Charlie. It's going to be just fine." A beatific smile crossed her features and her eyes drifted shut. Scooping her up, murmuring a heartfelt thanks to Amelia, Charlie started to stand.

"Wait! My flowers!" Twisting in his arms, Jennilee reached back to the bare ground. Reached out...

...and plucked a bouquet from out of nowhere.

A single cobalt iris, a cluster of yellow roses, a spray of pink lilac.

Carrying Jennilee to his truck, Jewel scampering ahead, the fragrance of his woman and the flowers wafted around Charlie with each step. She slept all the way home, didn't move when he carried her inside, snuggled closer when he sat in the rocker. Mumbled incoherently when Grandy took her flowers.

"Easy, Jennilee-love. Grandy's just going to put them in a vase."

Something else unintelligible and Jennilee went out like a light.

Charlie set the chair in motion. "She was at our house, Grandy, asleep. Let everyone know I found her, please."

"At your house? But Cyrus checked there, and Mac, and Mose, that I know of for sure, probably half a dozen others. And where'd she get the flowers? And especially the lilacs?"

"At our house."

"Your house? But…"

Charlie gave a snort that sounded suspiciously like laughter. "You wouldn't believe me if I told you."

Del was still puzzling over the incongruity. "I know your yard's a veritable treasure trove and there's always something blooming, but fresh flowers, this time of year? And those? They don't even bloom at the same time when they are blooming." Paused as something struck her. "That particular color of iris was your mother's favorite, and the yellow roses were Cynthia's."

Charlie laughed softly. "Do you remember Mr. Clyde Goodwin's wife?"

"Sure. Amelia was her name. Pretty little thing, loved to garden. Clyde and Benjamin, and gardening, were her passions, her entire life."

"Where was she from?"

"Somewhere up North, as I recall."

Another snort of laughter. "Did she ever get lilacs to grow here?"

"Lilacs? Lord, no. It's too hot here. She tried and tried…" Del stopped, looked from the lilacs to Jennilee, back to the lilacs. "I'll just go make those calls."

"Thanks, Grandy."

∽

Jennilee slept like a baby the rest of the evening and all night. Woke early, stretched, opened her eyes and looked up at Charlie.

A slow smile creased her face. "Mornin', handsome."

An answering one swept across his. "Hey, beautiful."

"How come…"

"You didn't answer your phone and no one knew where you were."

A slight frown flitted across Jennilee's face. "I woke early and went out to our house, went to the cemetery first, like I usually do, to say hi. I remember apologizing because I forgot to pick any flowers. I must've fallen asleep because I had the most wonderful dream."

Charlie indicated something with his chin.

Turning her head, Jennilee stared. Sat up in Charlie's lap. Reached out a shaking hand to the unusual bouquet in one of Grandy's ordinary vases. Picked up the vase and buried her face in the fragrant flowers. Looked at Charlie, the same beatific smile on her face she'd shown him yesterday.

"It wasn't a dream. Everything's going to work out just fine, Charlie."

"That's what you told me yesterday."

"I can't…explain this."

"Don't try, Jennilee-love. Just enjoy it, Rip."

"Rip?"

"As in *Van Winkle*."

Jennilee's laughter rang out. "So how many classes did I make you miss?"

"Only a couple, and you didn't make me. You're the most important thing in my world, Jennilee. Don't scare me like that again."

"Sorry. Talk to Amelia."

"Un uh. That's your department."

Jennilee laughed again. Kissed him. "I'm starving."

"Me, too."

"Well, since you're already home for the weekend, what would you like for breakfast?"

"Wrong question." Charlie growled and attacked Jennilee, pretending to bite her everywhere, bestowing kisses instead.

Hearing the commotion, Del rushed to the living room. Jennilee was laughing wildly, high pitched and continuous like a little girl at a slumber party. Charlie was placing smacking kisses and blowing zerberts on any patch of open skin. Jewel danced around them, barking ecstatically.

Scrubbing impatiently at her eyes, Del knuckled away the urge to cry. "Something I should know about, guys?"

Both kids looked at her, went off into gales of laughter.

When they could look at each other and keep a reasonably straight face, they helped Grandy fix breakfast. Charlie and Grandy watched as Jennilee cleaned her plate, filled it and cleaned it again.

Tony and Angel showed up, mid-morning. Charlie and Jennilee took them out on the boat for awhile, taught them how to fish with a bottom rig and a saltwater reel.

Showed them how much noise a fish could make—supposedly silent, they could make a surprising variety of sounds. Croakers croaked, hogfish grunted like, well, like a hog.

Back at Grandy's, the girls left the guys to clean fish and went inside.

Washing up, Angel asked, "So, where's this wedding dress Charlie mentioned?"

"You really want to see it?"

"I wouldn't ask if I didn't."

"I'm nowhere near finished."

"So?"

Shooing Jewel off her bed, Jennilee laid a clean sheet on it. Ran a loving hand over the cedar chest at the foot off her bed. Procrastinated. "Charlie made this for me."

"He made it?" Angel moved closer, ran her hands over the satiny finish just as Jennilee was doing.

Jennilee gestured toward her dresser. "He made that, too."

"Your dresser?"

Jennilee laughed. "No, we mostly leave the furniture making to Mose. The jewelry box on top of the dresser. Actually, Mose crafted the box and Charlie carved the flowers and stuff." Sounding just a tad desperate, Jennilee asked, "Are you sure…"

"Jennilee. If you don't want to show me your dress…"

Jennilee said softly, "I haven't shown it to anyone."

"You're kidding, right?"

"It's…personal."

"It's supposed to be, dingbat."

"I am no dingbatter. I'll have you know my family's lived here for…hundreds of years."

Giggling, the girls shared a glance.

Jennilee took a shaky breath, took the plunge. Got the words out in a rush. "I've been working on the embroidery mostly, but I have all the pieces cut out and I can sort of show you how it's supposed to look."

Lifting the lid of her cedar chest, Jennilee began taking muslin wrapped pieces out carefully. "Charlie found this picture a long time ago and gave it to me. This is pretty much what it's going to look like when I'm done." Handing the worn picture to Angel, Jennilee started unwrapping the delicate fabrics, laying them out on the bed.

A single glance had Angel exclaiming, "You're kidding, right?"

"You already asked me that."

"I thought that dress you were wearing the first time I saw you was something. Jennilee, this is…" Taking her eyes off the picture, she fastened them on the reality.

Gasped. "Jennilee—Charlie is going to shit a brick when he sees you in this."

Jennilee's laughter pealed out. "I hope not."

Dress put away, Angel sworn to secrecy, the girls headed downstairs to help cook supper. Big doings tonight, almost everyone who mattered to Charlie and Jennilee was coming, even Mr. Carlo and Miz Teresa.

Busy helping Grandy, moving around like a happy sprite, Jennilee lit up the room with her smiles and laughter.

Standing in the doorway, Charlie feasted his eyes. Whatever Amelia'd shown Jennilee had lifted her spirits immensely. Sensing him, Jennilee looked up and winked.

"Hey big boy, how about a…"

"…kiss?"

"A hand, you lech."

"How 'bout a kiss and then a hand?"

Laughter rang out, echoed and bounced throughout the kitchen.

The kitchen and dining room filled as the others drifted in—Chief Mac, and then Miz Sadie and Mr. Jubal, followed by Mr. Tom and Doc and their spouses, then Mose and Mr. Donnie, even Mr. Cyrus. Mr. Carlo and Miz Teresa were welcomed and introduced, accepted into the circle. Josh and Will came, both with a girl on their arm.

Raising a brow at Josh and Will, Jennilee grinned, swiped the back of a hand across her forehead. That brought another ripple of laughter from the assembled crowd, and more than one admonishment.

Mose started. "Don't think this lets you off the hook for yesterday, missy."

Jennilee sobered instantly. "That's partly why we wanted all of you to come for supper tonight. I want to thank you all for…caring so much." Her voice broke, and she swallowed. "And I want to apologize for scaring you all. I swear to you, I was at our house the whole time. I fell asleep."

Mose again. "Then where'd you park? It's not like I don't know your car. Everyone in town knows that vehicle." Crossing tree-trunk arms, he glared.

Mac gave her the same look. "I checked there, too, Jennilee. I wouldn't have missed your car, and I walked all over that place."

"Me, too." Mr. Cyrus added his two cents.

Jennilee threw a desperate look at Charlie. He might believe her, but the rest of the crowd would be calling for men in white suits and butterfly nets.

"She was there, all right. Just…out of sight." Charlie vouched for her, and the rest of them accepted his answer, still grumbling. He wasn't going to quibble. He'd walked right past her the first time he'd checked the cemetery. She'd been there, just not *there*. If he could accept that Amelia could conceal Jennilee from sight, it was no stretch to think she could hide Jennilee's car as well. And who was he to argue with the motives and methods of a ghost?

"I had a really good dream while I was there."

Everyone waited, and Jennilee rolled her eyes at Charlie's leer.

"It's going to be alright—this whole mess with…them. It's going to work out."

Charlie smiled at her, a smile full of love and promise. "Confession and penance time is over. Can we eat now?"

"You and your stomach!"

"Yeah, but it loves you nearly as much as I do."

"Loves my cooking, you mean."

"That, too." Charlie couldn't stand it any more. He had to kiss her. Had to.

Tony ribbed, "Hey! You're supposed to eat dessert *after* supper."

Jennilee came up for air, laughing. "Pineapple upside down cake. I made it this morning."

"If it's as good as your coconut cake, I'm not sure I want any supper."

Tony had rhapsodized to his parents about what a good cook Jennilee was, and after the blessing and the first few bites, they more than believed him. "Jennilee—what is this? I have never…" Miz Teresa took another bite, savored.

"Spoonbread? It's like…mushy cornbread, almost a custard. That's why it's called spoonbread, because you have to eat it with a spoon. We always have it with fish."

"Are you sure this isn't dessert?"

"I, uh, improved the recipe."

"I want it. Write it down for me, please."

Tony and Angel and Charlie and Jennilee and Grandy shared a look and went off into gales of laughter. Jennilee laughed so hard Charlie had to pound her on the back.

Gasping, half choking with bubbling laughter, she managed to say, "Yes, ma'am."

"Jennilee, speaking of writing things down, I'm still working my way through your books." All sound and movement ceased as Mr. Jubal made his statement, a veritable speech for him.

"Not mine, Mr. Jubal. I told you—you rescued them—they're all yours." Jennilee elaborated as they filled their plates and started filling their bellies. "Mr. Jubal found a bunch of the Judge's books that had been thrown away. He rescued the ones that were salvageable and he's been working his way through them ever since."

Platters of fried fish, shrimp, and scallops were passed around, bowls of cole slaw and baked beans, home fries and pans of spoonbread, gallons of sweet tea. There weren't any leftovers.

Loath to break up the gathering just yet, they made their way to the back porch.

Charlie played his guitar and the others joined their voices or not, some content to just listen and rock. As always, Charlie and Jennilee mixed and matched, some old stuff, some new, country and gospel and whatever else they felt like.

Tony couldn't carry a tune in a bucket, but he enjoyed good music. "What was that last song? I've never heard it before."

A deep voice spoke out of the darkness. *"The Porch Song?* That's theirs. Can't you tell? It's all about family and making music and making memories. It's got Charlie and Jennilee stamped all over it."

Jennilee jumped up with a glad cry. "Jeff! You're home! Why didn't you call?"

Jeff stepped into the light and Jennilee threw her arms around him.

Hugging her back, Jeff closed his eyes for a moment, opened them and locked gazes with Charlie. "I just got in, stopped by my folks' for a bit and took a chance you'd be here."

"For a bit or a bite?" Knowing laughter followed that query.

Charlie and Jeff stepped together, pounded each others' backs heartily. "Good to see you, man."

"Yeah, we keep missing each other."

"Jeff's going to college to be an FBI agent, in forensics." Jennilee tossed that tidbit in proudly as she tucked her arm through Jeff's, let Mr. Carlo and Miz Teresa know.

Jeff directed a look at Chief Mac. They all knew why Jeff was interested in that particular field. Chief Mac had steered him as best he could. It was up to Jeff now.

Stretching up, Jennilee pressed a kiss on his cheek. "You're too late for supper, but I can fix you something, or we're just getting ready to have dessert."

Jeff perked up like Jewel when she heard the word treat. "Dessert?"

"Pineapple upside down cake."

"Yours?" Jeff waited expectantly.

Jennilee put her hands on her hips. "Why do y'all act like I'm the only one that cooks around here? Grandy and Miz Sadie and Miz Teresa…"

"You put us to shame, Jennilee."

"Grandy, how can you say that? You and Miz Sadie taught me everything I know."

"We can say that because it's the truth." A hearty course of agreement had Jennilee blushing and burying her face in Charlie's shoulder.

A bit later and an empty cake platter, save for a few crumbs, upheld their faith.

CHAPTER 39

A few days later, in Mr. Tom's office, a livid Charlie paced back and forth, fury etching every movement, every gesture. Jennilee stood quietly, looking out the window at nothing, while Grandy watched her two chicks worriedly.

"So what you're saying is because we kept records and she didn't, her lawyer's twisted everything to make us look like the guilty party. Because we can account for every cent, earned or spent, and Celie has no idea where her funds went or what they were spent on…what we have must be hers."

Fingers interlaced, tapping his thumbs together, Tom nodded. "That's what it boils down to, yes. Pretty much so. And three cents."

"Three cents?"

"I've had an outside auditing firm go over your receipts and disbursements, and you're off three cents."

Jennilee laughed. "Charlie's always been better at math, but he insisted I keep the books."

Charlie snorted. "Even if my math's better, they couldn't read my writing. How can you laugh?"

"Because all those years, and I'm only off three cents, and because—this is going to work out just fine."

Jennilee obviously believed just that because she'd put weight back on in the last few days. Her eyes were clear, no shadows in them or under them. Charlie was trying to believe, but hard facts were more real to him than dreams and portents.

"I called you here today, not just to brief you, but because Celie's lawyer, Joe Pettit, has offered to settle out of court for an undisclosed sum."

"Everything, you mean. Like calls to like. Celie's lawyer—humph! I've seen his ads on TV—Joe Pettit's nothing but a glorified ambulance chaser."

Charlie's outburst startled another laugh out of Jennilee. "She must've promised him half."

Charlie smiled crookedly. "Half of nothing's still nothing."

"It's going to work out, Charlie. Stop worrying."

More worried about Jennilee than the outcome of Celie's troublemaking, Jennilee had that same fey look on her face he'd seen before and wasn't sure he trusted.

"When?"

"Today's Tuesday, your court appearance is scheduled for Friday. That doesn't leave us much time."

"Tomorrow." Jennilee stated it decisively and walked over to hug Mr. Tom, ready to go. She had things to do.

"Fine, Jennilee. I'll set it up for…2:00? Here?"

"Sounds good. See you tomorrow."

In the truck, Charlie started it, sat there staring at nothing. "How can you be so calm about this, Jennilee?"

"Charlie. Her whole life's fabric is woven of lies. I've got a pretty good idea what she told her lawyer, and it's all a fabrication. Just like the lies she told…" …*Mort*… "…her husband and her friends, the people at church, it's all unraveling. She's going to trip herself up but good, and after this, no one will believe a word she says. I told you, everything's going to work out just fine."

"You're scaring me, Jennilee."

"I don't want you to worry about anything except acing your exams, and when we're going to cut our Christmas tree this year."

"Jennilee..."

"Charlie, I'm not crazy and I haven't been out in the sun too long."

That made him laugh, as she'd known it would. Charlie pulled her close for a sweet, sweet kiss, forgetting all about Grandy sitting on the other side of Jennilee. Breaking off he growled, "Woman..."

Del cleared her throat. Jennilee turned and threw her arms around the older woman. "Sorry, Grandy. Didn't mean to embarrass you."

∽

In Mr. Tom's conference room by 1:30, Jennilee sat calmly embroidering. Charlie pacing, Del watching. Mac leaned up against the wall and stared at the ceiling.

Tom, in his office going over some last minute details, came in at five 'til and sat, drumming his fingers on the polished table.

2:00. No Celie, no fancy-schmantzy lawyer. Ten after. Fifteen after.

Charlie kept getting up to wear another layer of varnish off the floor. Jennilee kept right on doing whatever she was doing. Del kept darting nervous looks between Tom and the kids as Mac shifted from one foot to the other.

Knotting her thread, Jennilee clipped it, folded the fabric and put everything in a canvas tote at her side. Smiled and held out a hand to Charlie. "Sit down, love, or we're going to have to add refinishing this floor to our to do list."

Charlie sat, Jennilee wove her fingers through his. Lifting their joined hands, Charlie pressed a kiss over her ring. Making kissy lips back at him, Jennilee kept her eyes on his and smiled.

Celie blew in at twenty-eight after, lawyer in tow. Fire engine red mid-thigh skirt and white, barely there blouse beneath an equally red bolero jacket, stiletto heels.

Looking at Celie standing too close to her lawyer, at him hovering just a little longer, touching just a little more than necessary as he seated her, Jennilee figured he'd gotten all the pay he was going to. Serve him right if he got an STD.

Tom started the proceedings. "Let's get down to it. This is being recorded, both written and spoken." Nodded at his secretary.

Clinging to Joe Pettit, dabbing a lacy handkerchief to the corners of her eyes, Celie moaned pitifully. "I just want what's rightfully mine."

Jennilee's smile widened and she squeezed Charlie's hand reassuringly.

Del and Mac rolled their eyes at each other.

Glancing at Mac and Del, Celie stage whispered to her lawyer, "Make them leave. I don't want them here. This is embarrassing enough without…"

Patting her hand, Celie's lawyer said, "My client…"

Jennilee cut him off. "Too bad, Celie. I stopped caring a long time ago what you wanted. *I* want them here. They stay. Besides, we're none of us going to be here long."

"What ever do you mean?"

"Drop the act, Celie. I'm telling you now—you're getting nothing. Not a dime, not three cents."

"I just want what's owed to me! You…you left me with

nothing! How could you, after all I did for you? All those years I…"

Shrugging one shoulder, completely unconcerned, Jennilee responded, "More like—to me. I'm sure you'll reap exactly what you sowed. *Nothing* is exactly what you thought about all those years while you were spinning lies and blowing my inheritance, and *nothing* is what you deserve."

"How can you say that? You stole my home right out from under me!"

Jennilee flicked a desultory glance at Celie. "I'd be careful using that word if I were you. *I* haven't stolen anything."

Celie's lawyer cleared his throat. "Now see here…"

Jennilee held out a hand to Mr. Tom for a folder. "I see fine—right here. This is a binding contract, which you already have a copy of, with the terms spelled out clearly. Celie and family had all rights to stay in the Judge's house as long as it was kept clean, inside and out. Here are the pictures—before and after."

Lawyer Petit barely spared a glance at the photos. "My client couldn't focus. She was so upset about you leaving… …utterly distraught. That's why her house looks like that."

Jennilee shook her head, a slow, side to side denial. "*My* house looks like that because Celie's a lazy slob and because she'd rather spend money on herself than hire a housekeeper."

"How can you be so cruel? I'm practically the only family you have left in the world!"

"I had a good teacher."

"Be that way! I came here hoping to make you see reason, to…"

"You came here hoping to intimidate me, to browbeat me, to try and steal more from me—from us. No more. I'm no longer a helpless child at your mercy. I'm an adult, a seriously pissed adult, and you'll not get one more drop of blood from me." Jennilee smiled, the same ferocious smile Celie'd seen the day Jennilee informed her she was going to DC with Charlie and Grandy, that she knew the Judge's house was hers.

Shoving back from the table, pretense forgotten, Celie opened her mouth to blast Jennilee.

"Ah, ah, ah. Better shut that vicious mouth before you say something in front of witnesses."

Celie rose. "You won't get away with this, you little slut. The presiding judge was a friend of my father's and he'll…"

Jennilee tightened her grip on Charlie's hand as he gathered himself to stand.

"Thanks for the heads up, Celie. That's probably grounds for dismissal." Tom stacked his folders.

Celie's lawyer stood behind her, hands on her shoulders, whispering in her ear, trying to calm her.

Bracing both hands on the table, face twisted into a hate-filled mask, Celie spat, "I should've taken care of you a long time ago!"

"Careful, Celie. Your true colors are starting to show. Your *lawyer* might not be as willing to put up with your crap as your *husband* was, especially when he finds out all the lies you spun him."

"You bitch. You've always been a pain in my ass! You think you're so smart! I'll…"

Celie's lawyer clamped a hand over her mouth, muffling her threats.

Jennilee grinned. "You've had your fun for a lot of years, Celie. Time to pay the piper."

Joe Pettit yelped and cursed as Celie bit him.

Jennilee laughed out loud at that. "Still think she's such a charmer? Better go start rabies treatments."

"I'll make you pay for this! I'll see you in court." Livid fury showed in every line of Celie's overblown body.

"Just remember perjury will get you jail time, just like child abuse and stealing."

Shaking his throbbing hand, Joe Petit snarked in an oily tone, "Slander's a crime, too."

Jennilee flicked a contemptuous glance over Celie's lawyer. "It's only slander if it's lies. If anyone's going to be punished for slander, it'll be your client." Jennilee smiled. "Did you know that the ninth circle of Hell is reserved for slanderers? Slanderers are considered worse than mere liars, even though *Thou shalt not lie* is one of the ten commandments."

At his disbelieving look, Jennilee continued. "You didn't get any money up front, did you? Too bad. You won't get any now, no matter what she promised you, because she hasn't got any and she's not getting any of ours."

"I told you she's a selfish, scheming bitch. Do something, Joe! If you won't, Judge McPherson will."

Rising, Jennilee braced her hands on the table. Looked Celie dead in the eye. "Sit down, Celie. This isn't going to court—it ends here and now."

Her face as red as her outfit, Celie screamed, "You won't get away with this!"

"SIT!"

Celie dropped into her seat. She'd never heard her niece raise her voice before.

Jennilee's voice went soft, and they had to lean closer to hear. "You will listen, and listen well. There is no dungeon deep enough, dark enough, to lock you in that would repay you a tenth of the hell you made my childhood. If there was, I'd deliver you personally."

Crafty now, Celie smirked. "Ask anyone. I did the best I could with you—you've always been a problem child."

"You did nothing but betray me, abuse me at every turn, convince Mort and half the town I was the spawn of the devil. You could've saved yourself a lot of trouble and just looked in the mirror. You'd have gotten a much better picture of a demon."

Craftiness turned to smugness. "You've got no proof."

"That's where you're wrong—dead wrong. It's truly amazing what a good private investigator can dig up." Jennilee raised her voice. "Mr. Talton, would you come in here please?"

∾

A SHORT, stocky man with graying hair and twinkling eyes answered Jennilee's request. Jennilee assured him, "The recorder's still on and Miz Rose is still taking notes."

"You can't do this—threaten my client like this." Joe Pettit sounded righteously indignant.

Jennilee answered silkily. "No one save Celie has made any threats."

Tugging Celie to her feet, he told her, "Come, Celie. You don't have to put up with this."

"Oh, I think you'll want to sit and listen." Jennilee smiled, a cold, knowing smile, driving Celie's temper a notch higher.

"This is bullshit! I'm leaving, and you can't stop me." Celie made a great show of twitching her mini-skirt into place, pulling her blouse down to showcase more cleavage, fussing with her jacket, her rings and bracelets. Gaudy and tacky as always, but cheap imitations now, not the real things.

"You'll want to sit—now." Jennilee looked to Chief Mac, who moved in front of the door. "You're going to look, and to listen, and keep your mouth shut while you're looking and listening, or Chief Mac will take you straight to Beaufort. When I'm done, if you have any complaints or any more ideas about getting your hands on our money, I will press charges, and you will go to prison." Jennilee looked toward Mr. Talton, an *it's all yours*.

Placing a briefcase on the tabletop, he opened it and took out a folder. "At the behest of my clients, Charlie and Jennilee, I've been tailing Cecilia Johnson for a good while. I've also done some digging into her past." Taking 8 x 10 glossies out of the folder, one at a time, he slid them one at a time, to Jennilee.

"Let's see. This is interesting. 'Subject under surveillance, one Cecilia McRae Johnson, commonly known as Celie, in a parked car with a man.' Gee, Celie, that sure doesn't look like Uncle Mort you're lip-locked with."

Another picture. "You and the same man, going into a motel room. The room receipt is signed *Jenny Lee*."

Took her time perusing the next one and the attached explanation. Tsk'd. "Celie, Celie. What were you thinking? This is a picture of you at Bob Clark's Pharmacy in Havelock, picking up a prescription. Here's a copy of the write up, and it says the prescription is for…me. Birth control pills. There's also a photocopy of the patient form from the doctor's office that wrote the prescription. It says Lee, Jenny right at the top. It's got the right Social Security number and the Judge's address on it, my birth date. That's funny. This says Lee, Jenny is 5'4" and weighs 145. Brown hair and brown eyes. That doesn't sound right at all. I'm 5'6" and 125. Golden blond hair and blue eyes. Who do we know that fits the first description?"

Jennilee tapped the picture against her chin. "Sounds like —let me think—my cousin. That would be your daughter. All this time I thought it was illegal to use someone else's personal information."

On and on and on. Jennilee kept picking up pictures and reading summaries. Celie got whiter and whiter until she was almost transparent. Joe Pettit got grayer and grayer, shifted farther and farther away from Celie until he was nearly falling off his chair.

Starting to read another page, no pictures this time, Jennilee hesitated, swayed just a little. Reached for Charlie's hand. It was right there. "This...this is a consent form for...an abortion. Signed by Cecilia Johnson for one minor ward, Lee, Jenny. All my identification information is right, but the personal information sheet fits Sylvia's description—again. That's low, Celie. Even for you. You condoned that, you knew, and you still let Mort put me, put us, through hell about this. How could you?"

"What was I supposed to do?" Crying in earnest now, actual tears streamed down Celie's face, mascara making bold black stripes down each cheek. "Sylvie's my little girl. I couldn't just..."

"You could've told the truth for once in your miserable life. Faced reality. That was your...grandchild you let them murder." Picking up the rest of the pictures and summaries, Jennilee handed the stack to Mr. Tom, sick at heart, sick of the whole mess. "Get out of my sight. If you know what's good for you, you'll never cross my path again."

Charlie stood as Jennilee turned, enfolded her and shot daggers at Celie over Jennilee's head.

Flipping through the rest of the information, Tom pinned Celie with his glare. "If it was up to the rest of us, charges would be pressed and you'd go to prison. Jennilee's declined to do that as long as you drop this court case and agree to leave her alone. Before you leave, Celie, I want it on record, in your voice and in your writing that you're dropping this suit. That you will not attempt another one—ever."

"But...what will I do? I have no money—nothing." Celie's tears were all for herself now.

"Too bad. You brought all this on yourself. I happen to know the Judge left you a right smart amount of money as well as stocks and bonds and investments. If you'd played your cards right, you could've lived comfortably all your life and never lifted a finger. You've blown all yours, and Jennilee's as well. Say the words, Celie, and sign this form. I assure you, it is binding." Tom pushed a pen and the official document in Celie's direction.

Mac swung his handcuffs off one finger, a wide grin on his face.

Sobbing, Celie did as she was told.

A soft knock sounding at the door, Mac opened it and Miz Emma stuck her head in.

"Excuse me, Tom. There's something you should see."

Mr. Jubal entered, a book tucked in the crook of his arm. Nodded, let his gaze touch on the occupants.

"Tom, I know you're in the midst of something important, but this concerns Jennilee. You know I love her like she was my own. All of you know this book I'm holding," he held it up so they could see the leather cover and title written in gold leaf, "is part of a big bunch. A bunch I rescued from the dump. Y'all also know these books belonged to the Judge."

Celie started to make a stink, changed her mind, rolled her eyes. So what? So she'd gotten rid of some stupid old books. Stupid old man, scavenging at the landfill.

"I told Jennilee these were hers soon's I noticed the Judge's bookplates in them. She refused to have anything to do with them, told me they were mine to keep, to read and enjoy. I've been doing just that for a long time, working my way through them."

Admiring her manicure in a bored, dismissing gesture, Celie waggled her fingers and drawled condescendingly, "Yeah, so what? So you can read, old man. Good for you. Can I go now?"

Fisting both hands, Jennilee faced Celie down. "Don't you dare talk to Mr. Jubal like that."

"What more do you want? I gave my statement and signed your stupid paper. I'm leaving."

"Not just yet, Celie. This concerns you, too." Jubal smiled.

Examining her nails from a different angle, Celie snorted, "What could any of my father's worthless books have to do with me? I've never even read any of them."

Taking great pleasure in disabusing Celie of her erroneous assumption, Mr. Jubal grinned as he imparted his information. "Maybe you should've. And they're not worthless, so the joke's on you. Most of these are rare first editions. Some even belonged to your grandfather and great grandfather. The whole bunch, and I didn't even save all of them because some were beyond redemption by the time I found them, would've been worth a fortune—an extremely huge fortune."

As if he'd been saving them up for just such an occasion, Jubal certainly had no shortage of words today.

Celie screeched, "They're mine! I want them back."

Jubal looked to Tom for confirmation. "The Judge left the house and contents to Cynthia, and through her to Jennilee, right?"

Tom nodded. "That is affirmative. So Celie, not only did you steal Jennilee's money, you willfully threw away her belongings as well."

Still stuck back there on *worth a fortune*, Celie squalled, "They're mine! I *need* those books."

Jennilee spoke up. "Not according to Mr. Tom. They were mine, you threw them away, and I freely gave all rights to them to Mr. Jubal a long time ago."

Celie screeched again. "How can you be like that? He just said they're worth a fortune. That's just like you to let a n…"

"Don't you say it! Don't you dare."

Facing each other over the width of the gleaming table,

whatever Celie saw in Jennilee's eyes had her backing down, dropping her gaze first.

Jubal beamed proudly. Despite everything Celie'd thrown at her, Jennilee'd grown into a fine young woman. "I picked this particular one up today, intending to start reading it. When I cracked the cover, it opened to...this." Jubal held the open book out to Tom, as he'd once held one out to Jennilee.

An envelope.

Tom took the yellowed offering. All eyes on him, he turned it over, stared at it. "This is the Judge's handwriting and it's addressed to Tom Stimpson—my father or myself, I'm not sure which. Just the name, no junior or senior. Dad was the Judge's lawyer, so it could be either."

"I thought you were."

Tom answered Jennilee absently. "I was, but I didn't take over the Judge's affairs until after Dad got sick, sometime after the Judge had his first stroke." Opening the envelope slowly, he carefully took out the enclosed pages. Scanned the first few lines. Looked up and held Jennilee's gaze.

"It's to me. Jennilee, you're going to want to sit down."

Dropping heavily into her chair, Jennilee clung to Charlie's hand.

Tom read out loud, and rocked their world.

Tom,

It's hard to apologize for being such an ass in person, so maybe if I write this down, I'll get it done without making more of an ass of myself.

I've made some good choices in my life and some bad ones. Done good things and some not so good. I've made a really bad choice this time, backed it up by doing a worse thing. I'll tell you in detail when I see you. Let's just say I'm trying to—going to—make all the amends I can, try to repair what I destroyed.

We talked about my will, and you weren't happy the way I left it, with Cynthia getting the house and land, and Celie getting half the money. I was rude, didn't want to hear what you tried to tell me. I respect your judgement, and in hindsight, you always had the rights of this.

I'm changing it, here and now. I'll formalize it with you as soon as possible. Everything I have goes to Cynthia, and through her to Jenny. Celie gets just what she deserves—nothing.

You tried to tell me, Del tried. Hell, half the town tried to tell me how Celie was, and I wouldn't listen. She looks so much like her sweet mother—I let that sway me, influence my decisions and behavior. I accept complete responsibility for Celie, for the way she turned out.

Your father knew full well why I had a stroke, and who I caught Celie with. I'll tell you in person. You need to know. If anything happens to me, look to the two of them. I don't trust either one of them—my own daughter especially.

Cynthia's on edge after Iris' disappearance, and why shouldn't she be? She's always seen through Celie, tried time and again to tell me without sounding like a jealous, spiteful sister. I didn't listen, not once. I'm listening now. She left the letter you'll find enclosed in this packet, along with her will, for me to give to you.

Cynthia's gone out, and Celie's on her way over. I called and told her to come, thought it best not to have both girls here at the same time. I'll see Celie knows about both the change in my will and Cynthia's will.

I plan on giving you this in the morning, before I lose my courage.

McRae

THE SILENCE WAS thick as marsh mud, and just as nasty. Black and slimy and oozing. Broken by Celie's outburst, like a gas bubble popping up through the mud, noisy and smelling to high heaven.

"He's lying! You're all lying. That letter's a fake! You can't prove it—Daddy never changed his will. How much did you pay that stupid nigger to lie for you? To pretend he *found* that letter in that book? The ink's probably still wet."

If looks could kill, Jennilee would've been flat out on the floor and stone cold. The look she sent Celie was even colder and deadlier.

"Jennilee doesn't lie. She'd never encourage anyone to lie on her behalf. You, on the other hand, do nothing but. Your whole life's been a web of nothing but deceit and lies. I can hear the strands snapping, can't you?" Del, unable to keep quiet any longer, stepped up to bat for Jennilee.

"I'm not done." Tom sucked in a deep breath, blew it out. "Jennilee, I have no idea how your grandfather came into possession of this, but here's your mother's marriage certificate."

Jennilee looked to Celie. "You gonna tell me I bribed Mr. Jubal to forge that as well?"

Tom cleared his throat. "There's more."

CHAPTER 40

*A*ll eyes swung back to him as he moved another sheet of paper to the top and read the first few lines to himself.

"Son of a bitch. Son...of...a...bitch! This is Cynthia's letter." Scrubbing a hand over his face, Tom read aloud.

Tom,

I know you won't ask for one, but I need to explain.

Daddy helped me draft this, so it's airtight. If something should happen to me, please make sure Del gets custody of Jennilee. Keep Celie away from her at all costs. She's evil, and I won't have that foulness touch my baby.

My Albert disappeared without a trace, and now Iris. My gut tells me neither was an accident. Things are coming to a head. If not for Daddy's worsening condition, I'd take Jennilee and leave right now.

Daddy told me he's changing his will. I don't care about his money, or this house. Celie can have the whole mess as far as I'm concerned. I've got my degree and my trust fund mother left me, and it's more than enough.

My precious baby girl is all that matters. I want to make sure if something happens to me, she'll be taken care of. I told Daddy my fears, and this time, for some reason, he listened. What a relief to have him believe me for a change.

I was going to bring this to you, but Daddy said you were coming back tomorrow. Please file mine along with his, and I'll tell Del about it.

I'll come by the office and sign whatever needs to be signed.

Thank you,

Cynthia

"These are both dated the day Cynthia was murdered."

Mac echoed Tom's sentiments. "Son of a bitch. The Judge knew Celie was coming over, probably stuck this in the book so she wouldn't see it. Had another stroke when they told him Cynthia'd been murdered, never got a chance to get it to Tom. Son of a bitch."

Del confronted Celie. "You knew! You knew Cynthia didn't want you near Jennilee. Knew she wanted me to have custody. I begged you—begged you, time and again. And you refused—refused for the sole purpose of tormenting that child!"

Celie snarled, "You think I wanted the care of that brat? It was the only way I could keep what was rightfully mine. Daddy's will stated I was to get half the money, and if anything happened to Cynthia, as long as I had custody of her bastard, I got to live in *my* house, under *my* roof. Spend *my* money."

"His old will, not the newest one. None of it was yours. You knew that, too."

"Prove it."

She had them there. No doubt she was guilty. Proving it was a different matter.

Del dropped into the chair beside Jennilee. "All those years. Baby, I am so sorry. So very sorry." Gripped Jennilee's hand tightly in hers.

Face wet with tears, Jennilee whispered, "She wanted me. My mom loved me. She wanted you to have me, Grandy. Didn't intentionally leave me with her."

"Of course she wanted you, loved you. You were all she talked about, all she thought about."

A great weight lifted off Jennilee's soul. Grandy'd told her that, over and over, but hearing it in her mother's words made it real as it had never been, counteracted all Celie's ceaseless venom. Her eyes sought Mr. Jubal. "Thank you, Mr. Jubal. Thank you for rescuing those books, and for reading them, and for finding my mom's letter and bringing it here."

"Let's just have a group hug, shall we?" Celie's contempt ran rampant. Would have, had anyone given any credence to her nasty outburst.

"Thank you, Celie. If you weren't the bitch we all know you to be, I wouldn't be the person I am. Good bye."

"And good riddance," came simultaneously from Jennilee's supporters.

Letting out a half-scream, Celie shoved her chair back so hard it fell over. Stomped from the room, giving Mac an evil glare as she passed him.

He smiled back. Celie was going down, it was just a matter of time now. Jennilee might not want to press charges, but the stuff Celie had done, and what the Judge had hinted at would be enough to send her away for a very long time. Mac just needed to uncover absolute proof, and he was very good at digging. He watched Celie leave, her ex-lawyer trailing behind her, and stood, lost in thought for a minute.

When he turned back around, the tableau had changed. Del was talking earnestly to Tom and Jubal.

Charlie and Jennilee moved off to themselves, bread and peanutbutter close. His head bent, hers tilted up, Charlie murmured, "Beautiful, Jennilee. Just beautiful." Thumbed the tears off her face. "Seriously pissed?"

"Seriously."

"Hope you don't ever get mad at me."

Laughing, Jennilee threw her arms around Charlie's neck, stood on tiptoe to kiss him. Danced around the room bestowing hugs and kisses and thanks.

Working her way back to Charlie, Jennilee caught his hand in hers, needing contact. Wanting more, but not here, surrounded by the others.

Understanding, he brought her hand to his lips reverently. Let their joined hands drift down to rest over his heart. "Hard to believe inside our quiet little Jennilee is such a ferocious tigress. All of us were more than ready to spring to your defense, but you didn't need us—not at all. You did great all by yourself."

"I always need you, Charlie."

"Right back at you. Hey, did you notice the title of the book?"

Jennilee shook her head.

Charlie's grin almost split his face. *"War and Peace."*

Jennilee's laughter filled the room, joined by everyone else's as Charlie imparted that nugget.

∽

ACING HIS EXAMS, Charlie came home to Jennilee, for awhile. Making several trips to Raleigh to visit Tony's family, the first one back AC—after Celie—the whole Marcellini clan threw Charlie and Jennilee a surprise party. Jennilee cried some, laughed more.

The second visit, Grandy went with them. Mr. Berto, eager to show them his latest soon-to-be photography exhibit, could hardly sit still during the superb authentic Italian dinner.

Ushering them to the huge family room full of cloth-draped easels, motioning to the couch, Berto instructed, "Here. Sit here, Charlie, Jennilee, Del."

The Marcellini's crowded around, watching expectantly, giggling and grinning.

"Close your eyes, please." Whisking the coverings off, Berto stepped back. "Open, please." The three on the couch did, stared with identically shocked expressions.

A whole series of photos of Charlie and Jennilee, individually and together, and as the centerpiece, the day Jennilee'd been playing a singing game with the children when Charlie arrived.

Berto stood back and watched, needing no greater praise than the raw emotions on their faces.

Charlie and Jennilee shared a look, rose as one, walked closer. Stared. Grandy sat on the couch, tears streaming down her face, fingertips to her lips.

"Mr. Berto, I...*we*...want copies, please." Charlie knew he had to have some of these photos. "You've captured Jennilee perfectly."

"Not just Jennilee. You too, Charlie." Grandy came to stand beside her two, tears falling freely. Stared at the set of them with the children, at the love shining around them like halos.

"I'm going to call this exhibition—*Love Brought To Light*. That's what the two of you do—you glow with love, so much so that it's visible. If you're amenable, that is. I won't use these without your permission."

Charlie and Jennilee nodded as one. "You have it, Mr. Berto."

"Let us know and we'll come see it when you open it to the public."

Berto grinned. "The two of you are going to New York City to see this? I can't wait."

"New York?"

"Big exhibit. Thousands of people." Berto's grin widened.

"New York?"

"New York," he affirmed.

Looking at each other, Charlie and Jennilee burst out laughing and Jennilee said, "No, thanks, Mr. Berto. Raleigh's far enough away from home."

"How much?"

"How much what, Charlie?"

"How much for copies?"

Berto shook his head decisively. "Nothing. I refuse to take a dime from you. It's a pleasure just to work with you, to watch the two of you. There's not enough money in the world to get someone to pose like that, and no amount of money could buy your expressions. This one..." He pointed to the picture of them just after they'd kissed in the circle of children, "...this one here, whatever the two of you were remembering—it's written on your faces. Such a memory of love, right there."

Charlie and Jennilee locked gazes, remembering dragonflies and kaleidoscopes and heated skin.

"That look—that very one!" Mr. Berto crowed in delight.

Tony threw a wicked jibe. "Don't suppose you'd let us in on it?"

"Not a chance." Wrapping his arms tight around Jennilee, Charlie kissed her thoroughly.

Grandy was entranced. "You've done a marvelous job,

Berto. So… It looks like you could reach out and hold the love in your hands."

A hearty round of agreement came from all of Tony's family.

Berto handed Charlie a manila envelope.

Opening it with shaking hands, Charlie shared the contents with Jennilee. "Mr. Berto—we can't just…take these."

"You can and you will. This is a prestigious showing. If these do as well as I hope…" Berto shrugged. "This series could establish me as a premier photographer. Even if it doesn't, you've given me a great memory."

Jennilee shuffled slowly through the stack. Caught up in Tony and Angel's family, she seldom paid any attention to Mr. Berto—he was just always there, snapping endless pictures. And they had been endless.

A picture of the first day she'd come here, holding the baby and looking at Charlie. Numerous pictures of her and Angel and Tony and Miz Teresa. Jennilee and Angel, heads together, whispering and giggling, faces lit. Angel's dark curls and Jennilee's blaze of gold complementing each other perfectly.

Jennilee and Miz Teresa, in the kitchen, hovering over a meal, satisfied smiles on both their faces. Charlie and Jennilee, singing. Jennilee and Bella working on some kind of craft project. Jennilee lying on her belly on the floor, surrounded by coloring books and children, a shaft of sunlight pouring over them like a benediction. Charlie and Jennilee interacting with the Marcellini's, young and old alike.

Jennilee smiled radiantly at Charlie. "We'll get Mose to make frames and we'll place these on the walls up and down the stairs, scatter them through our house."

Sharing one of their looks, they turned to Mr. Berto.

"We'd like you…"
"…to photograph…"
"…our wedding."
"Please." Finishing together, they looked hopefully at him.

A slow smile creased his face. "I'd be honored. Name the time and place."

"Our house…"
"…in the spring…"
"…after Charlie…"
"…graduates."

Well used to it, Tony burst into gales of laughter as he watched his family try to keep up with Charlie and Jennilee's disjointed conversations.

The Marcellini's and Grandy drifted off, left Charlie and Jennilee with their likenesses. Charlie and Jennilee, hands clasped, took their time, stopping in front of each picture, absorbing it. Stood rooted in front of the one of Charlie braiding Jennilee's hair—her eyes closed and a look of pure bliss on both their faces. Right next to it, and every bit as intimate, one of their backs. Frozen in time, Charlie stroking a hand down the length of Jennilee's unbound hair.

∽

THE RIDE HOME WAS SILENT. A joyful, contented silence. Charlie drove, Jennilee right beside him, with Grandy in the passenger seat. They were almost to Chinquapin Ridge when Charlie spoke lazily.

"Going with us tomorrow, Grandy?"

"Going where?"

"To cut our tree. We thought maybe we'd head up Harlowe Creek and see if we could find a nice cedar on one of the hummocks in the marsh." Jennilee's voice was drowsy, and she was snuggled against Charlie, his arm around her.

"What time?"

"Tide's high around 10:00."

"Sounds great."

"I'll cut some magnolia leaves and some yaupon and holly to decorate the mantle and over the doors and make a centerpiece. Ooh, and some of that pine with the tiny pinecones. Want some for the Diner?" Jennilee was coming awake, excited by her plans.

"Jennilee, you don't have to…"

Jennilee reached out a hand to Grandy. "I know I don't have to—that's why I want to. Oh, and a wreath. I'll make a big wreath."

"Want me to shoot some mistletoe down?"

"Oh, yeah." Jennilee fairly purred and Charlie snickered.

Grandy snorted on a laugh, "Not like you two ever need mistletoe."

That set them off, and they were still laughing when they pulled up at Mose's. Mose heard them, waited 'til Charlie turned the engine off and let an ecstatic Jewel out. The little dog ran circles around them, danced on her hind paws, spun in place like a dervish. Jennilee held out her arms and Jewel launched. Jennilee caught her, got her face washed thoroughly, buried her face in her companion's shiny coat.

"I missed you, too, baby. Were you a good girl for Mose?"

"She talks to that mutt like she's expecting an answer." Mose imparted that with his usual straight face and low tones.

"Jewel does talk to me. Didn't you hear her?"

That brought on another round of laughter.

"They're goin' after some mistletoe, Mose. What do you think about that?"

"What for?"

Jennilee's laughter rang out. "Why, for everyone else, of course!"

"It's certain sure the two of you don't need it."

"I second that."

At the sound of voices, Jennilee turned to see Josh and Will coming across the yard from Garner House. "Hey, guys. You gonna be here for Christmas?"

"Yeah, we've both volunteered to stay here for duty so some of the guys with families could be with theirs for Christmas. If your Christmas is anything like your Thanksgiving, we wouldn't miss it for the world."

"We're decorating our tree tomorrow. Wanna help?"

"Is there food involved?"

"I'll take that as a yes. Tomorrow, then. Come about lunch time."

CHAPTER 41

She'd always helped decorate for Christmas, but this year, with the threat of Celie completely removed, Jennilee went all out. The big cedar they'd chosen stood regally in the living room, the star at the top brushing the eleven foot ceiling. Covered in ornaments, old and new, dominating the entire room, it radiated love and goodwill, a reflection of Jennilee.

Jennilee got her magnolia branches, and yaupon covered in bright red berries, and some type of pine with itsy-bitsy pinecones. Lined the mantles and the stairs, made gorgeous wreaths to hang on the doors, draped swags over the windows.

Charlie got an inkling of just what their house was going to look like when they were finally married and on their own. Jennilee decorated Grandy's house and the Diner until both house and restaurant ended up looking like something out of a magazine.

Set up a big tree at the Diner, no ornaments as such, just garland and lights. The ornaments were signature cards bearing needed items, with a space on the back of each card for pledging a donation to that needy family—money or food or whatever was needed.

She baked. And baked, and baked. Iced sugar cookies in Christmas shapes—Santas and reindeer and Christmas trees and bells and ornaments and holly. Peanutbutter balls and coconut balls, popcorn balls and candies. Banana bread and zucchini bread and squash bread and cranberry-eggnog bread. Sugared pecans. Peanut brittle. Fudge. And gave most all of it away.

Every room in the house had a little bowl or basket of homemade pot-pourri, dried orange slices and dried apple peels with a few cinnamon sticks thrown in. Jennilee kept a pot of the mixture simmering on the stove. The whole house was filled with not just the sights of Christmas, but the scents as well. And the sounds—Jennilee sang carol after carol.

Her happiness contagious, it spread to everyone who came in contact with her, friend and stranger alike.

∽

Waiting tables, Jennilee watched two small children holding hands and staring hard at the Christmas tree. Their mother, at least Jennilee assumed it was their mother, was filling out a job application, looking up frequently and keeping an eye on her two in between.

Picking up a couple coloring sheets and some crayons, Jennilee headed in their direction.

"Hey, guys. Would you like to enter our coloring contest?" Jennilee crouched and spoke softly. The kids, a boy and a slightly younger girl, looked like they'd spook if she moved too fast or spoke too loud. Their clothes were worn, obviously not new, but they were clean, the children well behaved.

The little boy, definitely the oldest, spared a worried

glance at his mother, shook his head. "No, thank you. What are those cards on the tree?"

"They're for people who need something. People who have…more…can adopt one of the families on the cards and help them."

The little girl's eyes lit and she piped up excitedly, "Can we have a card?"

"Hush, 'Lizabeth."

"Why, Timmy? We need…"

"I said hush." Timmy tightened his grip on his sister's hand in subtle warning.

"Miss, I'm finished with this. What do you want me to do with it?"

Rising, taking in the woman's brown hair and tired hazel eyes, full of worry, Jennilee held out her hand. "Jennilee, and I'll take it."

Handing Jennilee her application, the young mother asked nervously, "They weren't hurtin' nothin', were they? They're good kids, most of the time."

"Good as gold. We were just talking. I asked them if they wanted to enter our coloring contest. Winner gets free desserts for a year."

The young mother flashed an anxious look at her children. "We just got into town. I don't know how long we'll be here."

Jennilee quickly scanned the application. Rachel Tyndall, no address listed, nor phone number.

"I see you've waitressed before."

"In high school." Twisting her hands together, Rachel asked, "How soon will you know if I'm hired?"

Jennilee looked around at the full tables and grinned. "Well, Mrs. Tyndall, how does tonight sound?"

"I've got the job? Just like that? Are you the owner?"

Jennilee shook her head. "Not the owner, but I do the

hiring. When can you start?"

"When do you need me?"

"Right now."

Rachel looked at her kids, obviously torn. "I can't... I don't..." Went down on one knee in front of her children and took a deep breath. "Timmy, take your sister back out to the car and tell Daddy I got the job."

"Mrs. Tyndall..."

"Rachel, please."

"Rachel, walk the kids out and tell him yourself. A few more minutes isn't going to make any difference."

∽

JENNILEE WAS TAKING A WELL DESERVED break, hiding in a corner of the kitchen when Charlie came in. Giving her a thorough kiss, he snagged a handful of cookies. "What's up with the car in the parking lot?"

"What car, and what've you been doing? You smell like... outside. Wind and sunshine."

"The station wagon, and I smell like fresh air because that's where I've been—outside. You know better than to ask questions this close to Christmas."

"Secrets, huh? Maybe I'll just torture them out of you." Swiping a cookie out of his hand, Jennilee laughed and kissed him. "What station wagon?"

"The on-its-last-legs one that was here when I dropped you off, over on the edge of the parking lot. It's still here, and there's a guy and a bunch of kids in it."

"I hired a new waitress earlier."

"And?"

"And I think I need to talk to her. I'll get her if you'll go get him and the kids, please."

Making her way toward the dining room as Charlie

headed out the kitchen door, Jennilee snagged the first waitress she saw and motioned Rachel over, knowing if she went out on the floor, she'd get caught by someone wanting to talk. "Rita, take Rachel's tables for a bit. Rachel, come with me, please."

Worried frown instantly blossoming, tensing, Rachel blurted, "Jennilee, have I done something wrong? I told you I haven't done this for awhile."

"Calm down, Rachel. You're doing fine. You need a break, and we need to talk." Jennilee headed back to the kitchen, and the table there for the staff.

"Talk?"

"Sit down and eat something."

Rachel sat heavily, Jennilee slid a loaded plate in front of her.

"Relax, Rachel. You're not in trouble. You want to tell me what's going on?"

"What do you mean?"

"You didn't put any address on your application, and there's a car full of people waiting outside for you."

"I told you, we just got into town. I…"

"I can hear your stomach growling from over here. Eat."

"Not without… I…can't." Rachel covered her face with her hands and burst into tears. Attempted to speak. "Tim—he's my husband…"

"Rachel? What's wrong? What happened?"

Jennilee looked up as the back door to the kitchen opened. Charlie held it for Tim and the kids. Not just Timmy and Elizabeth, but two more. A toddler and a baby. All the kids looked like they were getting ready to start bawling right along with Rachel.

Timmy and Elizabeth each held one of the toddler's hands, while Charlie held the baby in the crook of one arm and the door with the other. Tim balanced awkwardly on crutches, both legs in casts.

Jumping to her feet, Rachel bee-lined for them, tears forgotten. "I'm fine. You shouldn't be... How come..."

Tim jerked his head at Charlie. "He insisted. I thought something was wrong, and when I saw you crying..."

"Sit. You need to sit." Urging Tim toward a chair, Rachel herded the children toward the table as well. Scooped up the toddler, gave Timmy and Elizabeth quick pecks on the cheek, murmured reassurances to them in a loving tone. Glanced at the baby and decided she was fine right where she was.

"Eat, all of you. We'll finish this discussion later. Charlie and these fine ladies will take care of you. I'll be back in a bit."

Jennilee waited tables, carried on with the customers and thought. Looking around the finally half empty Diner, she turned over the now dwindling customers to the other waitresses, headed to the kitchen. Grandy and Miz Sadie were cleaning up, cooking pretty much done for the night. Charlie was helping and trading knock-knock jokes with Timmy.

The toddler sat in a highchair beside Rachel, head bobbing. Timmy and Elizabeth were side by side, coloring, bracketed by Tim and Rachel. Rachel held the sleeping baby on her shoulder, softly humming a lullaby and patting her back, rocking gently.

All motion ceased when Jennilee came in, for just a beat, picked back up. Taking the mug of cocoa Charlie handed her, she sat. Taking the couples' measure, she sipped while her eyes weighed them, probed to their very souls.

"Timmy, Elizabeth—let's go put your pictures up on the wall with the others." He might not know exactly what Jennilee had in mind, but he knew her well enough to know it was something important. Charlie held out a hand to the brother and sister, Grandy swooped down on the baby and Miz Sadie crooned to the toddler as she picked him up.

In a blink, the kitchen emptied except for Jennilee and Rachel and Tim. Jennilee asked point blank, "Y'all livin' in your car?"

Rachel darted a look at her husband. "We're just…"

"We're not askin' for charity." Tim's face closed like a slamming door.

"We're not offering any." Jennilee answered him calmly. "Seems like you could use some help, though. Even if you don't want it for yourself, those kids deserve better."

Bursting into tears again, Rachel moved over against Tim, buried her face in his shoulder. Curving an arm around her, he pulled her tight against himself, brushed a kiss across the top of her head.

"We've hit a rough spot. We'll be alright."

"Tim—may I?" At his curt nod, Jennilee continued. "Seems like you've hit more than a rough spot, Tim. From where I'm sitting, looks more like the Grand Canyon. Pride's a good thing, most times. Pride in your accomplishments, in your work, in your family. Sometimes it's nothing but a burden. No loss of pride to admit you need help or to accept help when you need it."

Wandering back in as she was speaking, Charlie stood behind Jennilee, put his hands on her shoulders. Loud and clear, Jennilee heard his unspoken *Look who's talking*.

"Nobody's taking our kids away from us—not you, not *Family Services*, no one! Do you hear me?" Tim's grip on Rachel tightened, but she didn't let out a peep, only burrowed closer. His other hand clenched into a tight fist on the table.

From Tim's inflection, Jennilee figured he had about as much use for Child Welfare as she did.

Charlie pulled a chair out and sat. "Nobody said a word

about taking your kids away from you. Jennilee offered help, that's all.

"Tim, please. Jennilee's right. We can't go on like this. And it wouldn't be forever, just 'til we get back on our feet." Rachel's teary voice softened the harsh look on Tim's face, gentled his words.

"Rachel, honey..."

Continuing her interrogation, Jennilee asked bluntly, "How much longer do you have to be on crutches?"

"The doctor said he had to wear the casts two more months, at least. And that's if he stays off his feet." Rachel's watery gaze met Jennilee's, woman to woman, and *stubborn men* flashed between them.

"Let's say...six months, then."

"Six... No way." Tim shook his head stubbornly.

"I figure at least six, Charlie. What do you think? Two to three months until the casts come off, then therapy and a little bit of time to get back to his old self."

"Sounds about right."

"Six months it is." Jennilee completely ignored Tim's denial. "Rachel can't work, at least not much, not with all those kids to chase after. You can't chase kids without prolonging your recovery."

"Tell me something I don't already know." Tipping his head back, Tim closed his eyes tiredly.

"What kind of work do you do?" Charlie swiped Jennilee's cocoa, sipped.

Opening his eyes, Tim held Charlie's gaze. "I'm a... I used to work construction."

"Tim's a carpenter—an extraordinary one. He can build anything, and he's a whiz at getting the most from his crews." Rachel's pride clearly evident, she gave a half laugh. "I don't have a job, never had one besides high school and this one tonight. Never wanted one. All I've ever wanted to do was be a wife and mother and make a home. Look after the kids and Tim. We never planned for me to hold a job, got married as soon as we graduated high school. I'm afraid I'm sorely lacking in marketable skills."

"So what you really need is a place to stay, somewhere with enough room for the kids and some kind of work Tim can do until you get back on your feet, literally." Jennilee held Rachel's gaze.

Tim sounded bitter and defeated. "Yeah. Any suggestions for an out of work cripple?"

"As a matter of fact… Let me make a few calls." Rising, Jennilee swiped what was left of her cocoa back from Charlie.

Tim didn't say anything, started putting on his mule face.

Waiting until Jennilee left Charlie let his laughter spill out. "You might as well give in. She won't take no for an answer."

"Why is she so adamant about helping us? You don't know us from Adam."

"You've no reason to fear her motives. Jennilee loves kids, loves family. Besides, it's Christmas. 'Tis the season, and all that."

Jennilee came back, face wreathed in smiles. "We've arranged to borrow some baby things for the night—a crib and a playpen. You're welcome to spend the night at Grandy's—Miz Del. It's too late tonight to do much more, but you've got an interview tomorrow with Charlie and our business partner, Mose. He's black, by the way. If you have a problem with that, now would be a good time to say so."

Rachel and Tim shook their heads. "No. No problem."

"Good. Let's go home. It's been a long day."

CHAPTER 42

Charlie helped Grandy and Jennilee settle the Tyndalls in the downstairs bedrooms. Uneasy about being very far from the kids, the playpen and the crib and two old Army cots were set up in the room adjoining Tim and Rachel's, the connecting door left open.

In the hallway, Rachel caught Jennilee's hand, switched her gaze between Jennilee and Miz Del. "I don't know why you're doing this…"

"I'm doing it because I want to, and because I can."

"Thank you, from the bottom of our hearts. Where's Charlie? I wanted to thank him, too."

"Gone to his dad's for the night. He'll be back first thing."

"Dad's? Back? I thought you two were married?"

Jennilee's laughter rang out softly. "Not yet, but we're working on it. Soon. I can give you days and hours if you want, minutes if you give me a bit to do some figuring."

Del laughed, gave Jennilee a hug. "These old bones are tired. I'm going to bed. 'Night, sweetie. Don't stay up too late."

"Right behind you." Jennilee hugged her back, silently conveying her thanks and her love. " 'Night, Grandy."

"Miz Del's your grandma?"

Jennilee shook her head.

"Now I'm really confused. I heard you and Charlie both call Miz Del *Grandy*. Whose grandma is she?"

"Sorry." Jennilee didn't sound sorry—she sounded like she was trying not to laugh. "Miz Del is Charlie's grandma. Both our moms died when we were little and Grandy raised both of us, for the most part. Charlie lived with her while we were growing up and now I'm living here."

"Oh, well. That clears it up some."

At Rachel's dry tone, Jennilee clapped her hand over her mouth so the laughter threatening to burst out wouldn't wake the kids. Voice still full of laughter, she said, "We're all early risers around here, but don't feel like you have to get up at the crack of dawn."

Rachel sighed and smiled. "The kids are up with the roosters, so don't worry about waking us. I'm afraid we'll wake y'all up."

"Not a chance. 'Night, Rachel."

" 'Night, Jennilee."

∼

BREAKFAST well under way when Charlie slipped in the back door, Jennilee sighed in welcome, floated into his arms like they were practicing for a ballroom dance contest. Kissed. Kissed some more.

"Umm. I missed you."

"Missed you, too."

Starting to kiss again, they got distracted by giggles. Charlie kissed the tip of Jennilee's nose instead. "I think we've got company."

"Sounds like it."

Timmy and Elizabeth stood in the kitchen doorway. More giggles. "You two look just like our mom and dad. They're always kissing."

Jennilee laughingly informed the two, "Kissing's a good thing."

"If you say so." Timmy scrunched up his face, his tone doubtful.

Jennilee's laughter rang out and she gave Charlie another smooch for good measure.

∽

Following the sounds of giggling and teasing to the kitchen, pushing Tim in a wheelchair that had appeared after they went to sleep, Rachel knew it was far later than the kids usually let her sleep. She and Tim had woken to find all the kids' beds empty, a heartbeat of total panic before the scents and sounds lured them down the hall.

The wheelchair wasn't the only thing that had appeared. Both toddler and baby were ensconced in highchairs. Timmy and Elizabeth were sitting at the table, surrounded by Charlie and Miz Del and Jennilee, all laughing. Rachel'd already noticed Jennilee had that effect on people—her happiness filled the air, buoyed everyone around her.

Spotting Rachel and Tim, Jennilee rose. "Mornin' guys. Hope you're hungry. I've got plates in the warming oven for you. Coffee?"

Scrambling down, Timmy and Elizabeth ran to their parents.

"I feel like I've been snatched from the jaws of a never-ending nightmare and plunked down smack-dab in the middle of Heaven." Rachel sounded breathless, on the verge of tears.

Twisting, Tim reached a hand back over his shoulder to cover one of hers.

Only Charlie heard her muttered, "Been there myself," as Jennilee busied herself getting plates and pouring coffee.

Leaning close, Charlie whispered, "They're some of your lost ones, aren't they?"

Their long ago conversation at Amelia's grave echoed in the kitchen, audible only to the two of them. Jennilee's whisper-soft reply reached no farther than Charlie. "Yeah, Charlie. They are, but now we've found them."

Timmy and Elizabeth clamored for hugs. Hugging each in turn, Rachel picked them up one at a time, leaned over Tim and let the kids hug him too, patiently reminding them to watch out for daddy's boo-boos.

Pushing Tim to the table, Rachel gave the toddler and the baby the same loving attention she'd lavished on the older kids, dropping a kiss on top of each little head and cooing to them. Timmy and Elizabeth talked over top of one another, telling about their morning so far.

Urging Rachel to sit, Jennilee placed well-filled plates in front of her and Tim. "The kids've eaten. I told Timmy and Elizabeth they could go out and play as long as it was alright with you."

Rachel granted permission, along with all the standard mommy admonishments. Timmy and Elizabeth excused themselves, hurried to their room for their jackets, came tearing back and disappeared out the back door.

"They're great kids." Jennilee watched their noisy departure with all the tolerance of an indulgent aunt.

"Thank you. We think so too."

Giving Charlie and Jennilee each a peck, Grandy snagged her own jacket from a hook by the back door. "We'll go keep an eye on those two. C'mon Jewel."

The two young couples fell into easy banter.

Jennilee gestured to their nearly empty plates. Rachel and Tim shook their heads. "Thanks, but no thanks. You fed us well last night, and after this, we're stuffed."

Charlie laughed, pulled Jennilee close and pressed a kiss to her temple. "That's the way she likes to keep everyone —stuffed."

"What about the job interview?" Tim flashed a worried look at Rachel.

"Mose will come over when you're ready. Got any tools?"

Tim grimaced. "Sold what I could, pawned the rest."

"You can borrow some of ours."

Tim looked Charlie in the eye. "I'll work hard for you, whatever you want me to do. I'm no slacker, and we're not looking for handouts."

"Never said you were." Jennilee admonished softly, "If you were, you'd be down at the Welfare office holding your hand out instead of trying to live in a station wagon with four kids."

Rachel got a stricken look on her face. "Everything just happened so fast. We were doing fine—struggling, but making it—and then everything just…fell apart. Went to pieces like a pair of panty hose in a briar patch. Seems like it's just been one bad thing after another."

Rachel choked, recovered. "We had a nice little house—renting with an option to buy. We had Timmy and Elizabeth and Tim had a great job. Foreman at the construction site, making good money." Smoothing a hand over the baby's downy head, she blew kisses and smiled at the toddler.

Jennilee looked at the toddler and the baby, both sitting contentedly in their highchairs, obviously well loved and well taken care of.

Rachel caught the unspoken question in Jennilee's eyes. "Corey and Cassie aren't ours. I mean, they are, but we're not their parents. I mean, we are now."

Tim shook his head. "What Rachel means is—we're not their real parents. We've legally adopted both of them, couldn't love them more if they were really ours." Covering Rachel's hand with his, he squeezed consolingly.

Rachel fought back tears. "Corey and Cassie are my sister's children. She and her husband were killed in a car wreck when Cassie was just a couple weeks old. We got them, got custody. Things got harder, but we were still fine until Tim's accident. After that... It went downhill fast."

Jennilee moved to stare unseeingly out the window.

Giving Jennilee time, Charlie asked, "How old are the kids?"

"Timmy's almost six, Elizabeth's almost four. Corey's two and a half, Cassie's seven months. We always planned on having a bunch of kids, this just wasn't quite the way we planned to do it."

Charlie threw a glance at Jennilee's white-knuckled grip on the sink, knowing she needed a moment more to compose herself. "You don't have any family to help you?"

"Tim's a foster kid—he has no family except the one we've made. I only had my sister. Her in-laws opposed the marriage, refused to have anything to do with the kids. Their loss. I won't let Corey and Cassie forget their parents, but they'll know nothing but love from us."

High pitched children's laughter and Jewel's higher pitched barking rang in the sudden quiet.

Getting to her feet, Rachel peered out the back door. "Oh, that's such a good sound. The kids haven't laughed like that in ages. Thank you from the very bottom of my heart, Jennilee. You've done so much for us. If there's ever anything we can do for you, anything at all..."

Tim voiced his agreement. "Anything."

Jennilee stirred, demons banished. "There is one small thing."

"Jennilee-love, are you sure?" Enfolding her in his strong arms, Charlie stroked his hands up and down her back, touched foreheads.

"I'm sure, Charlie."

Rachel and Tim shared a glance, shrugged. Jennilee seemed upset, but when she turned to face them, her smile nearly blinded them. "Excuse me, please. I have to make a few phone calls."

Charlie watched Jennilee disappear down the hall, grinning like a possum.

Rachel gulped. "Who's she gonna call this time? Santa?"

"If anyone has a direct line to him, it'd be Jennilee."

Jennilee came back to find everyone outside. Stepping out on the back porch, she stood beside Tim in his wheel chair.

Tim held a content Cassie, Grandy sat on the steps, Corey standing between her knees. Charlie and Rachel were involved in a mad game of keep away with Jewel, her ball, and Timmy and Elizabeth. Bounding down the steps, Jennilee joined the melee, her laughter as carefree as the children's.

∼

PEOPLE, then things began arriving. First Miz Sadie, then Mose. Grandy and Miz Sadie occupied the kids in the living room while Charlie and Mose closeted themselves with Tim. Jennilee took Rachel shopping, she said, for necessities.

Coming home with enough stuff to bog down Santa's sleigh, they were just getting out of Jennilee's car when a big conversion van pulled up. The driver stepped out. "Jennilee —Merry Christmas. Any particular place you want this?"

"Merry Christmas to you. Right where you are is fine. Thanks, Dan."

"Any time."

Another car pulled up, Dan got in and they left.

Rachel protested futilely, "Jennilee, that better not be for us."

"Your station wagon's on its last legs. Not even Charlie's dad can revive that piece of junk, and he's a mechanical wizard."

"Jennilee, you have to stop. You can't just...give us all this stuff."

"Why not?"

"You...can't. That's why." Rachel put her hands on her hips and pursed her lips.

Jennilee laughed. "Okay, Mom. *Because I said so* never carried much weight with me. I'm more of a *give me a real reason why* type of girl."

"Jennilee..." Rachel was trying hard not to laugh, like a parent trying to discipline a child who's done something wrong but at the same time hilariously funny.

"Who said I was *giving* it to you? Tim's going to work for us, and we're slave-drivers, or so we've been told." Jennilee's eyes twinkled. "Consider this stuff...perks. Side benefits of the job."

"You are *hopeless*."

"Hey, Jennilee. Need help?"

Rachel watched Jennilee's whole face, her entire body, light at the sound of Charlie's voice.

"Need you." Tipped her face up for his kiss.

"Got me." Charlie swept her close, kissed her like his life depended on it.

"Y'all have to stop. You're embarrassing me." Rachel fanned her face with her hands.

"Better get used to it. They're always like that. And they are slave-drivers." Mose's quietly amused rumble got through to Charlie and Jennilee.

"You should be..."

"...well used to it..."

"...by now, Mose."

Giving a snort, Mose reached into the car to pick up packages. Shook his head. "You two..." Rachel caught his grin as the huge man turned, winked at her, and headed for the house, arms loaded.

Grabbing the remaining bags, the trio followed.

"Just what is it Tim's going to be doing for you?"

"Charlie and Mose and I've been business partners for a long time. We've bought a bunch of houses, refurbished and resold them. We're thinking about branching out, building our own. Mose wants to devote more time to making furniture. Charlie's in college, and I help Grandy at the Diner. We need a good, responsible person to supervise, take care of day to day details."

"And Tim's that person?"

Charlie answered, "Seems to be. Mose and I grilled him pretty good. He gave us all the right answers. If we don't suit each other or he decides he doesn't like it, we'll figure out something else."

Jennilee chimed in, " 'Course, he's going to have to do what Doc says until Doc releases him, or all bets are off."

Rachel laughed and shook her head. "He didn't even want me to go into the Diner last night, much less ask about a job."

"So, how'd you manage it?"

Rachel admitted, red-faced, "I waited until he and the babies were asleep."

"Great. Just what Jennilee needs—a partner in crime." Charlie rolled his eyes, his grin ear to ear.

"Mommy, Mommy." Two small bodies barreled into Rachel, almost knocking her off her feet the instant she stepped inside.

"Grandy said we could stay here 'til Christmas, so Santa'd know where to find us."

"Please? It's only two days."

Two hopeful faces looked up at her. Rachel melted, corrected them absently. "Miz Del, and we'll have to see what Daddy says."

"He said to wait and see what you said."

Elizabeth poked out her bottom lip. "She said to call her Grandy."

"It's not polite…"

Grandy came down the hall to help carry stuff. "This house might as well be a barn, 'cause it's sure enough full of mules."

"What's a…mule?" Elizabeth perked up, looked around interestedly.

"Like a horse, dummy."

"Timmy—little boys who are rude to their sisters might not have a Christmas. Tell Elizabeth you're sorry, and say it like you mean it." Rachel eyed her offspring sternly.

"Yes, ma'am. Sorry, 'Lizabeth."

"Go tell your father I'll be right there." The kids tore off, back to the living room. "What am I saying? *Might* not have a Christmas? And don't you dare, Jennilee."

"Who, me?" Jennilee looked at Rachel, all wide eyed innocence.

Rachel groaned. "Do you know what the definition of *incorrigible* is?"

"One of the synonyms for incorrigible is…persistent." Jennilee grinned, unrepentant.

Rachel rolled her eyes. "Like I said—incorrigible."

Charlie bumped shoulders with Jennilee. "It also means impossible to change, hopeless…"

"Charlie! Who's side are you on?"

"Yours, Jennilee-love. Always yours." Pinning Jennilee against the wall Charlie lowered his lips to hers.

"And they're off. Might as well come to the living room,

Rachel. Those two will be awhile." Del tucked Rachel's arm in hers and left the two lovebirds to it.

While the babies napped, Jennilee and Jewel took Timmy and Elizabeth out to see the dock and the boats. Sitting on the back porch, Charlie, Rachel, and Tim watched them.

"Charlie, can you talk some sense into her? She doesn't even know us, and she's treating us like we're really family. Spoiling us rotten, and I don't mean just the kids." Rachel pleaded their case.

"Rachel, Tim—Jennilee's a very giving person. She truly doesn't want anything from you. Please don't reject her gifts. Like you, she has a tremendous amount of pride, and also like you, she has no family except what she makes. She does have an unlimited capacity for love. Once she pulls you into her circle, there is nothing, and I mean nothing, she wouldn't do for you. Don't spoil this for her. Just accept it, and her. I know you feel like it's too much and you can't repay her, but acceptance is the greatest gift you can give her. She already thinks of you as a sister, Rachel, and she's taken all of you under her wing. Let her have this pleasure. You won't be sorry."

Tim asked straight out, "What about you? How come you're so gung-ho about what she's doing?"

"Me? Whatever makes Jennilee happy makes me happy. She's my world."

Watching Jennilee playing with the kids, Charlie explained. "Once, a long time ago, Jennilee...dreamed, and told me about it. Said because our mothers died so young, and because we ended up being only children, there were others out there like us. People who should've been our brothers and sisters. Lost ones. Brothers and sisters who needed us as much as we needed them. She's...gathering. Gathering the lost ones. Making a family, just as you have."

Tim made a disbelieving snort. "You're saying we're… some of her lost ones?"

"You don't have to believe me. I'm just telling you because you have a right to know why she feels the way she does, why she does the things she does."

Tim asked dryly, "So, just how many lost ones are there?"

Charlie laughed long and loud. "I have no idea, but Jennilee dearly loves family."

Sounding adamant, face set, Tim shook his head. "We can't stay here forever, sponging off the two of you and Miz…Grandy."

"Not forever, just 'til Christmas. Give her that, please."

Jennilee and the children raced across the yard to the porch. "We're ready for some hot cocoa. How 'bout you guys?"

"Definitely getting chillier." Charlie glanced at the overcast sky. "Wind's come to the north. Gonna get colder before it's done."

Charlie held the door as Rachel and the kids streamed inside, trailed by Tim in his wheelchair. Snagging Jennilee's hand, he held her back, closed the door, wrapped her in his arms and kissed them both breathless.

"I thought you said it was getting colder." Jennilee grinned up at him—her love, her life.

Touching a fingertip to her reddened nose, Charlie brushed it across her glowing cheeks. Her eyes sparkled with merriment, with love. His. His Jennilee. "Did I say colder? I must've been mistaken. It's a regular heat wave out here."

"Have I told you lately how much I love you?"

"Not in the last half hour or so."

"Well, consider yourself told."

Melting together once more, they heard the door open and Timmy's exaggerated sigh. In the thoroughly aggrieved tone only little boys can achieve at the sight of adults embracing, he hollered, "They're kissing—again."

Laughter, inside and out.

Escorting Jennilee in, Charlie ruffled Timmy's hair. "I'll remember that when I catch you kissing your first girlfriend."

"Kissing...a girl?" Timmy made choking sounds and pretended to gag. "I'm never gonna kiss a *girl*."

More laughter followed his heartfelt declaration.

Accepting mugs of hot cocoa from Grandy, they sipped gratefully.

"Ooh. Just the way I like it—hot and sweet with extra marshmallows. Thanks, Grandy." Cupping her mug in both hands, Jennilee grinned like a kid in a candy store. Threw her invitation out casually. "A bunch of us promised we'd go sing at the nursing home this afternoon. Wanna come with us?"

Rachel said the first thing that popped into her head. "What about the Diner?"

"We're closed 'til Monday."

"Closed?"

"Yep. Grandy's the owner. She said we're closed, so we're closed. Wanna argue?"

They piled into the van that had appeared when Jennilee waved her wand, made her magic phone calls. The front passenger seat had been modified, courtesy of Mr. Donnie, so Tim could get in and out easily.

Jennilee let Charlie and Tim figure out how to situate him while she and Rachel and Grandy got the kids ready. They filled the back seats, with much laughter and jockeying for position, Jennilee having procured three car seats and a booster seat from somewhere.

The singing was a great success, and so was the caroling afterward.

Part of a large caravan, Charlie drove them around, stopping at different places, pulling the van as close as possible so Tim could participate without having to get in and out. They sang until Corey started getting fussy and Cassie fell asleep.

Arriving back at Grandy's, the tired but happy group headed for the bathrooms first, then the kitchen. By the time Rachel and Tim made it to the kitchen with the kids, Jennilee and Grandy had it smelling good. Warmed up leftover chicken and dumplings, the ultimate comfort food.

Cassie, awake from her nap and having sucked down a bottle, willingly went to Jennilee. Giving Rachel time to eat and take care of the other kids, Jennilee stripped Cassie and plunked her in the kitchen sink. Rachel took a bite of chicken and dumplings, savored. Watched Charlie watching Jennilee with the baby. Shared a half-embarrassed grin with Tim. Being around Charlie and Jennilee was like...like watching an exquisitely tender love scene in a movie. Beautiful, but you didn't necessarily want someone catching you doing it, just in case the beauty made you cry, and mostly because you felt like you were intruding on an intensely private moment.

"Your chicken and dumplings sure are good, Grandy. Mind letting me in on your secret?"

Grandy and Jennilee exchanged a poignant look. Grandy had taught Jennilee to make chicken and dumplings right here—a blink ago, a lifetime ago. Jennilee flicked a glance at Charlie, saw the same memories dancing in his eyes.

"Better ask Jennilee. She does most of the cooking around here now."

"You taught me." Jennilee blew Grandy a kiss over her shoulder.

"Hey! I help." Charlie laughingly protested.

"Help yourself to seconds," Jennilee teased.

Charlie got up and stalked her, mock growling. Jennilee giggled, snatched up a dripping Cassie and held the baby in front of her like a shield. "Charlie…"

"Charlie, what?"

"Charlie, hold the baby while I get a towel. I forgot to get one."

"Practice makes perfect."

Everyone in the room, including the kids, knew Charlie was talking about more than bathing babies.

CHAPTER 43

Charlie's prediction proved right. Christmas eve day dawned clear and cold. A screaming nor'easter had torn through during the night, leaving icy blue skies, a biting wind, and much cooler temperatures behind.

Jennilee and the kids were up and fed before Rachel and Tim woke up. Making her way to the kitchen, Rachel smiled wanly. "Mornin'…Grandy. Y'all must think we're terrible parents."

"Hush that right now, Rachel. What you are is worn out."

"Still… Where are the kids? With Jennilee, I know, but where?"

Grandy snickered. "Right now, behind the closed door of the living room, with strict orders for the rest of us to keep out."

"What's Jennilee up to now?"

"Only time will tell. She'll be out soon. Charlie'll be here shortly, and nothing keeps those two apart for very long."

"Well, as long as I'm not needed elsewhere, what can I do to help you?"

"Eat first. There's plenty of work to go around." Taking a

plate out of the warming oven, Grandy set it in front of Rachel. Opened a drawer, took out an apron, laid it on the table beside Rachel.

Jennilee appeared in the hall door—Cassie on one hip, holding Corey by the hand, Timmy and Elizabeth and Jewel bouncing around her—just as Charlie came in the back door. Looking from one to the other, Rachel felt a quick flush of color sweep her face. The love radiating between them was palpable.

"Mommy! Jennilee said not to wake you. We've been…"

"Hush, 'Lizabeth." Clapping a hand over his sister's mouth, Timmy informed his mother importantly, "It's a secret."

"Let your sister go. She won't tell, will you, sweetie?"

Elizabeth shook her head, eyes wide over Timmy's restraining hand. Dropping his hand, both of them ran to Rachel. Corey, not about to be left out, toddled across the kitchen.

Rachel knelt and enfolded all three. "Mornin', angels. You behaving'?"

"Jennilee said…"

"…we have to be 'specially good today, cause it's Christmas eve."

"She's right."

Jennilee turned at the quiet sound of Tim's wheelchair behind her. Seeing Tim, Cassie cooed delightedly and held her arms out. Jennilee let Tim get into the kitchen fully before handing him the baby and pushing him closer to the table.

"You guys up for another round?" Jennilee looked to Rachel, who looked to Tim. They both shrugged.

"More singing? Yesterday was wonderful, by the way." Rachel grinned at Jennilee.

"Charlie and Jennilee are gonna…"

"She said we could help." Elizabeth interrupted Timmy.

Jennilee pinned both kids with a firm look. "Ahem. That's not exactly what I said."

Timmy clarified. "Jennilee said we could help as long as it was okay with you."

"Much better." Taking Tim's plate out of the warming oven, Jennilee slid it across the table and spun in one graceful move, like a dancer executing a perfect step and returning to her partner. Spun right into Charlie's arms for her morning kiss.

"Missed you."

"Missed you more."

"Soon."

"The sooner, the better."

Laughter threatening to bubble out, Rachel goaded, "Um, remember us? Are you gonna tell us what we're supposed to help with, or are we supposed to guess?"

Charlie never took his eyes off Jennilee's face. "Rachel sure is a spoilsport."

Jennilee nodded and stretched up on tiptoe. Charlie kissed her again, murmured against her lips, "Maybe we should make them guess. That way we could…"

A wadded up dishtowel hit Charlie upside the head. "Then again, maybe not."

Jennilee wrapped her arms around Charlie's waist, kept the side of her head against his chest, right over his heart and looked at Rachel. "We've got baskets to deliver."

"Wrong holiday." Rachel's delivery was droll.

Jennilee burst into laughter. "We do Easter, too. Right now, gift baskets, for special friends and some of the elderly and shut-ins around town."

"Just around town? For a moment there I thought we were going to have to hitch a ride with Santa."

Charlie rolled his eyes and squeezed Jennilee tighter. "Don't give her any ideas."

"Are we gonna take the van again?" Timmy danced from foot to foot.

"That's up to your mom and dad."

"Can we, please? Last night was so fun, and Daddy got to come. Please?"

Elizabeth added her *pleases* to Timmy's.

Rachel shook her head. "Like we'd tell you no, anyway, Jennilee. You..."

Jennilee denied what Rachel was about to say. "It's your van."

The baskets and kids were loaded up, the baskets delivered. Back at Grandy's, a late lunch finished and Corey and Cassie down for their afternoon naps, Grandy settled in the living room with Timmy and Elizabeth. Totally engrossed listening to Grandy reading Christmas poems and stories, the kids paid no attention when the adults slipped out to meet Mr. Tom in the room Charlie used for his office.

Introductions made, Jennilee paced, wove her fingers together, faced Rachel and Tim. Charlie and Mr. Tom watched, giving their silent support.

"Yesterday, you said you'd do something for me. Does your offer still stand?"

"Anything, Jennilee. After what you've done for us..."

Waving her hand impatiently, Jennilee propped one hip on the corner of the desk. "We want you to think carefully about this before you give us an answer. We're not pressuring you in any way, and if you say yes, we've had Mr. Tom draw up a contract. He'll explain and answer any questions you might have. It's totally up to you—your choice."

Hands fisted, white knuckled, Jennilee gnawed on her bottom lip.

Tim reached out a hand to Rachel. "Jennilee, calm down.

You have to tell us what you want before we can make any decisions. You're scaring us. You don't want us to make a hit on somebody, do you?"

That startled a half laugh out of Jennilee. "We..." Breathing hard, she trailed off.

Charlie cupped her cheek, touched foreheads. "Easy, Jennilee. Want me to ask?"

A quick shake of her head. Clasping Charlie's hand like a lifeline, she looked at Rachel and Tim.

This wasn't the bubbly, laughing person they'd come to know. Jennilee looked…anguished.

"Jennilee, just spit it out. Or, if you don't want to say it, you don't have to. We can see how much whatever it is bothers you." Throwing a panicked look at Mr. Tom, Rachel started to get up. Jennilee's upraised hand had Rachel settling.

Jennilee wheezed a laugh, a brittle sound, not the joyful one they'd become used to. "Y'all must think I'm completely crazy."

Rachel cocked her head. "We were starting to wonder. I mean, no one takes in strangers off the street and treats them like long lost family. So, yeah, we pretty much think you've gone round the bend."

Jennilee blinked at Rachel's dry sarcasm, gave her a lopsided smile. "I thought this would be easier—I thought I could do this with no problem."

"Jennilee-love…" Charlie wrapped both arms around her.

"I can do this, Charlie. I…have to."

"I'm right here."

Remaining in the safe circle of Charlie's arms, Jennilee opened her mouth, closed it. Took several deep breaths. Closed her eyes. Opened them, and said in a rush, "You'd be doing us a big favor. We have a house…an empty house. We'd like you to live in it, rent free, and before you pitch a hissy fit, consider it another perk. We'll cover the utilities. After you get back on your feet, you can decide whether you want to stay there or not. It's all in the contract, and you don't have to decide right now."

"Jennilee, you are crazy—crazy as a loon. You've taken us into your hearts, your home, you've already given us so much, and now you're giving us a place to stay, no strings attached?"

"Keep it clean."

"That's it?"

"I have to...go." Pushing herself out of Charlie's hold, Jennilee bolted out the door.

"Charlie, you gonna tell us what that was all about?" Tim kept his voice low, in case Jennilee was still close enough to hear.

Charlie paused on his way to the door. "Nope. If Jennilee wants to tell you, it's her call. Fill that house with love and laughter, and more children. That's exactly what it needs. That'll do more good for Jennilee than anything. Go look at it and see what you think. Mr. Tom'll take you through it. 'Scuse me."

Rachel and Tim looked to Mr. Tom as Charlie disappeared, hot on Jennilee's heels. "Charlie's right. Fill the house with love and laughter. As their lawyer and long time friend, I will tell you that you couldn't have landed in a better place, or found better people."

Hearing the back door slam, Charlie grabbed his and Jennilee's coats on his way out. She was standing at the end of the porch, oblivious to the bitter cold. Arms wrapped around herself, hunched as if in tremendous pain. Putting his coat on as he walked, Charlie turned her to himself and draped her coat around her shoulders.

"Jennilee-honey, I am so proud of you." Held her, just held

her. Brushed kiss after kiss over the top of her head. Crooned wordlessly until her shaking abated.

"Come on, Jennilee. Let's go somewhere."

Jennilee tilted her face up to his, her eyes fathomless pools against her waxy skin. "South Carolina?"

Charlie laughed, tightened his hold and spun them both in giddy circles. Teased her back as he set her on her feet. "We could be back before morning."

"Let's don't and pretend we did." Jennilee clapped both hands over her mouth, her eyes flying wide and her face instantly going red.

"Jennilee—I can't believe you said that! I'm...flattered... and tempted. If I wasn't such a stand-up guy..." Grinning down at her, Charlie molded his body suggestively against hers. "That'd be a Christmas present to top all Christmas presents, but no." Kissed her thoroughly. "We've waited this long, a little more won't kill us—maybe. I do have an idea, though. We both deserve a reward for being good."

A short truck ride later, Charlie pulled up at their pond. Indulging themselves with some heavy petting, heavy enough to fog up all the windows, they got in some serious one on one time.

"Jennilee, it gets harder and harder to leave you. A little over a year, and I'll never have to leave you again, dream about you, because we'll finally be married." Charlie started softly singing the Beach Boys—*Wouldn't It Be Nice?*

Charlie sprawled across the length of the seat, leaning against the passenger side door, Jennilee draped on top of him. Chest to chest, hip to hip, thigh to thigh. She could feel his hard arousal, right at the juncture of her thighs, right where she wanted it—almost. She wiggled, trying to center him.

Charlie held her still, practically begged, "Don't move, Jennilee-love."

Slipping a hand between them, Jennilee fumbled at the metal snap of his jeans.

Groaning, Charlie stopped her. "Jennilee-sweet, you can't..."

"Charlie, please." Her softly whispered plea almost undid him.

Gently removing her hand, he brought it to his lips. "What is it about this place that turns you into such a wonderful wanton?" Charlie held her, stroked her, fought himself. "Again, I'm flattered, extremely so, but I'm afraid I'm going to have to disappoint you once more. I have very specific ideas about our first time together, and none of them include taking you in the cramped front seat of my truck like we're a couple horny teenagers."

Jennilee snickered, "We are horny teenagers."

"What are you wearing?"

"Wearing?" Drowning in sensations, in emotions, his question made no sense. "Jeans and a sweater."

"Not right now. On our wedding night. I picked your dress, it's only fair you get to choose your lingerie. Of course, if you can't think of anything... I have some very specific ideas about that, too."

His words fanned the flames Jennilee was trying to tamp down. A guttural sound of want, of need, was wrenched from deep in Jennilee's soul. Plastering herself to his hard body, she covered his lips with hers, squirmed like she was trying to worm her way inside his skin.

Charlie came up for air first, broke the kiss, attempted to put some distance between them. Impossible, considering where they were and the position they were in. "Jennilee, I can't take much more. You have to stop, before I break my word to you." His desperation got through to her.

Jennilee pushed away. "I'm... Oh, Charlie. I'm so sorry. I didn't mean it."

"Ah, Jennilee-honey. I sincerely hope you did mean it. Don't ever, *ever*, apologize for letting me know how much you want me. It just makes me want you more."

Everything she was feeling showing on her face, Jennilee threw herself at him, buried her face in his neck and burst into tears. Charlie let her cry, wrapped her in his arms and his love, started singing quietly. *You Are The Woman. Heard It In A Love Song. Just An Old Fashioned Love Song. Let Your Love Flow. Your Kiss. Lady.*

She cried like her heart was breaking, cried as she hadn't let herself cry through all the years of torture and abuse, all the loneliness and despair. Cried like a desolate child, cried for the childhood denied to her. Cried for what could've been, what should've been. Throughout the storm, Charlie held her, sang to her, stroked her hair from the crown of her head to the tip ends.

The storm had abated, the sobs had dwindled to hiccuping breaths when Charlie started talking. "That's it, Jennilee-love. Let it out. You've held it in far too long. The last few months have been an emotional roller-coaster, one high and one low right after another. Today was the last straw. Tim and Rachel won't be like them. They'll fill the Judge's house with love and laughter and children, just like we're going to do our own home. You picked good people to entrust it to. Believe this, if nothing else—I want you with every fiber of my being. And Jennilee, once we're married, you'll get so tired of me wanting to make love to you, you'll be begging me to stop. I'll be like some randy old goat, never satisfied."

Jennilee sniffled. "Never happen. I'll never get enough of you."

"Easy enough for you to say now, when I'm denying us both. We'll see."

"You'll be the one begging me to stop. I'll never be able to keep my hands off you. We'll have to move far, far away where no one knows us."

"What good will that do?"

"You're right. None."

"Guess you'll just have to learn to live with it."

"We. We'll have to."

"Wanna go walk for awhile?"

"Sounds good. Then let's go shopping."

"For the kids?"

"Yeah."

CHAPTER 44

Going outside, Rachel and Tim automatically headed for the van.

Tom cleared his throat. "This way, please."

Rachel pushed Tim's wheelchair across the winter dead grass, across the expanse of yard and around the tall hedgerow separating Grandy's house from the nearly identical one next door.

Rachel stopped. "This house? This is the one they want us to live in?"

"What? You thought they'd put you in some hovel?"

"No, but…"

"You don't have to decide right now. They just want you to look." Tom continued, almost talking more to himself than the couple beside him. "The house has been empty for months. It's been professionally cleaned, so you won't have to start with a mess. I'm afraid the furniture is mix and match, somewhat sparse. If you decide to accept their offer, Charlie and Jennilee will…"

"…do nothing more. They've done enough." Tim's quiet declaration vibrated between them.

Raising a brow, Tom smiled to himself, kept walking.

Several fresh-cut boards formed a makeshift ramp up to the front porch, just like at Grandy's. While Rachel pushed Tim to the top, Tom unlocked the door. "Feel free to look around. I'll answer any questions I can. There are two bedrooms downstairs, six on the second floor, and a full attic. This floor also has the kitchen of course, dining room, den, a family room…"

Rachel asked, "Mr. Tom? How come if Jennilee and Charlie own this house, she lives with Grandy and he lives with his dad? Why don't they just get married and live here? Or if they don't want the house, why don't they just sell it?"

"I'm not at liberty to discuss details, but you need some facts. Jennilee was orphaned at a young age. Her mother's sister and her husband got custody. They also got to live in this house until Jennilee came of age, as long as they took care of Jennilee. This house is all Jennilee has left of her mother. That's all I'm willing to say about that. I can tell you she'll never step foot in this house again—not even for you and your family. Take what she's offering. As Charlie and I said earlier, fill this house with love and laughter and children. That's the greatest gift you can possibly give Jennilee."

Drifting through the rooms, Tim lingered behind. This was an old house, well built, constructed of the finest materials and utilizing expert workmanship. Rolling his chair around, Tim listened to the echoes of footsteps and fading voices as Rachel and Tom headed upstairs. The house needed some work, all old houses did, but little things. From the looks of the place, the previous tenants had left in a rage. The walls showed signs of recent repairs, there were deep grooves and gouge marks in the beautiful hardwood floors, what furniture was left was definitely worse for wear. All of it bore the evidence of not just rage, but retaliation.

Tim made his way into the kitchen. The layout of this

house mirrored Grandy's. Rolling to the kitchen door, he opened the inside door so he could look at Grandy's house. The door squeaked and stuck just a bit—it needed some oil on the hinges, and a touch planed off the edge so it wouldn't stick. A bit of the porch rail trim was coming loose—it needed re-nailing and a coat of paint wouldn't do the porch any harm.

His eyes lifted, following the beaten dirt path from the back steps of this house to…not to Grandy's kitchen door, as it should've. Ending at the unbroken line of shrubs, the bush where the path should've been was decidedly smaller than the rest. He'd had plenty of time to look around yesterday from Grandy's back porch, enough to know there was no path on her side. It had been deliberately and thoroughly obliterated.

Whatever Jennilee's relatives had done to her had been horrible. Tim didn't need details—hadn't he grown up in foster care? He'd never been hurt, not like this, but he knew others who had been. Jennilee's abuse had been long term, and secret, or they would have lost custody. Words from yesterday replayed themselves in Tim's head. No wonder Jennilee was so adamant about making a family.

He'd been full of misgivings at first, not trusting Jennilee's motives. Jennilee was the most loving, giving person he'd ever met in his life, almost too good to be true. She adored the kids and they were crazy about her already. He and Charlie'd hit it off, just like Rachel and Jennilee. Tim couldn't wait to start working with Charlie, and Mose.

Tim's mind was made up, long before Rachel came back downstairs, eyes shining with hope and possibilities. If their being here would help Jennilee, they'd stay as long as she needed them. They'd wait 'til tomorrow to tell Charlie and Jennilee—the only Christmas present they had to give.

CHARLIE AND JENNILEE came back to Grandy's just after dark, grinning, sharing smug, knowing glances. Rachel and Tim shared a few looks and eye rolls of their own. Charlie and Jennilee looked like kids trying to keep a secret—eyes alight and about to explode.

"Jennilee, what have you done?"

"Had a most enjoyable afternoon with Charlie. We went to one of our most favorite spots and necked in his truck. Then we..."

"Jennilee!" Rachel clapped her hands over Elizabeth's ears.

Laughing, Jennilee finished. "...went for a walk in the woods."

"Yep. You're up to something, alright."

The girls started getting ready for this evening's party. The guys, including Mr. Donnie, disappeared to do important guy stuff.

Jennilee and Elizabeth made eggnog while Grandy and Rachel readied platters of cookies and various goodies for the friends and family who'd be dropping by. Putting the eggnog in the frig, Jennilee excused herself.

Came back downstairs in an exquisitely embroidered dress. Velvet. Blue. Not quite midnight blue, but a lighter shade, the same color as the outer rim of Jennilee's eyes. No color Rachel could put a name to, but it looked stunning on Jennilee.

Around the loose cuffs and scoop neck, sprinkled down the mid-calf length skirt, glittery snowflakes were artfully embroidered. Shimmering and winking with each movement, looking like real snowflakes dancing and whirling. Charlie reappeared right behind her, his white silk dress shirt embroidered around the cuffs and over the breast pocket with the same glittery snowflakes. Dark brown cords set him off to perfection. Matching his eyes and fitting his muscled form, the sight made Jennilee's mouth water.

Looking at her the same way, like he was getting ready to take a big bite, Rachel stepped between them, laughingly headed them off. "I'm gonna call the fire department if you two don't cool it!"

Charlie laughed outright and moved purposefully around her, eyes on Jennilee. "That's a new one. You'll have to tell the rest of the crowd. It won't do you any good. The fire department's all volunteer, and they're all busy tonight."

Stopping in front of Jennilee, he looked her up and down. "Jennilee-love, I swear you get more beautiful every time I see you."

"You're pretty easy on the eyes yourself, handsome."

Putting his hands on her shoulders, Charlie bent his head. Jennilee tipped hers up, her lips hovering just shy of Charlie's. "Rachel, none of my dresses will fit you, because you've got a much curvier shape than I do, but if you don't mind wearing my clothes, I left a Christmas sweater on your bed. Charlie's shirt should fit Tim."

"I heard that loud and clear. You don't have to tell me twice! I've just been dismissed!" Laughing and sharing a look with Grandy, she took Elizabeth by the hand and they left.

∽

THE HOUSE FILLED with an ever changing mix of people, and love and laughter. Charlie and Jennilee sang off and on, and everyone there gathered as Charlie read the passages from Matthew and Luke that told the Christmas story. The company all scattered to their own homes and their own Christmas Eve traditions, the excited children finally fell asleep.

Christmas morning was just as wonderful. The adults had

JENNILEE'S LIGHT

helped the kids put out cookies and milk for Santa and carrots for the reindeer. Nothing left of the cookies but crumbs, the glass of milk was empty, all that remained of the carrots was stumps with obvious teeth marks. The kids were ecstatic.

Rachel and Tim exchanged glances. Rachel whispered when Jennilee got close enough that the kids couldn't over hear her, "What are you guys doing? Practicing?"

Jennilee's delighted laughter rang out. "You could say that. Thanks for lending us your kids."

Charlie and Jennilee didn't go overboard as Rachel and Tim feared they would. A wagon for Timmy, a tricycle for Elizabeth, a Tonka dump truck for Corey, a soft rag doll for Cassie, all from Santa. One outfit apiece. That and their full to bursting stockings.

Engrossed in the children, the adults forgot to open their presents. Timmy finally reminded them. "Hey! There's more presents, and they're addressed to y'all." He delivered each present, in his wagon.

Tim opened his to find a new tool belt, filled with tools —from Santa.

Rachel got—from Santa—some bubble bath and a new novel and a box of pricey chocolates.

Grandy got another exquisitely carved animal from Charlie to add to her collection, and from Jennilee, an intricately embroidered blouse. From the both of them, framed shots taken by Mr. Berto. A shot of them together, and one of Charlie and Jennilee with Grandy.

For Charlie and Jennilee, knit by Grandy, a new sweater for each—matching, of course—and a big, colorful afghan addressed to both, which Jennilee promptly draped over the back of the rocker.

Charlie and Jennilee looked at each other and said simultaneously, "Your presents are at the house." Threw their heads back and laughed.

"Hey! You guys didn't get any presents from Santa!" Elizabeth sounded like she was about to burst into tears at the injustice.

Grinning, Jennilee disagreed. "Sure we did."

Elizabeth shook her head sorrowfully. "Nun-uh. There aren't any more presents under the tree for any of us."

Jennilee tipped her head to one side and squinted like she was measuring something. "Be kinda hard to wrap y'all up, but I'm sure we could find a box big enough somewhere."

"People can't be presents," Timmy informed them with all the wisdom of his almost six years.

"A present is a gift you weren't necessarily expecting, but it's something you really, really wanted and finally got, right?"

Timmy and Elizabeth nodded, their eyes on Jennilee.

"Well, then. I've always wanted a big family. You're my present."

"Mommy, is she joking?" Two solemn faces looked beseechingly at their mom, awaiting a verdict.

Swallowing past the lump in her throat, Rachel clasped hands with Tim, shook her head. "We have a present for you, too, Jennilee. We've decided to accept your offer. We'll take the house."

"That's wonderful!" Jennilee closed her eyes for a moment, opened them, her face radiant. "Grandy, you gonna ride out to our house with us? We won't be long, and we'll help get dinner ready when we get back."

Grandy smirked. "I've seen some of y'all's presents to each other, and the results. Am I gonna get my eyes scorched again?"

"Grandy. I'm shocked, shocked I tell you, that you'd even

think that." Catching her up in a bear hug, Charlie grinned unrepentantly while Grandy rolled her eyes.

"We can start dinner. Just tell us what you want us to do." Rachel jumped to her feet.

"You're not coming with us?" Jennilee's smile dimmed.

Rachel clasped her hands nervously. "I guess we can. I didn't know you wanted us to."

"Why wouldn't we? Besides, we've got something, a project, to show you, and it's a great part of what we need Tim for." Jennilee smacked the heel of her hand to her forehead. "Project! Something to show you! Kids, what did we forget?"

Timmy and Elizabeth raced each other to the tree, reached carefully into the branches and pulled out small, crudely wrapped packages. Timmy handed his to his dad, and Elizabeth handed hers to her mom. Rachel unwrapped a necklace of beads and different shaped macaronis. Tim unwrapped a picture frame made of twigs.

Putting her necklace on, tears in her eyes, Rachel hugged Elizabeth. "It's beautiful."

"The necklace is from me and Cassie. Jennilee helped her pick out the colors and shapes, and I stringed them."

Tim hugged Timmy as the child told him, "Corey helped me pick up sticks. Jennilee said that's a special picture frame. We need a picture of you and me and Corey doing guy stuff."

Rachel and Tim looked at Charlie and Jennilee. Instead of the dismal Christmas they'd envisioned, they'd been blessed beyond measure.

"Timmy, Elizabeth, you forgot something else." Jennilee tipped her head in the direction of the tree. Timmy and Elizabeth were off again.

They handed the obviously homemade envelope of red construction paper to their parents, Corey helping. Opening the envelope, in the middle of a piece of green construction paper in bright crayon and childishly written letters, laboriously copied, were the words *Merry Christmas!* At each corner, in finger-paint, was stamped a child's handprint, with one of the children's names in the palm of each hand.

"I wrote my own name!" Timmy announced proudly.

"I did, too." Elizabeth crowed and then added, "Jennilee helped."

"I wrote Corey's, and Elizabeth…"

"I wrote Cassie's."

Charlie said, "Let me go get the skiff, cause there's fixin' to be a flood."

Instead of tears, Jennilee and Rachel burst into laughter, eyes overly bright.

Charlie pretended to nag. "Guys, we need to get moving if we're going to go out to the house and make it back in time to fix dinner."

"Wait!" Timmy grabbed Elizabeth's hand and dragged her back to the tree. Came back giggling, several more packages in their hands.

"While you guys were talking to Mr. Tom yesterday, we made you some presents."

"Grandy helped us."

Charlie opened his to find a picture frame just like Tim's, only bigger.

"We made it bigger 'cause we gotta fit more people in that one. Me and you and Jennilee and Grandy and ever'body. It's from all us kids."

Taking the lumpy package Elizabeth handed her, Jennilee opened it and smiled through her tears. Knelt down so Elizabeth could put the necklace over her head.

"This is from all of us, too."

At Timmy and Elizabeth's urging, Corey solemnly handed Grandy a smaller package.

"A bracelet! Thank you, kids." Grandy gave all of them a big hug, blew a kiss to Cassie.

Making one last trip to the tree, the kids brought back another homemade envelope, handed it to their parents.

All three women went to boohooing.

Everyone finally calmed down and got in the van, including Jewel. Rachel and Tim's reaction at their first sight of Charlie and Jennilee's house was the same as Tony's.

"Holy cow!"

"How big a family are the two of you planning on having?"

While they were gawking and getting Tim out of the van, Jennilee and Jewel slipped off to the cemetery. Laying a bright red camellia blossom on Amelia's grave, Jennilee wished her a Merry Christmas. Came back before anyone but Charlie had time to miss her.

Grandy teased, "Well? I've got thirty-some people coming and they expect food. Are we going to get to this sometime today?"

Charlie won the lightning game of PSR.

"What's that?" Timmy didn't miss a trick.

"A game Jennilee and I play to decide who gets to go first."

"First at what?"

"Anything. That way nobody gets to go first all the time and nobody gets their feelings hurt."

Jennilee informed Charlie, "Your presents are in the shop."

Walking across the yard, Charlie explained the intricacies of paper, scissors, rock, played several trial games with Timmy. Unlocking the door and ushering them all inside, Charlie flipped on the overhead lights. A lot of neat looking stuff, but nothing that looked like presents.

Beaming, eyes alight, Jennilee clarified. "Upstairs, Charlie."

Everyone except Rachel and Tim, holding Cassie and Corey, trooped up the stairs to the open loft. Charlie's exhilarated whoop rang out.

Charlie spun in a dazed circle. Finished walls, electrical outlets, track lighting, skylights, cupboards, drawers, benches, shelves. They'd talked about turning this loft into a studio for his carving, but talk was all they'd done.

"Jennilee! I can't believe you did this!"

"Mose and I…"

Charlie caught her up, kissed her thoroughly. Setting her down, he kept possession of her hand. Opening the cupboards brought still more surprises. Different types of wood, in all shapes and sizes. Charlie's hands itched to get started.

"You've got one more." Grinning, Jennilee indicated a wide drawer.

Charlie opened it, stared. A set of woodcarving tools. A really, really good set, each tool in its proper slot. He had tools, but just stuff he'd picked up here and there. Inside that drawer was a carver's dream. Charlie continued to stare, turned the same intense gaze on Jennilee.

"Your turn. Downstairs."

Back at the bottom, Charlie told Tim excitedly, "I can't wait 'til you're healed enough to climb stairs. You're not going to believe what Jennilee's done. I've got a whole woodworking shop up there, and tools." The way he drawled out *tools* made Tim's eyes light.

"Don't even think about it," came from Rachel and Jennilee at the same time, followed by laughter.

"Over here, Jennilee." Charlie indicated a tarp covered pile in a far corner. "Close your eyes."

Jennilee did, smiling, and he whisked the tarp off.

"Okay."

JENNILEE'S LIGHT

Jennilee caught her breath, as entranced as Charlie'd been upstairs. Glass, in every color and a variety of textures. Sheets and sheets of it. And not just glass. A grinder, and a polishing wheel, glass cutters and a soldering iron. Everything she needed.

Putting both hands over her mouth, her eyes darted hither and yon, taking it all in. Spun and threw her arms around Charlie.

Rachel ventured, "You do stained glass?"

"I...dabble. I love doing it."

"Jennilee's being modest, like me saying I whittle. She's a genius, and she wants to do all the fanlights in our house."

"*All* of them?" Tim looked at Charlie and raised his brows. Charlie gave a half shrug.

"Charlie's worked out a way I can put stained glass inside, behind the old glass without having to remove the old glass. Sort of...using the existing window for a frame." Jennilee's voice was getting dim, her mind already a million miles away, plotting and planning.

Rachel asked, "Where are you going to do all this, Jennilee?"

"Upstairs. Half the upstairs is hers."

Jennilee beamed and Charlie started lowering his head.

"Hey! Don't start that you two, or we'll never get out of here today." Grandy set them all to laughing again.

"Jennilee's still got another present. Outside."

"That's what you were doing the other evening when you smelled like wind."

Grinning from ear to ear at Jennilee's on-the-mark deduction, Charlie led them out of the shop around the far side of the house, steering Jennilee from behind with his hands over her eyes. He stopped, removed his hands.

Opening her eyes, Jennilee's delighted laughter echoed off the forest, rang out over the river.

"The school system was getting rid of them and I couldn't pass them up, Jennilee."

"Race you!" Jennilee took off, fleet as a deer, Charlie and Timmy and Elizabeth flying after her, Jewel running with the pack and barking madly. Grandy and Rachel and Tim, with the babies, followed more slowly. By the time they caught up, Jennilee was swinging as high as the top bar on the swingset. Charlie was pushing Timmy in one swing and Elizabeth in another. They went from there to the merry-go-round, to the slide, to the monkey bars, Cassie and Corey and Rachel included.

Jennilee cried out gleefully, "Look, everybody! It's snowing!"

Whirling in circles, catching snowflakes on their tongues, they laughed themselves silly watching Jewel as she dashed about in a frenzy trying to catch this strange white stuff falling from the sky.

Grandy didn't say a word, not one, when they left a bit later and the snowfall got lighter and lighter as they drove down the long driveway, fizzled just where their driveway met the paved road.

CHAPTER 45

Their birthdays came and went again, spring passed in a blur, and then Charlie was home for a bit before summer classes started. Jennilee had completed a little more than a third of her panels for the fanlights and Charlie and Mose installed them.

Each fanlight was a different size, just enough that they couldn't use the measurements of one for all her panels. Jennilee had a unique design in mind for each room. The one for their bedroom would be water lilies and dragonflies, of course. She had patterns drawn for the ones she didn't already have completed. Flowers. Birds. Intricate geometric designs. Tropical fish. Dolphins. Ocean scenes.

Back on his feet, for short periods only, Tim was turning out to be the perfect foreman, the deal between them working out far better than any of them had anticipated. Having finally gotten to see the inside of Charlie and Jennilee's house—and Charlie's shop—he was as excited as they were about restoring the old place.

A big chunk of land beside the Diner came up for sale, and Jennilee and Charlie amended their plans. Instead of building houses, they decided to try a small motel, maybe include some efficiency apartments. No motels in Chinquapin Ridge, one right on Highway 70 was bound to do well.

Putting their heads together, Charlie and Tim came up with a workable plan. Set it in motion. By the time Charlie went back to college in late summer for the fall semester, ground had been broken and work started.

Everyone settled back into their routines. Charlie, finished with football practice, headed to the Marcellini's to pick up Jennilee.

Mr. Carlo and Mr. Berto met him at the door.

"We need to talk, Charlie, before Jennilee finds out you're here. She's in the pool with the kids, so we've got a few minutes."

"What's up, Mr. Carlo? Sounds serious."

Mr. Berto took over. "It is, Charlie. You know I won all kinds of accolades for my photo exhibit of the two of you. It was featured in a lot of magazines, even made some national TV programs."

"Yessir. Is there a problem? Jennilee and I gave you our permission, verbal and written. Do you need something more from us?"

"Nothing so simple, I'm afraid."

Charlie's radar was pinging. Whatever it was involved Jennilee.

"Charlie...there's a man. He keeps calling, wanting to know anything I can tell him about Jennilee."

"What? Like a stalker or something?"

"He seems desperate, but not like that. He...wants to meet her. He's asked and asked. I didn't give any personal information to him, but I decided I had to tell you. I think you need to meet him and you can decide whether to...call the police or just what to do. I'm at my wit's end. He insists he's not out to hurt her, and he seems very sincere."

"Arrange it, and let me know where and when."

∼

A FEW DAYS LATER, Charlie waited in Mr. Berto's office for the unknown man to show. He and Mr. Berto watched through the one-way glass as a distinguished middle-aged gentleman leaning heavily on a cane limped across the gallery floor, straight to the office.

A firm knock, and Berto bid him enter. Before they could even begin to introduce themselves, the unknown man looked at Charlie and exclaimed, "You're the young man from the photos. I can see you love her very much." His voice broke. "Tell me she's fine, tell me…anything…everything about her, please. Please."

Charlie's eyes met those of the pleading man and the truth hit him like a heart punch.

Mr. Berto demanded impatiently, "I ask you again, what right do you have to ask any questions about my subject?"

"Easy, Mr. Berto. His name is Albert Marvin Lee…and he's…her father."

The older man staggered, sank into a chair. "How…"

"How did I know? No one else has ocean eyes like Jennilee's."

"Jennilee? Cynthia named her Jennilee?" His own ocean eyes strayed hungrily to a framed photo of Jennilee on the wall.

"I nick-named her that when we were toddlers. The name on her birth certificate, her real name, is Jenny Lee. Before I answer any more of your questions, you'll tell me why you left Jennilee's mom."

"I didn't *leave* her. I'd never have left Cynthia! Her father took a sudden turn for the worse and she went flying home in a panic. SOB—pardon my language— wouldn't even come to our wedding. Wouldn't even acknowledge it—but Cynthia loved the old...man. I was at work and she couldn't get ahold of me, left me a note to follow her ASAP. I don't remember anything after that except waking up in a hospital. No ID, more dead than alive, I'd been found in an alley in a seedy part of Raleigh. They just assumed I was a homeless person, or someone rolled in a bar brawl. I tried repeatedly to tell them who I was. All that got me was an extended stay at Dix Hill." His voice was bitter. "They wouldn't listen—not to anything I told them. The harder I tried, the more drugs they pumped into me, until I didn't know which way was up."

Charlie didn't know the details, but he'd bet anything Celie'd had a great hand in whatever had happened to him, topped off by the Judge's vast influence. "Did you ever meet Cynthia's sister?"

"Celie? Yeah." Albert's scathing tone left no doubt as to just what he thought of his wife's sister. "She came to our apartment once, while Cynthia was in class. Put the moves on me. I told her what she could do with it, and herself."

Charlie had his motive, as if Albert being married to Cynthia wasn't enough. Celie'd probably gone home, bided her time, waited 'til the time was right to go boohooing to her father. Told the Judge something along the lines of how she'd made a visit to see her sister to set things to rights, and Albert attacked her. She was so ashamed, afraid to tell anyone.

That's what had gotten Albert beaten and landed him in Dix Hill. Was probably also what the Judge meant in his letter about a bad choice, and trying to make amends. It was a safe bet that's how the Judge ended up with Cynthia's Certificate of Marriage.

Mr. Berto shook his head, still skeptical, his tone accusing. "That's a good story, but the truth of the matter is, you left Jennilee alone, just like you left her momma."

"I..."

"Mr. Albert, I believe you."

"You do? I didn't know about Jennilee. I swear I didn't—not 'til I saw the photos, and I had no idea where to look for her. After I finally got out of Dix Hill, I went to Chinquapin Ridge straightaway, to try and find Cynthia. Went to the Judge's address. Celie answered the door, told me my beloved Cynthia'd been murdered. Brutally murdered. Laughed when she said it, and slammed the door in my face."

Taking a deep breath, Charlie kept his eyes glued to Albert's face. "Celie raised Jennilee."

Turning so gray Charlie feared he was having a heart attack, Albert managed to wheeze out, "Cynthia would never have left our child for Celie to raise. Cynthia didn't trust Celie as far as she could throw her."

"Cynthia didn't, not intentionally. We just found Cynthia's will, right before Christmas."

Twin spots of color appeared in Albert's cheeks. "That bitch! She knew! She knew, and she never said a word."

"That's pretty much the general consensus."

"I want to kill her—strangle her with my bare hands!"

"Ditto. You and everyone else who's ever met the bitch."

"Ah, God. My sweet baby in the hands of that sadistic witch..." Albert put his face in his hands, rocked back and forth. "How'd she ever survive?" Looked to Charlie.

"I've been protecting her, as much as I could, since our mothers died. My grandma, Grandy, pretty much raised us both. Don't be too hard on yourself. We were right next door, and still Celie managed to make Jennilee's life a living hell. We knew some and we've found out more bits and pieces just recently, but I doubt we'll ever know the full story. Jennilee refuses to talk about it."

"All those years—lost." Albert rested his head wearily against the back of his chair.

Charlie'd had serious doubts when Mr. Berto told him there was a man who wanted to meet Jennilee, had a few more when he actually met the man. Had no doubts whatsoever now. Jennilee craved family, and here was a chance to give her some.

"Swear to me you have no intention of hurting Jennilee, or trying to take her away from us, and I'll arrange a meeting."

"You'd do that for me?"

"Not for you. For her. She's my world, and Jennilee adores family. I have to warn you, once she accepts you, she won't let you get far away. If you have any other family, they better be prepared to share you."

"No—none. There's no one. Not like you're thinking. I never remarried. Plenty of extended family, though. Jennilee's got aunts and uncles and grandparents and cousins. You have my word of honor—I will never do anything to harm my child."

"We're getting married in the spring, after I graduate."

Notice and warning, served all at once.

"Married? This is…so sudden."

"Not to us. We've been talking about getting married as long as either of us can remember."

"You have my blessing, not that you require it. Tell me about her. All this time, I've been so alone, and I had a piece of Cynthia left." Albert sounded unbearably sad.

Charlie enthused, "Jennilee's…Jennilee. My Jennilee. They broke the mold when they made my Jennilee. She's funny, and sweet, and unbelievably talented, and she can cook like you wouldn't believe."

Mr. Berto closed his office door quietly behind himself.

JENNILEE'S LIGHT

Charlie could rhapsodize about Jennilee forever, and Albert looked like he could listen as long as Charlie talked.

∽

CHARLIE MERELY TOLD Jennilee he had a present for her.

Albert was a lost soul, and where better for a lost soul than their house? Amelia'd understand perfectly, might even help things along.

Just finished planting snap dragons and pansies and dwarf sweet peas for the winter on Amelia's grave, Jennilee rose and dusted her hands and knees off at the sound of a car. One Jennilee didn't recognize. Charlie tugged her toward it.

"Jennilee-love, I've got someone I want you to meet."

"Charlie?"

"You'll see. I'm right here for you, and so's Amelia."

"Charlie... What in the world?"

Having done everything he could to ensure this went well, Charlie'd taken the added precaution of talking to Amelia's headstone when Jennilee was out of earshot. Told Amelia everything, hoped she was listening.

Charlie wrapped his arms around Jennilee from behind and waited.

Watching the man coming toward them, Charlie holding her like he thought she'd bolt otherwise, Jennilee recognized the emotion on the man's face for what it was—love. She ought to know—she'd seen that exact look on Charlie's face more times than she could count. Why would a stranger be looking at her like that?

Albert couldn't take his eyes off Jennilee. Even more beautiful in person, and the spitting image of Cynthia, except for her eyes. They were his, all his.

"Jennilee, this is Albert. Albert, Jennilee."

Jennilee cocked her head as she noticed the unusual color of his eyes. "Are you some of my daddy's kin?"

Albert could only shake his head, mesmerized.

Jennilee blushed prettily. "I'm sorry. I just thought because of your eyes... I've never met anyone else with eyes the color of mine."

Albert still didn't say anything, couldn't.

Whether Amelia gave Jennilee a nudge, or whether she put two and two together, Charlie knew the instant she realized the truth.

"You're my...father?"

Nodding, Albert swallowed audibly.

When he was sure she could remain standing on her own, Charlie leaned down, murmured over her shoulder, "I'll be in our shop if you need me."

"I...I don't understand. Charlie?"

"Celie." All the answer that was necessary, giving Jennilee a good hard squeeze Charlie left them to it, whistling as he walked off. *What's Your Mama's Name, Child?* Not Wilson green, but Lee blue.

CHAPTER 46

*L*ike the giant jig-saw puzzles they so adored, the pieces were falling in place and the picture emerging, bit by bit, the puzzle nearly complete.

Another Christmas, another birthday.

Charlie was days from being done with school, Jennilee's dress was finished.

The day of their wedding dawned, a picture perfect May day. Friends and family gathered, and Jennilee had a huge family now, both real and made. Everything in the yard was in full bloom, even things that had no business blooming right now—or at all.

Jennilee wowed everyone, looking like a radiant fairy princess in her dress, carrying a bouquet picked from her gardens. Pink lilacs, yellow roses, and cobalt iris with some trailing gardenias mixed in—and a woven circlet of colorful flowers on her head. Her hair was just as Charlie loved it— loose and flowing down her back like a wimple of gold cloth.

Charlie, looking like a modern day Prince Charming, wore the pearl gray suit Jennilee'd sewn for him.

Angel and Rachel, Jeff and Tony filled out the party.

Bella and Elizabeth were the flower girls, enough petals in their baskets to have stripped the gardens. Scattered them like a floral carpet ahead of Jennilee as her father escorted her down the aisle between the rows of folding chairs set up on the lawn.

She had eyes for Charlie only, and he for her.

Breaking tradition, when Albert placed her hand in Charlie's, Charlie didn't turn immediately to Brother Anderson, instead faced Jennilee directly and looked his fill. Leaning forward he feathered a kiss across her cheek. "Mine. My mermaid."

Jennilee smiled radiantly at him. "My love."

Unable to hear what Charlie said or Jennilee's answer, there wasn't a dry eye in the crowd, except Jennilee's—she'd shed enough tears. And she'd certainly waited enough— today was a day for rejoicing! As one, they turned to face Brother Anderson.

Charlie and Jennilee held hands and looked at him, just as they'd done so long ago. Faces filled with the same love he'd seen then, magnified a thousandfold, they waited for him to say the magic words.

Well pleased, he fairly beamed. "Well, you two. We've waited a long time for this day."

"Yessir," came from two throats.

"Do you remember what you told me, so long ago?"

Charlie didn't miss a beat. "There is no other for me."

"Nor for me." Repeating her vow, Jennilee handed her bouquet to Angel.

Charlie and Jennilee faced each other and held hands as Brother Anderson began the familiar litany.

Repeating each vow as he asked it, each promise he intoned, giving their solemn oaths.

"With this ring, Jennilee."

"With this ring."

"I now pronounce you husband and wife. You may kiss the bride."

With no veil in his way, all Charlie had to do was lower his head. Jennilee tipped hers up in a well rehearsed move. Their kisses before had been sweet, but this one, this kiss, was almost unbearably so.

One wasn't enough. They went back for seconds.

Timmy, ringbearer, huffed out an aggrieved sigh. "They said *one*." His soft mutter could be plainly heard in the hushed quiet.

Breaking their kiss long enough to burst into laughter, one beat ahead of the audience, Charlie and Jennilee kissed again. Charlie kept an arm around Jennilee as they turned to face the crowd.

Behind them, Brother Anderson announced, "It is with great joy that I present to you... Mr. and Mrs. Charlie Meyers."

A rousing cheer followed, led by Charlie. When the noise abated, he told the assembled crowd, "We have to do some pictures, but please feel free to walk around the gardens or the house, and we'll join you as soon as we're done."

Jennilee added her invitation. "There's plenty of finger foods and punch and soft drinks on the tables on the porch. Don't fill up on that, though. Mose and Mr. Jubal cooked a pig. It'll be served shortly, along with all the trimmings, and Grandy did the wedding cake."

Mr. Berto herded them here and there, taking pictures like a madman, adding and subtracting and rearranging people like a world class sheep dog.

Insisting on taking some pictures in the family cemetery, Charlie and Jennilee let Mr. Berto decide where else. On the long dock, down by the river, here and there in the gardens, on the porch, in the gazebo. Ended up on the side of the house where the swings were.

The kids claimed the playground equipment while Mr. Berto took shots of the rest of the wedding party. He turned to say something to Charlie and Jennilee only to find them missing.

Jeff tipped his head toward the swings, grinning.

Starting to protest, Berto grinned instead, seeing another show in the making.

Charlie was pushing Jennilee in a swing, not very high. In front of her, and every time the swing brought her back to him, he stopped it for a beat and stole a kiss.

Getting behind Jennilee, Charlie pushed her higher and higher. Mr. Berto got a perfect shot—Jennilee, head thrown back, laughing, skirts billowing and unbound hair streaming back toward Charlie. Charlie, behind her, arms outstretched, giving her wings but standing ready to catch her. Having ditched her shoes, Jennilee's bare feet peeked enticingly out from under her dress.

Taking shot after shot, from every angle, Mr. Berto took plenty of Charlie and Jennilee by themselves, and loads with the children. The little girls looked at Charlie and Jennilee, visions of their own someday weddings plain on their dreamy faces. The little boys watched, and wondered what all the fuss was about.

Jeff finally dragged them away from the playground. "Come on, you two. Mr. Berto wants to take some pictures inside."

Lining them up on the curving staircase, Mr. Berto rearranged and snapped until Jennilee laughingly protested.

"Enough, Mr. Berto!"

"Throw the bouquet and the garter, and then I'll…"

Giving Mr. Berto no chance to change his mind, Charlie said, "Done!"

The crowd assembled, Angel caught the bouquet and Jeff caught the garter. While the ribald jests and comments flew fast and furious, Charlie and Jennilee escaped upstairs.

Closing the bedroom door behind them, Charlie drew Jennilee close, kissed her thoroughly. "Next time we come up here, we're not coming out for days."

"Sounds good to me."

"I love you, Mrs. Meyers."

"Say it again."

"I love you."

"The other."

"Mrs. Meyers, Mrs. Meyers, Mrs. Meyers. I really like the sound of that."

"Me, too. I love you, love you, love you."

"Have I told you yet that you look ravishing today, Mrs. Meyers?"

Jennilee shook her head.

"Well, you do, and you are."

"Right back at you, Mr. Meyers."

Charlie held her at arm's length. "Let me look at you before you take off your dress." Walking slowly around her, he ended up right where he began. "Jennilee, do you have any idea how beautiful this dress is? It hardly looks real, and with you in it…it looks like something out of a fairy-tale."

"Thank you, Charlie. I…sewed my heart into it, and all my dreams."

"And mine." Another kiss, and another, each one sweeter than the one before.

"My suit, Jennilee. You said you were making it, but I had no idea." Shrugging out of his suit coat, Charlie ran a hand lovingly over the intricately embroidered vest. Dragonflies and water lilies, just like on Jennilee's dress. Gray on gray, silk on silk, so unless you looked closely, it just looked like a random, raised pattern.

Amid many giggles and whispers and kisses, they helped

each other out of their wedding finery. Unbuttoning Charlie's vest, Jennilee slid it off his shoulders, laid it over a chair back. Unbuttoned his shirt, removed his dragonfly cufflinks, and did the same.

Draping her hair over her shoulder, Charlie unlaced the back of Jennilee's dress and slid it down, kissing each inch of skin as he exposed it. Helping her step out of the puddle of fabric, turning her to face him, he caught his breath. "Jennilee, what in the world are you wearing?"

Jennilee blushed at the praise in his tone. "I didn't want to ruin the lines of the dress with a bra and panties, so I copied, sort of, the design for an old fashioned chemise to wear underneath."

Nearly transparent silk, it molded to her every curve, held together at the top just over the swell of her breasts by a ribbon. A row of tiny hooks descending between her breasts and down past her waist fitted the material to her like a glove.

Charlie definitely sounded strangled. "If what you're wearing tonight is any better than this, I may not survive."

Laughing low in her throat, Jennilee ran a hand up his chest. "I'll make sure the rescue squad's on standby."

"Jennilee, hot and bothered does not begin to describe what I'm feeling right now."

She offered hesitantly, "We don't have to go back downstairs."

"Yes, we do. We're only doing this once, and we're not missing our own wedding party because I can't keep my hands off my wife."

Untying the ribbon, Jennilee started undoing the hooks, one at a time, slowly.

Sucking in a deep breath, Charlie put his hands on her shoulders, spun her. Gave her a gentle, desperate shove in the direction of their dressing room. Jennilee's laughter floated behind her as she obeyed him, somewhat.

Unfastening as she went so that the chemise got looser and looser, dropped lower and lower, by the time she reached the doorway, it was barely resting on the swells of her buttocks. The image of her naked back and that scrap of silk seared into Charlie's brain as she disappeared from sight.

Staring at the empty space for a long moment, Charlie picked up Jennilee's dress. Ran his hands over it reverently. She'd never cease to amaze him. Her dress should be in a museum somewhere, or showcased on a runway in Paris. His glance went to the bed, covered in the Irish chain quilt she'd given him for Christmas years ago. It wasn't cold enough for a quilt, by any means, but he'd wanted it on the bed on this, their first night together as man and wife.

His gaze traveled around their bedroom. Just like Jennilee'd told him so long ago, everything in their bedroom reflected their love for each other. Her dress and his suit, their quilt. The dresser scarves he'd given her graced the dressers they'd had Mose build for them, one for each. On top of hers, the jewelry box he'd carved. On his, the kaleidoscope she'd made. A rocking chair, made by Mose and as close to Grandy's as it could be, including a delightful squeak, sat waiting on one of Jennilee's braided rugs.

The stained glass of their fanlight, water lilies and dragonflies, of course. The antique lace curtains at the windows and French doors. The crocheted afghan over the back of the rocker. The cedar chest he'd made her, filled with quilts and only Jennilee knew what else.

Jennilee came out of the dressing room, wearing a cream colored skirt and a silk blouse the color of her eyes. Barefoot, her circlet of flowers still on her head, she was holding out her left hand. Her shaking left hand. "Charlie…"

"You made your dress and my suit. That's your wedding present to me." Holding up his left hand, he wiggled his fingers so that his ring winked. "That's your wedding present *from* me."

He'd said he'd take care of the rings, and she hadn't given it a second thought. He had. Not merely regular gold wedding bands, custom made ones, just like her engagement ring. Just like her engagement ring, white gold banded in gold on the outside edges. Wide. The gold edges were studded with a band of diamond chips each, the white gold boasted an elaborate raised design of interlocking hearts.

"My eyes were glued to your face when we exchanged rings."

"And?"

"Oh, Charlie. It's beautiful." Crossing the room to him, Jennilee curled her hands over his biceps and rested her head on his naked chest, directly over his heart. "Let me see yours."

Charlie held his hand up. Clasping it in both of hers, Jennilee examined his ring. Like hers, but wider, and instead of just elaborate hearts, a single mermaid frolicked in the white gold. A very detailed mermaid with a tiny bright aquamarine for her eye.

Raising his hand to her face, Jennilee nestled the side of her face into his palm. Placed her hand over his to hold it in place, turned a bit and pressed a kiss into the center of his palm. Trembling from head to toe, she took a deep, shuddering breath.

Charlie sounded like he had that day at their pond when she'd asked to touch him. "Jennilee, let me go change so we can go back down, or we're not going back down."

~

THEY MADE it back downstairs a while later, eyes bright and lips swollen. Danced, and mingled, and ate. Charlie only let go of Jennilee's hand so she could dance—with her dad, with his dad—with all the male acquaintances they knew, as far as he could tell. When he finally got her back, he refused to let go her hand again.

"I never realized how many male friends we have," he growled in her ear.

"Me, either. There's Mose, and Jeff, and Mr. Tom, and Chief Mac, and Doc, and Mr. Matt, and Tony, and Mr. Jubal, and..." Jennilee grinned.

Charlie grumbled. "You should have more women friends, then I wouldn't feel so left out. I've danced so many times with Angel and Grandy it's not funny, and if I even look at Rachel one more time, Tim's going to punch me or walk out on us."

Jennilee grinned wider, eyes twinkling. "So dance with some of the guys."

That got a disbelieving look and a shout of laughter from Charlie. "Un uh, no way. I'd rather dance with my ravishing wife."

The revelries and the feasting lasted far into the evening, and at some point, Charlie and Jennilee slipped away unnoticed. Or so they thought.

Made it inside their room, closed the door. Didn't even turn the lights on. Charlie pinned Jennilee against the door, kissing her and shaping her through her blouse at the same time. He'd unbuttoned the first button and was working on the second when they heard a soft knock on the door—the French door that opened onto the porch.

Mose's deep rumble reached them. "We know y'all got plans, but we've got a present for you first."

Jeff added his two cents. "The sooner you two get your butts out here, the sooner you can go back to...what you're doing."

Charlie flipped on a small lamp and they crossed the

room, hand in hand. Opened the French doors, not to Mose and Jeff, who'd quickly disappeared, but to...no one. Or so it seemed.

Someone was out there, alright. A lot of someones, back far enough where they could see anyone standing in the French doors.

The whole crowd clapped and cheered at the newlyweds' appearance, broke into song, some of Charlie and Jennilee's favorites. Arms around each other, Charlie and Jennilee listened.

Listened for a long time before moving. Holding hands, Charlie gave the singers a deep bow and Jennilee curtsied, as pretty as you could wish. They stepped backward and closed the French doors. The serenade continued for a bit longer, gradually fading.

CHAPTER 47

"Well, Mrs. Meyers. Was your wedding day everything you hoped it would be?"

"Perfect, Mr. Meyers. Absolutely perfect."

Charlie kissed her. "Your wedding night's going to be even better. Go get changed, and take your time. I'll let you know when I'm ready."

"You're not ready now?" Cocking her head, Jennilee looked him up and down.

Charlie gave her a hard kiss and a light push. "*I'm* ready. The room's not."

Jennilee walked through the dressing room with its floor to ceiling shelves and drawers and closets. Glad they'd left this room mostly as it was, merely enlarged it. Knocked out another wall that opened into the room that was now their sumptuous bathroom.

Taking off Grandy's pearls, she laid them gently on the counter. Passed down for generations, Grandy'd given them to Donnie, and he'd given them to Iris. Grandy'd kept them for Charlie, along with his mother's things. That was her something old.

Her something new was the lacy scrap of handkerchief Miz Sadie'd pressed into her hand just before the ceremony. Finely embroidered with both her name and Charlie's and the date, Jennilee'd tucked it in her bodice, close to her heart. It lay on the counter already, placed there when she changed out of her wedding dress.

The clip in her hair was something borrowed. Not that it could be seen underneath her circlet of flowers, but her hair was pulled back, twists on either side caught in the back. Angel and Miz Teresa'd loaned the clip to her. It'd come from Italy a long, long time ago. Angel's great-great-however many greats back had worn it at her own wedding. A filigree of gold, Jennilee decided to keep wearing it.

Taking her circlet off carefully, she undid the clip just as carefully. Brushing her hair until it shone, she redid the twists, refastened the clip.

Her something blue, well, that'd been her garter, Jeff's now.

Humming as she prepared herself, doing what women have done since the dawn of time to make themselves ready for their chosen mate, Jennilee stripped, looked at herself critically in the bank of mirrors. Not that either one would care when they were old and gray and everything wrinkled and sagged, but it was nice to come to each other, this first time, young and firm and shapely. That's what they'd see when they were unclothed. What they'd still see when they celebrated their fiftieth anniversary, hopefully their seventy-fifth.

Jennilee had no doubts Charlie'd like what he saw, and so would she. They'd seen each other enough in their summer wear, he in shorts and she wearing her bikini, but it wasn't the same as totally naked. Naked like they'd been for each other that day at their pond, and not since.

Letting her mind drift, Jennilee hit the high spots with a

dampened washcloth, imagined coming to Charlie fresh from a bubble bath. She'd do that, for both of them. Someday. Not tonight. Dreamily wondered what it'd be like to take a bath with Charlie, or a shower. They'd do that, too.

Dabbing *Windsong* at strategic points, she sniffed appreciatively. Put the stopper back in the bottle, an antique perfume bottle, to match the rest Charlie'd given her. Let her eyes linger on the water lily and dragonfly he'd carved. Felt her blood heat as she remembered his touch, how close they'd come to going all the way. How much they'd wanted to.

Remembered and warmed more as she let her gown slide over her head, smoothed it over her curves. Tonight there would be no more holding back, no more denying themselves or each other.

Charlie's soft call roused her out of her reverie.

Going to him joyfully, Jennilee stopped in the doorway, almost cried. Candles were lit—a multitude of them. Vases of flowers sat on every surface, petals scattered everywhere. The bed was turned down, the silk sheets covered with more flower petals.

Charlie'd dreamed some pretty good dreams about this night, but none of his dreams matched the reality of Jennilee standing in that doorway. The light behind her limned her every curve, the candlelight on her face highlighted the love and joy he saw there.

Unable to take a step, he opened his arms. Jennilee gave a half skip and ran to him, as she'd run to him from the Judge's house on the day of their eighteenth birthdays. Threw herself into his arms and clung. This time there would be no letting go, no leaving each other every night.

It'd been a long time coming, but they were home. They had each other, and soon the babies would come, had a huge group of people they considered family. They'd fulfill their promise to Amelia and to each other, would fill this house with love and laughter and children. They'd made a good start on the love and laughter, tonight they'd start working on the babies as well.

Charlie kissed her with everything he was feeling. She returned both his kiss and his love.

"Your turn."

"What?"

"I left a present in the dressing room for you. Go change."

"Jennilee, I want to get out of these clothes, not put more on."

"Humor me. Besides, I want to enjoy this…" Waved her hand at the lover's bower he'd created. "…for a moment."

"Jennilee-love, you're going to enjoy this for more than a moment." Charlie went to change.

Looking around, Jennilee smiled to herself as she heard him softly singing. *I can't seem to forget you…* Their bedroom was just as she'd imagined. Like Charlie'd promised after her last beating, only better. Filled with furniture and things, but above and beyond that, their room was absolutely filled to the brim and overflowing with love.

Positioning herself, she waited. Charlie stepped into the doorway and Jennilee forgot how to breathe. He was so good looking, so *yummy*, and he was all hers.

"Jennilee, I'm already so sensitized just thinking about you, I won't be able to keep these on long." Indicated the silk pajama bottoms, dark brown the very shade of his eyes.

"I don't want you to keep them on long. I only wanted you to put them on so I could take them off."

Charlie hit the dimmer switch. The room lights came on, low, but added to the candlelight, made the room glow. "Come here, Jennilee. My Jennilee. I want to see you in your gown, and then I want to see every inch of you."

Jennilee walked toward him, couldn't have kept the sexy

sway out of her hips if she tried. Charlie did that to her—made her feel like the most beautiful, most desirable woman on earth. Coming to a halt a few steps in front of him, she raised her arms and twirled slowly. Part of her hair draped over her shoulder, molding itself to the curve of her breast and waist. The rest hung free down her back.

The gown she'd designed was a thousand times better than anything he'd imagined, and he looked his fill as he hadn't done earlier. Floor length with spaghetti straps, the top vee'd over her breasts and laced together in the front. It fit snugly to her hips, then loosened, draping her in graceful folds.

Following her every movement with his eyes, Charlie noted how the gown alternately clung and flared. Peacock blue silk with gold overtones, Jennilee appeared wrapped in gold one second, the next as if emerging from the depths of the sea, water cascading everywhere.

They came together, bodies touching, silk whispering against silk. Charlie bent his head, Jennilee tipped hers up. They kissed for what could have been minutes, might have been eons. Reaching up, Charlie gently removed the clip from her hair.

"Nothing, Jennilee. I want nothing between us this night." Untying the laces of her gown, he drew it over her head, torturously slow. Dropped it. Let his eyes roam where his hands would soon be.

Reaching out, Jennilee undid the drawstring, all that kept them from being skin to skin. Pushed his pants down over his hips, every bit as slowly as he'd dragged her gown off. Let them fall of their own accord to puddle at his feet.

Kicking them aside, Charlie traced a hand from Jennilee's shoulder to her hip. Scooping her up, he carried her to their bed, laid her on the fragrant petals.

Kisses and sighs and dreams come true. Everything they'd

ever wanted, right here in each other's arms. Charlie did exactly as he'd promised. Left the lights on so he could see every inch of her delectable body, made her scream his name again and again, gloried in the sound. Made more than a little noise himself as Jennilee did quite a bit of exploring of her own.

Eventually left her, just long enough to turn out the lights, blow out the candles and open the French doors. Any other night, he'd have worried about mosquitoes and such. Not tonight. Tonight was magical.

Wrapped around each other, they watched dawn's first light paint their bedroom a rosy gold. A cool breeze off the river fluttered the lace curtains.

"We made it, Jennilee-love. We made it."

"Only because you were right beside me every step. No matter how dark it seemed, or how much I despaired, you were always right there to light my way."

Turning to each other once more, they lost themselves in the magic of their love.

Too engrossed in each other to notice anything outside their little world, neither paid any attention to the lacy curtains swaying softly in the breeze off the river. Neither one saw the transparent silhouette of a woman, as insubstantial as the lacy shadows cast by the curtains.

Amelia watched. Not the couple in the bedroom. The single boat, anchored out on the river, the waves of hatred emanating from it practically visible. Her work here wasn't done, not by a long shot.

JENNILEE'S LIGHT SYNOPSIS

JENNILEE'S LIGHT SYNOPSIS

Chinquapin Ridge, NC Early 1970s

A sweet, precocious child, the death of Jennilee's mother, Cynthia McRae Lee, changes her life forever. Only four and a half years old when her mother is brutally murdered, Jennilee's whole world is turned topsy-turvy overnight. No more happy, laughing child. No more inquisitive, talkative youngster. Jennilee becomes silent and withdrawn.

Most folks in the small, close-knit town of Chinquapin Ridge blame the changes on the shock of her mother's death. A few suspect the truth, at least some of it. All their suspicions don't come close to the horror her life rapidly devolves into. With no will to be found, Jennilee's childhood becomes a living hell. Her mother's younger sister, Aunt Celie, gets custody of Jennilee and the family fortune—a fortune that now technically belongs to Jennilee, and one which includes the ancestral home.

A huge old place that's been in the family for generations,

JENNILEE'S LIGHT SYNOPSIS

The Judge's house requires a lot of work to keep it spotless. Jennilee knows exactly how much, because she's the one who keeps it so. Jennilee says nothing about what goes on in The Judge's house, not a peep to anyone. Celie puts on a good show for the townspeople, all the while making Jennilee look as bad as possible.

The only thing that saves Jennilee, keeps her from running screaming into the night, is Charlie. More than just the boy next door, Charlie's the other half of her heart. Born on the same day, in the same hospital room, Charlie is older by just a few moments.

Jennilee and Charlie are connected by more than shared birthdays.

Charlie lost his mother, too. A few months before Jennilee's mother was murdered, Charlie's mother simply...vanished. Charlie's father can't handle his wife's disappearance, and he drowns his pain in alcohol. As a result, Charlie lives with his grandmother in the house right beside The Judge's.

Charlie is Jennilee's champion, protecting her as much as possible, doing everything he can to counteract Celie's evil. He has a better idea of what goes on between Jennilee and her aunt than any of the adults in their lives, but even his worst nightmares don't come close to the reality.

As Celie does her utmost to destroy Jennilee without losing control of the fortune she covets, Jennilee and Charlie become closer and closer. Jennilee puts up with everything her aunt dishes out, fearing any complaints to outsiders will land her in foster care. Jennilee can live with anything, no matter how horrible, but she can't live without her Charlie. Charlie is determined to save Jennilee, to keep her alive and sane until they're old enough to implement their plans.

Charlie and Jennilee have known they were destined to grow up and marry each other since they were little. Neither

JENNILEE'S LIGHT SYNOPSIS

can remember a time when they haven't counted on doing so. They have their life plan mapped out—all they have to do to make their dreams come true is outwit, and outlast, Celie.

Through many trials, their abiding love for each other and a great deal of help from friends, including a ghost, insures Charlie's and Jennilee's ultimate success.

Made in the USA
Columbia, SC
29 September 2019